P9-CMW-180

Grave Secrets

Published 2020 by Solaris
an imprint of Rebellion Publishing Ltd,
Riverside House, Osney Mead,
Oxford, OX2 0ES, UK

www.solarisbooks.com

ISBN: 978-1-78108-861-6

Copyright © 2020 Alice James

The right of the author to be identified as the author of this
work has been asserted in accordance with the Copyright,
Designs and Patents Act 1988.

All rights reserved. No part of this publication may be
reproduced, stored in a retrieval system, or transmitted, in any
form or by any means, electronic, mechanical, photocopying,
recording or otherwise, without the prior permission of the
copyright owners.

This is a work of fiction. All the characters and events
portrayed in this book are fictional, and any resemblance to
real people or incidents is purely coincidental.

10 9 8 7 6 5 4 3 2 1

A CIP catalogue record for this book is available from the
British Library.

Designed & typeset by Rebellion Publishing
Artwork by Gemma Sheldrake

Printed in Denmark

THE
LAVINGTON WINDSOR
MYSTERIES

Grave secrets

An adventure with zombies. And romance.
And vampires. And croquet.

Alice James

SOLARIS

To Barbara and Wendy...

Chapter One

THAT VERY NIGHT, I planned to raise Bredon Havers from the dead. He was the oldest corpse in the cemetery, and I've always liked a challenge. I knelt in the damp grass of the graveyard and sprinkled a generous circle of salt around the headstone. A wide margin is crucial. Tree roots and moles move things around and it's always disappointing when your zombie comes up missing a limb. Or a head. I really hate that.

Me: Lavington Windsor, estate agent by day, necromancer by night. I've never found a way of making my hobby pay, alas. There isn't much demand for mouldering corpses in the corporate world. And while poking around people's homes isn't as much fun as raising the dead, it's an OK way to make a living. Professional necromancer though? I'd certainly like that on my passport.

I sealed the circle with a perfume atomiser, spraying over the white line until it was damp. My grandfather used stout in a plant mister, but Robert Windsor lived in a time when no one raised an eyebrow if you travelled with an emergency beer supply. If I ever got caught out, I'd be packing Chanel.

I added a few drops of blood even though I probably didn't need them. Practice makes perfect, they say, and I'd done this almost every day since I turned eight. I have to: it's a Compulsion, and I don't think I'll ever be free of it. But then, I'd never raised a man who'd died more than two and a half centuries before. I'd summoned every other corpse in the graveyard—four hundred and twenty-three of them, to be exact. Bredon would be the last and by far the oldest, so this warm August night marked a rather special occasion. I had my pin ready just in case.

They started burying people here about three hundred years ago and stopped shortly after the Second World War. Many of the names on the tombstones read like a roster of unlikely vintage film stars. John Doo, Ashby Rainecourt, Bailey Culpepper... No matter; old and new, I'd raised them all. Or nearly all.

I stepped out of the circle, taking care not to disturb the moist salt, and opened my rucksack. I'd packed four family-sized packets of crisps and an entire loaf of white sliced bread made into ham sandwiches. Take it from me: a raised zombie is a hungry zombie. I opened the crisp packets and poured them onto paper plates, then arrayed them inside the circle, adding a final one with the teetering pile of sandwiches on it. Good to go, Toni.

No eye of newt, no toe of frog. People yearning for arcane ceremonies with candles and entrails would be disappointed by the real thing, because I'd never needed to sacrifice so much as a wasp. Salt, perfume, snacks, occasionally a drop of blood, and end of story. That's all I've ever needed. I suppose I'm just a natural.

"Bredon Havers, in peace I call you. I summon you this night. Come to me."

The words weren't necessary, but they gave me a little oomph, probably not a million miles from a weightlifter grunting as they hefted the bar. Words or not, Bredon Havers came.

He stepped out of the earth with a firm stride, nothing tentative about him, and looked around with a watchful air. I could have cheered. He was beautifully intact, not a digit missing, not a mouldering limb in sight. My first thought was how perfect he was for a zombie, and my second just how tall he must have been amongst my short English ancestors back in the 1750s. He had curly dark hair, big brown eyes and a cheerful smile. He was wearing some kind of wide trousers and a long coat embroidered with peacocks.

Sometimes, when I summon, there's nothing in there, no soul—just a body, compliant but empty. I let them go straight away. Nature abhors a vacuum, they say, but demons love one, and a nice unoccupied body walking about... that would be irresistible. Mostly there's at least a wisp of character left. But not one of my resurrected corpses had strode into the world like they were ready to ask for my vote. I beamed at Bredon.

"Hi, I'm Lavington."

He looked just a tad taken aback, and bowed very slightly.

"Havers, Bredon Havers. Delighted to make your acquaintance, Mistress Lavington."

His voice was a pleasing baritone and his English accent could have cut glass. He was in perfect nick, as though he hadn't spent three minutes in a mouldering tomb, let alone three centuries. Such a shame I couldn't show him off to the world. I wanted to ask him to show me his hands, to check each and every cuticle... but that might have been rude, so I just beamed a bit more.

"So, you're a necromancer," Bredon said.

Startled, I nodded. "Since I was a little girl. How did you know?"

"I am a man of intelligence, dear lady. I died, yet here I stand in a graveyard with you..." He gestured around the moonlit hill. "It seems the obvious deduction."

"Ten out of ten, Sherlock," I said.

He looked confused and I found myself wondering how long ago the detective books had been penned. Clearly after Bredon had shuffled off this mortal coil... No, not shuffled. Bredon clearly wasn't a shuffler. Believe me—I've raised a lot of zombies. There's nothing I don't know about shuffling.

"I'm a necromancer, yes. And before you ask, the food is for you. I know you're hungry."

That's the trick. Get them munching right away, before they go crazed with hunger and you can't get anything sensible out of them. I had almost forgotten with Bredon because he seemed so... so civilised.

"I thank you, Mistress Lavington. I am, I admit, more than peckish."

He picked up the plate of sandwiches and perched on the edge of his gravestone. He devoured about six of them in quick succession before pausing and looking up at me.

"Would you like one, Mistress Lavington?"

"Oh, please call me Toni. Everyone does. And no, thank you, I brought them just for you."

"It seems a little uncivil, um, Toni, to be eating like a wild beast while you stand there without so much as a goblet of wine."

Goblet. I was absolutely certain I had never heard anyone actually say that word out loud before. Goblet. What a splendid, unappreciated, underused word. But before I could interrupt, he continued:

"And goodness gracious, you have no chair. Where are my manners? Would you like to have my," he frowned at the lichen-flecked headstone, "my settle?"

Goodness gracious? He said that too? He drew a white handkerchief from his pocket and began to rather futilely scrub at the surface.

"Oh, don't do that," I said. "Really, don't bother."

But he looked a little wounded, so—rather against my own judgement—I stepped carefully over the perimeter of salt and sat next to him, helping myself to a butty.

"These are quite excellent, I must say, Mistress Toni. Such soft bread."

Ah, yes. The seventeen hundreds were probably not renowned for the availability of sliced white. Actually, I had absolutely no idea what they were renowned for. Infant death, no electricity and a distinct lack of female emancipation seemed likely, but beyond that I drew a blank. Bredon, meanwhile, had moved on to the crisps.

"Delicious," he pronounced, inhaling a couple of packets worth. "Most tasty—can these be potatoes?"

"Um, yes. I believe they are. Probably with about a zillion E-numbers."

"So many graves."

That threw me.

"What?"

"Here. In the cemetery. There were just a handful in my day. How long has passed since my demise?"

"More than two hundred years."

He nodded, looking thoughtful.

"And why am I here? To do your will? To slay your enemies and bring them to justice? With a sword in my hand, you will find no finer fighter than I."

"I don't think I have any enemies, actually, but thank you for asking."

"None? You are lucky. I lived in a time of conflict. A man needed to know how to protect his family. Tell me: is the world much changed since my death?"

Where to start, considering I had given up history up at the earliest opportunity? I hadn't a clue. Instead, I showed him my phone. He seemed surprised enough that I could read, explaining that—in his day—it was a skill few enough men acquired, let alone women.

All in all, I was having the best evening I could remember in a while, and I think I would have stayed chatting with Bredon until dawn—except that my phone rang. Caller ID said it was my brother, and at two in the morning that meant only one thing. William wanted me down at the police morgue to raise a corpse. It wasn't a favour he often asked, so I usually just said yes. Tonight, I would rather have stayed chatting with Bredon... but family is family.

"Hi bro."

My brother joined the police straight from school. Other kids played train driver, spaceman, cowboy... not William. Always the copper. His heroes were Starsky and Hutch, Inspector Morse, Hercule Poirot. And William had done well—there were a lot of uniforms his age still rounding up stray cats. Or in Staffordshire, stray sheep. And Wills really cared about the victims he encountered. He cared about justice. I felt he sometimes saw me as a useful tool in helping him achieve his ambitions, but I didn't mind enough to make a fuss.

"Hey, Toni. I need a favour." No surprise then. *"Where are you? How long would it take you to get to the slabs? There's not a soul here and shouldn't be until seven."*

"I'm at the old cemetery above Colton Hill—I could be with you in half an hour."

"Come as soon as you can. You'll understand when you get here."

He ended the call.

I looked up at Bredon. He had a quizzical expression...

"Bredon, I have to go. I want you to know how much I've enjoyed talking with you tonight."

"Mistress Toni, likewise. I hope we can continue our acquaintance very soon. Should you need a protector, my sword will always be ready."

I didn't tell him that he wouldn't remember our meeting; that if we did ever meet again, he would recall nothing of our conversations and our happy discussion of the literacy of women and the wonders of modern technology. He kissed my hand very chivalrously and I stepped out of the circle. I varied the words for him—my usual discharge seemed too brusque for someone I had so enjoyed my time with:

"Bredon Havers, I release you to your rest. Go in peace and friendship. Return to the earth from which I called you."

He ebbed like mist in a breeze. And then he was gone, and the circle of damp salt with him.

I felt a little wistful to see him go, and rather glumly walked the mile back to my house through the trees. In really bad weather I was occasionally tempted to drive, but there couldn't be good consequences from letting the rest of the village know that I visited the old cemetery in the middle of the night. Every night. In a little village like this... well, people talk.

I'd parked my car by the kerb, although 'car' was a kind term for it. It was an old green Morris 1000 with wooden boot frames. It went from nought to thirty in its own time with a following wind. It was, in polite terms, a big heap of rust: my brother used less affectionate words than the BBC liked broadcasting before nine o'clock. But it was my heap of rust. And this time around it started at the third attempt within only a token protest. One day, I would get it a fourth hub cap.

I had driven to the morgue in the middle of the night only twice before. Why so seldom? The fact remained that Staffordshire was a sleepy county—people just didn't murder one another. Most sudden end-of-life incidents in the county tended to involve tractors. Or cows. Sometimes both. My brother seldom called on me because he seldom needed to. The coroner wasn't kept busy—he moonlighted as a conveyance solicitor. Mysterious deaths? They just happened somewhere else. Maybe in London. Or Birmingham. You could try Liverpool. Round here we had Young Farmers' nights and the Women's Institute. Murder and mayhem? Indeed no—they passed us by.

But not tonight, it seemed. I pulled the car in a couple of streets away and walked to the back door of the morgue where Wills was waiting. He pulled me inside and gave me a brief hug.

"Thanks, Toni. I appreciate this."

"Hey, it's not a problem. This is my party trick remember. Our grandfather taught me well."

"Still…"

"Just leave the sheet on this time, OK."

He laughed. He'd seen it all before and wasn't squeamish. I hadn't seen very much of it and wanted to keep things that way.

We made our way to the cool room, where bodies were kept until they could be post-mortemed. It was super cold, and I kept my coat on. Usually the corpses that dwelled here were nothing suspicious—unfortunate cow-related events or the odd tractor accident—but today there was something bad, something Wills didn't want to risk messing up. Someone who needed justice.

"Her name's Fenella Hampton May—she's seventeen. She passed her driving test just yesterday and was beaten to death with her own wheel lock. Her parents and her boyfriend were waiting for her in a restaurant. She never arrived."

Fenella was under a sheet. I didn't ask Wills to remove it—nor did

I go any nearer than I had to. Raising the dead and buried is one thing. Raising corpses that have barely cooled is another. I drew the salt circle very carefully, trying not to raise my eyes above the tiled floor but failed briefly. There was a toe. It had a label on it. Ick. I lowered my eyes from the toe and took out my atomiser. Confined in the room as we were, the air took on a heady, dense aroma.

"I need to buy you better perfume," said Wills cheerfully.

I was less cheerful, down on my knees finishing off the circle, my ear just inches from a toe. *Don't think about the toe.* I stood up and moved back from the line of salt.

"God, but you're picky. Fenella Hampton May, in peace I call you. I summon you this night. Come to me."

She sat up, and the sheet fell to the floor, revealing pale skin with freckles. She was wearing nothing—her clothes probably heading right that moment to a crime lab—and I could see she had been a skinny teenager, flat-chested with a runner's legs. Her face was blood-stained still. I hoped to prevent her from turning round. I didn't want to see the back of her head. What surprised me was how little of her spirit was left. Bredon had been full of spirit, hundreds of years after his death. Fenella was barely there at all. If I'd waited a couple of weeks, I doubted there would have been anyone to question, just an empty corpse. My theory is that how long your spirit—soul?—hangs around depends on how much you influenced the world. Fenella had trod lightly through life.

No matter. Best to get things over with:

"Fenella, do you remember your death."

"Yes."

Her voice was soft and uninterested. She didn't look either at me or at Wills. I handed her an open packet of crisps, and she devoured them rapaciously.

"Tell me how you died."

"I was driving to the restaurant. It was sunny. I was nervous so I pulled over and drank some squash in the layby where the old pub burnt down." She paused, looking at her hands in a distracted way and picking at her nails. "I saw Max."

"Max who?"

"Maximilian Fisher. He was in the field with the sheep. Literally with the sheep. Can you believe it? My whole netball team wants to date him and he's a sheep shagger."

She stopped again. I wanted to prod her, but my jaw had fallen open and I couldn't make it shut. Eventually I managed:

"So, what did you do?"

"What do you think? I began to video it on my phone."

Of course she had. Because that's what teenagers did... I shook my head in disbelief.

"But then he saw me and ran after me. I left it too late and then when I tried to run, my heel caught and I tripped. I dropped my keys, and by the time I'd found them and got into the car he was nearly on me. I tried to start the engine, but it kept stalling—I was panicking, you know. Then he killed me."

Her voice trailed off. She didn't seem very interested in talking about her murder. She looked at me hopefully and I handed her a second packet of crisps. This time she just tipped back her head and poured them straight in.

"Where's your phone?"

"I dropped it in the field. I don't think Max saw where."

I looked at Wills.

"You have enough to go on?"

"More than enough. We didn't search the field because there was no reason to think she'd left the car. There's no signal from her phone, but if I know where to start looking... well, it hasn't rained and the video should be on there. And there are fingerprints on the wheel lock. We just didn't know whose and they aren't in the database."

I nodded and turned back to where Fenella was sitting.

"Fenella Hampton May, I release you. Return to the earth from which I called you."

There were no fireworks, no eerie mist and no organ music. She just lay back down and closed her eyes and I watched the damp salt leach away as though it had been sucked into the tiles.

Wills was taking notes on a little lined pad. I thought he was wise not to commit his thoughts to electronic media. He looked up when he had finished.

"I owe you."

"Yes, you do."

"Thank you."

"You're welcome, bro."

He paused. I knew what he was going to say. He just couldn't help it.

"Do you want to have another go at Jane?"

Ah, Jane Doe. His nickname for the morgue's longest-standing resident. She had been in a refrigeration unit for three months. She had been stabbed, and then beheaded, and her hands cut off. Her corpse had been dumped behind a disused grain silo and only found some weeks after her death. Her head and hands had never been recovered. My brother's team had no ID, no fingerprints, no motive, no murder weapon and absolutely no idea who had killed her or why. And they couldn't stand it. Wills had brought me here on several Sundays when it was quiet, but it was no good. I didn't know her name… so I couldn't raise her.

My brother had told me that in years gone by, police called unidentified male corpses John Doe, and the women Jane. They still do in parts of America, but these days in England a serial number is more common. Still, Jane Doe they had nicknamed her, and so she would remain until we found out who the hell she was and why someone had thought it worthwhile to kill her and mutilate her body so badly.

"I'll have another go, Wills, but honestly, I can't see it working."

"Try? Please just try. For me…"

"Alright, you win. But cover her up for me. I'm not looking at that again."

He walked to the rack of extra cold cabinets and slid Jane's drawer out. I carefully looked anywhere else while he covered what was left of her with a sheet. Then I drew my third circle of the night, spraying it until it glistened. I jabbed my trusty pin into my thumb—ouch, thank you very much, brother of mine—and added a dozen drops of blood. And then I tried to summon her. It's not easy to describe, but without a name there's nothing to grab, nothing to catch; it's like trying to knit with fog. I was scrabbling around in a big, dark place and getting nowhere. I could feel her, a little softer than the last time. With a name I knew I could have done it. Without? It wasn't going to happen. After a few minutes I shook my head.

"Not tonight, Josephine."

He looked resigned.

"Thanks for trying. I just hate the thought that whoever did that to her is out there, scot free, and could do it again."

I patted his arm.

"I know; me too."

"Thanks Toni. I feel we haven't done enough, you know. Not you, but us here. There've been so many missing persons recently— you would know all about that because of Benson Hood and stuff..."

I didn't mean to interrupt him, but I failed to stifle the world's biggest ever yawn.

"Listen, bro, it's nearly dawn, I haven't been to bed yet and I've got a big day ahead of me."

"You head off home. I'll clear up here and close up."

As I went, he was sweeping up salt and perfume. No summoning and no banishment, so it lay where I had scattered it. I walked back through the poorly lit building, unlocked my car and drove home. I cleaned my teeth and went to bed in my clothes. I hoped my makeup would rub off on the pillow. It usually did.

Chapter Two

I WAS SLUMPED asleep at my desk, drooling gently onto my keyboard when my boss Bernie wandered in through the glass entrance door to the office and slammed it loudly. I sat up with a jerk, and he looked amused.

"God almighty, you look like death warmed up. Did you go eleven rounds with a bottle of vodka and a kebab?"

I scraped a handful of tangles out of the way. God blessed me with pale English skin that burns under bright candlelight and curly tangerine-coloured hair that tangles when you are asleep. And when you are awake. And probably when you are dead. That morning it had a head start on me as I hadn't been conscious enough to find a brush. I squinted at Bernie. He looked horribly awake and was wearing a rather grim mustard-coloured shirt with his usual navy suit. That morning, he had paired them with a tie featuring a selection of nubile women who had apparently given up lingerie for Lent one year and never got back into the habit.

"I wish I'd done anything that much fun," I told him. "That's a really repulsive tie. Did you wake me up for anything in particular, or just because you're a sadistic tosser?"

"Mostly the latter, but if you can work this evening, I'll let you go home and sleep the rest of the day?"

"This evening? Have we finally picked up a vampire client?"

"We have—or rather you have. He asked for you by name."

"That's so exciting. God, I need coffee. But I don't know any vampires. And don't they all use Cadwallader & Penstone in Rugeley?"

"They did, but the entire firm burnt to the ground last week in a mysterious case of spontaneous litigious combustion. Come on, you must know at least one?"

I thought about it.

"There is one, actually. Old Farmer Hugh from the Black Mitre."

"Your watering hole? You have a resident vampire?"

"Yes, but don't tell anyone. He's been drinking there for years, long before the Heidelberg Accord, but no one realised. Since the Accord, he's kind of come out, but he's quite shy. Maybe he recommended me?"

"Maybe. Anyway, if you can make a house call after the sun goes down, I'll let you go home and pour Alka Seltzer down your throat."

"I wasn't drinking."

"Of course you weren't. And this tie isn't sexist. Offer holds..."

"Done. Done. I'll work tonight instead. Give me the details."

He handed me a scrumple of paper. Our office often had ambitious plans to meet the modern age halfway, but they'd usually faded by lunchtime.

"Can you be there by eight? He probably wants a house with extensive cellars..."

"Ha ha. But yes, I will."

"Thanks. And Toni..."

"Yeah?"

"Brush your hair."

I made a helpful hand signal at him, one which I hoped gave general directions on how I felt he should spend the next hour or two. He smirked and promised to try.

I didn't hate Bernie, and he wasn't actually the worst boss in the world. But our relationship had soured at the Christmas party, when he was newly single having split up with my friend Helen, and I was newly drunk, having consumed two bottles of champagne on an empty stomach. We had spent one of those hideously memorable nights together that both parties would rather forget, which hit a low point—after some sub-average shagging—when he suggested I should spank him. Lacking the sobriety needed for a really cutting response, I threw up on him instead. Two days later he got back together with Helen and they promptly got engaged.

I wasn't traditionally lucky in my choice of men. In the last term of school, my best friend Lawrence and I had decided that as we had failed to persuade anyone we actually fancied to help us lose our respective virginities, we would shed them together. Our resolution had culminated in a truly disappointing and rather gynaecological evening, during which the only fireworks that had gone off were at the golf club dinner next door. A week later, he came out, and shortly after moved in with a personal trainer called Hector.

Not my finest hours, either of them. Actually, scratch that. On neither occasion had the shenanigans come close to lasting an hour. Welcome to my world. Aged eighteen, I drove my best friend gay and a decade later drove my boss into the arms of his ex. It wouldn't be so bad if those events marked the low point of an illustrious career, but honestly... they were about par for the course. As I said, not great taste in men.

But Bernie had made me a generous offer, and I jumped at it. I tucked the paper in my handbag and drove home. I made a cursory search for the hairbrush, assured it we had an appointment later, and flung myself under the eiderdown.

When I woke later, the sun had a way still to go on its journey to the horizon. I took a leisurely bath, dried and plaited my hair, painted both finger and toenails a summery shade of gold, and added a few layers of lipstick and mascara. I tugged on black boots and a neon-green jumper—I called it a dress, but then I'm only five foot in my stockinged feet—and hunted around the bathroom floor until I found the address. It was less formal than expected, and written in our receptionist Bethany's spidery script: "*Please ask Ms Windsor to come to the Black Mitre,*" it read. "*Hugh will introduce us. Oscar Wolsey.*" There was a mobile phone number at the bottom.

It's nice to get paid for going to your local. I walked the half mile through the village instead of driving. Colton isn't the smallest village in the shire—it has a shop and three pubs—but it's fair to say that nowhere is more than walking distance. I'd lived in the village all my life. The house had been my grandfather's, and when he died, I'd stayed. Wills had already moved out by then, and was living in police accommodation. I don't know how many people live in the house they grew up in, but in the heart of middle England, it's not uncommon.

The Black Mitre had never been much of a pub: one bar with a couple of ales on tap. If you wanted lager, it came in bottles. One night they might shock patrons and upgrade from pork scratchings to crisps, but I wasn't holding my breath. Its unchanging nature was probably what had attracted Hugh to the place. He came every evening and nursed a lone glass of brandy. For literally decades everyone assumed the sunglasses were due to a sight impediment, and somehow no one noticed he'd been sitting at the same table for more than seventy years, outliving four publicans, two breweries and three name changes as the Black Mitre became the Golden Boar and the New Inn before reverting back to form. He was lucky the table had lasted, but those old Singer treadles can weather the odd bar brawl without buckling. But tonight, for the first time in all the years I had been drinking there, he wasn't sitting alone.

I had chatted with farmer Hugh Bonner over a pint of Old Badger more than once, but our conversations had never run past general pleasantries and observations on the weather. We were English after all. Tonight, though, he stood up and very civilly shook my hand.

"Miss Windsor, good you came."

His hand was ice cold. Of course it was. I looked up at his face, gently lined under white hair. He wore his sunglasses, as he always had. These days, though, I understood why.

"You're very welcome, Mr Bonner."

"Just Hugh is fine."

"Then you're very welcome, Hugh. And in that case, you must call me Toni."

He nodded gruffly. He intrigued me, this man who'd been gifted eternal life but had only ever wanted the simple one that he already knew. A farmer to the core, he must have found it bewildering only to be able to watch his flocks at night. Yet he'd persisted. The decades had grown old around him, but he still ploughed his lands and raised his livestock.

"Well then, Toni lass, this is Oscar."

At this, Oscar turned to look at me—and I almost wished he hadn't because after that I found it very difficult to concentrate on anything at all. He was one of the best-looking men I'd ever met, and exactly my type. He had straight, pale gold hair, not cut too short, and the vivid blue eyes that are the giveaway of vampires—an almost unreal cerulean hue, the blue favoured by eyeliner manufacturers in the 1980s or graphic designers who Photoshop sea views for travel agents. He was tall and built like an athlete, with broad shoulders and slim hips, shown off well by black cotton chinos and a crisp white shirt. No tie, but cufflinks. I love cufflinks. I tried to look professional and not drool.

"It's a pleasure to meet you, Miss Windsor," he said.

He had a lovely light baritone voice with deliciously English vowels, and a rather formal way of speaking.

"Toni, please," I said on autopilot. "Everyone calls me Toni."

"Toni, then. But it's still a pleasure. And you must call me Oscar."

I blushed. I actually blushed. Oh my gosh, for the first time in months I had met a man who could make me glow... and he was a vampire. Way to go.

They did the very English thing of standing up until I sat down, standing up again when I went to the loo, and then insisting on getting me a drink before we could actually all three of us sit down together. I took a gulp of my beer and a bite of my pork scratchings, and attempted to remember why I was in the pub in the first place.

"So, Oscar, what is it that I can do for you?"

He raised an eyebrow, and I laughed. He was as charming as he was scenic.

"Forgive my levity, Toni. You're not quite what I expected when

Hugh said he knew an estate agent. I'd pictured a dapper little gentleman in a chequered suit carrying a briefcase."

"And it's clear I have never owned a briefcase?"

"I have my doubts that you own a suit."

He was right. I didn't.

"Whereas you, I can tell, own many suits. Some of them black tie."

"Touché. I even have a white tie one left over from a visit to America."

"Do you have…" I left it open.

"No. I do not have a full-length black cape lined with scarlet silk. Nor do I play the organ."

I snorted into my beer. Oscar rolled his eyes. Hugh sat back and watched us with some amusement.

"But seriously, Toni, I'm moving into the area and I intend to stay. Since the Accord, we vampires can openly hold property." He gave me a quirked eyebrow. "We no longer have to produce a fake heir every thirty years or so and pretend to be our own grandchildren."

"Have you actually done that?"

"More than once."

"So—a two bed semi in Castletown?"

"Not exactly. I am looking for a rural property…"

I interrupted: "…with extensive cellars."

"As you say." He looked a little embarrassed. "But no need for turrets full of bats. Or gargoyles."

"Not at all—I'm sorry I teased you. And I'm delighted to help you. But don't you all use Cadwallader & Penstone?"

"We… I should say, the vampire community… have had an affiliation with the firm, it's true. But recent events have changed that."

"If you don't like my bill, will our office mysteriously burn to the ground too?"

"I assure you, disagreements over your hourly rate will not incur violent penalties."

Hang on, was he... Oh he was. He was almost definitely flirting with me. I batted my lashes hopefully.

"You promise, Oscar, that you won't be trying to light any fires at the humble premises of Bean & Heron?"

"I promise you, Toni, the only flame I plan to kindle is in your heart."

OK, full on flirting. I suppressed the urge to fling myself on him and took notes. He wanted somewhere remote, stone built, ideally walled... it was quite a long wish list. Not that I would have a problem finding places that fitted the bill. People forget just how old the villages of rural Staffordshire are. You'd find more than one pub in the county claiming to have been in business since the 1100s, and almost every village had houses dating from the 1500s and 1600s. I could find him a dozen old walled manor houses with acres of cellars by throwing darts into an ordnance survey map. These days, I had to wonder how many of them had already been snapped up by the fanged brigade.

We filled in a few forms and I noticed what beautiful cursive handwriting he had. My own looks like the mating ritual of the rare Amazon ink dancing spider, but he kindly didn't mention it.

"What's brought you to Staffordshire, Oscar?" I asked, mostly to get him to speak again so that I could drown in his lovely voice. "Do you have family here?"

"As it happens, I have no living relatives."

"No living relatives... how old are you?" It slipped out before I could gag myself with my own pork scratchings wrapper. Thankfully, he seemed amused.

"Older than you, Toni."

In for a penny:

"Are you too old to enjoy parties?"

"Absolutely not."

"Would you like to go with me to my work party tomorrow night?"

He didn't miss a beat.

"I would like that more than life itself."

Which was slick, but given that he was already dead, I decided not to read too much into it.

"Thank you. You'll probably regret it but I'm not going to tell you that in case you change your mind. It's a grim industry event with a free bar, dodgy canapés and a local band."

"Well, I've spoken to your boss, remember. If we can avoid him all evening, that would probably be best."

I looked at my hands, terribly happy for some reason to discover that that my varnish was perfect. I looked back up at him to find him smiling. He had a smile that set my pulse racing.

"And if you give me your address, Toni, I'll pick you up a little after sunset."

"Thank you."

I wrote it down carefully on a beer mat and gave it to him, and he made a little show of tucking it carefully in his pocket. My heart, which was already somewhat gooey, melted a little further. Then he stood up and nodded to Hugh, who had not appeared to mind playing gooseberry to our flirting.

"Hugh, thank you for arranging this evening. Toni, I will see you tomorrow. A very good evening to you both."

And he left. I watched his elegant figure shrug on a soft-looking wool coat, and stride out of the bar. Maybe I emitted a little sigh. I didn't mean to. At some point I would have to ask my moral compass if it was OK to date dead people, but I wasn't sure I'd drunk enough beer for that.

I looked at Hugh shyly.

"It was very generous of you to recommend me," I said. "I appreciate it."

"You're welcome, lass. You've a kind heart yourself, you know. You made no big fuss, but I did see it—how you still made me welcome, even after you knew what I was. Few were as quick, and there are plenty of folk who still won't speak my name."

He was lucky. Not everyone was of my mind. The Heidelberg Accord had become EU law just four years ago, and most of us were still reeling from it. Some statistics-obsessed German journalist had noticed that, in Heidelberg's small hospital specialising in childhood cancers, recovery rates from acute myelogenous leukaemia were one hundred per cent. Moreover, children being treated showed no side effects from the chemotherapy and stem cell transplants they were apparently having. The journalist uncovered the secret of Herr Doktor Lenz Lange: the man was a vampire. He had discovered that his blood cured children with the condition, and every day, patients received a tiny drop. The good Doktor Lenz was estimated to have saved the lives of more than two thousand children. He pleaded to be allowed to continue his work, and Germany embraced its vampire healer.

Lenz's story proved to be a very tiny snowball that triggered a Europe-wide avalanche. His kindly face—with its electric blue eyes—was on every screen, as were the grateful smiles of his patients, their siblings, their schoolmates, and their parents. He became the third man ever to receive the Großkreuz in besonderer Ausführung, Germany's highest civilian honour. Lenz had gone viral.

There were dissenters, more than a few, but Germany passed laws recognising the legitimacy of vampires as people, and giving them human rights. A year later, the EU followed suit. And from the crevices of society where they had been hiding, the creatures of the night emerged, with their odd blue eyes and their chequered pasts.

It was very different in the Americas of course. There, of course, the Mason-Schelling Act had instead come into force, also known as the Stake-on-Sight Act, and though the likes of California and Mississippi had declared it unconstitutional... well, put it this way: you wouldn't want to be a vampire in Texas or Ohio.

Hugh was a retired farmer, but no one had noticed that he had retired seventy-five years before, or even guessed that his relationship with his housekeeper and her stockman husband might be more than that of employer and employee. He continued to frequent the same table each night that he ever had. He had told our current publican Albert Winner that he had been propping up the same bar for a century. Faced with customer loyalty of that calibre, Albert had made it clear that he expected the rest of his clientele to be liberal-minded when it came to socialising with the undead. I don't think he lost much custom over his stance. Neither of the other two pubs in the village stocked decent beer, and one of them had recently started selling alcopops.

As always, Hugh was nursing a small glass of cognac. Did he ever drink any of it? Hard to say. Maybe he just liked the smell. Sometimes he bought snacks and fed them to Albert's dog. Sometimes he brought his own dog.

Suddenly Hugh leant forward and took off his dark glasses. It's hard to think of an old man with a flat cap and a stick as a member of the living dead, but looking into his eyes, I had no doubt. There was a sense of power and age, not unlike being around Bredon the previous night. Hugh's eyes were the same hypnotic blue as Oscar's, but they looked at me with unexpected kindness.

"I knew your grandfather, lass. Did you know that?"

"I hadn't thought about it, but I guess you would have done. Were you friends?"

"Yes, Robert Windsor and I were friends. In our way."

"Did he know what you were? That you were a vampire."

"Yes, he did. But more to the point, I knew what he was—and what you are."

I was honestly shocked. I thought absolutely no one knew outside of our family. I thought my secret was very, very well kept.

"Lass, listen to me. I'm under an obligation to your grandfather. He saved my life once, and that debt went unpaid. So I'll give you a warning. No other vampire must ever know about your powers. The Children of Diometes don't look kindly on you and yours, and we've all but wiped out necromancers over the millennia. Most believe your kind were driven to extinction centuries ago. Keep it that way, Toni. Heed me on this."

Why was it that everyone I met these days seemed to want me to stand around with my mouth open? Somewhere in between catching flies and dislocating my own jaw, I stared at Hugh in disbelief.

"Why on earth would vampires try to wipe out necromancers? Why would they even care?"

Hugh looked at me and shook his head. When he spoke, I thought he was quoting something—the words didn't sound like his.

"The slaves of Diometes betrayed him when they filled the empty souls of revenants with the seeds of Satan. They thought to control an army of the dead, but we slayed both master and servants to live our stolen lives."

"Oh, for goodness' sake Hugh, now you're just being obscure. And I've had two pints of Old Badger. Don't please be like that stupid Greek Oracle woman. I had to study her for classics. She'd take your money and then give you a prophecy so incomprehensible that you only understood it when you were being wrapped in your own stupid Greek shroud. Or whatever they buried you in back in Ancient Greece."

He sighed theatrically, but telling me he was some kind of honorary uncle had dented my deference towards him, and I knew he was putting it on.

"Toni, your kind is feared for good reasons. Don't raise the dead except in times of great need. Lass, don't do it at all if you can help it, because if other vampires find you out, you won't see another sunrise. Now, young lady, run along and let an old man pretend to drink in peace."

So I did. He had put the tiniest damper on my lovely evening, but only just. I had a date for the office party, something that had never happened before, and it was with Oscar, the most beautiful man in Staffordshire. Not even dire warnings from the oldest farmer in the village could quell my spirits for long. I was full of excitement, and—thanks to my afternoon nap—wide awake. I needed to tell someone all about how wonderful life was. The trouble was, my dearest friend Claire was on a spa break with her mum, and Helen was probably smooching on a sofa with Bernie at that exact moment. Then it struck me—there *was* someone else. I'd made a new friend. I walked back to my house and changed into tougher boots. On impulse, I grabbed the entire roast chicken I had planned to eat over the week, and headed up the hill, salt cellar at the ready.

It was only after I'd drawn my circle, moistened it and was ready to go that doubts came. Why was I bothering? The summoned dead—what had Hugh called them? Revenants, a much nicer word than zombies—had no memories. Did I really want to introduce myself to Bredon all over again? But I had come all the way, so I ploughed ahead. I always was stubborn.

"Bredon Havers, in peace I call you. I summon you this night. Come to me." After a moment, I added: "again".

So much easier tonight... The second time you raise a corpse, it's always the case. It's like they've learned their way. The earth released Bredon Havers without a tremor. But to my complete surprise he turned to me and smiled with recognition.

"Miss Windsor, Toni. What a most delightful pleasure to meet with you again."

Chapter Three

I COULDN'T HELP it—it was so unexpected that I jumped into the circle and hugged him.

"Bredon, you remember me!"

"But of course. My social life has been somewhat limited since I was interred, Mistress Lavington. I was unlikely to forget."

"You don't understand. They never remember. No one I have raised more than once has remembered the first time. I'm so happy."

I handed him the roast chicken and perched on his headstone again. He absentmindedly ate about half, bones and all, before remembering his manners and offering me a bite. Two packets of pork scratchings hadn't made much of a dent in my appetite, so I accepted a drumstick and we munched together. After a while he seemed sated enough to chat.

"So, Toni, since we last met, have you acquired enemies who need smiting?"

"Goodness no, Bredon, quite the opposite. I have a date, and I wanted to tell someone."

"A date?"

I sought a better word.

"It's just possible that I'm being courted."

"I see. Congratulations. You seem excited."

"Bredon, of course I'm excited. I haven't had a date in months. I've *never* had a date for our office party. This is big news for me."

"And you're here to ask my advice?"

"I hadn't thought of that, actually. I'm pretty sure that I can mess things up all on my own. But since we're together, by all means: go for it."

He laughed.

"Well, Toni, is he of good family?"

"I don't think he has any family left. In fact, I'm sure of it."

"Do you know of his people?"

"Not really. I think he might originally be from round here. To be honest, Bredon, I didn't get around to asking. I was too busy fluttering my eyelashes at him and admiring his smile."

"You're as bad as my daughters. Let us approach this from another angle, young miss. How did you meet him?"

"That one I can answer: a friend of my grandfather's introduced us."

"That's good. And this friend, he is well disposed to you and your grandfather? He has your best interests at heart?"

"Definitely, yes. Apparently, my grandfather saved his life, and he wants to look out for me."

"And he approved of your—how did you phrase it?—your date?"

"Golly, he seemed to, yes."

"Well then, Mistress Windsor, we will assume that your beau is of good family. Is he of means?"

"Of what?"

"He can support you?"

"Oh, lord yes. He's minted."

"And do you think he has honourable intentions?"

I was pretty sure Oscar had dishonourable intentions. I was really hoping he did. I thought we should skip that question.

"You don't need to worry about that, Bredon," I said carefully, not wanting to lie to him. "It's not a concern."

"Then I wish you good luck on your date, Toni."

"Thank you."

After which we fell back into chatting about what else had changed since Bredon had died, which turned out to be quite a lot—though not, it appeared, the weather. He had been a great swordsman in his day, I learned, and fought in many duels. Bredon was in the middle of reminiscing about how he had met his wife—at church it transpired—when there was a wonderful clap of thunder and the heavens opened.

"Bredon, I'll have to go. I didn't even bring a coat."

"You can borrow mine." He tugged off his lovely peacock-embroidered coat and arranged it around my shoulders. "How odd. I certainly wasn't buried in this coat."

"No?"

"No indeed. It was my favourite coat for some time, but eventually it grew sadly shabby, and I gave it to our gamekeeper."

"I have a theory that revenants like yourself, who have a strong memory of themselves and their lives, come back as the person they see themselves to be. How old were you when you died?"

"I was fifty-two."

"You see, I'm right. You don't look anything like fifty-two. You barely look forty."

We could have sheltered under the trees at the far end of the cemetery, but I'd never broken a binding circle. It's a barrier the summoned dead can't cross either way, hence the occasional missing limb when you summon but you draw your circle too small. Like every other corpse I'd ever raised, Bredon didn't notice he couldn't cross the salt—he just didn't try. Just like he didn't notice he always answered my questions and did what I told him to... but then, he was much more vibrant than anything else I had ever encountered, so maybe he would eventually twig.

The rain intensified, and even Bredon's coat was becoming soggy. I threw in the towel:

"Bredon, I should go."

He stood up, and courteously helped me up from the headstone.

"And you should get some sleep, Mistress Windsor, if you are to look your best tomorrow night for your 'date', I think. Perhaps you would like to come back soon and tell me how it went."

"Thank you. It's a promise." I took off his coat and handed it back to him. "OK: Bredon Havers, I release you to your rest. Go in peace and friendship. Return to the earth from which I called you."

I really needed to vary my lines.

It was raining so heavily by then that I decided to make my way home through the woods rather than by the road. The route through the trees was darker and muddier, but also rather shorter and more sheltered, and the rough path ended at the back of my garden. My boots already looked destined for gardening tasks, so I climbed over the low wall that surrounded the old cemetery and sheltered in the dark for a few moments while my eyes adjusted. I managed to make my way without incident to where the trees gave way to the lawn at the side of my house and was just about to cross when I realised that someone was waiting for me. Someone was hiding in the dark just where they could catch me as I unlocked the front door. Someone large. Someone wearing a balaclava.

Call me cynical, but I couldn't see a good motive for them. I crept back under cover, moved slowly out of hearing range, and dialled William.

"Hey, Toni, is this urgent? I was just heading to bed…"

"I'm in the woods behind my house," I whispered. "Some jerk in a balaclava is camped outside my front door."

There was a moment of silence.

"Gods on a bicycle! Toni, don't move. I'll be there. I'll get a unit over there right now. Stay quiet. Don't let him hear you."

He cut the call. I stood, shivering now, in the dark. Must keep quiet, Toni. Do not make a sound. Silent as the grave… Then, of course it happened. My phone rang, the tone horribly audible in the blackness. I scrabbled at the screen and turned it off, but too late: balaclava jerk had already begun to run across the lawn towards me. I turned and fled.

I had the tiny advantage that I was on familiar territory and had been walking in the dark while he had been looking into the bright lights of my porch. He had the rather larger advantage of being more than twelve inches taller than me, über fit, and not wearing a dress. I made it about fifty feet back into the woods before tripping up over a combination of my own feet and a tree root. I fell into an abyss of blackness that seemed to go on for a while and ended in a lot of mud. Perhaps fortuitously, I had tumbled into the small stream that ran behind my house. If balaclava jerk hadn't heard me fall, I thought I might be safe here until the police turned up.

I lay very still and very cold. Who could want to harm me? I was an estate agent, not an international jewel thief. The last time anyone had chased me into a wood I had been eight years old and stinky Billy Pomeroy had got carried away in a game of kiss chase. That hadn't ended well. I was worried this would end worse.

My pursuer ran past the spot where I had tumbled off the path. I heard him go maybe another fifty feet or so. Should I creep out and try to make it to the house? Before I had made up my mind, I heard a second figure approach.

"Have you got her?" he called,,, in an English voice. A Birmingham voice to be exact. How galling: I wasn't going to die at the hands of an escaped zombie or a blood-lusting vampire. I wasn't even going to be shunted off this mortal coil by a ninja or a Chicago hit man. I was going to going to meet my maker at the hands of some thug from Shirley. Thanks, posterity. You suck.

"I don't think she's come this way," Balaclava Jerk called back. Another Brummie accent. "I don't think she could have come this far."

"How did you let her get into the woods in the first place, you prawn?"

"Hey! She came out of the woods—you're lucky I spotted her at all."

Just as I thought things couldn't get any worse, they did. Balaclava Jerk turned on a huge blinding torch and headed back my way. And I felt a sneeze brewing. Wonderful: my hay fever actually was going to kill me this time. I buried my face in my shoulder to muffle it, but it was one of those high-decibel explosions that usually waits for the romantic bit of a live Shakespeare play to make its move. It wasn't enough to raise the dead—believe me, you really can't do that sneezing—but it was quite enough to alert the Moseley mafia to my presence.

I scrabbled to my feet and began to squelch as fast as I could downstream. Upwards would take me deeper into the woods, which I didn't fancy. This way and I would hit the road in about three hundred yards.

"There she is!" I heard Thug Number Two call out. "This way."

The streambed was mostly empty—it only really filled up in spring or after a few weeks of rain—but it was still slippery and covered in slick, rocking stones. I fell heavily a couple of times, and had a feeling I had done some not-so-nice things to my hands, but I seemed to be making progress. But not enough. I had gone a hundred yards at most when my hunters drew level with me at the top of the bank.

"Stop there. We won't hurt you," one called down.

Of course not. And I was just playing hard to get... I didn't slow down. Instead I fell flat on my face, slipping on the rocks a third time and failing to recover my balance. I clambered back to my feet again, but the road seemed an impossible distance away now. The only reason I hadn't been caught yet was because the sides of the stream were high and slippy. They shallowed off closer to the road. Once my fan club realised that, I wasn't going to make it. I decided not to think too hard, and staggered on. Bredon had been right after all—I had acquired some enemies who really, really needed smiting.

Ahead of me, the bank had partially collapsed, making a slope down to the bottom of the gully. A season of rain like tonight's would soon wash it away, but for now it provided easier access to the streambed. Even as I drew close, Balaclava Jerk came down it in a rush of limbs. He caught his balance, and stood up, blocking my way and blinding me with his torch. Behind me I heard a thud as his colleague leapt down and cut off my escape route.

"Take it easy, little lady," said Balaclava Jerk. "You don't make a fuss, and no one gets hurt."

"Little lady! Who the fuck do you think you are, Clint Eastwood?"

I bent down and picked up a couple of rocks from the streambed. Hope springs eternal, much like the supply of mud I seemed to be encountering that evening.

I didn't get to use them. While I was being blinded by the man in front of me, Thug Number Two came up behind me in a rush and pinned my arms behind my back. I struggled frantically, but he was big and strong, and I was small, tired and terrified, and I doubt he even registered my flailing. So I stopped struggling and concentrated on something I thought I would be better at—I started screaming.

I'm a good screamer. I was always in the school choir, so I'd had plenty of practice, and I really let rip.

"Stop her, someone will hear," said Balaclava Jerk. My captor obediently let go with one hand and tried to clamp it over my mouth. But with one wrist free I spun round and whacked him in the face with the rock in my free hand. He gave a yell of pain—which warmed my heart—and let go of me momentarily. I spun off into the dark somewhere, filled my chest with oxygen and carried on shrieking.

"Shut up, you stupid bitch."

Balaclava Jerk seized me and tried to wrestle me into a grip where he could keep one hand over my mouth. He managed it briefly but incompetently, letting a nice bit of fleshy palm into the range of my teeth and I bit down—hard. He yelled and drew his hand away but kept hold of me by the scruff of my dress. I dropped to the ground and he fell with me, but sort of on top, and I got a faceful of mud. I curled up and put my arms over my face so that I could carry on screaming through the gap in my elbows.

"Christ, can't you gag her?"

"What with?"

"Club her with a rock or something."

"We're not meant to kill her, you twit."

No? That was good news. I continued to scream with abandon, but my good run was coming to an end. Balaclava Jerk levered me onto my back and sat on top of me, yanked my hands above my head and held them with one hand while slapping the other over my mouth. Carefully this time.

"Now listen here, you dim cow, let me tell you..."

But I never got to learn.

"Police! Let the woman go and step into the light."

I was thrust to one side in a rush, and then heard fleeing footsteps heading away along the streambed at top speed. I lay in the mud, feeling the raindrops falling on my face. They felt good.

Two hours later, I had showered and nice PC Fiona Miller had dabbed antiseptic on my scratches or—to put it more accurately—over most of my body. My hands were covered in steri-strips and my knees in bandages. Whatever dress I wore the next night… well put it this way, it would have to be one that looked good with gloves. My face had somehow escaped damage, but Fiona thought I might have cracked a rib, so she had bound up my torso to help me sleep. A plain-clothes officer was watching the house for the rest of the night—given that my attackers had fled into the night without a trace—and my shaken brother William had announced he would sleep on the sofa. For now, we sat together on the old sofa, clutching mugs of tea.

"Do you have any idea who would want to hurt you?"

"Of course I don't. Do you?"

He hesitated before replying. He put down his cup of tea, and then took mine and put it down too. He took both of my hands in his.

"Toni, I think that I do, but it doesn't make any sense. You heard about the arson attack on Cadwallader & Penstone?"

"Yes, but everyone thinks they must have pissed off some vampires."

"Heavens, no. The opposite. They were threatened by two anonymous representatives of the EDL two weeks before the fire."

"What the bloody hell is the EDL?"

"It stands for the English Defenders League, and it's the militant arm of the UK Anti-vampire Party, UKAP. You must have seen them campaigning on social media. They hope to win seats on a ticket reversing the Heidelberg Accord."

Now I knew who he meant—I'd seen their slogans on buses: 'Send 'em back to the grave!' and 'Up stakes and at 'em!' to quote just a couple.

"Might they get in?"

"At this rate, they will all be arrested first. Two masked men with pronounced Brummie accents—sound familiar?—smashed Cadwallader & Penstone's window and told the staff that if they continued to look after their vampire clientele, they would regret it."

"No one was hurt in the fire, were they?"

"It's not staffed at night, so no, but both old Mr Cadwallader's daughters worked there, and he's thrown in the towel. The buildings were well insured, so he's decided not to reopen."

"So that's why the vampires are coming to us now."

"What!"

"We got our first vampire client this morning. I'm finding him a house in the area."

"Well we at least know why they were after you, then. Could you persuade Bernie to turn them away? There are two of them in Stafford prison right now; I put them there myself. And Toni, they are not nice people and they have some serious firepower behind them."

"And give in to these blackmailing thugs? No way, José."

I decide not to tell him about my date. There had been quite enough fireworks for one night. And while dating the undead might be legal, I doubted it was going to go down well with an overprotective elder brother.

"I suppose not. Well, look, I'll stay here tonight. If we don't round these thugs up by tomorrow, we'll think again."

"Thanks, big brother. I might turn in now."

He hugged me.

"I thought I might lose you tonight. I heard you screaming in the woods. It was the worst moment of my life."

I hugged him back.

"I wasn't enjoying it myself, you know."

"You did well, though. You kept your head. Might this finally persuade you to sign up for that self-defence course I keep going on about?"

I elbowed him in the ribs.

"Don't push your luck, Wills," I said. "I have the dexterity and coordination of a deckchair. I'd never live through the first class."

And I headed up to bed.

Chapter Four

I WOKE IN a world of pain. My ribs might or might not be broken, but they hurt enough for me not to care either way. My knees were nearly covered in blue and green patches, but they had kindly decided to leave some gaps in between for the purple and red patches to show to their best advantage. How thoughtful. My knuckles under their bandages throbbed and itched, and my neck had stiffened to the point where I could turn my head about two degrees to the left and maybe one and half to the right.

Thinking about the evening ahead of me, I hoped Oscar didn't want to dance. I also hoped he didn't expect to get beyond first base on a first date. After all those close encounters of a painful and muddy kind the previous evening, I wasn't up to encounters of the up close and personal kind. Picture it: he'd caress a knee, I'd shriek in pain; he'd maybe go to stroke a breast and I'd accidentally break his nose with a full-body wince. No, tonight I would be a lady and stop at a goodnight kiss. Who was I kidding? If I was really, really lucky, I might get a goodnight kiss. Still, after the past night's narrow escape, I was feeling pretty lucky.

I tugged on some clothes over my bruises—my usual work uniform of jumper and boots—yanked a comb most of the way through my hair, added lip gloss and drove through a selection of traffic lights—well, the red ones—in order to get to the office. Wills had left a note saying he'd keep a plain-clothes man on me for the rest of the day. I hoped my bodyguard didn't also do traffic enforcement.

I also had a bone to pick with Bernie because I knew that he and old Mr Cadwallader were friends. In fact, I had a feeling they were distantly related. Was it likely that somehow Bernie didn't know about the EDL threats? Not very. Was it more likely that he knew perfectly well, but had decided that it was just fine to put me and our sweet seventeen-year old receptionist Bethany in harm's way to boost his bottom line? I thought that was much more likely.

And that didn't please me at all.

Our office is off the main square in Stafford, opposite the beautiful old court buildings. They'd become a mixture of museum and community space, often holding little exhibitions and craft fairs. I would often size up what was on as I walked past in the morning, working out whether it was worth a wander round in my lunch break. That morning I stormed past—or rather limped—without looking. I was unable to prevent an earnest looking lady in a tweed printed mackintosh from thrusting a flyer into my hand, though I nearly crashed into a rather good-looking dark-haired man sporting a Barbour jacket as I futilely attempted to give her the slip. I rounded the corner to the offices of Bean and Heron, and shoved the door so that the bell jangled angrily and Bethany looked up in surprise from her marmite and toast.

"You're late," said Bernie, not looking up at all from a paper, "again."

"And you, you inconsiderate tool, are in trouble."

Bernie dropped the paper and looked up at me with a distinctly sheepish and guilty air. Then he took in the bandages on my hands and the cuts and bruises on my legs that I had deliberately not hidden in leggings or tights.

"Bloody hell, what happened? Oh God, are you OK?"

"I am OK, no thanks to you. You knew perfectly well when you spoke to me yesterday that we were only getting vampire business because Cadwallader & Penstone are too scared to do it anymore. And you didn't warn me. You let me go out—at night I might add and made out you were doing me a favour letting me have an afternoon nap. I nearly died last night because you are a selfish, avaricious twat and you can take your stupid job and your dumb commission schedule and shove them."

I paused long enough for Bernie to run forward and hug me.

"Let go, Bernie, I'm only here for my things."

"Toni, I am so sorry. I never dreamed this would happen. I didn't think—look, sit down and I'll get you some coffee. Bethany, get Toni some coffee! Toni, think about this. We are friends, special friends. You like working here. I like you working here. Why don't you tell me what happened last night? Tell me everything. Bethany, when you have made that coffee, go out and get some lardy cake."

To be honest, we both knew I wasn't going to leave. I threatened to resign about every six months. Today was overdue. Bernie would give me a small raise—and compensation for a ruined pair of boots this time around—and honour would be satisfied. As I've said, he wasn't the worst boss in the world.

He and Bethany listened to my tale of woe, and were appropriately shocked and sympathetic. I got the raise I'd planned to ask for anyway and two hundred quid for new boots. I could probably have swung the day off too, but I wanted to make a shortlist of properties for Oscar.

The sort of houses my future husband was after do come up on the open market—but more often they are on the 'grey list', an informal roster of top-tier dwellings that owners would like to sell, but discreetly. So there are no adverts, no for-sale signs and no open days—just an entry on an under-the-radar inventory that can take some chasing down. I rang four solicitors, ineptly bashing at the keys with my bandaged fingers, and gave them Oscar's wish list. The local firms all like me—I'm a fully qualified lawyer myself, so my sales tend to be a little more glitch-free than most—and all of them phoned me back within the hour.

All except one. My old friend Benson Hood of Deanthorpe, Duncan & Delaney didn't answer when I rang, which was unusual, and he didn't call me back either. I particularly wanted to get hold of him because I knew he had Butterbank Lodge on his books, a very secluded vampire-friendly dwelling hidden at the end of half a mile of wooded driveway. I rang him a second time before giving up. Thinking about it, Butterbank Lodge wasn't on mains gas and the roof leaked. I would find Oscar somewhere better.

Come time for elevenses, I had five potential dwellings, one of which sounded perfect. The kind of people who live in these kinds of houses in this kind of county ... well, they can be old-fashioned. So I was slowly and incompetently writing an introductory letter to each, which I planned to hand deliver, when—joy of joys—Mrs Amelia Scott Martin rang.

I was lucky enough to pick up the call. White-haired, petal-skinned Amelia had bought a house through us some five years ago, but nonetheless, when anything went wrong, she would ring. Door handle stuck? We were her port of call. Tree needed trimming? We were on speed dial. Vegetable garden infested with butterflies (infested—her word not mine), we got the job. The thing was, she was so adorable, none of us could say no at first. And then later on she simply bribed us. She baked like a goddess, huge mounds of fluffy pastry things, cakes crammed with enough cream to drown a cat, raised beef and ale pies, some kind of strudel thing the size of a cream-drowned cat. You name it. Whoever came to her rescue would stagger back to their car, weighted down by boxes of suet crust.

I'd given my week's catering to Bredon and been praying for a call from Amelia. But before I headed out, I put on a pair of opaque black tights. No point in scaring off the clientele with my injuries.

Amelia lived in a tiny terraced stone-workers cottage on the edge of Salt, a pretty village blessed with two pubs, the tiniest little church and a croquet green. I could have sold her house for her a thousand times had she wanted. It was a chocolate box property with the thick stone walls that would get it a good energy efficiency rating. It also had one of those big cellars with a coalhole by the front door. A century ago, the horse and dray would have pulled up and your coal cellar would have been filled up without you even having to open the front door. Not that many people use their cellars for coal these days. Most of them get converted to games rooms that are always damp and never get natural light. I don't like lying, so I use the words 'flexible accommodation' in my brochures. Bernie says words like damp and dark kill your commission rates stone dead.

Amelia hadn't used her cellar in years. She used the mixing bowl a lot though: I swear that as I parked my car in her driveway, I could already smell the cooling spun sugar.

As I walked up to the front door, a gentleman was carefully polishing the windscreen of a pale blue vintage mini parked on the verge, and I realised I had spotted my undercover guard. His cover was really blown by his good looks. As I admired his dark eyes, shiny black hair and high cheekbones, I suddenly recognised him as the same man I had crashed into outside the court that morning. He had shed his waxed jacket, but I was in no doubt. I gave him a little finger wave as I passed which he pretended not to see.

Amelia answered her door almost before I released the bell.

"Miss Windsor, how kind of you to come. I hoped it would be you."

"Hi there, Mrs Scott Martin. Don't worry about that—it's much nicer here than in the office with Bernie scowling at me."

"That nice young man, I am sure you don't mean that. Oh, gracious me! What happened to your hands?"

What indeed.

"I, um, fell off my bicycle. So annoying. Just scratches, you know."

Her hall was painted a cheerful yellow colour, with bowls of flowers on little tables set at hip-banging height. The doorways were far too low for anyone taller than Mrs Scott Martin, which was probably everyone except me. I avoided the tables, sneered at the low lintels, and was then caught out by the stupid little step down to the kitchen. I staggered in, arms wheeling, but managed to stay upright. Goodness, I was earning my cake already.

Today it was a nice moist coffee cake, served with the lapsang souchong I had agreed to try the first time I had called on Amelia. Unable to bring myself to admit how disgusting it was, I subsequently had to drink the wretched stuff on every single visit. After about two years I had developed a taste for it. These days I even drank it at home.

"It's so good to see a young person with an appetite," Amelia murmured. "So many of you seem to live your whole life on a diet these days."

I couldn't answer for a moment, due to a vast mouthful of coffee cake, but gave an encouraging smile. Her kitchen was a very welcoming place, with an old model cream Aga next to which her elderly cat Winchester spent his days. He was a vast, benign tangerine-coloured English short hair with a wide good-natured face. It was slightly lopsided in appearance, one fang having been shed some years before. He deigned to briefly curl around my ankles, generously fuzzing my tights, before returning to his warm base. I wanted to stay all day.

Amelia was saying something, and I tuned in.

"… so difficult after my husband died, but then of course I moved here and started to make friends. And now Winchester and I are so happy."

"And how's that troublesome son of yours, Mrs Scott Martin? Didn't make parole again I guess."

"He didn't turn out very well, did he? I wonder where we went wrong, but perhaps I shouldn't blame myself. He got in with boys who took a lot of drugs, and nothing was ever the same after that. He would steal money, steal my jewellery to sell… He sold my father's medals once. Fortunately, that nice jeweller in Lichfield sold them back to us for the same price. They wouldn't even let him out when we buried his father."

She started talking then about her husband's funeral, a tale I'd heard before, and I tuned out again, thinking how sad it was that she was alone when there was a perfectly healthy son out there who should be changing her lightbulbs and ordering her a new recycling bin. Perhaps to overcompensate, I not only changed bulbs and phoned the council waste office, I also promised to mend the jammed cellar door in the hallway and put up a new shelf in the garage once my fingers worked again, and to tie back an escaping rose. Finally, I arranged to renew her subscription to *Private Eye*— who knew this dear old thing was a left wing firebrand?—and at the door saying goodbye, I felt a flood of warmth towards this brave old lady, pottering around with her baking trays and her orange cat.

"Goodbye, Miss Windsor," she said. "It's so kind of you to come again."

I put down my pile of bounty: two meat pies, a coffee cake of my very own, and a tray of profiteroles. I leant forward and gave her an uninvited hug, which she returned with some surprise. Thank goodness she wasn't a rib crusher. My ribs were crushed enough.

"You call me anytime you like, Mrs Scott Martin. Don't hesitate. And don't wait until you need something doing. Call even if you just want to chat or if you want me to take you shopping."

"I will do that, Miss Windsor," she said with her lovely smile.

We really needed to get to first names soon. Still, we were both English and it had only been five years...

I drove home via five addresses that I had shortlisted for Oscar. As I had anticipated, the one at the top of my list, Lichley Manor, looked like a dream destination. It was pretty little moated house originally built in about 1350 and renovated at the height of the craze for all things gothic in the 1750s. The place had been unofficially on the market since Sir Martin Lichley died two years previously. His sole heir, a socialite daughter who was occasionally pictured in newspapers hanging out with the offspring of D-list popstars, hadn't let the dust of Staffordshire taint her kitten heels since graduating from a Swiss finishing school and wasn't about to start.

There was a tiny gatehouse, currently unoccupied and missing part of its roof. The main house, deliciously turreted and with an agreeable frontage of leaded glass, wasn't large or labyrinthine, but I had found out earlier that it sat on top of two storeys of extensive wine cellars, which apparently merged with some natural caves. Oscar would love it, I was sure. The building was sound, but in dire need of modernisation. The electrics were half a century old, the heating non-existent and the plaster fifty per cent horsehair. A fixer-upper.

Oscar was my first vampire client, but statistically, that put me behind the curve. In the south and around London, there had been a big influx of North American vampires. Scared away by the Mason-Schelling Act coming into force, they had flowed into liberal Europe, treading on each other's toes and starting turf wars. This far north, we seemed immune. I'd heard talk of some Chicago vampires in Wolverhampton, but little to indicate it was more than gossip.

I took the time to wander around the gardens. They were lovely, ancient and massively overgrown, rhododendrons a couple of hundred years old sheltering under cedar trees three times their age. I was here out of sheer nosiness, truth be told. I hadn't written a letter to the absent Lady Serena Lichley. She wanted money, not old-fashioned courtesy. I'd discovered the name of her lawyer in London, and emailed him. He'd got back giving me directions on getting hold of a key and permission to nose around—or 'view the property on behalf of my client' as we prefer to put it in estate-agent speak. Well, I'd viewed the property and it was exquisite. Scratch that. If Oscar wanted to spend about a quarter of a million in improvements, it would be exquisite. Right now, it had the charm of a Tim Burton film set, or in estate-agent speak it was a 'dwelling with great potential'.

Nosing completed, I headed home. I wanted plenty of time to get ready for my date. I waxed my legs in between the bruises, redid my nails and drank tea. I picked out a gold-coloured shift dress I'd found at Oxfam and not yet worn. It was long enough to hide my multi-coloured knees, low-cut enough to say come and get me, and plain enough to get away with wearing gloves. I hung it in the bathroom while I showered and assured myself that the creases would drop out in the steam. Maybe they did—truth be told, the dress was too tight to tell. I drank more tea, applied whatever unguents and lotions caught my fancy, and added mascara, lipstick and some bangles. As the sun set, I poured myself a gin and tonic to calm my nerves, adding two slices of lemon and three cubes of ice. I liked tea as much as the next girl, but the sun was over the yard arm.

I sat in my garden watching it set, and wondered where my mysterious plain-clothes guardian was hiding out. I wondered where my attackers from the previous night were holed up, and whether I was insane to think about dating a vampire, a man who'd died before I was even born. I wondered all these things briefly and without much attention. To be honest, I was mostly wondering whether I would get to snog Oscar that night.

He pulled up in a cute little car that I tentatively placed as a Lotus. It was a dark aubergine colour and it tucked itself in next to my heap-of-rust-mobile in an embarrassed way. Oscar levered himself out, a procedure that I had a feeling was going to prove a challenge later on for me and my dress. He was wearing black linen trousers and a polo shirt, which I considered nine out of ten. Cufflinks would have been better.

I ran down the porch steps to meet him.

"Hello. You made it. You found me."

He took my gloved hand and bent down to kiss my cheek. How tall was he, I wondered? Five ten? Five eleven? A lot taller than me, but then everyone is. School children are generally taller than me. Even Amelia looked down at me. His lips were very cool, which threw me for just a moment, but cool is better than hot and sweaty, right?

"I did. Toni, your village is very pretty—have you lived here long?"

"I grew up here."

"Here? In Colton."

"Right here. In this house."

"Are you like vintage port? Do you not travel well?"

He helped me into the passenger seat. Yes indeed, getting out was going to be fun. Or limb breaking. Definitely one or the other.

"I am exactly like vintage port: when I travel, I need a lot of expensive packaging. This car will do just fine."

"Do you like it? It's new."

"It's delicious. Next time I will wear purple to match. If there is a next time, of course. I was going to invite you in for a drink, but you distracted me."

"Actually, I am not a great drinker."

"Oh, of course not. I completely forgot. Do you drink at all? I mean, apart from…"

"…apart from human blood? No, not really. There's no point. I can't really enjoy the taste in the same way. But some aromas are still intoxicating… hence Hugh and his brandy. He just inhales it really."

"What's the best aroma?"

He gave me a toothy grin and I realised that his canines really were longer than mine… quite a lot longer.

"Raw steak isn't bad."

"Ugh."

"But fresh bread is good too. And roasting coffee. I never get tired of that one."

Fine. After we were married, I would make coffee and drink it and he could just appreciate the scent. He drove down the hill slightly too fast for the old biddies in the village to appreciate. I saw the odd lace curtain twitch.

"Where are we going by the way?"

"It's near Stafford at the County Show Ground. Turn right after the bridge."

We drove on for a little while. I sneaked the odd glance to my right. Oscar looked just fine in profile too.

"If you don't mind talking work, I found you the most amazing house."

"Already?"

"Yes, already. It's called Lichley Manor and it's got everything you asked for and more. Provided you want to absolutely throw money at it, of course."

"May we visit it one evening soon?"

"As soon as you like. I have keys. Turn right here."

"Tomorrow? Could you make tomorrow?"

My social calendar had no entries until Christmas, but Oscar didn't need to know that.

"I'll check, but I think so," I said. "I think tomorrow is free. And left here."

"Thank you. Do I park anywhere?"

"You are welcome. Yes, but close to the building please."

He slid the little car into a space, and got out to open my door. I am a feminist, and don't usually have much time for chivalry, but in this skirt I would take whatever was going. He held out a hand, which I gripped in both of mine and hauled on. Ah gravity, I defeat you!

He offered an arm, and we walked to the entrance of the suite. I was on cloud nine. It was the Institute of Staffordshire Estate Agents' annual summer bash and I had a date. He was a little older than me, and dead, but he was also drop-dead gorgeous and so was my dress.

"Let's go in," I said.

Chapter Five

THE THING IS, there aren't that many estate agents in Staffordshire, so it wasn't the world's biggest party. Pretty much everyone in the room knew me, and they would notice I had a date. Which was exactly what I wanted, but also slightly terrifying. I gripped Oscar's arm, and he reached over with his hand and gave mine a squeeze. I winced without meaning to.

"Were you going to tell me at some point why you have bandages on both your hands and are limping slightly?" he asked.

"Yes, I was. I am. Just not exactly now."

The party had been going since six, and there was some enthusiastic dancing going on at the far end of the room. On the stage, the Seighford Swingers were in full flow, surrounded by members of my profession who had clearly partaken more of the free booze than the free canapés. Some of them had probably been drinking since lunchtime. One or two looked like they had started the previous day.

Oscar smiled down at me rather enigmatically.

"I take it we won't be dancing?"

"I might manage a very slow waltz."

"But not a tango."

"No."

"Or a foxtrot."

"A whatnot? Oh that. Definitely no."

"Or indeed," he squinted at the dance floor, "whatever it is that they are doing now?"

"That's called the drunken estate agent. And actually, if I drink enough of this free champagne, I will probably do that one anyway."

He laughed. "I am holding my breath."

"Somehow I doubt that. Do you even have breath?"

"No. But I do have the ability to persuade the man with the champagne bottle to come over to you with a full glass."

"And a tray of those prawn dumplings?"

"Probably."

"OK, that tops breathing."

A loud and familiar voice inches from my ear made me jump.

"Oh my giddy aunt, who is your completely hot date, Lav?"

"Claire! You're back. How was your spa weekend?"

I hugged her. Claire and I met at university under rather unfortunate circumstances when we discovered we were dating the same rower. We'd been inseparable since. After graduating with a 2:2 in law, I'd offered her a room in my little cottage while we found our feet jobwise, and she had never left the area. She worked at the showground as an events organiser, and I should have expected she would be around that evening. Claire was a posh platinum blonde, six inches taller than me, and she was working her Nordic looks with a pale green silk number that hung just below see level, as opposed to see everything level, and was apparently held up by crossing fingers and wishing very hard. She was also loyal and kind, despite appearances.

"Was amazing," she drawled in her low Sloany voice. "Turns out that a one-hour Swedish massage is what it takes to shut my mother up for minutes at a time. I wanted to leave her there, but they wouldn't let me. Now stop distracting me, Lav, and introduce me to this completely delicious creature you have on your arm. I warn you; our years of friendship won't be enough to stop me trying to steal him off you."

I turned to introduce my completely delicious date to find him holding out a full glass of champagne and a plate stacked with prawn dumplings.

"I missed seeing you do that," I complained. "Did you use arcane powers or just a compelling manner?"

"You will have to watch more carefully next time," Oscar said, placing the fruits of his labour in my hands. "Or you will never know."

"Ha. Oscar this is Claire. Claire and I are bosom pals from uni. She is not as scary as she looks. Claire, this is Oscar. He is a friend of Hugh Bonner's and I am finding him somewhere to live."

Oscar looked down at Claire.

"How did you plan to steal me?" he asked, deadpan.

"I was going to offer sex, and failing that money," said Claire firmly.

"I am sorry, but Toni outbid you."

"What the hell did she offer?"

"She has promised to dance the drunken estate agent for me later."

"Yah, I cannot top that. We will have to be just friends." Claire stuck out a hand. "Most delighted to meet you, friend."

"You also."

They shook hands. Claire looked down in shock at the cold hand holding hers, and then up at Oscar's rather canine-heavy smile.

"Arcane powers. Hugh Bonner. Cold hands. Ohmygod. You're a vampire."

"Guilty as charged."

"An actual vampire."

"Still guilty."

"Lav, you have bought the world's coolest date ever. Wait until I tell Bernie. He's been watching you in drunken jealousy since you walked in."

"Please don't tell me he's here without Helen to keep his groping hands in check?"

"Sorry. He's been muntered since six thirty and just nearly got thrown out for goosing a waitress. Oh lord, got to go and talk to the catering manager. We are running out of those stupid little bamboo boat plates. Oscar, I will come and give you the third degree later. Ciao."

And she vanished in a swish of blond mane.

I looked up at my date. He looked smug. And he was delicious. And fun.

At that moment Mr Cadwallader spotted us from across the room and headed our way. A big grey-haired, dark-eyed man, he'd played a lot of rugger in his youth, including a season for England as well as several for the county, and it showed. Even now he was an impressive figure, and unlike most of the partygoers around him, he was very formally dressed in a black suit with a well-knotted tie. He had a neat triangle of matching silk handkerchief poking out of his breast pocket, and a watch chain dangling in exactly the right place.

"Oscar."

"Lewis."

They shook hands with great courtesy.

"Oscar, I didn't expect to see you here tonight."

"I am a guest of the lovely Miss Windsor here."

"Is that wise?"

"Wise?"

"Are you putting her in danger?"

"I don't…" He broke off and turned to me. "Is that what it was? Your bruises, the bandages… Toni, is this my fault?"

"Oscar, please don't ruin this evening. Yes, it was the EDL, the police think. But I'm fine."

He looked shocked.

"I was so thoughtless, I never meant this to happen. Toni, I was too impulsive. I shouldn't be here with you."

"Yes, you should. This is exactly where you should be. Right here, on my arm. Making my evening amazing, you daft prawn."

"No. I should go. You shouldn't be seen with me."

"Please stop talking bollocks, Oscar. I actually acquitted myself pretty well. I mean, here I am, all alive and unkidnapped."

But he wasn't looking at me—he was exchanging a meaningful glance with Lewis Cadwallader. Something seemed to have been agreed between them, because Oscar nodded his head curtly, and began to lead me towards the exit.

"What's going on, please?" I asked, by then thoroughly irked.

"I'll explain," he said. "Please, come with me. This won't take long."

"Can't it wait? Just a little Oscar? I was having such a lovely time."

"So was I and that's why it can't," he said. "It has to happen now before I lose my resolution."

We headed outside and I was bewildered when he led me to a dark corner behind the catering wing. There was a smell of prawn dumplings, but hell, I was alone in the dark with my hot date. I had a hideous premonition I was about to be dumped, and I knew only one way to stall that.

He turned to me and put both hands on my shoulders.

"Toni," he began gently.

"Oscar, please shut up now," I said.

And I stood on my tiptoes and kissed him.

It's fair to say he hadn't expected it—goodness only knows why—but his reaction was so perfect that I forgave him his blond moment. His hands slid decisively and firmly down my back to my waist and he held me against him while we kissed. I wasn't sure how many centuries old Oscar was, but I was absolutely sure he had spent all of them practising his kissing technique. His mouth was doing deliciously evil things to mine, and just when I thought things couldn't get any better, his tongue joined in and I melted into his arms like syrup.

His hands were cool through the sheer fabric of my dress, and so were his lips. But I was getting quite warm enough for both of us as he explored the contours of my lips and mouth with his and began to slide his hands lower and start to caress me.

He bit my lip softly and his hands crept just that little bit lower to massage my curves. He pulled his mouth the tiniest bit away from mine and murmured into my ear:

"Are you wearing nothing under this dress?"

I dropped little kisses onto his neck, which was all I could get at.

"Nothing else was going to fit under this dress," I said.

One hand left off exploring the curve of my buttocks to slide the skirt of my dress up and come to rest on the flesh of my thigh. He stroked his way gently between my legs and up.

"I know something that would fit perfectly under your dress," he whispered, beginning to graze on my earlobe, "beautiful, intoxicating, lovely Toni."

"You'll have to show me," I said sliding my tongue down to his collarbone and tracing it with my mouth. He wasn't wearing any aftershave that I could tell, and just smelt of man.

Suddenly, there was a sound from the kitchen, a tray of crockery meeting its maker on a tiled floor. There were shrieks and laughter, and the moment—so perfect—was shattered.

Oscar pulled back from me with a jerk and held me at arm's length. He looked mortified.

"Toni, this wasn't what I intended."

"Don't worry. It's exactly what I intended."

"No. Lewis was right. It's not fair on you."

"Please Oscar, try shutting up again. It was working really well."

Instead he put his hands on my shoulders as he had when we first stood together, and the light from the kitchen window fell full on his face, illuminating his crazily blue eyes. He looked at me very intensely, and when he spoke his voice had a melodic, throbbing quality to it. My head felt slightly fuzzy.

"Toni, after tonight you won't remember me. You won't care about me. You will forget we ever met. If people mention me, you will shrug and say you don't understand. You will throw away the notes you made about our meeting. You won't even remember my name." He looked into my eyes and the fuzzy feeling intensified. "After I leave you here, you will walk to the taxi rank and take a car home."

I shook my head in disbelief.

"Oscar, what are you talking about? Of course I won't forget you. This is creepy."

He reeled in shock.

"What? You aren't... this isn't working. You aren't compelled?"

"I'm pissed off and confused, that's what I am. Now will you please either start kissing me again or take me back to the party, because this is just weird."

But he just stood there, staring at me as though I had sprouted horns.

"This has never happened before."

"Yes, well, Bernie said that too."

"What?"

"Nothing."

He shook his head and took hold of me again, and gazed at me a second time in that oddly focussed way and began to speak in those throbbing tones again.

"Toni, listen to me–"

"No, listen to me, it's not warm enough out here for me unless you plan to start canoodling again."

He let me go again and glared at me. "You're immune. This makes no sense. Have you ever drunk vampire blood?"

"Drunk what? Yuck no. I don't even like my steak rare."

"I can't compel you. I have never met a mortal who can't be compelled, apart from a tiny few who have drunk vampire blood for many decades. It's not possible."

"Can't be compelled. What is this compelling?"

He ran his hands through his hair in exasperation. A few minutes earlier, I would have found the gesture adorable, but I was cooling towards my date faster than a martini on ice, especially now that it didn't look as though I was going to be stirred, let alone shaken.

"We can impose our will on mortals, a geas or an enchantment might be another way of putting it."

"You were going to impose your will on me? Compel me to obey you." I was suddenly incandescent with rage. "Why stop there? Why don't you just rape me then tell me to forget about it afterwards. Who do you think you are to force me to do what you want? Take your stupid wanky penis-shaped car and bugger off back to your coffin, you undead creep."

I tugged down my skirt, and swivelled round, combing my

tousled hair with my fingers as I headed back towards the lights of the main entrance.

"Toni, please wait."

I turned round and looked at the man who just moments ago had embodied all my dreams.

"Oscar, dumping someone is never fun, but it's not OK to brainwash them into forgetting it just for your convenience. I actually preferred being dumped by Bernie. Goodnight."

I stormed back into the party and walked straight into Claire.

"What happened to your hot man?"

I groaned.

"We'll always have feelings for one another, but our lives are heading in different directions. Yada yada. He's a creep."

She swiped a full glass of champagne from a passing waiter and tucked it into my hand.

"Wow. Is that a record? Your shortest relationship ever?"

"Let's see. If we consider that it started when he picked me up at around eight, and it's now shortly before ten, so even including the drive here... yes, I think that's a record even for me."

"Darling girl, I'm so sorry. But tonight I'm also in charge of a room full of boys who have now drunk enough that they are inhaling the helium from the balloons to sing the girl's lines in *Grease*. And I need to you to remove your lovely boss from my waitresses, and either run him over a few times or run him over a lot of times. Your choice."

What a perfect end to my evening. This office party was going to end exactly like all the ones before it. I would be single and getting groped by Bernie. At least it was unlikely to contain any more unwelcome surprises—I knew the script from here.

I found him trying to explain the offside rule to a terrified Bethany. He had cornered her behind a buffet table and was waving a sausage roll and a canapé fork at her.

"So this is your ball, geddit? And this," he made a swoop with the fork, "this is your striker. And this," he looked around for another prop, tried to pick up a small bamboo boat plate, dropped the sausage roll and fell over trying to catch it.

Bethany took the opportunity to escape. I sat next to the sprawled Bernie, picked up a bottle of champagne that someone had thoughtfully left on the table and took a swig. I glared at my boss, who was starting to look green about the gills. I'd had to ask about a dozen taxi drivers at the last party before I had found one who would let him in their car. Then I remembered something... strictly speaking, Bernie was someone else's problem these days; someone else could have their evening ruined. Feeling only slightly guilty, I took out my mobile. I dialled Helen's number. She answered on the third ring.

"Hey, Toni. Aren't you at the party?"

"Hi Helen. Yes, and why aren't you?"

"I have an early start tomorrow, and you know how crazy these office events always get..."

"I do, indeed. This one just got so crazy that you need to come and take Bernie home."

"Is he OK?"

Was he OK? That was a dumb question. He was selfish, avaricious, sexist, lecherous, shit in bed and couldn't hold his drinks. Even his clothes were offensive. The answer to that question was never, ever going to be yes. What was she even thinking? The man in question began to stroke my ankle so I stood up and took a step away.

"Yeah, um, Helen, he's a wee tiny bit pissed. You need to come and get him before he passes out in a puddle of his own puke. And I think that gives you about ten minutes, so put your foot down."

And I disconnected before she could argue. I looked down at my employer. He was lying on his back, gazing up my skirt as though it was Christmas. Great. I delivered a few spleen-venting kicks and asked security to drag him to the pickup point. Finally, I commandeered a couple of trays of canapés and three bottles of champagne from the kitchens and walked to the taxi rank.

I let two cars go, before taking one where I recognised the driver. I didn't really fancy ruining a second outfit running through the to certain death. I settled myself into the passenger seat, piling the bottles around my ankles and taking the canapés onto my lap.

"Where to, miss?" the cab driver asked.

"The old cemetery above Colton," I said.

He looked perplexed.

"Are you sure, miss? It's not very warm and it will be very dark."

"I'm quite sure," I said, close to tears but knowing that out there one person would understand. "Please hurry. My friend is waiting for me."

It took about twenty minutes. Normally I am quite chatty, but I didn't say a word as the car made its way along the bypass, through the village, and then up the hill.

"I don't like leaving you here on your own, miss," the driver said. "Are you quite sure you are OK on your own?"

I pressed a twenty pound note into his hand.

"It's OK," I said, placing two trays of prawn dumplings, a rack of honey-roasted spareribs, and two dozen chilli chicken skewers at my feet and clutching the champagne to my bosom. "I'm not alone."

I waited until his headlights had moved out of sight. Then I took off my shoes and padded up to Bredon's grave. I didn't have any salt, and I didn't have any perfume. And I was buggered if I was going to waste good champagne—or even just free champagne—on a circle of protection. I just sat on the gravestone in my gold dress and sent my power into the damp, dew-filled English earth.

"Bredon Havers, in friendship I call you. I summon you this night. Come to me. Please." And then I burst into tears. "Oh God, Bredon. I just had the worst night of my life ever. I messed up everything. And I don't even think it was my fault. I don't think I was ever so unhappy."

He put his arms around me, and I buried my face in his coat.

"There, there," he said. "Tell me everything. Tell me everything that happened."

Chapter Six

THE CHAMPAGNE WAS gone. The food had gone too. Without a circle to constrain him, Bredon could wander at will, so we were sitting on the cemetery wall under the trees, where it was dry, just behind the headstones of John Doo (1872) and Maryrose Bletchington (1899). I was wearing Bredon's coat.

"I think it makes sense," he was saying. "You have power over the dead. Vampires are dead... so it's logical for you to be immune to some of their influence."

"Do you think I overreacted?"

"No, in no manner. My dear lady, freedom and free will—those we should never surrender without the fiercest battle. To have them stolen away, and in secret... that is a great betrayal. But in your love's defence, he did want to protect you."

"I suppose so. So what should I do?"

"Your new world is very strange to me. In my day, we would stake vampires wherever we found them. We were taught they were the very spawn of the devil."

"You don't sound so certain."

Bredon shook his head. He looked troubled.

"I am an undead creature myself, yet I am not evil. I feel I could do good in the world. I am no tool of Lucifer. So it seems quite possible to me that your vampire could be a good man too."

"Thank you. I'll give him another chance. If he'll have me, that is."

Bredon very chivalrously kissed my hand.

"If not, Mistress Toni, he is a fool and not worth the curls on your head."

"Thank you. You're really sweet. Would you mind walking me home? There are some people who have been causing me trouble and I really can't cope with anything else this evening."

"Of course. But you must tell me the way. Much has changed since I walked these roads, you know."

I decided to leave the debris of our midnight picnic to pick up in daylight with my car, and we walked down the hill from the church together. Bredon told me which buildings had been there in his day—not many—and which were new. He was very impressed by the smooth tarmacked road surface.

"How did it come to pass that the vampire kind are accepted among you?

"It's quite a new thing. And only in Europe, of course."

"What about further afield? Are the undead less accepted?"

"They're completely illegal in North America and Canada. They passed laws making it OK to stake them on sight."

"Why the divergence?"

I explained about Silvio Gambarini, Chicago Mafioso-turned-vampire. Silvio was the worst kind of vampire—he killed when he didn't need to and had total contempt for humans, seeing us as little bags of blood on the move. He'd moved to America from Sicily more than a century before and built up an impressive power base in the city, taking control of much of the drugs trade, controlling prostitution and extortion rackets left, right and centre. He'd made a lot of enemies—and he'd killed most of them too.

In the end, though, it wasn't his business interests that caused his downfall, but his underestimation of human love. He had a devoted coterie, the term used for a vampire's mortal household, and when one of them, Maria Acquarone, gave birth to a little boy, Silvio drank the infant's blood and casually told her to bury the body. It was the last order he ever gave.

Maria's loyalty was broken. The next morning, while Silvio lay in the daytime coma of the undead, she bound him in silver and called the police. It turned out Maria had kept meticulous records of her master's dining habits over the previous quarter of a century. Silvio was found guilty of 1,779 counts of first-degree murder. The Mason-Schelling Act came into force, pitting Europe and the US head-to-head on vampire rights, and Mr Gambarini was staked through the heart at the Metropolitan Correction Center. More than a billion people tuned in live to watch him turn into a cloud of grubby ash. He didn't ask for salvation.

"There are a lot of American vampires coming over to Europe now," I explained, "and according to the paranormal press, they all hate each other."

Bredon and I had plenty of time to chat as we walked back to my house, being as I was wearing a long tight gold dress and little kitten-heeled shoes designed for lingering in rather than actual walking. As we grew close, I warned him:

"There were two men waiting for me the other night. I'm paranoid that they'll be back. My brother had a man protecting me, but I have a feeling he knocked off at midnight."

I had just one advantage when it came to sneaking up on them—they would be expecting me to come from the bottom of the hill or through the trees. The road upwards meandered through the village and ended at the old church. They certainly wouldn't be looking for us to come from the old cemetery at two in the morning. And my hope was that—even if they had been staking out the house—they would have got bored long ago.

No such luck. As we rounded the corner and my porch came into view, I saw a figure on the opposite side of the road, partially hidden by the bus stop. And yes, he was wearing a balaclava. Next time there was a work party, I was going to lock the door, take the phone off the hook and watch all three *Lord of the Rings* movies with a kebab, an entire tub of ice cream and a bottle of vodka. If there was any evening left, I would start on *The Hobbit*.

"Is that your enemy?" Bredon whispered.

"One of them," I whispered back. I took out my phone to call the police, and realised with horror that the battery had died. "This is so unfair. Damn it, Bredon. I think we will have to try to make a run for the house so I can call the police."

"I am more than equal to two assailants," he assured me.

"OK, that's my porch there." I took off my shoes. "I can't run very fast in this dress, and I'll have to unlock the door when we get there, so I am pretty sure they will catch up with us. If you can just fend them off for long enough, then I can get to the phone."

"Have no fear."

"Let's go."

We did quite well. The thug by the bus stop had lost interest hours ago and didn't even see us until we were within moments of the porch. But as luck would have it, that was exactly where thug number two was hanging out. Even as I bounded up the steps to the door, he barrelled into my already-bruised ribs and I went flying. There was a sound of expensive gold fabric tearing, and I think I smacked into the wall and then maybe all of the stairs at least twice each before I tumbled heavily onto my arse.

I looked up, dazed. My attacker wasn't wearing a balaclava. Instead, he was sporting a splendid crusty black eye, the sort you might get if a small, terrified estate agent whacked you in the face with a rock. He smiled, revealing a couple of decades of poor dental hygiene and a disregard for flossing. Perhaps blinded by the porch light, he did not seem to have noticed I was not alone this time.

"Got you now," he said, and took something large, long and shiny out of his belt.

"Leave her alone," Bredon said, stepping in between us.

"Bredon, be careful, he's armed!" I called, but too late.

He stabbed Bredon three, four, five times through the torso. The final thrust was so vicious, I saw the blade emerge from the back of Bredon's shirt. I stared in horror, unable even to scream. Bredon, on the other hand, didn't appear to notice.

"I said leave her alone," he said, and reaching forward, he seized the man on each side of his face. "What sort of low creature attacks a woman?" he asked in disgust and with the most casual of twists, he tore my attacker's head off and hurled it onto the lawn.

Yes. That's what he did.

There are about seven pints of blood in a human body, they say. At least six of them hit me head on, along with a couple of vertebrae and the odd chunk of neck. I gazed in revulsion at the top of a torso, which lay sprawled on my lawn. Bredon seemed as surprised as me and we both gaped in silence for some time. Across the road a car engine started up, and a vehicle drove off at top speed, the sort of speed you would drive away at if you'd just seen a man have his head ripped clean off. I didn't blame him at all.

"I do apologise, Mistress Toni," said Bredon. "I was worried about you."

I looked at him. He was blood splattered too and the hilt of a bowie knife was protruding from the centre of his chest. The hydrangea was covered in something I would broadly term 'viscera'.

"Um, don't worry about that. Oh arse, this is awful. What am I going to do with this body?"

"I could eat it," suggested Bredon.

"Please tell me I heard that wrong. Did you really just offer to eat it?"

"Well, to be honest, it smells rather good. And it's been a while since we finished those marvellous little snacks you brought me."

He looked a little dazed, and licked some blood off his hand in a rather embarrassed way. Hungry zombie, no circle of power, corpses springing up around me... this was exactly the kind of irresponsible behaviour my grandfather had warned me about.

"Don't eat him!" I snapped, struggling to my feet and leaving half my skirt behind. "Please don't eat him, it's just too icky. Stay there and I'll get you something."

I clambered up the steps and unlocked the door. I staggered up to the bathroom, where I found the scrap of paper with Oscar's number on it still on the floor. I grabbed the phone from its cradle, and then headed into the kitchen, to collect one of Amelia's meat pies. Under the bandages on my hands, blood had begun to leak out and mingle with the blood that had sprayed onto me. I was starting to smell decidedly of abattoir. I limped back out to find Bredon standing on the lawn, clutching a severed arm and looking peckish.

"Put it down," I said crossly, and he dropped it guiltily. "Eat this instead."

He sat on the steps of the porch, and began to devour the pie. Just the thought of food made me gag, but I pushed it to the back of my mind. I dialled Oscar's number. To my despair, an unknown man's voice answered, quite posh and rather friendly-sounding.

"Hello! Hello, this is Peter."

"Oh, bollocks to that. I need Oscar."

There was a pause, and then the nice voice said rather carefully: "He's really tied up right now."

I heaved a deep sigh. Something squelched under my bare foot. Looking down, I rather thought it was a bit of oesophagus. Or maybe trachea—I was never a hot shot at biology at school.

"Peter, please listen very carefully, because I have had exactly the worst evening of my entire life and it's all one hundred per cent Oscar's fault. My dress is ruined, my shoes are toast, I have had to give away a meat pie that I was really, really looking forward to and—are you still listening, Peter?—there is a decapitated corpse on my lawn that so needs to be gone by the time the milkman drops by in around two hours. So please would you ask Oscar if he could kindly unbusy himself and sort it the fuck out."

There was another pause.

"You must be Toni."

"Yes."

"Right. If you could hold on for a mo, I'll just go and tell Oscar to bestir himself."

"You do that."

"Righty ho."

After about a minute Peter returned.

"Hello Toni. How's your decapitated corpse doing?"

"It's finished bleeding over me, and now it's just oozing onto my lawn."

"They do that. Toni, it's your turn to listen to me. Go inside, leave the door unlocked and have a nice bath. Leave anything that's bloodstained outside the door. Oscar and I are on our way over with some friends."

"Um, OK."

"Give me twenty minutes, Toni. Time for a deep condition if you are quick."

And there was a click. I looked up at Bredon.

"I can't let vampires see you," I said. "I'll have to let you go." I hauled myself to my feet and hugged him stickily. "Thank you for everything. You saved my life tonight."

"You are welcome, my dear."

"Bredon Havers, I release you." That was all it took. I was getting better. It never becomes any less strange, the way the earth just swallows up the summoned dead, like a lake of soil. Bredon receded into my lawn as smoothly and as suddenly as he had emerged from his grave. I was not sure I would ever get used to it. The bowie knife lay on the grass. I left it there.

Whoever Peter was, he had sounded nice. And competent. If you ask someone for help, you should probably take what's on offer. Somehow, I made it upstairs to the bathroom. I ran a bath, dumped my ruined and repulsively meaty dress and shoes outside the door, and soaked off the blood-encrusted bandages from my hands. I shampooed my hair. I shampooed my body. I cleaned blood out of my ears. And my nose. And my teeth. I soaked gravel out of both my knees. I was combing conditioner through my hair when I heard my front door go. There was murmuring, some scuffling, and then Peter's voice called softly up the stairs:

"Toni, is there an outside tap?"

"Behind the dustbin," I called back.

"Okey dokey."

I rinsed my hair and sat on the side of the bath, feeling dizzy. There were bloody footsteps, mine, across the tiles. I wrapped a towel round myself. There was the sound of machinery. A carpet shampooer? Then a tap at the door.

"Toni, it's Peter."

"Come on in."

Peter was short and broad with dark hair that had been trimmed almost to his scalp. He was wearing jeans, some kind of rock tee-shirt and little round glasses. And bless him, he was clutching some kind of crystal decanter and a fine-looking tumbler. He seemed un-phased by my damp, semi-naked state.

"Come into the bedroom while they do this room," he said cheerfully. "Gosh, your hair *is* curly, isn't it?"

"Oscar mentioned my hair?" I asked as we navigated the landing.

"Among other things. I am Peter Hilliard, by the way."

He handed me a glass. I took it gratefully.

"Thank you. I'm Lavington Windsor."

"You are welcome, and I know."

I sat on the bed, and he poured me a generous slug of whatever was in the decanter. I took a gulp. Cognac. Nice cognac.

"Do you clear up a lot of bodies?"

"More than I'd like to."

He rather competently scrabbled through a heap of clothing and unearthed my dressing gown, which I slid into without embarrassment, and then very kindly found me a pair of slippers. Somewhere outside I could hear what sounded like a jet wash going. I finished my recuperative glass and Peter idly refilled it.

"I'm really curious to know how you ripped his head off."

I glared at him over the rim of my glass.

"Maybe I'm just very strong."

He shrugged good-naturedly.

"So don't tell me."

I sighed, feeling very tired suddenly.

"Peter, my house is full of people."

"I know, but on the plus side, I can tell you that your lawn is free of corpses."

"OK, that's good news. Is Oscar here?"

"Yes, but Toni, it's nearly dawn. He can't stay long."

I hadn't realised how much time had passed. Peter patted my

shoulder and stood up. A few moments later, I heard him talking to someone on the stairs. A familiar voice answered. Oscar's. I was either going to have an awkward chat with my date—or my ex. And I had no idea which.

He tapped gently on my door.

"Come in."

He didn't quite come in; he stood in the doorway looking at me. I looked into his lovely blue eyes and quite without meaning to I held out my hand. He walked over and took it gently, careful not to press on my bleeding, torn knuckles.

"I did a very bad job of protecting you, didn't I?"

"In your defence, I think I told you to sod off and let me protect myself."

"Sod off in my wanky penis-shaped car, actually."

"I take that back. I like that car."

He took my other hand and sat on the bed next to me.

"Toni, I promise that no matter how much you annoy me, I will never, ever try to compel you against your will again."

It sounded good, but then it was an easy promise to make, as his vampire compelling stuff didn't work on me in the first place. But I decided to give him the benefit of the doubt.

"Thank you, Oscar. I promise not to call you an undead creep."

He bent his handsome head and kissed me on the forehead. And then the cheek. And then the lips. He traced the outline of my cupid's bow with his tongue, and slid one hand around my waist and the other up my thigh where my hastily knotted dressing gown was doing a very bad job of protecting my modesty. His fingers crept up the inside of my leg and were just making an exquisite foray into the invitation-only area between my legs when there was a tap on the door.

"You have to get below ground," Peter's voice said.

Oscar cursed softly. He dropped a final kiss on my neck.

"I have to go. I will leave Peter to guard you."

"He doesn't look like a bodyguard."

"You'd be surprised."

"Do you want to see that house tomorrow?"

"Yes, but I have business first. I will pick you up at midnight."

I supposed I could sleep when I was dead. Which given the events of the past few days might be soon.

"I'll be ready," I said.

And he was gone.

Chapter Seven

I SQUEEZED OUT my hair with a towel. My knuckles were oozing, and my knees looked like a rugby player's halfway through the season. I looked up at Peter—he was standing in the door holding a massive first aid box.

"Do you know how to use that thing?"

"I was going to spread antiseptic over your entire body and say 'there, there' a lot."

"Honestly, right now that sounds quite nice."

"Thank you for the vote of confidence. As it happens, I am a doctor."

He sat down next to me on the bed, opened the box and began taking out little sealed packets.

"Of, like, physics or theology?"

"Of medicine, smartypants. Have another glug of my nice anaesthetic and hold out your hands."

He was gentler than the PC who had seen to my injuries the previous night. He needed to be. After he had carefully re-dressed and bandaged my poor hands, I watched as he knelt by my bed, removing the last of the gravel from my legs with tweezers.

"Ouch!"

"Cry baby."

"When I jab your bleeding flesh with sharp metal objects, we'll see how brave you are."

"I'm very brave. No whinging at all. Other leg."

"This one's worse."

"Drink more cognac. I'll do your back next."

"It hurts but I have no idea why."

"I think you fell backwards into the porch steps at some point. I was wondering how the blood got there. Hold this roll of plaster, will you?"

"Good God, Peter. Just how much sticking plaster are you going to use?"

"Let me think... have you seen that film, *The Mummy*?"

"Oh, so very funny."

But he was patient and thorough. I also decided that his voice wasn't quite as English as I had first thought.

"Peter, where did you train to be a doctor."

"Heidelberg. Why?"

"Your voice."

"Ah. Yes, I have been in Heidelberg since I was a small child."

"Do you speak German?"

"Ja. Vorsprung durch Technik."

"Why are you with Oscar?"

"I have always lived with Oscar."

"Always?"

"Ja, always."

"Stop being evasive."

"You ask a lot of questions. I am only being evasive because it's a long and rather sad story. Pass me those scissors. My mother was part of Oscar's coterie. When I was very small, I was extremely ill, and Oscar took me to Germany for treatment. My mother died in a car crash while we were there, and we never came back."

"OhmyGod. You're one of Dr Lenz's children."

"Yes. Oscar stayed in Heidelberg and worked for Lenz until very recently."

"You know Dr Lenz?"

Lenz was Europe's superhero, the saviour of Heidelberg. I was impressed.

"Very well. He didn't manage to cure me entirely though. I need vampire blood every month or so to keep things stable."

"So why did you and Oscar come back?"

Peter snipped at a length of tape.

"Coming out hasn't been unremittingly good for the vampire community. There has been a lot of resistance to it. You know how unpopular they are with the far right! And the London Assemblage has been a pain for over a century—Oscar was one of a small group of vampires who was asked to try to talk them into agreeing to some better ground rules. And Oscar wanted to come back to England. But you know all this, surely?"

I really didn't. Why did Peter seem to think I was so enmeshed in the vampire community? He knew Oscar and I had only just met, right? We'd been on exactly one date. Actually, maybe half a date. It didn't make sense.

"Go back, Peter. You lost me at London assembly."

"Not assembly, Assemblage; a community of vampires with its own rules and hierarchy."

"And these London vampires are in charge of the rest of England?"

"Lord, no. I think I need to explain. It's easy to think of the city as sophisticated and the countryside as simple and provincial. With vampires, it's exactly the opposite way round. City vampires move very seldom, they become entrenched in their ways, very closed to change... they see the march of the world around them as irrelevant. They tend to be very arrogant, very focussed on rituals. They view mortals like us as slaves, as just food."

"Like that mafia guy from Chicago? Gambaretti?"

"Silvio Gambarini, yes. He's a classic example. Part of the behind-the-scenes negotiations of the Heidelberg agreement included a commitment that we would force the worst of the urban Assemblages in Europe to behave better. Oscar has been in London for six months working on that."

"How's it going? Did you guys make progress?"

"It's a farce! They are insanely insular. Their mortal coterie is uneducated and inbred. They are obsessed with their crazy hierarchy. I doubt a single one of them has accessed the Internet, let alone used a mobile. But the group is old, and clever, and hugely powerful. Worst of all they have allowed the New York Assemblage to take up residence in the city and it seems to be a competition as to which of them can behave the worst."

Many of the vampires of North America had fled to Europe. Others had stayed to fight the new legislation. Mississippi and Louisiana, where the undead had been an open secret for generations, were heavily opposed to the new law, as was California, where two medical facilities had been working on similar projects to that of the good Doktor Lenz.

"Did you give up?"

"Not exactly—we may have a worse problem here now. It seems that our lovely London vampires have given the remainder of the Chicago Assemblage permission to come and live in Staffordshire."

"What? That lot who inspired the Mason-Schelling thingy? Gambarini's crew?"

"Self-same."

"Can they even do that? Give them permission to come up here and settle…"

"Absolutely not. Toni take a deep breath; I am going to yank this last bit out."

"Ow!"

"That's better. No, they can't, but they have. While I would rather deal with Chicago than the London Assemblage, they are bad news. And they can't stay. But they've been buying up property under the radar, and missing persons reports are already on the up. They target the homeless and lonely older people who live on their own. And friends of the resident vampire community. When you told Oscar you had been attacked he assumed it was them—not the EDL."

He'd told Peter about that too?

"They were pretty incompetent, to be honest."

"Probably was the EDL then. The Chicago bunch may not be

very evolved, but they are extremely good at violence. I have a suspicion that they fell out with their hosts in London, who decided to suggest Staffordshire as a good place to settle in the certain knowledge that Benedict will wipe them out to the last fang. OK, you are ready for interment in a sarcophagus now. Is your tetanus up to date?"

"I don't think I have ever had one."

"Hmm." Peter took out a fat syringe that made my stomach drop. "Arm, thigh or bum, fräulein?"

"None of the above?"

"Sorry."

"Arm, then. Left one. Ouch!"

"You are such a wuss."

"Bully. You have a crap bedside manner."

"I have a lovely bedside manner. All my patients say so."

He unexpectedly gave me a very careful hug. It turned out to be exactly the wrong thing to do because I burst into tears.

"Oh Peter, there was so much blood. And his head came off. And my dress is ruined, and Oscar never got to take it off me."

"Oh Christ, I am so sorry. And here I am being an arse. The blood-soaked scraps of it that I saw did look very sexy. There, there."

I gave a rather watery chuckle.

"That is the first time you have got round to saying that."

"There, there. Come on, let's get you into bed."

He found me pyjamas, and poured me another glass of cognac.

"Do you want me to give you something to help you sleep?"

"No. I don't think so. I want to be able to wake up like a cat when the next person attacks me. Will you stay?"

"Yes, I'll stay."

I crawled under my eiderdown. I didn't seem to have spent nearly enough time with it recently.

"Peter."

"Yup."

"The vampires in Heidelberg don't all sound bad."

"They are very different. But Toni, they are a very young Assemblage. The original vampires of Germany were almost all wiped out in the Second World War. The current crew are free thinkers. The inhabitants of Chicago and London have lived there for centuries, with no one to challenge the way they behave. You really don't want them on your doorstep. I understand the Chicago mob think it will be trivial to just wipe out the resident Assemblages here and move in."

"It won't, will it?"

"No. The Assemblage here is one of the most powerful in Europe. Their leader is the oldest vampire I have ever heard of."

"What is his name?"

"Benedict Akil."

"What's he like?"

"Not very nice. But fair. Mostly."

"I take it vampires don't do democracy."

"Gott no. Leadership is based on power. That's a lot of the problem. Are you sleepy?"

"Maybe."

He said something, but I couldn't quite work it out. It was the last thing I remembered of that night. Thankfully, I didn't dream.

When I woke, the sun was high in the sky and there was a pleasing smell of coffee. I blearily opened my eyes to see Peter carrying a tray in one hand—all good—and his enormous first aid kit in the other. Not good. I tried to sit up but all the bits of my body that had ached the previous day ached even more. Worse, all the bits that had been fine had decided to feel left out and joined in on the pain front.

"Please, just kill me now," I said miserably. "Please don't take any more sharp things out of that box."

"Don't panic. I've bought you coffee, croissants and morphine. In five minutes, you'll be bouncing round the room. You'll probably offer me sex."

"Nope, I am living the rest of my life celibate. I tried to get laid last night, and I got dumped, beaten up, my dress ruined and had to watch a zombie rip the head off the only guy I have ever met who looks worse in a balaclava than me. I am becoming a nun."

"A zombie?"

Oops. That wasn't clever of me. Peter was looking at me curiously, his brow furrowed behind his glasses. I tried to look clueless and sleepy, which wasn't hard.

"A what?" I asked vaguely.

"You said a zombie."

"Did I? Are you sure?"

"No, but I thought you did."

"I don't know what I am saying. Give me that coffee and those nice pills now."

He sat down on the side of the bed and handed me the mug of coffee and two bright pink torpedo-shaped tablets. I got the impression he had been up all night. A strong smell of bleach was drifting in through my bedroom door.

"There you go. It's noon on Saturday, by the way. Do you have anything to do today?"

I gulped down hot coffee.

"I have to pick the keys to Oscar's house, and I have to play croquet. Why, are you planning to guard me all day?"

"I was if that's alright. Oscar would like me to keep you alive until nightfall, and I think we are all impressed by your ability to get into trouble."

"Thank you so much. Absolutely none of this was my fault. And can you even play croquet?"

"No, but I can learn. And what were you even doing out on your lawn at four in the morning wearing half a dress?"

"Trimming the sodding leylandii. Give me those croissants."

It's hard to stay mad at someone who brings you coffee and croissants in bed. And it's impossible after two of those little pink pills. By the time I had finished my coffee I was full of warmth and affection for the whole world, and my aches and pains seemed like just a bad dream. Peter had made himself comfortable at the foot of my bed.

"Who are we playing croquet with, then?" he asked.

"Oh, that. He's known as the eighth dwarf."

"What? Who?"

"Mr Allardyce—or Gropey as we call him. He has wandering hands."

George Allardyce had been chief constable of Barchester. He knew how to network, and he'd finessed that into an appointment at the House of Lords on his retirement. He still worked as a consultant for the police force, and was always wandering round Will's place of work being smarmy and patting down the WPCs. He liked a bit more luxury than a police salary stretched to, but he'd coped with that quite recently by marrying Lulu, widow of a millionaire beef importer. The talk was he'd better be careful though—Lulu was a staunch Catholic, and she'd not forgive Gropey George his wandering hands if they became public.

Lulu Allardyce had never had children, and she adored Wills—and me. So whenever the weather turned warm enough for croquet, Wills would drag me round. He would hobnob with any senior officers present and I would try to get my ball through the hoops while keeping my arse unfondled. I'd been too slow to think of an excuse for this weekend. Maybe Peter could protect me from more than the EDL or the Chicago undead mafia.

I picked out a white chiffon sundress with spaghetti straps that was long enough to hide the bandages on my legs, and teamed it with black lace gloves and black strappy sandals. I added a soft white shawl to hide the plasters on my back and I was nearly there. I tried and failed to brush my hair with the fat bandages on my hands.

"Shall I do that?" Peter asked.

"I don't think you can," I said. "No one can brush my hair when it's in this mood, not even me."

"Let me try," he said, taking the brush out of my hand and in about four minutes he had reduce my frizz to a headful of neat and obedient ringlets.

"How do you even know how to do that?" I asked in amazement.

"Can't you guess? There are always dozens of little girls at Lenz's hospital. None of them has been away from their parents before and they all burst into tears if you snag a tangle."

"That's so sweet. Do you miss it?"

"My work? Yes, every day, but I hope in time there will be facilities like that in the UK. Hold out your hands and I will try to get those gloves onto them."

"Ow."

"Do you want more painkillers?"

"Goodness no! I am already floating. You are right about this morphine. I might start offering sex in a minute."

"Good lord, girl. Why couldn't you have decided that before we brushed your hair! I am not doing it twice."

"Fair enough. But no, no more painkillers unless you want to carry me."

He took my handbag and helped me down the stairs.

"I'll drive," he said, "so as to avoid certain death. Which is your car?"

It was said with a note of doom as he looked at the sad specimens on offer.

"Um, that one there," I said in embarrassment, pointing at the piece-of-crap-mobile.

Peter shuddered.

"There goes my street cred. Forever. Hop in."

We drove first to the office to pick up the hefty bunch of keys that the Lichleys' solicitor had couriered over and then to the Allardyce house, a pretty 1920s heap of red brick to which Lulu had added a tennis court, croquet lawn and a swimming pool. The pool was memorable for its sub-zero temperatures, the croquet lawn for its population of flying ants. My brother and his boyfriend had arrived ahead of us, and Wills was already schmoozing. I caught sight of his shock of red hair amid the throng around the bottles. He's got my colouring, but fortunately for his career, not my height.

The dress code was smart casual. I looked around at a sea of chinos and white shirts and then back at my escort. He was still wearing his jeans and trainers, but had swapped the previous night's tee-shirt for a black one that sported a large skull on the front, skewered on a dripping dagger. He caught my look and smiled, all innocence.

"Tell them I'm from Germany," he said sweetly, "and don't understand your strange English ways."

"I was going to pretend you were my stalker," I said, "but I don't think I can hold the mallet, so you might have to be my deputy instead. You had better come and meet my brother."

Wills was inevitably chatting with Gropey George. We look very alike, my brother and I, the same copper curls, freckly skin and green eyes. But as I said, like most other humans who have graduated to lace-up shoes, he's a lot taller than me.

He did a double-take when he saw that I wasn't alone, raising one quizzical eyebrow at my unconventionally clad consort.

"Hello Toni. Who is your friend?"

I decided to make him suffer the pangs of curiosity.

"Hey, bro. This is Peter."

They shook hands, and William called over his rather lovely boyfriend Henry Lake. Henry described himself as an actor, but he never seemed to have much work, and paid his way by taking off-on modelling contracts. He'd recently been thrown off a reality TV show and bookings were up, mostly to pose scantily clad in glossy magazines or clutching new model mobiles for handset adverts. Henry was third generation from Jamaica, with a physique designed for being photographed. He'd been a gold medal fencing champion four years before, and you could easily see why, with his long, elegant limbs and beautifully coordinated, lithe loping gate. I would bet he never ever tripped over his own feet or actually slapped himself in the face. He was very sweet, and I was never sure that Wills deserved him.

Henry also shook hands with Peter, who smiled affably and disclosed nothing.

Wills said with unconvincing nonchalance: "So, um how do you two know each other?"

"We met through work," I said as unhelpfully as possible. Peter stood by me quietly, pretending he had no idea anyone was interested in him. My brother looked from Peter to me and back again... and then nosiness got the better of him.

"OK, enough sis. Who's this guy, is he a boyfriend? What does he do? Yada yada. Spill the beans."

I laughed. "I knew you would break. Seriously, Peter is moving to the area, we actually did meet through work. He's not my boyfriend and I don't think you will ever have to arrest him for anything. He doesn't sell drugs or jack cars."

"Unlike your previous boyfriend."

"Unlike my previous boyfriend."

"Who did both..."

"As you say." I punched him on the arm. "Lighten up. I am only here because you bullied me. Let's get this dumb game over—Peter is going to play for me because I hurt my hand and because it's not possible for him to be any worse at it than I am."

Croquet is a game with two teams, six hoops, eight mallets and too many rules.

If the damn ball is too close to the edge, you have to move it. If it's over the edge, you move it. If someone else hits it, they move it for some complicated second shot. Anyway, the way it works is that someone is always moving my ball around, and while I am asking them what the bloody hell they're doing, the opposition has shot theirs through another two hoops. And then whenever I bend over to try to hit the ball myself, Gropey George starts fondling my bum... At which point I arse up the shot and someone starts moving my ball around a-bloody-gain. The worst rule is that you are not allowed to use the mallets to club the opposition to death, and the best rule is that when the game is over, you all drink a litre of Pimm's and lemonade. It's a wonderful game; everyone says so.

Peter proved to be rather good at it, and without the need to bend over and sight through the hoops, I was getting rather less fondled than usual. The Pimm's mixed swimmingly with the morphine and all in all, it was the best croquet match I could remember.

When we sat down for lunch—the inevitable quiche, rice salad and strawberries and cream—my team had won for the first time on record. Lulu congratulated us with genuine pleasure while Gropey George consoled himself by sitting next to me and squeezing my thigh.

"Been meaning to talk to you about the clear up rate, my boy," he said to Wills. "You know what I am going to say."

My brother sighed.

"I know what you are going to say, but please don't. Someone killed her. Someone we haven't found yet. Someone who is out there and could do it again."

Ah. They were back to poor headless, handless, and generally hopeless Jane Doe.

"Windsor, let it go. You can't bring that poor lassie back, and you haven't made any progress. Let her be buried, and move on."

"Give me time. Just a little more time. We found Fenella's killer in record time."

George Allardyce shook his head.

"There are other things to be done, my boy. My mind is made up."

Wills looked despondent. I understood his frustration, but George had a point. In all the months that she had been lying in a freezer, they had come no closer to finding out who Jane Doe was or why anyone would want to kill her. She was just a poor sad statistic ruining the station's record. Maybe it was time for her to rest in peace.

"So, more Pimm's anyone?" asked Lulu cheerfully, appearing at my elbow with a jug. No one declined.

Peter and I left soon afterwards. I was falling asleep in my strawberries, and he thought I should take a nap before trying to show Oscar round Lichley Manor.

"After all," he said as we drove back home, "think how embarrassed you will be if you fall asleep mid-shag."

He parked the rust-mobile at my kerb, and patted it kindly as he helped me out.

"Are you planning on playing gooseberry?" I asked.

I was starting to like Peter very much, but I didn't want him on my date, and I really wanted to find out if Oscar was as good at second, third and fourth base as he had been at the first.

Peter seemed amused.

"No, I was planning on getting some sleep myself, as it happens. If you could manage not to decapitate anyone tonight, or break any limbs, I would appreciate it. I'll head off when Oscar arrives. If you are really lucky, I will brush your hair free of flying ants."

"It's a deal."

Peter gave me two more lovely pink pills and I curled up on the sofa and slept the sleep of the dead. Well, not quite the sleep of the dead. Or even the undead. But it was a good nap just the same.

Chapter Eight

I woke to darkness and the smell of frying steak. Someone was singing something in German in my kitchen.

"Peter," I called. "Is that you?"

The singing stopped. A few moments later my living room door opened, and Peter turned on the main light. He was wearing my apron and looked cheerful.

"I love your stove," he said. "I've never seen one before."

"It's an Aga. My grandparents had it installed. I got it converted to gas about five years ago. Are you cooking me dinner?"

"Ja. Your fridge assured me that you weren't a vegetarian."

"Goodness, no. And you?"

He looked amused.

"Toni, I grew up in Germany, remember. There we think sausages are vegetables."

We wandered through to the kitchen together. Peter hadn't just de-corpsed my house. It had been spring cleaned to within an inch of its life. My old wooden table—which I usually kept piled high with washing up waiting for the washing stage—glowed. I had never seen it so unsticky. It sported a bottle of wine and two place settings. Peter had even dug out two crystal glasses that I kept for best. Who was I kidding? I had never used them.

Something was sizzling. A saucepan was filling the room with steam. I sat down at one of the place settings. Peter, his glasses slightly fogged, poured something sparkling into my glass. It was the colour of sunshine on water. While I was appreciating that it tasted exactly as good as it looked, my guest started heaping two warm plates with hot food. A couple of minutes later, he placed them on the table and sat opposite me. We chinked glasses.

"Peter, are you bored or something?" I asked, picking up my knife and fork and poking at my plate. It appeared to contain a cross section of cow, all of my five a day and a potato cake. They were bobbing along merrily in a golden sea of butter; as I watched, a broccoli floret sank to happy, saturated doom.

"I have been bored since we came here," he said. "Gott im Himmel, but I'm not used to all this free time. At the clinic, I never had a moment to myself, in London we were constantly under siege and fearing for our lives. Here, in this green and pleasant land, I have nothing to do and no one to talk to. When you rang last night, it was the first time I had felt useful for a month."

I shook salt liberally over my plate. Peter winced.

"My blood pressure is fine," I protested.

"Not if you keep that up," he retorted. "If you don't mind, I'll sleep here while you and Oscar view this house."

I speared a garlic mushroom on my fork.

"Where are you living until Oscar finds a house?"

"At the home of the Assemblage leader I mentioned, Benedict Akil."

The mushroom was delicious. Peter topped up my glass.

"And you don't like that," I asked.

Peter shook his head, his glasses still steamy.

"I can't like him. He is very used to having his own way, very autocratic. We need our own place."

I leaned over the table and squeezed his hand.

"I do think after tonight, you will have it. I can't imagine a more perfect place for you and Oscar to settle in."

He nodded.

"Thank you."

We ate our meal in companionable silence after that, and Peter served us each one of Amelia's apple turnovers for dessert. After scarfing the last curl of pastry, I got up from the table and hugged him.

"Thank you for everything."

He hugged me back.

"You're welcome."

I took my final glass of fizz out onto the porch. Perfect: no blood, no corpse, no assassins. I sat on the steps and waited for midnight. I really hoped my second date would be better than my first.

At any rate, he was on time. His little aubergine-coloured car slid in next to mine bang on the dot of twelve. Tonight, my date was wearing beige linen trousers and a white polo shirt. Hmm. Seven out of ten, but I wasn't feeling picky. I ran over to the car and when Oscar stepped out, I gave him a hug. Someone else could play hard to get, because I really couldn't be bothered.

Oscar returned the hug.

"Did Peter look after you?"

"Are you joking? I have been looked after almost to breaking point. If he nurtures me any harder, I am going to fake my own death."

He laughed and kissed my cheek and then my lips. The kiss got a bit out of hand, and rather shortly I was leaning back against his car and he appeared to be trying to count my tonsils with his tongue. It seemed too late to tell him I'd had them both out six years before. Anyway, he seemed to be enjoying the search. After a few minutes he pulled back and looked at me rather intensely.

"How am I meant to resist you while we view this property?"

I shook my head.

"We can take breaks," I suggested. "Frequent breaks."

He peeled himself off me and we got in the car. I saw a few lace curtains twitching. Ah well, let them have a bit of a thrill, I thought to myself. I was hoping for a much bigger one later myself.

As he drove, I told him what I knew about the history of Lichley Manor. Along with the keys, I had been given a half-hearted marketing brochure that some flunkey who didn't work as hard as me had flung together. I wasn't sure how much of the house and gardens had working electricity or floodlighting, so I had bought my largest torch. As an estate agent you pick up a lot of essential kit; my work bag contains a torch, lock picks—and yes, I know how to use them—hand wipes (don't ask) and a rape alarm. The latter I have only used twice, once to scare off a dog and the second time when the lock picks didn't work. But I keep it charged.

The house by moonlight was a dream. We drove through the rusting gates and parked in front of the dilapidated porch. No lights came on, so I turned on my torch and began to try keys in turn. Oscar poked at a windowpane, and something fell off with a clang.

"Toni, this is fabulous. All we need is some bats and I will be my own stereotype."

He couldn't see how embarrassed I looked in the dark, right?

"Actually, there are some bats in the roof of the gatehouse. They have a protection order on them; it's in the brochure."

He laughed.

"Don't be too embarrassed, Toni. I like wildlife."

Oh, hang on: he was a vampire. He could see in the dark. He could see exactly how embarrassed I was. Thankfully, the seventh key I tried fitted and the door opened. It let out the corniest and most unearthly creak. I started to giggle.

"Honestly, Oscar, you could at least have driven us here in a coach piled high with coffins. You're rather letting the side down. After all, I've provided the bats and the sound effects."

He slid an arm around me and kissed my neck. I detached myself for long enough to slip through the front door and into the hallway. I found a light switch that surprisingly came on at the first press, and blinked into the sudden brightness of a dusty wood-panelled room with an elegant curved staircase. Lord Lichley had lived in the house until he'd died, but he'd last done it up decades ago. It needed rewiring, replumbing, replastering and redecorating, not to mention the addition of trifles such as central heating—but even in its current rather dilapidated state it was a remarkably pretty house.

"Do you want me to show you round?" I asked Oscar, who was looking about in a pleased manner that boded well for my commission.

"Hmm? No, you wander. I will explore," he replied, and vanished into the dark of one of the corridors off the hall.

Hey, Toni: want to explore a spooky old house in the dark on your own? Bats and vampires guaranteed? But naturally, of course, bien sûr; it's what Saturday nights were made for.

As it happens, I am not easily spooked, so I wandered around the rather lovely rooms, trying light switches at random. Some of them worked. The house was still largely furnished, and I knew a cleaning service occasionally spruced it. My favourite room was above the arc of the front porch—a curved wall studded with deep cushioned window seats looked over the front lawn, which was illuminated sufficiently by moonlight for me to appreciate the vista. Someone had installed one of those lovely round daybeds, and a green silk cover still lay on top. Bored of waiting for Oscar, I turned off the lights to that I could better appreciate the view and sat on one of the window alcoves. Starlight came into the room in an appropriately romantic manner. All that was missing was my swain. Then:

"I wondered where I'd find you."

I spun around. He was standing in the shadow of the bedroom door, head to one side, watching me. How long had he been there?

"Oscar."

He crossed the room and sat down next to me, wrapping his arms around me.

"I like this house."

I nestled into his embrace.

"Me too. It's beautiful. And cosy."

"This is your favourite room?"

"Definitely. Imagine the sun streaming in through the windows on a lovely summer's day. The brochure calls it 'the sun room'."

He looked around at the moonlit room.

"Toni, I will have to just imagine it."

Oops. Vampire. Mental face palm.

"It's probably at its best right now," I hastily amended.

He drew me closer.

"It's at its best with you in it," he said, and tightening one arm around me and with his other hand tilting my face up to his. "Please don't make me wait, Toni. I want you."

Make him wait? The man could have had me on the pool table at the Black Mitre!

"Don't wait, Oscar."

He gazed into my eyes.

"Truly?"

I met his gaze head on.

"Really truly."

Be careful what you wish for. He kissed me until my head was spinning, and then lifted me into his arms and carried me over to the day bed.

"Beautiful Toni," he said, lifting one hand to the neckline of my beautiful white sundress. He ran a single fingernail down it, slicing through with vampire speed and—with just that little flick— reduced it to the base elements of dusters.

"Um," I had time to say before my knickers went the same way, leaving me clad in my watch and sandals. He somehow shed his own clothes in the time it took me to even start to wonder how he planned to drive me home nude, and then he was lying over me, whispering my name again.

"Lovely Toni," he murmured into my ear, doing unspeakable things to my earlobe with his tongue and the pointy bits of his teeth.

What the hell... I kicked off my sandals. The watch was too much to worry about.

Indeed, I had other things to think about. Maybe nice things... an alarming amount of Oscar was pressed into my stomach, and he began kissing me with a fierceness that I hadn't expected from his rather well-mannered demeanour out of the sack. He moved both his hands from my waist to my breasts where his cool fingers began to stroke and tease in a way that would have left me breathless if his kisses hadn't already managed that. He was biting my lips hard enough to hurt, but it felt so good I held back my protests. Then he began to move down my neck.

"Gently, Oscar," I managed to say, but he didn't seem to hear. He kissed his way down to one breast, sucking hard enough to make me whimper, and then soothing me with soft little kisses. His fingers mimicked his lips on my other side before he made his way slowly over with his mouth, moving his other hand to take over where his lips had left off.

"Oscar," I said, but nothing else would come out because his first hand had made its way lower, straight past my belly button and into ground zero. He caressed with soft fingertips before pushing them inside and making his way unerringly to my g-spot. Then he stopped kissing my breasts and returned to devouring my mouth, biting harder. It tipped me over the edge. I was lost. I vaguely realised that, as I lost control, he drew back to watch me, a little too controlling for my taste but I was too far gone to care. As my gasps ebbed, he slid his fingers out and laid his body along mine.

"Toni," he said fiercely, driving in.

I'd thought I was prepared, but I wasn't. Frankly, I'd thought I was done, but it turned out I wasn't even started. Oscar wasn't gentle, but I no longer minded because the golden peaks of pleasure that had just started to ebb away rushed back in waves and all I could do was hold on to him and close my eyes.

He took his time, wringing every tiny ounce of pleasure out of me before taking his own. Finally, I lay on the dusty silk daybed, my face buried in his neck, tasting the salt of his chest with my lips, trying to remember how to breathe. In, then out again, right? He moved to curl around me, pressing his chest into my back, and dropping kisses into my hair. I wondered how to break the ice after so much passion, before realising with a shock that we were nowhere near icebreaking time: he slid into me from behind and set up a glorious staccato rhythm. I cried out again, and then as he continued, again. I felt his climax match my own, but it made no difference to his appetite... pulling back from me, he was tumbling me in his arms, laying me back on the cushions, readying himself to take me again.

"Oscar," I was moved to protest again. "Gently."

He laughed in triumph.

"Gently?"

"Yes! Gently."

In response he caught me up into his arms and carried me over to the nearest window seat, gathering me sideways onto his lap and cradling me in one arm while caressing my breasts with the other.

"You are drenched in starlight," he whispered into my neck.

"Starlight is lovely," I murmured back. "I am kind of drenched in Oscar too."

He began to kiss my lips softly, over and over, while his hand crept lower. It made its way between my thighs and he stroked with insistent fingertips until I was whimpering with pleasure again. Then he lifted me up and impaled me on his lap. I gasped because at this angle he was even deeper and my whole weight drove me onto him. But this time he just rocked me gently to orgasm, keeping up the tempo until I was crying out loud. I felt his own spasms match my own; he called my name three, four, five times... and then I think we both lost the power of speech for a while. This time he seemed ready to rest and I curled up in his embrace with my cheek on his shoulder.

I would have been the happiest girl in the world except for two things. The first one was that I hadn't so much made love with my adorable Oscar as been ravaged. It was the best sex I had ever had, times fifty. If there were prizes, Oscar would have won gold, silver, bronze, all the runners up and the good spirit. But I thought making love should be more about sharing and frankly just a little less like being assaulted. But then, it was our first time. And given how unutterably crap first-time shags usually are, I was willing to give it another shot.

The second thing was more concerning: naked and alone with Oscar, I had finally worked out something that had been bothering me since we had met in the pub.

I could feel him.

I could feel him not just physically, but in the same way that I could feel Bredon Havers, Fenella Hampton May, John Doo, Maryrose Bletchington or any other corpse I had summoned from its rest. I could feel the shape of his spirit. I'd told him off for trying to compel me, but I was worried it was the other way round. I could boss around the undead like school children. Just suppose I could do it to Oscar?

I gazed at the tattered remains of my clothing on the floor and began to chatter a little frantically.

"You realise that this is the third dress I have gone through in three days. Dating a vampire is very hard on the wardrobe."

"I'm sorry; did anything survive?"

I looked over to the bed.

"My shoes, I think. Nothing else."

"You will probably be relatively modest if you wear my shirt."

He was right—it would in all likelihood come down to my knees. And I would get to lech at his torso as we drove home. A win all round, if you discounted the rather pretty sundress that might now have a second career polishing candlesticks.

I was daydreaming about this and other things when I realised that Oscar had begun to kiss my neck again in an interested and hopeful manner. Oh my goodness, he was gearing up for round two. Or in my case, about round eleven.

"Are you ready?" he asked confusing me.

"Ready for what, my darling?" I kissed his lips. "Do I get to go on top this time, because I am totally ready for that."

Tomorrow was Sunday, and I didn't have to walk anywhere. Ha! Bring on round eleven.

He cupped my face in both his hands, and looked into my eyes with his own blue gaze.

"Toni, let me taste you," he said. "Let me taste your essence."

A cold wave washed over me. I didn't think he was talking about a bit of oral foreplay here.

"Oscar, I don't think…"

And he ruined everything.

"Toni, let me drink your blood."

Ugh. It wasn't quite as gross as Bernie asking me to spank his behind, but it was close. Way too close. I couldn't help myself cringing.

"Yuck, no!"

He recoiled in shock.

"Toni, you don't mean that."

Oh no. Second date was going to be a complete washout if I wasn't careful.

"Of course not. It's just way too sudden, too soon." I was blathering; slow down Toni. "You've taken me by surprise. Dearest, darling Oscar, I adore everything about you. I am sure this will be fine. But not tonight."

Could vampires tell if you were lying? Because I wasn't at all sure it was going to be fine. It sounded thoroughly unpleasant; I really didn't want to be Oscar's little post-coital snack. I'd tried to give blood twice and both times I had felt thoroughly nauseous watching my life drain out of my arm. I certainly didn't fancy it as a recreational activity. It sounded like minor surgery, not extreme heavy petting.

"Toni, dearest, the exchanging of blood is the most exquisite of sensations, I assure you. Even making love cannot compare. You will see…"

Of course I would. I'd never sawed off a limb either, but that sounded just about as nasty. And he hadn't finished.

"… and once we begin to exchange blood, the bond between us will strengthen."

He was going on about something, but I tuned out. This was getting worse. It was going to be just like when you were a teenager, and as soon as you got past first base, your boyfriend was clawing for second. We did that on Friday, now let's do this on Saturday. Last week you let me take off your bra, now take off your knickers. Every time we made love, Oscar would be badgering me to let him partake of a little haemoglobin hunt. And just as soon as I buckled, he would be on at me to drink his blood in return. I gave a little involuntary shudder at the thought. Just as I thought my bad run with men was ending. I wasn't so much unlucky in love as damn well cursed.

"Hush, darling," I said soothingly. "I should have expected this. It's my fault. Now, take me home."

Oscar looked wounded. Or maybe he was just hungry. I didn't care. I was sick of hungry undead men. I wanted my eiderdown and a cup of tea. Or maybe a mug of gin and tonic. Tomorrow I would regret being short with Oscar—tonight he would have to lump it. But he very courteously helped me into his shirt, which was big enough to get me passage into a mosque, and we walked down to the car, turning out lights as we went.

I chattered aimlessly about the house, mostly to ward off any more neck-biting discussion.

"So, do you want me to put things into motion?" I asked. "I mean, do you really like it?"

"Like it? It is perfect. I suppose you will want the little sun room as your bedroom?"

I tripped over my own feet and Oscar gently caught my arm. Two dates, one shag and our first quarrel and we were moving in together. I decided not to fight fate.

"Yup," I said. "Definitely my room. I can set up two months of rental while the purchase goes through."

"Good, yes of course. Peter and I can move in tomorrow?"

Tomorrow was a Sunday. I was good at my job, but not that good. I turned off the hall light and we stood on the porch while I fought with keys again.

"Tuesday," I assured him. "Give me until Tuesday."

He looked a little disappointed. It was a look I was getting used to. "Of course, that will be quite agreeable."

And we walked across the gravel to his little car. He opened the passenger door and I slid into the leather seats. He got in next to me and we drove home in a silence that I hoped was less sullen than it seemed.

At my house he parked behind my little car. He opened the door for me.

"Can I leave Peter with you?" he asked. "It seems a shame to wake him when I'll be going to ground in a few hours, and I doubt he has had much rest recently."

I realised suddenly that all Oscar's years hadn't given him much understanding of people. Peter was frustrated and craving activity—and Oscar was arranging a lie-in for him. I decided to tackle that problem another day and just nodded.

"Sure, I'll make him some breakfast when he wakes up. Wait here while I put something on and then you can take your shirt back with you."

"I don't need it."

"You're driving an open-topped car in a pair of trousers. I think you need your shirt!"

I ran up the porch stairs. No attackers tonight—good, I didn't need another corpse on my lawn. I scurried up to my bedroom and tugged on a nice grey jumper, a cousin of the green one that had been ruined in the woods by my EDL thugs, and then hurried back out to join Oscar. He had walked out to the pavement and was standing rather disconsolately against my neighbour's garden wall.

"There you go, sweetie," I said, handing him his shirt. "But for the record, I think you look just fine without it."

"Thank you."

He shrugged into it and I watched his torso disappear with regret. I started to walk back up the porch steps but stopped when I saw him standing on the pavement looking at me wistfully. Clutching my handbag to my chest, I looked back at him. I had a million things to say: I wanted to tell him how much I fancied him, standing there in his rumpled polo shirt with his hair ruffled and sexy. I wanted to tell him he was being insanely impulsive assuming I would move in with him after two dates. I wanted to tell him that drinking blood was icky and creepy. But most of all, I realised with a rush of warmth, I wanted to tell him that I had fallen in love with him and that he was amazing.

As it happened, I didn't get to say anything at all. I was just standing there looking back at him, wondering whether my life was coming together or falling apart, when a Range Rover roared up the hill at about a hundred miles an hour, mounted the pavement, slammed straight into Oscar and crushed him into the wall of the house.

"Oh my God," I heard myself say.

I ran over to the bonnet, which had sprung open and was smoking. Amazingly Oscar was alive. There was more blood than I could imagine and, after the week I'd had, I could imagine a lot of blood.

"Oscar, are you OK? What do I do?"

He opened his eyes and looked at me.

"Run, Toni," he said. "Just run."

Too late. Something heavy and hard whacked into the back of my head and I crumpled to the pavement.

Chapter Nine

I WAS SEVEN years old when I raised the family dog. Raising pets isn't a good idea. Raising animals is a bad idea full stop. Their spirit leaves the moment they die, and what you get back is hungry, angry and confused, and—if you wait too long—demon infested. It didn't get that far because my grandfather came into the room as I was hiding on top of my own wardrobe from a foaming mass of enraged zombie Jack Russell and he banished the hell out of the thing. I nearly lost a toe from zombie dog bites and I was grounded for a month. Goodness knows what would have happened if we'd had a German shepherd.

But I couldn't help it after that—it was a Compulsion. I raised a wasp and was stung six times until it ran out of venom and I squished it. Grounded for a week. I raised a mouse and then had to crush it with a croquet mallet. Two weeks. Then I practised in secret on my brother's dead hamster. I dug it up and locked it back in its cage, which I hid in my wardrobe. I raised and commanded the poor little sod for days on end until it smelt so bad that grandfather worked out what I was doing. I'd been experimenting by feeding it muesli to see if it would calm down, but it never did. On about day three, it started to rot. By the time I was found out, it was a maggot-infested lump running round the cage on two festering stumps trying to bite me whenever I dared to throw muesli at it.

After that Robert Windsor realised that it might be better to teach me some basic safety techniques rather than just keep grounding me. He'd tried shouting, threatening and taking his belt off, and nothing had worked one iota. So we cut a deal: in the day he coached my brother in football. At night, he taught me to raise the dead. In return, I agreed not to practise on my own. And he was a good tutor, thorough and strict, and excellent at setting coursework. He taught me how to lay a circle of protection, how to summon, how to tell if a raised body was empty and vulnerable to demons. He taught me how to banish efficiently, and how to command the undead. And in between learning how to put on mascara, wear high heels and dance the Macarena, I think I was a pretty good student.

But it took a long time to get to that point: the first time he and I raised the mortal human dead together was on my eighth birthday. We summoned Ethel Maybank, who until five days previously had run the village shop. I think my grandfather had underestimated the strength it takes to call the deceased back from the underworld—he didn't start until he was in his forties. After I had brought back and dismissed dear old Ethel, I threw up and then slept for two days.

But like singing or ice skating—or snogging to be honest—it got better. Though nothing compared to the rush I got that very first time when Ethel had slipped out of the fresh earth of her grave rather more easily than I shrug off my bedcovers in the morning. Blink and you'll miss it. The dead creep easily from their graves and return with just as little fuss: the earth—like a lake of sinking sand—welcoming them back to their rest.

My teacher laid down some ground rules for me. Number one: never raise without a circle. Number two: never break the circle. Number three: never linger with an empty corpse, send it straight home. And if you messed up number three, there were a whole load more rules and one very, very cross grandparent. If you were lucky.

The thing is, necromancy is something you can get better at, but not something you can learn. You can do it—or not. Bernie can't roll his tongue or wiggle his eyebrows. Claire can't digest milk. Wills' boyfriend Henry can't tell the difference between red and green. None of them feel the spirit of the undead.

I can. Even with my eyes closed, I can feel their strength and their presence. And I can tell them what to do.

And that night, as I crawled back to consciousness, I could feel them around me even through the pain in my skull, just as I had when I lay in post-coital bliss with Oscar. I didn't move or open my eyes. I reached out to explore with my sixth sense—my undead eye, if you will. I could feel Oscar himself, weak but awake. And there was another—not such a strong presence, but definitely in the room. I was starting to understand that the vibrancy of a vampire is different from that of a revenant—but not by all that much.

I was lying curled on my side, having apparently been dumped in a heap on a tiled floor. My back was wedged against a cold, lumpy wall. I didn't move. There didn't seem to be any upside in letting whoever had lamped me know I had woken up. I felt the second presence recede. Was there anyone else around? I cautiously opened my eyes to take stock.

I seemed to be in the corner of a well-lit stone cellar. Ahead of me, there was a shoe, no two shoes. I squinted closer... two feet, and Oscar's feet at that. I cautiously tilted my head to look up at him. Well, he wasn't dead, far from it. He certainly didn't look like someone who had just had a close encounter with a Range Rover. He was covered in odd purplish dried blood, and there was plenty of scuffed bodywork, if you get my drift, but he looked more like someone who had fallen down a flight of stairs than survived a hit and run. He was secured to the wall by solid silver-coloured chains and appeared to be asleep. Or unconscious.

I could still hear a hint of movement somewhere, so I kept very still. After maybe a minute I heard footsteps coming down some steps and then the sound of someone stomping across a stone floor. I closed my eyes.

"He got away through the woods, Signore Gambarini."

It was a man's deep American voice, the Chicago accent clear as a bell. He sounded apologetic, a little respectful.

"You were outrun by that little Kraut sawbones?"

The second voice was the other vampire's, a lighter male drawl with the Chicago twang not quite masking Italian vowels.

"Sorry, boss. He had a long head start."

"Damnation. I've been looking forward to draining that holier-than-thou Mother Teresa wannabe. Who's the girl?"

"Oscar Wolsey's latest addition, I am guessing. Word is he petitioned Akil for formal protection for her tonight."

"He doesn't waste time. What did Akil say?"

"Told Wolsey to bring her in and he'd decide."

I was trying to make sense of things. I was pretty certain that we had fallen foul of the Gambarini Assemblage that Peter had spoken of. I seemed to be an accidental addition to a kidnap attempt that was intended to scoop up Oscar and Peter. So far so bad. They hadn't caught Peter, which was nice for him. They'd got me instead, which frankly sucked. The vampire's words indicated they'd planned to kill Peter, which didn't make my odds look good. What was planned for Oscar, I didn't know.

"What state's that car in?" the vampire asked.

"Pretty much dead. It's barely an hour until dawn: you want to get the video equipment down here now?"

"Yes. Now."

And two sets of footsteps made their way away from me and up a flight of stairs. Oscar and I were alone…

I opened my eyes and rolled over. A stone room about twenty-foot square, no doors, no windows. Just the stairs as a way out. It seemed mostly empty, apart from some farm machinery in the far corner and one chained-up vampire boyfriend. He seemed to be coming to now. He blinked his eyes for a moment or two. Then they focused on me and widened in shock. I put a finger to my lips, and he nodded. I tried to scrabble to my feet and something yanked me back down. A locked metal cuff around my left ankle shackled me to a massive ring in the floor on a chain about eighteen inches long. I got to my hands and knees and shuffled backwards, trying to get close enough that I could stand up. Something brushed my elbow as I did. God be praised—it was my handbag. I tipped the contents onto the floor. Rape alarm: fat lot of use. Lipstick: ditto. Condoms: maybe later. Phone? Yes... but damn, no signal in the cellar. Lock picks? Yes!

I looked up at Oscar—he was chained to the wall, and too far away for me to reach. To help him, I would have to get free first.

I sat back down and crossed my chained ankle over my thigh. It was the simplest kind of mechanism, just one barrel. Not sophisticated, and that was a good thing. Picking locks requires two things—calmness and patience. I was short of both, so I forced myself to close my eyes for a moment and take a single deep breath. OK. Good to go. I took out two narrow rods, and worked one into the lock, feeling for the corners of the little flange. The key would normally flick it out of the way—the trick was for me to try to do it by hand. I got it once, twice, three times but it slipped off the edge of the rod. The fourth time it caught. I held my breath... and heard with relief the tiny click I was hoping for. I opened the metal bracelet, and slid it off my ankle.

Oscar's turn next: I ran across the room to him. Now I had time to look, he was chained to the rock wall at wrists and ankles by four similar manacles, but they were shiny and glittery, unlike the dull steel that I had been bound with. The metal seemed to be eating into his flesh in some horrible way. I averted my eyes.

"Can't you break these?" I whispered to him.

"No," he whispered back. "Not a chance. They are rhodium-plated silver."

I had no idea what he was talking about, but the important thing was that I had four locks left to pick.

"Stay still," I murmured. "These shouldn't take long."

But it's one thing to jinx a lock that you are holding on your lap, and another thing entirely to stretch your arms above your head and try to pick one you can barely reach let alone see. I tried again and again, but my hands were starting to shake and sweat and the little pointy rod to jiggle about in my grip.

"Oscar, I can't do it." Tears started to run down my face. "I just can't do it."

"Look at me," he said in a soft but commanding whisper, and I stopped what I was doing and gazed into his eyes. There was a bruise on his cheek. I wanted to kiss it better, but it wasn't the time. "Look at me, Toni. Of course you can do it. You can do anything. I know you. I love you."

I wiped my hands on my grubby jumper, covered in bits of road and smears of cellar. Maybe I needed to go shopping today... what would be open on a Sunday? I reached back above me to the chain above Oscar's right hand and began over again. Calm, calm, Toni. Maybe that new little boutique in the arcade opposite the prison? It took perhaps fifteen seconds this time before I felt the tiny satisfying click. I opened the bracelet of the manacle and eased out Oscar's mangled wrist. The skin stuck to the metal and tore. I winced. Three more to go.

"Toni! They are coming back."

Damn. I thrust the picks into Oscar's free hand, flung myself to the floor on top of my tipped-out handbag in what I hoped was a similar position to before. I had time just to close the chain back around my ankle—but not all the way—and shut my eyes. Moments later I heard footsteps returning back down the stairway.

"Set it up there."

It was the vampire's voice. There was the sound of something being dragged across the floor. I cautiously opened an eye. I could see the back of a shaven-headed man in leather trousers and a camouflage jacket. He was setting up some kind of video equipment, a camera on a big stand aligned in Oscar's direction.

"You got it," he said. "I'll run a power cable down."

And he headed back up the stairs.

I heard footsteps, and a pair of black lace-up boots appeared in front of my face. I tilted my head and looked up. I had the feeling that pretending to nap had stopped being an option.

He was a big broad-shouldered man with close-cropped dark curly hair and a rather jowly face with an enormous number of teeth—two of them very long, much more so than Oscar's. He was dressed in the same kind of leather trousers and army-style jacket as his flunky. His vivid blue eyes were ice cold and they were sizing me up like the Sunday roast. If I distracted him for long enough, might Oscar be able to break free?

"Well, look at this," Toothy said. "A little bedtime snack just for me."

"I am not your bloody snack, you pointy-toothed tosser," I snapped back.

He looked momentarily taken aback.

"Hell, Oscar. You picked one with a bit of spirit for a change. Have you lost your taste for German sausage?"

"You leave him alone," I said, desperate to stop him looking too closely at Oscar. "You've ruined my date and now you stand there pontificating as though you are something special. Well, you are not. And what is more, you have terrible taste in clothes and those trousers make you look like a failed heavy metal star."

It worked. Toothy stopped trying to taunt Oscar, and crouched down by me. He took my chin in his hand and squeezed hard enough to grind my teeth together.

"You are full of words, bedtime snack. How full of words will you be when I rape you until the blood runs down your thighs and then rip out your throat?"

Not very was probably the answer. I hoped Oscar was making progress. I decided to be very calm and grown up about things—and spat in my tormentor's face.

He backhanded me and my head smacked into the floor. Perhaps I was trying too hard to distract him from Oscar. He grabbed me by my hair and pulled me towards him. Then he ran a fingernail down the fabric of my jumper from neck to hem at crazy vampire speed. It was a version of what Oscar had done to my dress just hours before—but without the love and care. My jumper opened like a crisp packet—sodding wardrobe-mutilating vampires—but so did a slash the length of my torso to my thigh that began to ooze blood. Toothy looked at my bandaged body.

"Wolsey, you have been bruising the fruit. Tut tut."

And then he threw me onto my face. I got my hands out just in time—just in time to scrape open my palms to match my knuckles.

"Get ready for snack time," he said from behind me, and I heard a belt being unbuckled.

Damn it. I had distracted him too much. I reached under my body and let my hands close around the little square box of my rape alarm. I grabbed the cord and yanked it out. An eardrum-shattering klaxon filled the cellar, triggering a stream of curses from behind me. I was hurled over onto my back and my attacker crushed the box with his foot. He didn't look particularly cool with his trousers at half-mast and his todger wagging about, and I could tell he knew it.

"Now I am angry," he said. "Really angry."

I had only one option left that I could think of, and I had no idea if it would work.

"Tell me your name," I said to him.

He looked surprised.

"So that you can beg for mercy?"

"So that, beyond the grave, I can curse you for eternity," I replied. I like to be honest—I didn't say which sides I expected us to be on.

"I am Claudio Gambarini, and I will be the last thing you ever see," he said, not very nicely, and frankly, not very originally either.

I took a deep breath and closed my eyes. I reached out with my senses. There he was, much easier to take hold of now I knew his name.

"Claudio Gambarini, I banish you. Leave the world of the living and return to the earth from which you crept."

I opened my eyes to see him slam back all the way into the wall next to Oscar as though a horse had kicked him in the chest. He was clawing at his throat and his face. His hands were opening up tears in his own skin. He made a keening noise, high and panicked. That same purple blood that I had noticed on Oscar was dripping out of him.

I was trying to push his spirit back into the earth and it was like stuffing a greased octopus into a rucksack. His spirit fought tooth and nail—while the man himself simply flailed. He should have just throttled me, and he'd have been alright, but he seemed to be intent on ripping out his own organs. He scratched at his chest, opening it up to the ribs. Blood sprayed across the cellar, across me and across Oscar who was gaping at the scene in horror.

"I said: I banish you, Claudio Gambarini. Leave the world of the living right now, you bloodsucking pain in the arse."

He seemed to have decided I was the problem and staggered over to where I lay on my back, largely naked and bleeding onto the tiles.

"It's you, you're doing this," he rasped. "I'll kill you, I swear."

But it was all too late; the octopus was giving up the fight. It was as though the vampire's spirit had been clinging on desperately to the edge of a cliff and his fingers suddenly lost their grip. He stepped through me and through the stone floor of the cellar, and I felt his power ripple through my whole body like honey. The rush made me gasp. He seemed to turn into liquid or sand or both together at the same time. And that was it. He was gone. A greasy, rough powder covered my body and the stones around me. That was all that remained.

I rolled on to my front and had almost got to my hands and knees when I heard steps on the stairs. I was exhausted, sweat was dripping off me and mingling with the blood on the cellar floor. The right thing to do would be to leap to my feet and carry on fighting. It seemed an awful lot of effort.

"Boss, I got the cable. I…" he broke off. I couldn't blame him. Nearly naked woman covered in blood. No vampire but lots of purple vampire blood. "No, what have you done?" His voice was filled with a despair and rage I hadn't expected. "Where is he? What have you done?"

Hands seized me around the neck and began to shake me.

"What. Have. You. Done!"

He paused for breath and I heard two sounds. The first was the noise that a pair of foot manacles makes when it hits a stone floor. I hadn't heard it before, but it was pretty distinctive, so I thought I had it nailed. The second one was more obscure, but I had heard it just twenty-four hours before so I could identify it right off. It was the exact sound you get when your attacker's head is ripped off. Had I not heard it before, the tip off would have been the two gallons of warm blood jetting over my body.

There was a third noise that followed. I wasn't absolutely certain, but I was nearly sure it was the noise of a hungry vampire, whose girlfriend hadn't felt like putting out earlier, taking advantage of a freshly headless corpse. It wasn't a nice noise. I put it from my mind.

After it stopped, I staggered to my feet. Oscar was standing about four feet away from me. At his feet was a bedraggled headless corpse. A little distance away was the head. What was it with the undead and head ripping? If I never saw another headless corpse again, ever, it would still be too soon.

I looked at Oscar, and he looked back at me.

"So you're a necromancer," he said carefully.

Really, where were his priorities?

"Oscar, sweetie," I said as gently as I could, "I am so pleased you worked out the lock picks. Now give me back your shirt."

Chapter Ten

MY GRANDFATHER LIVED with us when we were growing up. Or rather, we lived with him, my grandmother having died many decades before, slipping on the stairs in a patch of lamp oil and breaking her neck when my father was just a toddler. Anyway, the house was my grandfather's, and I thought had been in the family for a long time. No one in our family ever seemed to have much money, and my parents were rarely around. They certainly never stayed in one place long enough to make buying a house a sensible idea. They were both archaeologists, and there was always a dig here, a temple restoration there, a barrow to be excavated somewhere else. I rather thought they'd had children as a side thought and then discovered that we just weren't as interesting as ancient history.

They all three of them died just before I graduated from university, in that horrible train crash up in Derbyshire that was in the news for so many months and never really satisfactorily resolved. I had to learn younger than a lot of people to make decisions on my own. Assess, prioritise, act... that's my mantra. Also, don't panic.

Anyway, there I was, wearing only the remnants of a jumper that had been sliced into the world's worst cardigan, covered in blood, trapped with an injured vampire in the basement of what might well be a mafia stronghold. It was an hour before dawn, and we had no idea where we were. And Oscar wanted to talk about my necromantic powers. Well, I wanted a hot bath and a martini, but things have a time and a place.

Oscar stripped off his polo shirt, which was also filthy and blood splattered. The only advantage it had on my clothes was the virtue of still being in one piece. I wiped myself down with the remnants of my jumper and pulled Oscar's top over my head. I stuffed everything that wasn't broken back into my bag, failed to find my shoes, and decided that the basement had nothing left to offer us.

"I said: you're a necromancer."

Lord, he was still at it.

"Yes, and we can talk about it later. But right now, Oscar, we have to get you somewhere safe before the sun comes up. I can't feel any more vampires near us—are there any other humans?"

He looked a little sulky.

"I have heard nothing."

"Is your hearing very good?"

"Oh yes."

"Right then, it's probably safe to go up."

The stairs led to a shed that might once have held cows. Today it held the remnants of a Range Rover with a crumbled bonnet. The driver door was ajar, and I could see that keys were still in the ignition. Nearly dead it might be, but it had got four of us here—it could probably get me home. There was a wooden door, also ajar, leading out into the dark.

I stepped out, with little expectation that I would be able to work out where I was just from the view. Actually, I was pleasantly surprised. The shed was perched on the side of a hill, looking over a dark expanse of water. The moon was still bright, and it illuminated a road that led down a hill and across the lake. We were in the hills above Blithfield Reservoir on the Abbots Bromley side. The lights I could see a couple of miles away up the hill would be Rugeley.

I took out my phone—now that we were out of the basement, it registered thirty-five missed calls, eleven voice messages and several screens of texts from Peter. The last one just said: "Please don't be dead."

I stuffed the phone back in my bag and walked back to where

Oscar was scanning the view. I hugged him.

"Oscar, I don't know much about vampire powers, but you need to get below ground really soon. I could drive us to my house, if this car works, and you could be safe in my little wine cellar, but you might just be quicker without me. We are just a couple of miles from Rugeley—can you get to your Assemblage before the dawn comes?"

He hugged me back, a little stiffly.

"I could, but I don't like to leave you here alone."

"There's no one else here, I have a four-litre battering ram at my disposal, and the sun will be up soon. You should go."

He was still looking mulish. I pulled him down to me and kissed him. His bright blond hair was blood-spattered, but the bruise on his cheek was already fading, and he was my lovely Oscar who was apparently massively impulsive and not very good at covering up his emotions. I didn't really know him at all, but what I knew, I liked.

"Oscar, I love you. Please get to safety. You have seen I can look after myself."

He kissed me back, properly this time.

"You can. I can't deny it."

And then he turned and just seemed to vanish in front of my eyes into the blackness. I wasn't expecting it, or I would have watched more closely. Did he run? Did he fly? It was too dark to tell what had happened. I shook my head. Vampires were going to take some getting used to.

First things first. I texted poor Peter: "Hey. All good here. Oscar winging his way back to your Assemblage. Can he actually turn into a bat? Toni xxx".

There was a lot more I could have said. There was a lot I could have asked for too. But I couldn't face another night of being rescued and nurtured. No doubt, if I asked for it, Peter or another well-meaning and competent person would turn up. They would mop up bloodstains and make me feel grateful, and I had really had enough of that. All I wanted was a quiet night of sleep in my own bed. On my own. I turned off my phone.

A thought struck me, and I headed back down into the cellar. Ignoring the bloodless and headless corpse adorning the floor, I poked at the video equipment until the data card fell into my hands. Who knew what they might have forgotten to wipe? I stuffed it in a pocket and sprinted back up the steps. My sandals seemed to have been a casualty of my kidnapping, so I drove the steaming and complaining Range Rover home in my bare feet. One headlight was working, which was enough to see my way.

A smoking four-by-four covered in vampire blood would definitely draw attention outside my front door, so once home, I parked for long enough to put on a pair of trainers. Then I drove the car to the car park behind the old power station site. It could languish there for months without drawing attention. I was pretty sure that Oscar could despatch someone to remove all traces before then. I jogged the two miles back to the house, the sun rising to light my way. It was too early for cars to drive past me, which was good as a blood-stained woman wearing a polo shirt and trainers would raise more eyebrows that than a dead Chelsea tractor.

I wanted peace and quiet. I wanted nine hours of sleep. I doubted I would get them, but I might at least get a bath before someone knocked on the door and tried to kill me. Or protect me. I was pretty sure Peter had taken a key even though he hadn't mentioned it. I wondered about putting the security chain on the door, and then decided that perhaps he could sneak in really quietly and nurture me in silence while I rested in the arms of Morpheus.

At any rate, a bath was top of my list. I ran six inches of overly hot water and added rose oil. It might sting, but it would also help to soak off my bandages. They were thick with blood, but not mine, I hoped. I thought most of it belonged to the former Chicago mobster who had quite literally lost his head over me earlier in the evening. While the tub filled, I wandered down to the kitchen, poured myself a tall gin and tonic, and stuffed Oscar's polo shirt in the bin. It was past saving.

I climbed back up the stairs and settled into the warm, scented water. The terrors of the evening melted away along with the stiff bandages Peter had put on not so long ago. I scrumpled them into a wet, pink ball and threw them in the sink. I swigged half a glass of cold gin. Then I took a look at my hands and knees to assess the damage.

There wasn't a mark on them.

Not a bruise from falling into the river. Not a trace of the gouges on my knuckles. Less than two hours ago I had slid along the stone floor on my palms leaving a smear of blood on the slabs, but there wasn't even a tiny graze to show for it. I reached a hand behind my back to pat at the gouges that had made Peter break out his anti-tetanus shot. The skin was smooth and unbroken.

I thought back. What had happened and when? I tracked through the evening in my mind. When I had decided to jog back from the town? I must have felt well then. Further back then... When I had gone bounding back down the steps to help myself to the camera card I had been just fine, so it must have been before that. It was certainly after the vampire had thrown me over onto my face. I remembered the renewed pain in my knees as well as my hands. When then?

Then it came to me. As I'd banished him. As he'd flowed through me into the stone floor, I had felt that rush of power. I had sent him on his way to the grave and as a parting gift I had somehow stolen his power to heal myself. Was that even possible?

I lifted up one toe to take a look at the old scar I'd got from zombie dog bites two decades before. It had grown with me over the years to some two inches long and wound its way up the side of my foot. Or rather, it had once. Because there wasn't a scar on my foot anymore. I had a feeling there wasn't a scar on my body.

I found the small hand mirror I kept by the bath to put on a facemask. Well, I didn't need a facemask, that was for sure. Apart from the blood still matted in my hair, I looked amazing. I almost glowed. The little zit that I had worried would flare up and ruin the office party wasn't there. Neither were the three little scars on my neck where chicken pox had left its mark. I was as perfect as the day I left the womb. The only mark left on my entire body was the crescent moon-shaped birthmark just above my heart.

I put down the mirror and drained my glass. No wonder vampires hated necromancers. Without ever having practiced before, I had killed Claudio Gambarini and somehow used his vampire powers to heal myself. Or maybe he had the power to heal people and I had stolen it when I banished him. I lay back in the water and soaked my hair clean of blood. I shampooed it twice, and then slathered it with conditioner. It felt springy and buoyant, free of split ends and ready to go into battle with hot irons and some hairspray.

There had been times when I had yearned to be normal. While my friends were taking a bus into Birmingham to learn ice-skating and elementary snogging techniques, I would be packing for an exciting weekend at a cemetery in Bangor. Helen's parents did all her GCSE coursework for her. My grandfather would pull me away from my revision to practise my banishment techniques. And he never let me go to family funerals, just in case. Yes, there were times that I hated my talents. Not this morning. As the sun began to shine through the bathroom window and illuminate the flawless skin of my knees, which the previous evening had looked like an aerial photograph of the Andes, I loved my gifts. They rocked.

I realised something else. I wasn't tired in the least. Whatever healing powers I had experienced had also acted like the best night's sleep ever. I finished my bath, dressed, cleared the house of the remaining evidence of kidnapping and murder, and ate pretty much everything in the fridge that Amelia had given me, barring one last giant cream cake. After that, there was still a block of cheese sitting, lonely, on the middle shelf, so I ate that too.

I decided it was late enough in the day to call Claire. Reluctant to turn on my mobile and read a thousand reproachful messages from Peter, I rang her from the land line. I bribed her with the promise to tell her every gory detail about Oscar, while making a mental note to keep silent about the ones involving actual gore, and she agreed to come round at noon for lunch and shopping.

To my surprise, I realised that still left me with a couple of hours with nothing to do, so I curled up on the sofa with a suitably crap novel and a cup of coffee. I was on chapter two—tall blond heroine had met chinless wonder already, but not quite bonked him senseless—when the doorbell rang. All in all, I had been given more peace than I expected.

"Come in, Peter," I called. "It's not locked."

I heard the door go. His footsteps approached and then stopped. I looked up. He was leaning against the doorframe. He looked terrible.

"You look terrible," I said unnecessarily.

"Thanks," he said. He had a nice scrape down his cheek and the start of a black eye. "There's a gully behind your house in the woods. I fell into it in the dark. It's full of mud and brambles. And rocks. And nettles by the way."

"I know it well. The good news is, it wasn't full of vampires."

He ran a hand through his dishevelled hair. "No, I suppose not." Then he squinted at me through his glasses. "You look amazing."

"Thanks. Um, new conditioner."

He looked unconvinced and I couldn't blame him. He sat down on the sofa next to me.

"Did you get my messages?"

"Not really. My phone turned itself off."

"It does that when you turn it off."

"Sorry. I didn't know what to say. There was so much going on." He slumped against a cushion.

"Peter, do you need coffee and breakfast, or just sleep."

He looked touched.

"A couple of hours of sleep and then breakfast?"

I stood up and held out my hands. He took them and I helped him to his feet. He was swaying slightly.

"I think we can manage that," I said. "Do you mind sleeping in my bed?"

"Nein. The floor would be fine."

I followed him up to my room. He unselfconsciously stripped off his clothes and crawled under the covers.

"Will you wake me?" he asked sleepily.

"Yes. I am going shopping, but I will be back in a couple of hours with food."

"Besten Dank."

I wasn't sure what that meant, but it sounded positive. At any rate, Peter was asleep before I closed the curtains and left the room.

I returned to my novel, but had barely got to the first sex scene when I heard a loud revving outside. Claire was ready to shop.

She was driving the tiny yellow Caterham that her stepfather had given her at Christmas. She had tucked the blond mane up into a ponytail and was wearing jeans and a strappy white top, topped with expensive-looking sunglasses. I was similarly clad—but my sunglasses were fakes from Penkridge market. She beeped her little horn cheerfully a few times. Lace curtains twitched along the street. Behind them, I was pretty sure that brows frowned over their horn rims.

"Let's go in my car," I said cheerfully.

"Ha. Get in, darling. Seriously, how have you even managed to keep that thing MOTed?"

"I've been giving the mechanic blow jobs."

."It must take something like that. Where are we going?"

"Have you checked out the new boutique in the arcade? Opposite the prison. Then we can have lunch there. Oh, and there is a man in my bed. We need to pick up breakfast for him."

She changed gears very badly.

"You have so much to tell me, girlfriend. Start now."

The problem with having secrets is remembering what lies you've told. Years of practice had taught me to tell the exact truth wherever possible, and just to omit the rest unless people noticed there were gaps. And I always answered questions about why I wasn't at home in the middle of the night the exact same way. Oh yes. I couldn't sleep and I went for a walk. Isn't it annoying when you just can't drop off… so far, it had worked well. I wasn't sure how long that would last.

So, I told Claire the unvarnished truth—just not all of it. I also told her about my passionate encounter with Oscar in some detail, not only to distract her from noticing any holes in my account, but also because I wanted her advice.

"…and that is just it," I finished. "I really absolutely adore him. But I want to be his girlfriend, not his lunchbox."

"Picky."

"What!"

"Picky picky picky. He's lovely, he's funny, he's fab in the sack, he has nice friends and he's rich. He wants to get serious and he says he loves you. And you are all wound up because he has some kinky bedroom habits. So, yah, picky. Lav, I dated Rufus for two years and he liked to wear my shoes. Some heavyweight love bites don't strike me as a deal breaker."

"You kicked Rufus out."

"Yes, but that was because he slept with my stepsister and beat me at tennis. Totally different." She parked on a double yellow by the arcade. "Anyway, if you had decided against him, you wouldn't be rejuvenating your wardrobe. Just buy some polo necks and go with the flow. Or some nice scarves."

The boutique was nice. It was more than nice. And it was reassuringly and wincingly expensive. In the end I did the usual thing of spending far more than I should have, and Claire did the usual thing of paying for half of mine as well as hers and whacking the whole lot on her stepfather's credit card.

"Total shame, you know," she said as we gathered up our many bags and repaired to the little eatery next door. "He's an absolute poppet and I love him to bits, but he's convinced he has to buy my affection. Two steak and chips and extra onion rings?"

"Make it three with one as take out," I said. "The nice man in my bed will be hungry when we get back."

"Lav, darling, just to be clear: this is the nice man who is not your boyfriend but is spending a second night at your house, possibly naked?"

I tried not to think about Peter naked in my bed. There was a non-zero probability that he was Oscar's boyfriend, but I was busy building up a nice solid blind spot on that front, so I just wittered on about their relocation problems. Underneath, I knew I hadn't convinced Claire. I hadn't even convinced myself. She was right about one thing—love bites were the least of my problems.

Chapter Eleven

BACK AT MY little cottage, I made a few phone calls and sorted out a little light admin. Then I warmed up Peter's steak and chips on a plate in the Aga and dumped it onto a tray. I didn't attempt to emulate his swanky presentation of the previous evening by adding a napkin, but I did make him a mug of tea. I managed to get the whole lot upstairs without dropping anything and opened my bedroom door.

The curtains were closed, but they don't cut out a lot of light. I put the tray on my bedside table, sat on the bed and observed its occupant. It's kind of cheating looking at someone while they sleep. I did it all the same. Peter had very short dark hair. I thought it would be straight if it was longer, but it was cropped so close that I couldn't be sure. He had a broad face and very dark eyebrows, and he had eyelashes twice as long as mine. He had rather perfect lips, currently marred by a cut that was an extension of the scrape along his cheek. The black eye that had been on its way when I had seen him earlier had flowered into green perfection.

The covers had slipped off most of him and I was able to determine a couple of other things: he was definitely buff, and he slept in the nude. One point to Claire. He had broad shoulders and agreeably defined arms. I let my eyes drift lower. He didn't sit at a desk much, that was clear and… ah: that too. OK. I let my eyes drift back up again. Definitely cheating.

I deposited the eiderdown a little more modestly and drew the curtains. I was taking my time tying them back when I heard Peter stir.

"Hello there," I said without turning round. "I brought you food."

"It smells wonderful."

I sat down on the bed and handed him the tray.

"Why did you come here?" I asked.

He looked down, and speared a chip.

"I was worried about you," he said. "Your phone was off. Oscar shouldn't have left you."

"You didn't have to stay here once you knew I was OK."

He munched. I thought he was avoiding the question, so I just sat.

"OK," he said eventually. "I prefer it here with you to the Assemblage."

I looked around my room. It contained a bed, a bedside table and a wardrobe. It also contained about forty pairs of shoes in various stages of divorce. They clustered round a broken chandelier I had once had plans for and six or seven waist-high piles of ironing that were going to meet an iron when the ambient temperature in hell fell below zero. To add macho panache, there was also a rack of weights that the boyfriend from hell had left behind. I hoped one day to swap them for the Kate Bush boxed set he had borrowed. Maybe when he got out of gaol.

"Peter," I said in genuine confusion, "you must really hate it there."

"It's not really that. Well, maybe it is that, and Benedict Akil is frankly terrifying. And I think he blames Oscar for a lot of what's going on, so I am really just hiding out."

"How can he terrify you? You grew up with vampires."

"Yes, maybe, but not like this one. And of course, he is furious about you."

"Me? He's never met me."

"I should have explained: Oscar petitioned him for protection for you last night, that's why he couldn't meet you until midnight. And while Benedict wasn't pleased, he's agreed to meet you. I'll take you there at sunset."

I nearly knocked over Peter's tea recoiling in shock.

"You certainly will not!"

Peter didn't answer me immediately, mostly because he was eating, but I think also to buy a little time again.

"You will be in danger once it gets dark, you know. We still haven't found out how they tracked you and Oscar down last night."

A light bulb went off in my head. I knew exactly how. Oscar had still been unconscious when our captors had been talking, and only now did it really make sense to me. "He petitioned Akil for formal protection for her tonight." The man Oscar killed had said those words. I hadn't understood the implications back then, possible due to being clubbed unconscious and then nearly raped, but now I did. Benedict Akil might be powerful, but he clearly wasn't running a tight ship. I needed to tell him he had a Gambarini mole in his Assemblage.

"OK, I'll come," I said reluctantly. "You need to tell me more about this Gambarini mess."

Peter finished eating and pushed the tray to one side. He swung his legs over the side of the bed and stood up. I averted my eyes. A little late, but I did it nonetheless.

"It's complicated," he said, rifling through his clothes. "When Maria Acquarone turned Silvio in to the police, they also arrested several members of his coterie, but they didn't manage to get any other vampires. It was only a small Assemblage, but given what we know about it, that means there are probably seven others at large."

"Six now," I said, thinking of Claudio sinking through my body into the cellar floor. I wondered if Peter was decent yet, and took a peek. Nope.

"Good point. Still much more vampire than you want on your doorstep at night. Oscar said you took out Claudio between you, and while that's good, he wasn't a strong vampire—he would have been the least of your worries. It's Marcello and Livia you need to watch out for."

Peter walked to the window and looked out. He had put on jeans and shoes, which was a shame in many ways but made it easier for me to talk to him.

"Do the different Assemblages have a lot to do with each other, then?" I asked.

"Some more than others. Oscar explained to you about lines of power?"

I didn't like to say that shagging and not conversation had been the main feature of our date.

"We hadn't got around to that, to be honest," I said neutrally.

"I'll try to break it down a bit. You know that not all vampires have the same powers?"

"Peter, assume I know nothing. It's safest."

He sighed. He had by now finally found his tee-shirt—this one sporting a tattooed man wielding a burning guitar—and pulled it over his head.

"Oscar can compel people—though not you, I gather—and he is very, very fast. He is fast enough that he would beat most other vampires in a fair fight. Not that fights tend to be fair, as you found out last night. But neither of those skills is rare." He drained his mug of tea. "Is there more of this? I like it."

"An infinite amount," I said. "It's lapsang. Come down and I'll make some."

We trekked down to the kitchen. I put the kettle on the Aga and sprawled in a chair waiting for it to boil. Peter padded round the kitchen tidying things.

"Where was I?" he said, brushing crumbs into the sink. "Powers. OK, that makes Oscar sound not very special, but he has very strong compelling powers and speed. And he's not that old, so not only will his powers get stronger, but he will probably acquire more."

I thought about that. Peter was moistening a cloth.

"Do you mean that the really old vampires tend to be the most powerful," I asked.

"Ja, for sure. Take Benedict Akil. I don't think anyone really knows how powerful he is, and I expect he is happy to keep it that way. But he has abilities I have never heard of. Oscar says he can fly, and I believe he knows when people are lying to him. And of course, he has the gift of true healing."

"Like Doktor Lenz?"

Peter paused in the act of wiping down the taps.

"No, not like poor Doktor Lenz. His gift is very slight, and very specific. It took him hundreds of years to find a condition he could reliably cure. It's a constant frustration to him, poor man. Most vampires have a little—they can certainly heal themselves, but also small wounds. But Benedict's blood heals pretty much everything— the most serious injury, infection, deformity... you name it."

I wondered what the dead Gambarini's power had been? Had he been a healer? The kettle began to whistle, and I poured a fresh pot of tea. While it brewed, I poured milk into mugs.

"What has this got to do with the different Assemblages talking to each other?"

"The more enlightened Assemblages trade talent. They exchange vampires. Think how useful it would be to have someone who could heal? Or who could tell if someone was speaking the truth. All vampires can move with amazing speed, but very few can keep it up for longer than, say, a minute. So those that *can* make the finest warriors."

He accepted a mug from me and sipped. I thought about what he had said.

"So, what decides what talents you end up with? Why can Benedict heal people, but not Oscar?"

Peter nodded.

"Natürlich. I should have explained. A vampire typically develops skills similar to their creator, as though they inherit them. It's not a certain thing. You might not get them, or you might get something totally different. But it's a strong trend."

"Did the Gambarinis have a particular skill?" I asked just as casually as I could manage it.

He nodded.

"They were healers too," he said.

So that really was it. I had not only banished a vampire, but stolen his powers too. But I hadn't been casual enough. Peter's face changed.

"Gott im Himmel. You are healed. I was so tired I didn't notice." He pushed his tea aside and began examining my hands. "Perfect. Not a mark. Why did Gambarini mend you?"

Think quickly, Toni. Come up with a lie that holds water.

"Oscar forced him to," I murmured into my tea, "before he killed him."

But before he could ask me to embellish a story I was already struggling with, I was saved by the phone ringing. It was my brother Wills.

"Hey, you; come to the pub, right now and celebrate."

He sounded jubilant.

"Um, maybe. What's up?"

"Get this. Henry has a movie role."

"OMG. That's so amazing. Can I bring Peter?"

"Your completely hot heavy metal croquet guy? Sure—we're in the Black Mitre. I've been phoning your mobile all morning, but it's off. See you in ten."

I put down the phone and hauled a reluctant Peter to his feet.

"Come on, hot heavy metal croquet guy. You have a pint to drink."

"I do? I thought I had to find out what the hell you did with a mangled four by four, probably covered in blood, and arrange for it to be towed away before the police find it. Knowing you, you probably torched it in the town square."

"It's OK. I hid it well, and the local police are in the pub."

He yielded slightly.

"I'll come, but only if you promise to behave tonight."

"I'll try."

He looked a little reassured.

"And wear something pretty."

"Why?"

"Benedict likes pretty. It might make him look on your petition with favour."

"One, that's inappropriate behaviour in a world that needs more equality. And two, I am not petitioning him for anything. Oscar is doing that. Let him wear something pretty. It's time someone other than me totalled a dress in a good cause."

We walked together the few minutes down the hill, bickering agreeably. Peering into the dimness of the bar, we found Wills and Henry already there. My old schoolmate Lawrence was also in residence, introducing his artistic new boyfriend to Helen and Bernie. I squinted at Bernie; two days had passed since the office party, but he still looked hungover. Publican Albert Winner, keen to boost margins, had opened a couple of bottles of fizz and was assiduously topping up glasses. I glared him down and demanded two pints of Badger.

We toasted Henry, clapped him on the back a lot, and told him how happy we were for him. We demanded he remain friendly with us when he left us all for fame, fortune, and Hollywood, and told him not to join a cult or bleach his teeth too much.

"But seriously, Hen, how did you get it?" I asked when there was a pause. "I thought the only film job you were interviewing for was as a stunt double."

Henry let Albert top up his glass.

"That's the one," he said, his lovely face filled with excitement. "I was chosen because of my fencing skills, and we've done a lot of my scenes. Then the actor who I am doubling for fell ill, and they asked me to take his place." He drained his glass. "It's a dream come true. I am so sick of modelling mobile phones and men's lingerie."

I hugged him.

"You deserve it."

He hugged me back until my ribs ached.

"Thanks. I bought myself a present. Maybe two…" He went off into rapture about a new sword he had bought. Henry collected antique blades—his house was filled with glass cases. This time it was some buzz speak about a vintage English blade from like 1800 that he had been lusting after and I kind of tuned out.

"I am really pleased, Hen."

"Thanks, petal. I like your new boyfriend, by the way."

"What, Peter! He's not my..." I trailed off. "Really, he isn't. I mean, I like him. I really like him. He's adorable. But not like that."

"Whatever you say, petal," he said, clearly unconvinced. "Whatever you say."

I didn't say anything. My life was too complicated right there and then for me to get a handle on. I couldn't really expect anyone else to manage it.

At that moment, my brother came up. He slid one arm around me and the other around Henry.

"Happy days," he said cheerfully. "How are my two most favourite people?"

"Very happy to hear Henry's news," I said.

"Very happy to tease your sister about her new boyfriend," Henry said.

Wills laughed.

"We all like doing that. But seriously, baby sis, I had something I wanted to tell you." He paused and looked solemn. "We are burying Jane Doe on Tuesday."

"Oh Wills, I am so sorry," I exclaimed. "You must be gutted. Don't take it personally."

He shook his head.

"I am trying not to, but Allardyce won't budge. I wanted just a little more time." He sighed in frustration. "Who am I kidding? We haven't found her killer and now we never will."

I seized Henry by the arm.

"My giddy aunt, Henry, get some more champagne into this man before he ruins your celebration."

"Done," Henry said hastily, and giving me a last hug, he dragged my brother back to the bar.

Peter sidled up.

"I love all your friends..." he began.

"They all love you," I interrupted. "They all also think we are an item."

"How sweet," he said, looking faintly embarrassed. "I was going to say that I love your friends and I am having an excellent afternoon. But I need to get someone to pick up that car, you need to get ready for this evening, and if I drink another pint of this," he waved an empty glass of Badger in my face, "I won't be able to drive us to the Assemblage. Or walk upright."

"That's fair," I said. I drained my own glass. "You can help me pick out a dress."

"I am good at that."

We walked back up the hill together. I was starting to enjoy sharing my home a little more.

"I have a lot fewer dresses than I had when I first met Oscar, mind," I cautioned him.

He laughed.

"I take it that you don't need me to dose you up with morphine this evening though?"

"No. So I won't offer you sex, but you can brush my hair. I have to print off some files first though."

In the end he did choose my dress, an off-white sheath dress with little crystals round the neckline. I paired it with flat cream sandals in case I had to run away from someone who was trying to kill me, and added a string of pearls.

"Don't I look a bit..." I struggled to find a word "a bit virginal?"

He snorted, putting down my phone. While I beautified, he had spent the time calling some unknown people about the abandoned car.

"Maybe that will persuade Benedict to keep his hands to himself," he said.

"That's not fair," I said, locking my front door. We walked down to the kerb where he had parked Oscar's lovely car. "First you tell me to dress up for the guy, and then you tell me I might get groped for my pains. I get enough of that at work. And at croquet. I'd quite like my evenings to be grope-free."

We reached the car and I hefted my handbag onto my hip. I saw Peter frown at the bunch of files I'd stuffed in there and raise his eyebrows in enquiry. I didn't enlighten him. If I'd guessed right, he'd find out later. If I was wrong, there was no point in making more of a fool of myself than I had to. He shrugged, opened the passenger door, and helped me in. Tonight's dress wasn't too tight—I was starting to cool towards fashion that might hamper you in a fist fight—but it was short enough that climbing in and out of a sports car could cost me points in dignity if I wasn't careful.

"In Benedict's defence, most people would be tempted to grope you in that dress," Peter said. "Benedict is just more likely than most to give in to temptation. I thought about having a go myself when I helped you into the car."

He started the engine and headed down the hill. I glared at him.

"You picked out this dress and now you tell me it invites gropes."

"Not at all. I picked out the dress because it makes you look adorable." I blushed and was glad that he was driving and couldn't see. "I am just warning you that Benedict Akil is someone who takes what he wants. And there's probably a fine line between making him feel positive about you and making him behave badly."

The outing I really hadn't been looking forward to was getting even worse. And tomorrow was Monday. I needed a little moral courage.

"Peter, please turn around," I said on impulse. "I forgot to do something."

Looking a little surprised, he slowed down the car, and executed a neat three-point turn. "Will it take long?" he asked as we headed up back through the village. "I'd hate to be late."

"Not long," I assured him.

"I've heard that before. Oscar says it when he's getting dressed and half an hour later, I find he hasn't chosen so much as a sock."

"Wait here," I interrupted hastily as he slowed down at my house. I bounded up the steps. "I won't be long." It was the work of a minute to tuck Amelia's last cream cake into a box. Back at the car, Peter and I did some complicated tag team manoeuvring to get me into the passenger seat, clutching it on my lap. Peter paid me the complement of not asking why I needed an emergency cream cake at sunset.

"Up the hill to the church," I said as he restarted the engine.

He obliged.

"I know I haven't made tonight out to be great," he said, "but Toni, you probably don't need to offer special prayers. And I am not a Catholic, but I think lighting a candle is more the done thing than an offering of confectionary."

"It's not that," I assured him. "The church will all be locked up. I have to..." how to put things? "I have to briefly meet a friend."

He just looked at me and I crumbled. After all, if I couldn't trust Peter, who the hell could I trust? My lies were already starting to trip me up and anyway he deserved the truth.

"My friend is dead," I said. "I mean, really dead. I have to raise him from his grave. Look Peter, I'm a sodding necromancer, alright. And don't panic, Oscar knows but we have to keep it a secret."

He put his head in his hands.

"A necromancer. Historic enemy of all the undead and you're dating a vampire. You don't want an easy life, do you Toni!"

I blinked.

"Now you're just being melodramatic," I said. "And I'd love an easy life. I became an estate agent, for goodness sake. I could have been a lawyer, remember?"

Chapter Twelve

I DIDN'T BOTHER with a circle, and I didn't need blood. False modesty would be pointless. I was just better than my grandfather. He didn't start until his forties and it was always a huge effort for him to raise the dead. I started aged seven and almost immediately I was hooked. If a day went past when I didn't summon, I was like a forty-a-day smoker separated from their lighter: fractious, antsy, moody, depressed. Necromancy was in my blood in a way it had never been in his. It wasn't just that I called the dead from their graves to walk upon the earth—I had to. It was a Compulsion. And it was rarely an effort anymore—it was my daily fix.

And that night I wasn't calling some random corpse to briefly re-tread the mortal coil. I was going to get moral courage from my new best friend.

"Bredon Havers, in friendship I call you. Come to me this night. Oh, there you are."

He strode out of the earth. There was something different about him. He looked, he looked…

"Bredon, you look younger!"

"I do? How very gratifying. I feel extremely well. Though hungry."

OMG, I had forgotten. I levered the cake plate out of its box and handed it to Bredon.

"Sorry Bredon, I forgot to bring you a fork."

He broke a piece off delicately with his fingers and handed it to me courteously. I nibbled, careful not to get cream or raspberry juice on my dress. He munched the rest with remarkable speed.

"So, my dear Mistress Lavington," he said, brushing sugar from his fingertips, "when last I saw you, we had experienced a most unpleasant encounter. I hope that it has had no further ill consequences for you?"

"Um, not directly," I said. "And my second date went fine, actually."

He pressed my hand.

"I am delighted to hear it, young lady. Are you on your way out again? You look—if I might say so—quite exquisite."

Ha. I raised the best zombies, and anyone who disagreed probably had more friends than me.

"Thank you, thank you," I blathered, a little overwhelmed. "That was actually what I wanted to ask you. I wasn't sure about my dress."

"I am quite sure. You look in every way lovely."

I stood on my tiptoes to kiss his cheek.

"I am so glad I came to see you. I was thinking it looked a bit…" I took a deep breath. "A bit virginal…"

Bredon looked at me carefully.

"Yes, but in a most attractive way, I do assure you."

Even I had to laugh.

"OK, I give up."

He walked over to the wall of the cemetery where a rather lovely sepia-coloured rose was in bloom. He plucked off a blossom and brought it over. Between us we persuaded it to lodge behind my ear.

"Now you look perfect," he said very kindly.

"Thank you again. I should go now."

"You can't stay a little longer?" he asked, a little wistfully.

I hugged him.

"I really can't but I will come tomorrow."

"I will put it in my diary," he said formally, "so that nothing can disrupt our plans."

"Good night, Bredon," I said. "I release you to your rest."

And he went. I touched the flower behind my ear. In recent days, my life had become more dangerous, but also an awful lot more fun. I walked across the graveyard, picking up an empty cake plate and a sugar-smattered box. I tucked them into the bin provided for the church's rare visitors, and then levered myself back into the little sports car.

"Thanks for that," I said.

"Can I take it that was Mr Head Ripper?"

"The same."

"OK."

He didn't ask any other questions. He waited for me to talk. I really liked Peter.

I took a deep breath. I seemed to be doing that a lot.

"Alright. I summon the dead. I raise zombies. And don't think it's kind of arcane and exciting or anything. I mean, most of the time I never know what to do with them when I've woken them; they're usually really boring and really hungry. It's only recently that I have got good enough to raise ones that don't smell gross and fall to pieces. It's just a thing that I do. I never really thought about whether there was more of a big picture to it."

He looked worried.

"Have you done it for long?"

"I've done it since I was a tiny girl. Why do you ask?"

"You're really young to be a necromancer. There are records on this in Heidelberg—a lot of our key historical texts are kept there. I only ever heard of one or two necromancers who came into their talent before they were in their sixties or seventies. For you to be able to do it as a child... I've never heard of anything like that."

I thought about that.

"My grandfather Robert started in his forties. My great, great grandfather Ignatius was in his thirties."

Peter looked surprised.

"Ignatius was your grandfather? I should have twigged from the name; I mean he's famous. I've read all about him and that demon Azazel he bargained with."

"I've got all those creepy contracts. They're written in blood."

"I'd love to see them."

"I'll dig them out for you. They're pretty grim."

"Could you give it up? Raising the dead, I mean?"

That was a harder question. I'd never known quite what had turned my grandfather so against his necromantic heritage. Whatever it was, it must have been profound. He never raised the dead himself that I knew of, and he certainly didn't want me to either. But that had never been an option. Later in my life he'd said I was cursed and blamed himself. I never found out why. I shook my head.

"I don't think so, no. It's like an addiction, a Compulsion, particularly in the winter when the nights are longer. I couldn't hold back even when I was seven or eight years old. I knew how furious my grandfather would be if he found out, but I couldn't help it. And it's worse than ever now. As a teenager, I could hold it down to once or twice a week, though it was a struggle. These days, if I miss more than a night or so, it's awful."

Peter nodded.

"The literature said something on those lines. That it's an overwhelming Compulsion, like a vampire drinking blood."

"Yuk. It's nothing like that."

Peter laughed.

"You raise festering corpses from the grave and you are getting snotty about drinking a little blood."

"My revenants do not fester," I objected. "Most of them are perfectly formed. Some of them are even chatty."

At this he looked impressed.

"Really? I never heard of them talking. But seriously, Toni, this has to stay a secret. Vampire rules are strict on this. Necromancers are toast and the same goes for anyone who protects them. God help us all if Benedict found out."

I thought that through.

"Well, I will just stay out of his way," I said hopefully. "But Peter, I got the impression that vampires kind of thought they'd already wiped us out. You know, that there were no necromancers left anymore."

Peter nodded.

"That's true. But the laws stand, and I don't think there is any wiggle room in them. We're nearly here."

He drove down the hill and over the bridge, but then turned the car away from Rugeley towards the Bellamour Lane road. The hills above the river were quite heavily wooded and a little too steep for farming. Some tracks headed up into them, but I'd no idea where they went. We turned into one of them. After a few hundred yards of overgrown weeds and enshrouding trees, it transformed into a proper driveway. There were high hedges bordering each side, neat but unfussy. The trees of the woods beyond hung over the roadway still, making it into a tunnel that I had a feeling would be dark even in the day. We wound deeper into the trees for a little way further, and then they opened out into a wide clearing.

The house wasn't big—it was probably smaller than the one I had found for Oscar—and it was certainly less ornate. It was unburdened with any of the curlicues and turrets of either gothic period; I thought it managed this by preceding them both by several hundred years.

Because it was *old*. The stone was dark and worn. The windows were narrow and square. The moonlight revealed the building to be bracketed by cedar trees so vast that pterodactyls could have roosted in the branches. Sunset wasn't long past, but it was dark enough that I could only roughly make out the geography of the place.

"Peter, what is this place?" I asked. "I can't even remember a building here on the ordnance survey maps."

He shrugged.

"It was once called Stone Chase House. They tend to call it The Stone House these days."

He drove through a sloping expanse of lawn to the back of the main building. He parked the car in a courtyard lit only slightly by burning torches. I could see a hint of arches and ivy and wide double wooden doors up a short flight of steps. There were stone dragons to either side.

"Seriously, Peter, torches?"

He laughed, getting out of the car and opening the door for me.

"Be fair. Stereotypes have to come from somewhere. And they had a few hundred years to get set in their ways here. Listen, Toni, tonight…" He paused, and then gave up. "I give up. Just try to be polite."

"I am always polite. I say sorry after I rip heads off."

He gave me a hug.

"I very much doubt that is true. And I thought we had agreed that wasn't you."

I shrugged.

"Come on, let's get this over with."

At that precise moment, the doors opened and a slight figure rushed down them towards us. She threw herself on Peter.

"You are late. What were you thinking? And Benedict is in the foulest mood."

She had long, straight hair the colour of milk. I would have struggled to guess her age. She was one of those women who could have been anywhere between thirty and sixty. And while I couldn't tell what colour her eyes were in the torchlight, I would have guessed at sky blue. Basically, she was just gorgeous. To enhance her general gorgeousness, she was wearing a pale blue evening dress and court shoes. The footwear raised my hopes that people round here didn't have to spend their evenings fleeing from certain danger. Which was good, because by then my hopes weren't high. I didn't think we were heading into date night territory.

Peter held her for a moment.

"Camilla, he would be in a foul mood whatever time we arrived, and you know it. This is Toni, and she is a lot more nervous than she is letting on. Toni, this is Camilla. Camilla is the kindest person you will ever meet, so be nice to her."

As he spoke, he led us through the doors into the brighter interior. I found myself in a hallway lit entirely by torches and candle sconces. The Stone House was a tad austere for me, with un-plastered stone walls and a slate-tiled floor. I found myself mentally preparing a sales catalogue: many original features. Needs modernisation. Would suit vampire with sense of superiority and a bossy streak.

I was distracted from taking better notice of my surroundings by Camilla, who rushed over to hug me.

"Don't worry, Toni dearest," she breathed. "I am sure it will all be OK."

I gazed at her. Yes, her eyes were pale blue, and she seemed entirely genuine. But to my surprise, she wasn't a vampire. She was as human as Peter or me, and her hands where she held me were warm and gentle.

"Thank you, Camilla," I said gently. "I am sure it will."

She gave me another spontaneous hug and rushed off in a whirl of blue satin.

"Peter, is she for real?"

"Ja. She is always like that. Follow me. It's easy to get lost—I sometimes think that's the idea."

He led me to a staircase. It headed down. I looked at it with dislike.

"I take it that it is too late for me to back out?"

"Much."

He put a hand firmly on the small of my back and guided me to the top of the stairs.

"Really?"

"Truly."

We descended together. A long way. After far too many rotations, the staircase gave way to a long irregular chamber. More torches lit our way, rather unenthusiastically. I began to feel distinctly uncomfortable.

"Peter, what is this place?"

He took my hand.

"Don't be scared. It's an old coal working. Our Benedict likes a sense of occasion. And a lack of sunlight of course."

I couldn't make out nearly enough in the half-hearted flickering light, but we were approaching an archway. Through it, brighter light streamed. I could hear raised voices. A shouting match of epic proportions seemed to be reaching its zenith.

"Peter," I whispered. "I don't like this. Let's go home."

"Hush," he said. "You survived two decapitations this weekend. How bad can tonight get?"

We walked through the arch and I blinked. I had a feeling I was in vampire central. Dozens of wrought iron candelabras and great metal braziers illuminated a soaring space. It was warm, toasty warm, and lush rugs and elegant furniture clustered together in various recesses and raised areas. There was a soft smell of smoke and spices, and a just-audible crackle from the flames of the closest brazier. Everything was exquisitely arranged. My idea of tidying up and feng shui was to line up all the piles of rubbish in a visually pleasing manner. I figured the luck couldn't run out because it would get lost before it found an exit. But this place... I had never been in a more beautiful room, if it could be called a room.

Indeed, the vast space was more like a cavern, finished and carved in some places, but rough stone in others. There were pillars, some ornate, others looking as though they had grown there over the millennia. A raised central area held a cluster of lush velvet chairs and side tables surrounded by a ring of shorter braziers. There was also a heavy stone table arrayed with more formal dining chairs. Away from this central point, I got an impression of galleries on different levels, but the recesses were less well-lit and it was hard to work out the geography. I wondered if vampires had better eyesight than I did. Oscar hadn't needed a torch to explore Lichley, so perhaps the recesses were bright enough for undead eyes.

I also didn't get to gaze around the sidelines much because of what was happening in the centre—namely, a splendid row. The floor was currently being held by a tall man with long black hair. I'm not the biggest fan of long hair on men, but this was nice hair, shiny, and even curlier than mine. My necromancy told me he was very old and powerful, but it was the way he was striding round the chamber yelling blue murder that told me he was in a really, really bad mood. One that he seemed to be working off by having a right go at Oscar.

"No, not useless," he was yelling in a deep, very English voice.

"Worse than useless. Instead of providing any assistance, you made yourself a convenient kidnapping target. You found out bloody nothing about where the rest are holed up and left me with a second headless sodding corpse in two days to clear up. And now, rather than do anything useful, you want to make us extra popular by scooping up some feckless floozy to bolster your coterie. Great way to bring us into favour in the neighbourhood, Wolsey; start preying on the local girls just when it is my enviable task to try to improve our profile in the community. You make my fingers itch for a stake."

He turned round and caught sight of Peter and snarled:

"Wonderful. Just late enough to piss me off and not quite late enough for me to rip your throat out and improve my mood. Do you do it on purpose, Peter, or is it a natural talent?"

Peter didn't say anything. He looked like he wanted to find a dark place to hide, and I couldn't blame him. Benedict Akil in a good mood would have been scary. In a raging temper he was terrifying.

He was more than six-foot-tall and built like a rower, with broad shoulders, heavily muscled arms and an impressive chest. He was good looking in a way I didn't particularly admire but which was certainly eye-catching. His skin was several shades darker than mine, and he had very straight dark eyebrows. His eyes were such a dark shade of blue that they weren't at odds with his Mediterranean skin. He had rather perfectly curved lips. Oh, and teeth. Glittering white teeth and longer canines than any of the vampires I had encountered before. For moment I thought I recognised him, though I couldn't think from where.

He was wearing black jeans with low black boots and a dark green linen shirt with cufflinks, an ensemble that easily scored him a ten in my book. Oscar, irritatingly, was dressed in beige chinos with another polo shirt. At least, I assumed it was another. Several people had bled all over the previous one. That scored my boyfriend a measly seven out of ten, but I was fine with backing the underdog. I glared at Benedict, which turned out to be the wrong thing to do, because it meant he finally took some notice of me.

"Gods above, Wolsey, if you wanted something little and soft to stroke at night, why didn't you just get a kitten! Or a bloody hamster. Peter probably knows how to cook one of those when you've got bored of it."

Oscar rose from his chair and interrupted.

"Benedict, there's no need for this. I..."

Benedict cut him off.

"No need? If the precious Gambarini posse you have brought down on me carries on like this, The Hague will overturn your beloved Heidelberg Accord. You lot promised to stamp out rogue vampires with no thought as to who would do it or how. If the Accord goes belly up, they will stake the lot of us faster than you can say 'undead kebab'. But you don't have time to worry about that, do you, because you are busy expanding your coterie."

"You told me to do that," Oscar protested.

"I meant with something useful, for crying out loud," Benedict snapped back icily. "How about someone who could help us to work out how the hell Claudio tracked you down last night or where the rest of his amiable family are. What the hell use is this?"

He strode over to where I was trying to hide behind Peter and seized me by my hair, clutching it in one fist like a ponytail and tilting my face up to his.

"I swear, I got one of these in my last Christmas cracker. If you drained the whole thing, you would barely get enough blood to gargle." He looked closely at my neck, and let out a savage burst of laughter. "And goodness, Wolsey, you haven't even sampled the goods yet. What if you don't like the taste? I once spent weeks seducing an Egyptian princess only to find out that all the wretched wench tasted of was ass's milk."

I waited for Oscar to defend me. He didn't. I waited for Benedict to let go of my hair. He didn't. I was still seething when Benedict said in a calmer voice:

"This is pointless. I have lost the strength to argue with any of you. Let's get on with it. If your pocket Venus here will swear fealty to me, I will extend the protection of my house."

There was a relieved silence. I ruined it.

"Swear fealty to you?" I said in disgust, trying to tug my hair out of his grip. "I wouldn't pull you out of the Channel if you were drowning."

The silence changed. It was no longer one of relief. I wasn't sure exactly what emotions it did contain anymore, but they were none of them good ones. Benedict looked at me for the first time with something close to interest.

"I don't breathe, little hamster, so I don't drown."

I eyed him with loathing.

"Then I wouldn't lend you my bloody umbrella if you were toasting in the sun," I said helpfully. "Just so we are clear."

I finally managed to wrench my hair out of his grasp. I didn't even see his response it came so fast, again that freakishly swift vampire motion. Seemingly without moving he had pinned both wrists behind my back. Confusingly, his hands were burningly hot. He moved in and loomed over me, pressing me closely to him. I stared up at him, a little aghast at how quickly things had turned against me. For Christ's sake, he was at least fourteen inches taller than me; why did he have to do the looming thing?

"Your hamster has claws, Wolsey. Maybe it is a tiny little baby tiger? Does it have sharp little teeth as well? Shall we find out?"

He leant forward very slowly, but before I had an inkling of what he planned he dipped his head down and ran his tongue over the tips of my upper teeth. Where his skin touched mine, I again felt that fiery, feverish heat. I tried to jerk back but couldn't move. He pulled his face back far enough to gaze into my eyes. His expression was impossible to read. He bent forward a second time. I tried to turn my head away, but he changed his grip to hold both my wrists in one of his hands. With his free hand he cupped my face and turned it back to his. He moved his mouth back to mine, and with a sharp little motion, he bit my lower lip and traced it with his tongue.

I tasted blood, and realised he had deliberately caught me with one of his canines. I pulled away again. This time he let me.

Too late. A hot, burning feeling started in my lip, as though I had been drinking cognac or whisky. It spread through my neck into my torso. It crept sneakily down through my abdomen. There was never any doubt where it was heading. It took the scenic route, but without major diversions, and trickled gently into my groin. I was ready to ignite with desire. Through a haze of lust, I heard Benedict's mocking voice:

"Hmm. Well, Wolsey, take it from me—you don't have to worry about ass's milk."

I wrenched my hands free of his and stepped back.

"Sod this for a game of soldiers," I said. "Nothing is worth this."

And I turned on my heel and walked back the way I had come.

Chapter Thirteen

I STORMED TOWARDS the dark archway. He let me get through it and about halfway back to the stairs before passing me like mist and stepping in front of me to block my path.

"Come with me," he said without preamble, opening a door to my left.

"Nope," I said trying to step past him. He caught a wrist in his burning grip. I tried not to let the touch of his hand fire me up further. I didn't really manage it.

"You can come on your own two feet or be dragged by one of them, little tiger."

Call me a coward, but I went with him. He closed the door behind him.

The corridor was dark, lit by a single torch that Benedict casually unhooked. He used it to light a random number of its fellows as we passed them. The corridor had no doors opening off it for a long while, and it curved and twisted. Looking back, I could no longer see the entrance we had come in by. The passage finally ended in two solid-looking black wood doors embellished with heavyweight iron fixings. My heart sank a little further. Benedict opened the right hand one and gestured me in.

To my surprise we entered an elegant apartment, lit by hundreds of tiny candles. A black slate floor was dotted here and there with deep pile sheepskin rugs. The stone walls were broken up by emerald green swathes of curtains and old misty mirrors. I caught sight of myself in one, a soft, pretty version of Lavington Windsor, framed in bronze and lacking the sharp edges that sunlight or even a light bulb would have shown. Captivated, I stood looking at my reflection. I was jolted out of my reverie when Benedict moved into the image I was gazing at. Hmm, so that was one thing Mr Stoker was wrong about.

"What on earth am I going to do with you?" he mused, catching my hair in his hand again and holding me in front of the mirror while he brought his face down to my neck. "Oscar will be so cross if I kill you, and all the other options seem so dull." He nuzzled into the soft skin below my ear and I felt his hot hands slide on to my hips. "You could tell me what you are really here for, maybe? If you never intended to ask for my protection, I have to wonder why you turned up at all. I don't have the reputation of a natural host, you know. I am not famed for my parties."

I took a deep breath and looked at his reflection. He was holding me against him and looking at me in the mirror, his lips almost touching my skin. The radiant heat of them felt delicious. My body wanted to melt into his like caramel. The rest of me wanted to lamp him with a rock.

"You make me sick," I said thickly. "These powers you all have. You could do so much with them, but oh no, you utilise them like so much dead man's Rohypnol. I have three things to tell you. First, I know exactly where the Gambarini clan is holed up. And second, I also know how they found Oscar last night—you have been careless, Mr Akil. There is a mole in your camp. And third…" I paused and marshalled my resources. They were pitiful. "And third, take your hands off my body."

For a moment, he didn't move, and his expression didn't slip from its normal inscrutability. Then he slid his hands off my hips via the longest possible route and stepped away from me.

"Maybe Oscar isn't as stupid as he looks. Thinking about it, that would actually be quite hard. Wait here."

He turned and left, closing the heavy black door behind him. I let my breath out in a rush. I would have given worlds for a glass of cold water. Or a cold shower. My body had other ideas. It would have given a hell of a lot more to be shagged senseless, then and there, on the sheepskin rugs. Oscar himself had warned me that vampires were dangerously attractive, the more so the closer you got to them. What on earth had Benedict done when he had bitten me? I made a lifetime vow never to get close to the man again if I could manage it. After tonight, I hoped to never set eyes on him.

I couldn't shake the impression that I had seen him before, though, and I let the thought run round my head as I explored my surroundings. The main room was as luxurious as first impressions had suggested. There was a roaring open fire, a broad black ebonised wood desk, several vast swallow-you-up sofas, and even a neat little bar. I looked for bottles labelled B-negative but found only a fridge full of champagne. In a spirit of fuck-you-Benedict, I opened one and poured myself a glass. I sipped at it as I assessed my surroundings, inhaling the room's honey-soft aroma of burning wood and beeswax candles.

There were several doorways, one of which led to a study and another to a bedroom. Off the bedroom was a bathroom about the size of my entire house complete with a traditional Finnish sauna. I opened the door briefly and was hit by a wave of dry heat and the smell of roasting granite. I pushed it back to and sipped at my champagne. I rather thought I had discovered the source of Benedict's confusing body temperature.

"We love the heat," said a deep voice by my ear.

I jumped and let out a shriek. Benedict pretended not to notice. He put his hands on my shoulders and smouldered down at me. His touch was soft this time.

"We crave it. It is one of the attractions of your mortal bodies, their lovely warmth."

The vampire looked at me through his petrel blue eyes. I got the impression he was used to looking into people's souls and seeing their darkest secrets. Well, no one looked into my soul and my secrets... they were mine and they were staying that way. The dead didn't have power over me. I was only beginning to realise that myself—I certainly didn't want Benedict to know, so I just wriggled past him and made my way back through the bedroom into the lounge area. I curled up on a chair so that no one could sit next to me.

The door to the corridor opened and Camilla entered in a flurry of blue. She rushed over to me and hugged me.

"Are you OK? Oscar was having kittens and then Benedict came back and summoned us for a meeting here. What does he have to say that the Assemblage can't hear?"

Before I could answer her the door opened again. Oscar came in looking anxious, followed by Peter and a woman with sleek, short black hair. I didn't need the long white teeth to tell me she was a vampire. Her aura was strong enough that I could feel that from across the room. She gave me a look-what-the-cat-dragged-in look, so I ignored her. Peter hid in the most out-of-the-way chair he could find, but Oscar came over to me and enveloped me in his arms. He knelt by the chair and buried his face in my hair.

"My troublesome Toni," he said softly. "Life with you will never be boring."

"I could say the same to you," I replied, my voice muffled because I was speaking into his chest. "I have seen three headless corpses this week—though admittedly only two of them were your fault—and that is three more than I ever want to see again."

"Enough," Benedict's voice snapped.

Oscar drew back from me and moved behind my chair. I looked around. Benedict was standing in front of the fire, the snooty black-haired vampire woman stood next to me, facing him. Camilla was sitting contentedly at her feet. Peter continued to sit as unobtrusively as possible in his chair.

"Akil, it is of course a rapturous honour to be invited into your rooms, but can I ask what is so secret that we cannot speak of it in front of the others?"

It was the dark-haired woman who spoke. She had a deep, mellifluous voice and an English accent you could have cut glass with. I turned to look at her. She was wearing a tiny little black dress with fishnets and four-inch heels shimmering with diamante. Benedict nodded.

"According to Wolsey's little pet here," he began. I felt my fingers curl into claws. Benedict caught my eye and almost smiled. Almost, but not quite. "She tells me we have a little viper nursing at our bosom. Would you care to elucidate, little tiger?"

"It's not rocket science," I said, looking into the fire rather than at anyone in the room. "Last night before he came to meet me, I gather that Oscar asked you to offer me your protection. But just a few hours later, when we were ambushed, our attackers knew that. So unless there's a really cool bar around here where all the happening vampires go to hang out on a Saturday night, that means one of the Gambarinis that you are so desperately searching for is in regular contact with someone here."

A long silence followed.

"I can see why you separated the wheat from the chaff," said the dark-haired bitch. "I am flattered."

Benedict shrugged.

"Hmm. Well, if I can't trust you and Camilla, I might as well take up sunbathing. And I really can't see what axe our illustrious visitors," he nodded at Oscar and at Peter, who huddled back in his chair, "would have to grind from stabbing me in the back. At least," he added thoughtfully, "not over this."

"How do you want to do this?" It was the woman with black hair again. Benedict didn't reply, so she pressed: "Should we question people one by one?"

"No, I don't think so, Grace," he responded. "As it happens, I rather think I know the identity of our little mole."

"Who?"

"You should know, dear."

"Me!" She seemed honestly shocked. "What do you mean?"

"That nice little brunette of yours."

"Diana? What about ..." She broke off. "Oh. Oh, I see."

She sat down rather abruptly in the chair next to mine. Camilla, looking as confused as I felt, put her head on the vampire's knee.

"What?" interrupted Oscar. "What are you talking about?"

Benedict looked expectantly at Grace. She just looked at her hands and then began gently to stroke Camilla's hair.

"Grace's dear little Diana wasn't born in England, was she?" Grace said nothing and didn't look up. "She was born in Chicago. She came to England with her mother as an innocent child—isn't that right, Grace dear—leaving behind two older brothers."

"Oh," said Oscar. "I see. Perfect blackmail material."

Benedict looked at Grace. She was still just sitting silently, stroking Camilla's hair.

"Grace," he said, and there was a tiny touch of kindness in his voice. "Go for a nice walk. I won't make you watch."

Without a word, she rose and left the room. She slammed the door vigorously, leaving a nervous silence.

"Camilla," he said. "Go and fetch Diana."

She looked up from her spot on the floor, slumped by the chair that Grace had just left. Tears were pouring down her cheeks and dripping off her chin.

"I can't," she whispered. "She's like my sister. I just couldn't do it."

Benedict looked at her for a moment, and then shook his head.

"Go with Grace," he said. "Go on."

Camilla scraped herself to her feet and crept dejectedly to the door. Grace had left in tragic dignity. Camilla had no such defences. The door closed behind her, this time with a pathetic little click.

"Oscar, for the love of God go and get this wretched creature for me. Unless I have to bloody do everything for myself around here, which I am beginning to think is the case."

Oscar nodded, and headed out into the corridor.

"This isn't easy for them, Benedict," said Peter, bravely.

Benedict rounded on him like a snake.

"Then they shouldn't have bloody let it happen."

"I'm sure that was the last thing they intended," Peter protested.

Benedict positively growled.

"I wish someone could properly explain to me why I should

give a flying fuck about what they intended. Who cares what they intended? They messed up. And now there are tears and excuses. Excuse me for finding that pathetic."

I could see Peter was regretting his earlier burst of courage. I wanted to sit quietly, but felt I couldn't leave him to fight his corner alone.

"Who is Diana?" I interrupted.

Benedict looked at me as though he had forgotten my existence. I knew that was faked, so I ignored it.

"Diana Hansen, one of Grace's precious coterie," he said shortly. "Someone whose loyalty to their family turned out to be stronger than their wish to live."

I thought about that. It didn't sound good.

"Hang on: you mean…"

He didn't give me a chance to finish.

"What the hell else did you think? That I was going to ask her to write lines… Three hundred repetitions of 'I must not betray my vampire kindred'? Gods above. The one redeeming feature of this unholy bloody mess is that I at least get to kill someone."

Before I could protest, the door opened, and Oscar ushered Grace's mystery brunette into the room. She was no vampire. She was as mortal as me. Diana Hansen was a pretty, curvy girl with ringlets like Shirley temple and dimples about as cute. She was wearing a pale blue mini dress and a little denim jacket, the sort that doesn't keep the rain out or the heat in but looks chic. I didn't know what Oscar had said to her, but she clearly had no idea that her cover had been blown. She breezed into the room, talking to Oscar in a cheerful animated way. She was halfway to the fire before it dawned on her that the company in the room was not what she had expected. She looked around and took in the presence of Benedict, and the gaping absence of Camilla and Grace. The colour drained from her face. It was a term I'd heard said before, but never seen in action. Her face literally turned pale as I watched, and she almost lost her footing.

Benedict loped up to her. He was giving off vibes of barely

suppressed rage. He moved right in, close enough that she took a step backwards and still ended up chest to chest with him. She looked up into his face and whatever she saw there stripped away any remaining vestiges of courage. She folded up and crumpled to her knees.

"I'm sorry, I'm sorry, I'm sorry," she whispered. "I didn't mean any harm."

"What did they do?" Benedict's voice was icy.

She didn't look up. She looked at the rug in front of her, and traced the edge with a fingertip.

"They sent a video," she said miserably. "They sent it to my phone. It was my brother Louis. There was so much blood. So much. They said they would…" Her voice trailed off. That was fine with me. I didn't want to know what they had threatened to do.

"What did you tell them in return?"

She looked up at him and then straight down again.

"I gave them maps of this place," she said. "And I told them who was here and what they could do, and when people were going where. I gave them addresses. Last night they called and I told them about Oscar. I knew where Toni's house was because I went there the night the EDL man died to help clean up. I jet washed the lawn."

"Anything else?"

She shook her head.

"No. That's all, I swear. Are you going to kill me?"

"Yes."

"Oh God." She pawed at his hands. I felt sick. "Please, I never meant any harm. I had to do it. You understand, I had to. He was my family, my blood family. I couldn't just let him be tortured and die."

Benedict looked down at her impassively. He shook his head.

"Diana—we are your blood family. Blood you chose. Not some blood you were allotted by a random twist of fate. I promised you protection and that was no empty vow. Why didn't you come to me? To Grace? What did you think we would do? We would have come through for you."

She was crying, great hiccoughing sobs. She put her face in her hands, but the tears were trickling out and I could see them dripping through onto the rug.

"Benedict Akil!" I heard myself snap.

He spun round to look at me. I shook my head.

"Stop this right now. Do it if you are going to. Don't drag it out a moment longer."

He nodded. Looking straight into my eyes, he reached down and lifted Diana up by the front of her denim jacket. He turned his head to one side so that he could continue to gaze at me while he moved his mouth into her neck. Then he ripped out her throat.

Chapter Fourteen

I TRIED TO close my eyes. I really did. I tried not to watch him drink her life force as it spilled out of her body. But my eyes only closed properly when I slumped forward and passed out in a little heap by the chair.

I woke to find myself lying on a bed. A very soft and enveloping bed. Benedict's bed. Ugh. Through the open bedroom door I could hear raised voices. I didn't think I had been out for more than a few minutes, so I took my time. I lay and gazed at the ceiling (Mirrors. Really? People actually do that?) as I marshalled my resources and listened to a nice little row going on in the main room.

"That was totally uncalled for," I heard Peter say.

I swung my feet over the edge of the bed and sat up. The room span around disobligingly.

"On the contrary." Benedict's voice this time. "I think you'll find I did exactly what she told me to."

"She didn't know what she was saying!"

I hung on to the side of the bed and blinked a few times. The room began to slow down.

"Now that's unfair," Benedict drawled in his deep bass voice. "I think our little Toni knew exactly what she was asking for. I'm rapidly changing my mind about her. Indeed, Oscar has gone up immeasurably in my estimation this evening, a quite unique experience for me."

I put my feet on the floor. I kept them there until it stopped moving.

"You didn't have to make such a vile scene," snapped Peter. "There were a million better ways of doing that."

It was sweet of Peter to leap to my defence. I couldn't imagine it was going to do any good.

"Maybe. And why not? I get bored easily."

Nope. No good at all. I stood up. It didn't work very well. I sat down again.

"You should be more grateful." It was Oscar's voice this time. "She didn't have to come here tonight. She came of her own good will to help us."

I got to my feet again. This time I managed to stay there.

"I accept that," Benedict replied placidly. "I accept it, but I hate it. So I am going to change it. Toni," he raised his voice "get back in here."

I walked cautiously through. Where Diana had been standing, the rugs had gone. The floor had a scrubbed look. There was a smell of bleach drifting through the scent of burning wood and beeswax. Benedict was poised in front of the fire again, with his infuriatingly nonchalant air as if waiting for someone to paint his portrait. Grace, Peter and Oscar were sat uncomfortably in chairs facing him. Camilla was nowhere to be seen.

"Lavington Windsor," Benedict said laconically, not bothering to look at me. "Will you swear fealty to me?"

I scowled.

"Not while I am alive and breathing," I said nastily, "and probably not afterwards either."

"Such a surprise," he said. "If I had feelings, they would be hurt by now. Oscar Wolsey, will you swear fealty to me on behalf of Lavington Windsor?"

There was a pause. I tried to work out what was going on, but I wasn't quick enough.

"I will, I suppose," said Oscar. "I presume I don't have any choice?"

"None at ___ said Benedict pleasantly. "Do get a move on."

Oscar kn___ ___gantly at Benedict's feet.

"I swear ___ ___ou the fealty of my charge Lavington Windsor. Let her crime ___ my crimes. Let her forfeiture fall upon my shoulders."

This d___ ___t sound good.

"Ha___ ___n," I interrupted crossly. "What the hell just happened?"

Ben___ct ignored my question.

"___arvellous," he said. "And to Lavington Windsor, I extend the pr___tection of my house. Now we can get on."

I interposed myself between him and the other occupants of the room.

"No, we bloody can't," I said. "What does it mean, the oath that Oscar just swore? I need to know."

Benedict's expression remained as impassive as ever. The smugness was only evident in his voice, which was dripping with self-satisfaction:

"Your lovely Oscar has sworn that you will observe the conditions I place upon you," he explained kindly. "It's a win either way for me. Either you do as you are told, which will be a very novel undertaking for you I feel and one I am looking forward to gloating over, or I get to stake your boyfriend through the left ventricle. I can't lose. Now sit down and shut up."

I sat down because my legs were still shaky. I shut up because I couldn't think of anything to say. I glared at Oscar and Benedict in turn because I couldn't decide, between the two of them, who I was the most angry with.

Benedict continued as though I had never interrupted:

"Toni, earlier you were so obliging as to tell me that you know where our unwelcome American cousins are holed up. A little clarification on that front would be most welcome."

I sighed. Benedict merely waited.

"They are at Butterbank Lodge," I said reluctantly. "If you head ___wards Raunton from Stafford, it's about three quarters of a mile ___ the side road to Coton Clanford."

___nedict tilted his head to one side.

"And you are sure of this?" he asked.

"Pretty much."

"How?"

I nodded. It was a fair question.

"When Oscar asked me to find him a house, my first thought was the lodge. It's so secluded that I'm not sure a lot of people know it's there. I do, but that's because it was on our books for two years before the current owners decided Bernie was useless and gave it to Benson Hood at Deanthorpe, Duncan and Delaney. I rang him the day after I saw Oscar, to suggest we set up a viewing and split any commission, but he didn't reply or call me back. He had a table booked at the industry party the next night, but he didn't turn up. Today while Peter was sleeping, I rang Benson's wife, and she hasn't seen him for two weeks. She reported him missing to the police. My brother mentioned it, but I wasn't listening."

Benedict shrugged.

"Interesting, but circumstantial."

I continued as though he hadn't spoken. Two could play at that game.

"So then I rang his secretary. Butterbank Lodge was bought three weeks ago for cash by a secretive American millionaire with a fondness for discretion and privacy. He had asked Benson to find him somewhere secluded with cellars that didn't flood. Talked a lot of baloney about a wine collection."

Benedict said nothing for a moment. Then he nodded.

"You have convinced me. What else?"

I shrugged and played my joker.

"Benson isn't very good. I never thought he'd sell the house. I hoped we'd get it back. So I kept the file."

Benedict frowned.

"Meaning?"

"I still have the floor plans."

He nodded.

"With you?"

I walked over to the chair where I had sat earlier and p

up my handbag. It was the hand-sewn cream leather satchel I had bought at the county fair the previous year. It had pale blue stitching and little chrome studs on the pockets. It was also covered in blood.

"I brought them," I said. "You owe me a new bag."

For a moment I thought he might smile. The moment passed.

"Agreed," he said. "Pass them over."

I took out a folded wad of A4. Benedict took it with a gracious incline of the head.

"Oscar, I take it all back," he said. "Your hamster has hidden depths. Let's hope we had only the one mole and throw this open."

And he walked to the door, flung it open and stalked out.

"If you call me a sodding hamster one more time, I am going to explore your hidden depths with a sharpened snooker cue," I promised his retreating back. He graciously ignored me. Maybe he didn't hear. It was probably for the best.

Grace drifted after him, and Peter followed reluctantly. Oscar took my hand.

"You are amazing," he said. "I am looking forward to exploring your hidden depths."

I melted. How could I stay mad with someone so adorable?

"I am still cross with you for pledging my allegiance to that fangy tosser," I said. "You know that?"

Oscar hugged me to him and kissed me softly.

"I know," he said. "But I am sworn to him myself. I don't think I had a choice."

I sighed.

"Kiss me a few more times and I may forgive you."

He kissed me softly again and then harder. His lips explored the contours of my own and then pressed in more firmly to coax me to open to him. I was more than happy to oblige. At first his tongue only skimmed the soft moist inner edges of my mouth, but then he became more ardent, thrusting his tongue in to taste me deeply and rhythmically, and give me a promise of pleasures yet to come.

He drew me closer into his embrace and pressed our bodies

together. He slid his hands up from my waist to my shoulders. He gripped my hair at the base of my neck and softly tugged my head to one side. Slowly, he withdrew his mouth from mine so that he could kiss his way down my neck, his tongue tracing wet patterns from below my jaw to my wishbone before tracking back up and coming to rest in the hollow curve below my ear.

He bit me gently, not hard enough to draw blood but enough to make me gasp. I think he realised things were getting out of hand, because he pulled away from me and held me at arm's length. We were both ruffled, and I was breathing with difficulty.

"Am I forgiven, Toni?" he asked. "Please?"

"No, not nearly," I lied. "Why?"

"Because there is a council of war going on in the Chamber." He straightened his clothing and then tried to tug mine back into place. My skirt was all over the place and my neckline certainly hadn't started the evening that low. "And more importantly, we are virtually in Benedict's bedroom."

That was a turnoff.

"I still need more kisses, but you can pay me later."

He squeezed my hand as we walked out of the opulent apartment and back through the torch-lit corridor.

"You can redeem them at your convenience," he said. "Your account will be accessible whenever we are together."

We turned back into the main corridor. Ahead of us, through the arch, I could hear raised voices and chatter from the main chamber. We entered to find my maps had been strewn across the stone table on the central dais. Shadowy figures were clustered around. Benedict looked almost animated. He saw us enter, and said almost cheerfully:

"Oscar, over here. You are the fastest. I will need you ahead."

Oscar left me and joined him. I tried to work out how many people were present, and which were vampires, but I still couldn't see properly in the flickering torchlight. I closed my eyes and tried to sense them. It felt as though it might be possible, but it was also nothing I had ever tried to do. I was overwhelmed by the sensation of so many undead presences and gave up. People were coming and going. As they passed me, I could sense the vampire kind, but I felt like a child who had just mastered multiplication and is suddenly being asked to do differential equations. I played like Peter and hid in a corner. He had chosen the same hideaway ahead of me, so we huddled together on a pile of silk cushions, somewhat shielded from the main throng by a stone pillar.

"I understand now," I said. "I will sort out my spare room and you can stay over any time."

"Thank you. They are not exactly a warm and welcoming family bosom."

"In return you can cook me wiener schnitzel, or whatever it is that you actually eat in Heidelberg."

"You are so kind. I can cook wiener schnitzel, as it happens. It's rather nice."

Benedict's boots appeared in front of us. We looked up guiltily from our secret pile of cushions.

"Describe the roof," he said. "Are there access points?"

I closed my eyes and tried to remember. I'd had a preliminary survey done... why wasn't it in the file? Had I given it to Benson as a favour?

"There would be three access points if you could get up there," I said. "The two round windows that are on the map both pivot open. They lead into the front and back attic steps. There are no locks. And on the flat lead roof area behind the little cupola there is an access hatch. Again, no lock unless they have added one. That opens above the balcony in the hall."

"Good enough," he said. "We will play snooker another time, little tiger. Peter, Camilla's out of commission and I gave too many people the night off. Follow with Toni in case we need help covering our tracks. Take Oscar's car. And stay back. Don't get bloody killed. I have enough bodies to deal with this week."

Peter jumped to his feet.

"Are you leaving immediately?"

Benedict nodded shortly.

"Yes. If there is any element of surprise left, we would like to use it."

He rejoined the group around the stone table.

Peter pulled me to my feet. I looked down in horror at my party dress and sandals.

"I take it there isn't time for me to go home and get changed?"

"No!" Peter looked horrified. "We need to leave right away."

I sighed. "Let me grab my bag," I said. "It's still in Benedict's room."

It was still leaning up against my chair. As I bent to pick it up, I heard the trilling of a mobile phone. I traced it to under the chair that Grace had sat in. I picked it up, but before I had time to answer I noticed the caller ID. It was one letter: G. I had a feeling I had found Diana's phone. If no one answered, would her blackmailers be tipped off? I wasn't sure, but I couldn't risk it. I flicked it off and stuffed it into my bag just as Peter came into the room.

"Come on, let's go," he said. "There's no time to waste."

I followed him reluctantly back up the spiral stairs and through the hall. We exited into the courtyard and he hurried over to the car and opened the passenger door for me.

"I know the road well," I said. "Shall I drive?"

"Have you ever driven a sports car?"

"Goodness no."

He motioned me into the passenger seat.

"Then I will drive, but tell me all the twists and turns coming up as well as the junctions."

I settled myself in.

"This time of night, go onto the dual carriageway and take the Stafford road," I told him. "Do you care about speed cameras?"

He was already in fourth gear.

"Tonight, not at all."

Peter could drive terrifyingly fast. When we took corners I lost my voice. At this rate, I worried that we would end up in a hedge before we ever got to Butterbank. But after a few minutes I realised I had misjudged my chauffeur. He could really drive.

"The road curves to the left here," I said. "Very sharply. Then a swing to the right as you head up the hill."

He double-declutched instead of braking. The car nipped left neatly and then arced to the right.

"Have I just discovered your hobby?" I asked him, hanging on to the sides of my seat.

"One of them," said Peter. "Fast cars, wine and women, of course."

"Sex, drugs and rock and roll?"

He thought about it, revving the car back into fifth and peaking the hill at the full ton.

"The first maybe," he said, swerving slightly to avoid a rabbit. "But I am more of a jazz guy. And Lenz is pretty strict on recreational pharmaceuticals."

"There is a nice jazz club in Birmingham, you know," I said. "You get a straight run for the next mile."

The accelerator hit the floor and the car briefly left the tarmac at the top of the hill.

"If there is ever an evening when our lives are not in hideous danger, Toni, let's go there," he said.

"I'd like that," I said. "In about 400 yards, you need to hang a left. It's a single-track road and it's crap."

The brakes bit. My seatbelt had its work cut out. The car turned on a sixpence and we were trundling down a muddy, badly surfaced lane.

"It's straight until the hill and then it twists and turns for about 200 yards," I said. "The turn to the lodge is on the left after that. Peter, should we hang back?"

We hit the hill. Peter hit the brakes. My seatbelt hit my solar plexus and drove the air out of my chest. The car swerved up the hill and did another handbrake turn into the lodge drive and hurtled along it. Butterbank Lodge loomed up ahead of us.

"No," he said. "If there was a fight, it's over by now."

He was wrong. A figure loomed up ahead of us and we braked sharply. Whoever it was, they were down on their knees and covered in blood. I jumped out of the car before Peter could stop me.

"Toni, no!" he yelled. "It may not be one of us."

I realised what he meant too late. The figure turned to look at me. She was certainly a vampire, but no one I had ever seen before. Her beautiful face was marred by bruising, a gash opening up one chiselled cheekbone. Dark hair was slick and shiny with blood. Her blue eyes bored into mine.

"Give. Me."

Her voice was a weak breath. I had a feeling that once she had gorged herself on my lifeblood, it would be stronger. I reached out and felt for her. What was the name Peter had said? Livia. Yes, now I had her. So weak that it ought to be easy. Or at least possible.

She was crawling towards me. Blood dripped off her chin. She was just ten feet away, nine, eight, seven...

"Livia Gambarini," I said with as much conviction as I could manage. "I banish you."

Her eyes widened in shock even as she fell back into the gravel of the drive. But unlike my previous victim, she knew what she was up against, and there was no wasting time flailing and threatening like Claudio. She dragged herself to her hands and knees and continued to advance on me. I pushed everything I had into my words. It was like trying to lift a truck, but once I had started, I couldn't stop. I collapsed to my own knees on the drive. I thought I might throw up. We were face to face. I saw her blink blood out of her eyes. Then one hand, sticky with blood—hers? Who could tell?—snaked out and grabbed me by the throat. Her grip was like iron.

"Give. Me. Blood."

Her voice was already stronger. Vampires heal fast. I knew that. A vampire that isn't quite dead is likely to recover. A few pints of my blood and she would be ready to go clubbing.

I saw Peter come up behind her and try to pull her off me, but she backhanded him with her other hand, and I saw him tumble back into the darkness.

"Livia Gambarini, hear me," I gasped through the pressure of her fingers on my windpipe, "Livia Gambarini, I banish you from the world of the living." It was all I could manage. It wasn't enough.

I needed more power. I looked down at my hands, dirty with the dust and gravel of the driveway. Of course... I reached up with one for the rose that Bredon had tucked into my hair. The stem had a nice fat, sharp thorn on it. I rammed the ball of my thumb into it, once, twice, three times and then pressed my bleeding hand back on the ground, feeling the connection with the earth stronger and more resonant. I really had her now.

I looked back into her eyes. I still couldn't speak but I no longer needed words. The power coursed up through my fingers. I felt I was glowing. I trapped her spirit like a butterfly in a net. It fluttered weakly. It never stood a chance.

The grip on my throat softened and she surged through me, her collapse almost elegant. Again, there was a rush like sunshine or molten honey: a sweet, thick heat that burned into me as she ebbed into the ground. A soft fine dust covered my dress, covered my shoes, covered the road surface, covered even the skin of my face and hands. I felt it on my lips, a chalky grit with the taste of salt. She was gone and it was all that remained.

Chapter Fifteen

IF SHE HADN'T been near death, I could never have managed it. That much I knew. But it was hard to feel anything other than elation. I felt amazing enough that the potential ruination of my new dress paled into insignificance. I breathed deep inhalations of dark night air into my lungs. They smelt of jasmine, night scented stock, cut grass and dead vampire.

I came to my feet and tucked Bredon's rose back into my hair. Peter was at my elbow.

"Toni, what in the name of God just happened?"

"I might just have banished her," I said, a little embarrassed. "It seemed for the best."

It was Oscar's voice that answered.

"Better than you being killed, maybe. But what on earth do we tell Benedict?"

He walked out of the darkness. His hair was windswept, and he throbbed with energy. Whatever he had been doing before we arrived on the scene, he had been enjoying it. I thought about his question.

"We could tell him that Peter rammed her with the car?"

They both considered that. Then:

"Fine," said Oscar. "That works. It almost worked when they did it to me."

And before I could say another word he walked round to the

front of the little Lotus and kicked the bonnet in. It crumpled under his foot like a crisp packet.

"Poor little car," I said to Peter.

"I liked that car," he said forlornly. "Oscar does get through them."

We were just in time. Even as Peter and I gathered around the front of the car to inspect the damage, Grace and Benedict joined us. Half a dozen other figures drifted in behind them and my senses told me they were all vampires. Grace looked as though she had been apple bobbing in a vat of bolognaise. I wondered how much of the blood was Livia's.

"Did Livia pass you?" Grace asked. "I didn't quite manage to finish the bitch off."

"Peter got her with the car," I said as casually as I could manage.

"Good," said Grace with conviction.

Benedict gave me a look. Just a look but the bottom dropped out of my stomach. What had I done wrong? Had I given myself away? I glared at him—that seemed in character—but he just gazed back at me impassively. As Grace, Oscar and Peter huddled round the car, I tried to step away and hide in the darkness. I moved into the shadow of the trees that lined the driveway, but he followed me.

"You have blood on your neck, my dear," he murmured. "Fingerprints, unless my eyes deceive me. Which seems unlikely."

"You could try just being grateful she is dead," I suggested. "How does that sound?"

He stepped in very close and put his hands on my shoulders. I dropped my eyes from his gaze and just looked at his wrists. His cufflinks winked in the moonlight. Up close, they were little silver sickle moons set with tiny gems.

"Not good enough," he said in his deep voice. He sounded amused. "But I will let it go for now."

He stepped in and pulled me closer. He dropped his face to my neck. I felt him carefully lick Livia's blood off my throat.

"You are already so much trouble, little tiger." He spoke softly into my hair. "But amusing, so I will let you lie to me through your little white teeth." His own grazed my neck. "And not kill you tonight."

And he was gone. Just that quickly and leaving me standing in the moonlight with his saliva drying on my skin and my shoulders burning from his touch.

I hurried back to Oscar and Peter. Grace was talking earnestly. Her dress was wet with blood, heavy with it. It dripped off the hem onto the grass. Her fishnets were shredded and the diamante shoes suitable only for landfill.

"They had no idea," she was saying, "but apart from Livia, there were no other vampires present. Only the mortals. They fought bravely to the very end."

Peter looked serious.

"Was that truly necessary?"

"In this case, yes. You know they are not like us, Peter Hilliard. These Assemblages breed their followers from generation to generation, each one more brainwashed than its predecessors. Their undead masters are their gods, their culture is one of utter subservience. They would have fought us to the grave and beyond. I cannot see a way that they could have been redeemed. The Gambarinis use their blood for control and domination. It is a perversion of our gifts."

I couldn't help but interrupt.

"You use your gifts to compel people against their will," I said. "How is that different?"

She put her head on one side and looked at me.

"Are you more than a slave to give me pleasure?" she asked. "More than meat for my table and wine for my palate?"

"Of course."

She nodded vigorously. Blood sprayed across Peter's tee-shirt.

"Not if you were one of those we slayed in the house," she said. "They were no more and wanted no more. Truly Peter, we could not save them. Maria Acquarone was one of a kind, believe me."

I smelled smoke. I looked back at the lodge. An orange glow was building. Flames were flickering out of the lower windows. A blazing curtain waved in the gentle evening wind. As I watched, the flames spread to a first-floor window embrasure. We could feel the heat from where we stood. I began to hear it too, a dragon's roar audible above the evening breeze. Benedict had obviously decided that arson made the best cover up of the evening's activities.

Peter was looking down at his feet. In the limited light that was available, he looked pale. I touched his arm.

"Are you OK?" I asked.

He shook his head.

"No, not really," he said. "Toni, I'm a doctor. I save lives. I don't take them. I'm sick and tired of this violence. I am not cut out for it. Grace, Benedict, even Oscar... in their own way it's bread and butter to them."

"You helped when I was attacked the other night."

He shook his head.

"I didn't exactly like it, but it was more clean cut. Two thugs who tried to kidnap and beat up a defenceless woman then came back with a knife to finish the job once and for all... I don't mind so much that you took one of them out defending yourself. There's a sense of justice in that. But all these people... I can't help thinking there had to be a better way."

I thought about what he had said. It was hard to argue with him. But then, I hadn't seen a lot of flaws in Grace's words either. The world was more complicated than I wanted it to be.

"Can we just go home?" I asked him. "Do we have to stay?"

He shook his head.

"I can't see that we do. And I don't think that Oscar completely killed that car. If you can lend me a toothbrush, I will take you home now. This lot will be heading to ground. Hey, Oscar!"

This last he yelled across the drive to where Oscar and Grace were still talking earnestly.

"Oscar, can I take Toni home? You don't need us."

Oscar walked over. He looked elated. He had clearly had the best evening ever. I sighed and examined him for bloodstains. There were a few. They weren't a turn on. I tried to think of a nice thing that had happened since I left the graveyard earlier with Peter. There had been one little kiss. The rest of my evening had been unredeemably crap and while I didn't have a mirror, I didn't hold out much hope for my dress either.

"Go if you must," Oscar said. "It's not so long until dawn."

I thought of trying to steal a second kiss. Then I thought of the bloodstains.

"Goodnight sweetie," I said. I stood on my tiptoes and gave him a peck on the cheek. "I'll sort out your house tomorrow. I hope you will be able to move in in Tuesday night."

He smiled. He had a lovely smile. All my reservations melted away.

"Thank you, lovely Toni. Will you come tomorrow at dusk? Perhaps we can do something that doesn't involve near death experiences and arson?"

I hugged him and buried my face in his chest. He hugged me back.

"I would like that," I whispered. "I have a few suggestions on what we could do."

I felt him smile.

"Do you want to tell me?"

I pressed myself to him.

"I will show you," I said. "We can practise until you get it right."

He wrapped both arms around me and kissed the top of my head.

"What if I am a very slow learner?"

I raised my face so that he could drop his kisses on my lips.

"That will be fine," I promised. "We will keep going until you get the hang of it."

It seemed unfair on Peter to carry on, so I left the circle of Oscar's arms and climbed into the battered Lotus. Our trip back was much more sedate, partly because we weren't heading into battle, but also because taking the poor little car over about thirty produced a deafening screech that set my teeth on edge.

So we pootled at an extremely leisurely pace. Peter distracted me from thoughts of dead burnt corpses by talking about training as a doctor in Germany and his years in Heidelberg with Europe's hero, Doktor Lenz. I kept the light-hearted tone going with anecdotes about studying law in Bristol, meeting Claire, dating unsuitable men, and spending too much on shoes.

It didn't really work. We were about halfway home when I burst out.

"Oh Peter, I am tired and dispirited. Every time I close my eyes, I see Diana getting her throat ripped out. I think this dress is ruined and I only bought it yesterday. Let's please just go home and get drunk. I am buggered if I am going to go in to work until the afternoon."

He laughed a little forlornly, and then reached across the car to squeeze my hand.

"I feel much the same, to be honest. The good news is that I left the cognac in your kitchen so we can at least get drunk in style. Don't give up on the dress though—take it off when we get in and put it to soak."

I picked at the hem. It was a little gravel stained. I hadn't checked for blood higher up.

"I think it's dry clean only."

Peter laughed.

"Foolish English girl—nothing is dry clean only. Trust me, I am a doctor."

He parked the Lotus in front of my house and came round to the passenger door to help me out. No one tried to kill us. It made a nice change.

I unlocked the front door and put on a few lights. We wandered through to the kitchen, and Peter unearthed the decanter he had brought the other night and a couple of tumblers. He poured far too much into them. He handed one over.

"Zum Wohl!" he said. "Now, take off your dress."

I necked half the cognac thoughtfully. What the hell... The night had been weird enough that I no longer cared. I turned round to let Peter unzip my dress with his warm hands and then I peeled it off over my head. But he just took it from me, dropped it in the sink and turned on the tap. I stood for a moment in my lingerie—carefully chosen in the hope of a tête-à-tête with Oscar that had never happened—and then said lightly:

"I'll just put my jimjams on."

He turned and looked at me. There was an appreciative glint in his eye.

"If you must," he said. "I want to add salt and lemon juice to this."

"God, you're so domesticated."

"I hope that's a compliment."

"Maybe."

By the time I came down the coffee table had been pulled right into the sofa. It was supporting the decanter and glasses, along with a plate of buttered toast. Peter had removed his shoes and stretched himself out along the length of the sofa. An old black and white episode of Sherlock Holmes was playing on the television. Watson was looking for something on a moor. There was scary music.

"Shove up," I said.

He raised an eyebrow and opened his arms. I curled up in them and he passed me my glass. He fed me toast and cognac until I was full of buttery contentment and unsure how to stand. I ignored all the alarm bells going off in my head and licked butter off his fingers. When I started to drop off, he turned off the screen and carried me up the stairs.

"God you weigh a ton," he said conversationally.

"I'm a size ten, I'll have you know."

"Sure you are," he said, and then added carefully: "You were going to make me up a bed in your spare room."

I leaned my head on his shoulder.

"I was, but I am drunk now. You can sleep with me and defend me from marauding vampires."

"It's light, Toni. They are all below ground."

"Well, you can defend me from hangovers then."

"OK. I do actually know how to do that."

He pulled back the eiderdown with one hand and dropped me unceremoniously onto the mattress. After a few minutes fussing around in the bathroom he came back and turned off the light.

"You need a cat."

Where the hell had that come from?

"I need a what?"

"A cottage like this needs a cat," he said.

"I don't think…" I began. I didn't get any further. Exhaustion and cognac had taken their toll. I tumbled into sleep.

I woke later screaming. Diana pleaded with me over and over not to betray her. But each time I did, and had to watch her die in slow motion, her blood spilling onto the black tiles as her eyes glazed over. Peter held me until I stopped crying. He said soft things in German. I didn't understand them. It didn't matter. When I woke for the second time, the sun was high in the sky and I was alone.

Chapter Sixteen

MY GREAT-GREAT GRANDFATHER was the most eminent necromancer in our family. He summoned demons into the bodies of the empty dead, which is a crazily dangerous thing to do, and bargained with them, which is even crazier. He was a lawyer, though, and wrote long, complex contracts to seal the bargains he made. He must have been good at his job because he lived a long and happy life. He died surrounded by his children and Satan didn't get to collect. I suppose when your immortal soul is on the line, you will be extra careful with your proof reading.

I'd read those contracts and the sub-clauses were disturbing. And as I'd told Peter, they were written in blood, so pretty much everything about them was pretty disturbing. Most of them were with the same demon, Azazel. I think my great-great grandfather quite liked bargaining with Azazel. In his diaries, he describes with glee how the demon would try to snare him and how he would be foiled by cunning legalese time and time again.

Peter had told me he was famous, which I hadn't known, and it had piqued my interest. All of his remaining things lived in a chest on the landing, so I pushed my feet into slippers and wandered out. I knelt down and lifted the lid. There were the contracts I'd promised Peter, tucked in alongside dusty packets of other things I hadn't looked at in years. I leafed through diaries and fingered some fierce little tools I didn't know how to use, including a tiny golden knife, with little wings just above the tip of the blade, hanging on a well-worn chain. I laid them next to each other on the wooden floorboards. Other items had been stuffed into an envelope, things that screamed *gentleman* rather than *necromancer*—such as a pocket watch, a tiepin, a bone comb, a silver ring, and a cut-throat razor. I put them aside.

At the bottom of the chest was a photograph album. I'd looked through it many times, enjoying the strong family likenesses I found. My great-great grandfather, Ignatius Windsor, had a head of curls like mine. There are terrific photos of his brother, who not only had the curls but a fat, frizzy beard you could nest eagles in. The photos were black and white, but my grandfather told me those ringlets were the same fiery orange as the mirror shows me in the morning. I took the book out and began to leaf through. I wasn't sure why, but a nagging sense told me I was on the right track.

There was my great-great grandmother, a tiny little thing who had died of polio before seeing her twenty-fifth birthday. There were her two children, an aunt I couldn't remember the name of wearing a white lace dress, and my great grandfather wearing short trousers and little boots. There was my great aunt Marnie, the beautiful but notorious actress whose life had been dogged by scandals, misery and madness...

I turned the pages slowly. Ignatius Windsor, still young but by then a widower, a beautiful man with high cheekbones and white teeth... Had he bargained with Azazel for those good looks? Had he learned his craft too late to save his young wife? I turned another leaf over and my heart stopped. I stared stupidly, like a badly raised zombie. It was a photograph of my great-great grandfather arm in arm with another beautiful man. There were people in the background but too blurred to make out, and the room itself was badly lit. But was it a room or a cavern? Had I been in that room just a few hours ago? I thought maybe I had. Ignatius was standing arm in arm with someone I'd hoped never to meet again.

It was Benedict Akil.

I heard Peter at the foot of the staircase and stuffed everything back bar the contracts, slamming the lid shut just as he bounded up the stairs. He was wearing just his jeans, barefooted and bare-chested. I remembered licking butter off his fingers and blushed, but if he noticed, he had the tact not to mention it.

"OK," he said, holding out his hands and hauling me to my feet. "The Lotus has been towed, and I used your car to buy breakfast. How are you feeling?"

I followed him down the stairs.

"Better, thank you. I dug those contracts out for you."

"Brilliant."

There was a smell of coffee. There was a pile of croissants. I sat down at the kitchen table. Peter poured coffee into one of my mugs. I added milk and then dropped in cubes of sugar until he took the bowl away from me.

"I also rang your boss, by the way," he said. "I told him you were doing a second viewing on Lichley with me and would be in in the afternoon."

I beamed at him and gulped at my coffee-flavoured syrup.

"Thank you. I have to go in and do some paperwork if there is the slightest chance of you and Oscar moving in tomorrow."

I dipped a croissant into my coffee, and he winced.

"I hate to break it to you, Toni, but it's certainly afternoon already."

"Oh God. I'd better get dressed. If I have anything left that hasn't been covered in blood or ripped in half."

I started on a second croissant.

"You went shopping yesterday…"

I sighed.

"Yes, but I needed cheering up. I didn't buy anything practical for work."

He looked very amused at that.

"Well this should help. Camilla dropped it round about an hour ago. It's from Benedict."

He handed me a brown paper envelope. I took it with distaste.

"I am surprised it's not made of tanned human skin. What am I going to find in it? Finely grated eyeballs?"

He laughed.

"Camilla said to tell you that Benedict owes you a new handbag."

"What's with Camilla anyway?" I asked failing to open the envelope properly. In the end, I ripped one end off.

"She is Grace's consort."

"Oh." I shook out the envelope. It was full of twenty-pound notes. "O. M. G. Does Benedict think I need a bag studded with diamonds? There is about five grand in here!"

Peter reached over and counted.

"More like six. Well, he's a pretentious bastard. I suppose he likes grand gestures."

I put the money in a little pile on the end of the table.

"Well, that solves the clothes problem, provided I can find something to wear today." I looked over at Peter. "Who was Diana Hansen, by the way? She wasn't a vampire."

Peter looked grim.

"She joined Grace and Camilla about six or seven years ago, I gather. Grace has a fairly large coterie, and unusually for vampires, they are all women. Camilla and Diana really were like sisters."

I was a little afraid of finding out things I wasn't ready for.

"Vampires are open-minded when it comes to these things?"

Peter looked thoughtful.

"You mean sexuality? Open minded is one way of putting it. Vampires are creatures of desire—but they can't reproduce, as you know, so that desire isn't channelled strongly one way or the other. Grace is unusual in that I have never heard of her taking a man into her group, but then she is pretty unusual anyway. And she is very old."

I thought about that.

"Don't vampires bond with each other?"

Peter laughed rather sadly.

"No. It's the irony of their existence. In time, I expect Grace will make Camilla one of them, and soon if she can persuade her; she loves Camilla too much to lose her. But from that moment their affection for each other will begin to change. Vampires don't desire one another. There can be a strong bond of trust and loyalty, but not attraction or romantic love. They lust only after the living."

I thought about that.

"Is Grace Benedict's..." I struggled for a word. "Is she Benedict's protégé? Did he make her a vampire?"

Peter shrugged.

"I believe so. He trusts her completely, and I don't see him like that with any of the other vampires."

I wanted to ask: and what about you and Oscar? But I just couldn't. Peter had grown up in a world where normal meant something different than it did to me. I wasn't ready to see it yet. I decided to change the subject.

"I have to sort out this paperwork for you and Oscar, and I have to spend this money of Benedict's. Do you want to come?"

"On almost any other occasion, yes, but I will take the opportunity to catch up on my sleep."

I laughed.

"I can't blame you. Do you ever get enough sleep?"

He poured me more coffee and supervised me adding a mere four lumps of sugar.

"Not since we came to England."

"I am starting to worry that you'll put down roots in my mattress."

He looked at me rather penetratingly.

"I don't think that was what you were worried about last night."

I dropped my eyes and stirred my coffee with great concentration. "Peter, don't..."

He sat down opposite me. He took the teaspoon out of my one hand, the coffee cup out of the other and held both my hands in a compelling grip.

"Toni, Liebling, look at me. I don't think Oscar has been the world's best communicator. Actually, he never is, so I should have expected something like this. I think there are a lot of very essential things that he needs to have shared with you that he just hasn't. Am I correct?"

I held his hands nervously. They were very warm. If I hadn't fallen asleep last night, what would we have done? Would we have made love? And if we had, could I have blamed the drink?

"Yes, I think so. Probably. I mean, Peter, I have no real idea who you are! I didn't know your name when you answered the phone the other night."

He looked truly taken aback by that.

"Really? It's worse than I thought. I feel you are enmeshed in all of this, and no one asked you if it was what you wanted or warned you about the consequences. You've ended up sworn to Benedict, and I don't think you even know what that means."

I shuddered.

"I know it's bad."

"Yes and no. You couldn't have a better protector—but who knows what he'll demand in return one day? It won't be money. But that wasn't why I started this."

I looked at him nervously.

"Why, then?"

"Toni, you have never lived with vampires. I have never lived anywhere else. We do things differently and see things differently— it didn't occur to me that you didn't know that. Or Oscar, apparently."

I thought I should defend my boyfriend at this point.

"There wasn't a lot of chance, you know. We had one pint together, half a date, and then a shag that turned into a kidnapping."

"But that's what I mean. He is so impulsive. I've met you and I can see why." I blushed. "But it's still crazy. Anyway, the thing I wanted to say is that vampires within a coterie... they tend to share."

He wasn't talking toothbrushes...

"I'm not OK with that, Peter. I am a Staffordshire girl. We are broadly monogamous. Or at least serially monogamous. The closest I get to a threesome is sharing dessert with my girlfriends."

"I am beginning to work that out. I got an inkling when I realised how uncomfortable you were with me this morning."

"Are you saying that Oscar expects me to sleep with you?"

He shook his head.

"No, nothing like that. But he probably assumes that you will. I mean, given how impulsive he is himself, he probably thinks you already have."

"I am not like that!" I squeaked.

"I know. So, I just want to say that it's fine if you don't want anything like that."

He let go of my hand and walked around the table. He pulled me to my feet and held me so that he could look down into my eyes. He didn't loom over me. He just held me very gently.

"I'm no predator, Toni. I will be your brother if that is what you want. Whatever you want is fine. OK? Trust me. And when you need things explaining, ask me."

I hugged him back. I was confused and bemused. I had some inkling of what he was saying, but I really didn't want to think about it too closely. I understood that he was telling me I could trust him—and I knew that much was true.

"Thank you," I said. "You are always looking out for me. I don't think I have ever needed a friend as much as I need one now."

He laughed, a little ruefully this time.

"Then we will be friends. But Toni..." I looked up. He was smiling. "If you change your mind..."

I nodded and blushed again.

"I will let you know. Now do you want that last croissant, or can I have it?"

"You can have half. And only if you don't dip it in that syrupy travesty of coffee that you have created in that mug."

So I left him sleeping in my bed, once again, with a promise to come to Benedict's at dusk. I hoped Peter would smuggle me in if I got there before dusk.

The paperwork for a pre-purchase rental can be hideous, but the avaricious absentee landlady Serena Lichley clearly needed some new Manolos, because she was willing to sign just about anything that came with a cheque. I finished everything I could think of with time to spare, and even after popping in at the boutique next to the court and picking up some new clothes and a rather nice soft black leather shoulder bag, I had an hour in hand to drive over to Amelia's. I'd promised to mend her cellar door and put up a new shelf in the garage. I hoped to pull off at least one of these favours without looking like a needy hungry estate agent who was hoping to scarf pastry. I grabbed Bernie's office tool kit and headed out before he could work out what I had planned.

I drove down to Salt, which was looking particularly pretty in a summer afternoon kind of way, and parked at the curb outside Amelia's cottage. She didn't answer the door, which perplexed me. She didn't have a car, and I wasn't sure if she had other friends than myself and Bernie who would take her out for an afternoon. But the milk had been taken in that morning, so at least I wasn't worried. It would be rather nice if she had found someone else to run her errands—provided they weren't also desperate, impoverished, incompetent cooks. Still, I decided to call again the next day and reassure myself that she was fine.

As I left, I saw Will's plain-clothes man hanging around again in his waxed jacket. Why was he watching me again? Had the EDL resurfaced? The thug who'd fled at the decapitation of his partner in crime hadn't been seen since... was my brother concerned that I was still in danger? It was just one more thing than I couldn't be bothered to worry about, so I put it from my mind.

Arriving home, my house was starting to look disturbingly neat and tidy. The rubbish bins were lined up. The dead plants in my bedroom had vanished. I thought the rack of free weights had been dusted. I shook my head, took the world's hottest bath, and emptied a bottle of conditioner onto my hair. I wanted to follow up with about eleven gin and tonics, but I had a rendezvous with Oscar planned, so instead I waxed everything that looked furry and painted my nails. We hadn't really agreed on plans for the evening, except that they would involve smooching, so I picked flat black sandals and a strappy denim mini dress that would have benefitted from a bra but didn't make too much fuss at going without one.

I managed to drag a comb about two thirds of the way through my hair, which was about as far as I usually got, and added two layers of lipstick and three of mascara. Because it was a date, I also spritzed perfume and put on a bangle.

I packed my new handbag carefully. Salt and perfume? Always handy. Phone, lipstick, torch, (brand new) rape alarm, comb, lock picks. Done. Spare clothes in case of vampire emergencies. No problem. Oh yes, and just shy of six thousand pounds in used notes.

I drove over to the little manor house that Peter had taken me to. But even knowing where I was going, I couldn't find the entrance in the fading evening light. By the time I drove into the right narrow passageway, the sun had well and truly set. I coaxed the heap-of-rust-mobile up the irregular section of drive with every nut and bolt rattling. Then we hit the smooth avenue I remembered, and I drove up the elegant curve to where Peter had parked the previous night.

I got the impression that I was being observed as I parked the car in the torchlight. I wondered what would have happened had I not received some grudging acceptance from Benedict the previous evening... I didn't feel this place was without its guardians.

When we had arrived at The Stone House before, I had been too nervous to notice the flotilla of other cars in the courtyard. Today I registered that there were a fair few. Some were nearly as battered as my own, but others were more in the vein of Oscar's aubergine Lotus, as well as top line cars that probably cost as much as my house. I couldn't help stroking one, a racing green sculpted chariot of a car that looked like nothing so much as a sexy clutch purse on wheels. I opened the driver's door—the leather and walnut finishing glittered with chrome.

"It's Benedict's," a soft voice behind me said. "It's a Spyker."

I turned and saw Camilla. She looked pale, and there were dark shadows under her lovely eyes, and she looked as though she had spent the last twenty-four hours crying. She came up to me and I couldn't help opening my arms and holding her close.

"I'd quite like one," I said into her hair, "but he didn't give me quite enough cash."

She gave a rather watery chuckle.

"I was wondering if you would like to go shopping with me," she said. "We could go into Lichfield or Birmingham and have lunch."

It was the best offer I'd had in a week.

"I'd like that," I said. "I can't do tomorrow—I have a funeral to go to—but Wednesday?"

We swapped numbers.

"Shall I take you to Oscar's rooms?" she asked. "I haven't seen him yet tonight."

I followed her into the house and down the spiral stairs.

"Thank you," I said. "I only know the way to Benedict's rooms and I really don't want to go there."

She nodded.

"Now would be a bad time too—he will be hungry."

I thought about that.

"Doesn't he have his own coterie to feed on?"

She shook her head.

"No. He uses everyone else's." Ugh. She led me around some twisting corridors, half made, half natural. I was lost in moments. She stopped at a neat little oak door. "Call me tomorrow, Toni."

I watched her turn the corner out of sight. I tried the door. It was unlocked. It opened into a cosy room, again lit by an open fire and many candles. Dark blue walls and woven rugs gave it an opulent, vintage look. There were more mirrors, silk curtaining, crystal lamps... It was beautiful, and also warm and welcoming. Oscar's bloodstained shirt from the previous night was thrown over a chair. A second door led into what I assumed was the bedroom. I pushed it open cautiously.

Oscar lay on the bed. He was naked, his longish gold hair spread over the pillow. His arms were wrapped gently around Peter, who was fast asleep. I rather thought Oscar had just fed. There was a smear of blood on Peter's neck, shining wetly in the candlelight.

I tried to creep out the way I had come, but you don't get to sneak up on a vampire. Oscar opened his eyes. He sat up and looked at me. He smiled in a very welcoming way and held out a hand.

"Hello, my love. Will you join us?"

I couldn't say I hadn't been warned. I would say I hadn't listened. I shook my head in confusion.

"I will wait for you outside," I said. "I didn't mean to disturb you."

He looked a little confused, but I didn't stay to watch. I panicked. I turned and fled. I had no idea how to get back out. I hurtled along identical-looking corridors, getting hopelessly lost. Every turn seemed to take me somewhere deeper and less likely. The passageways were getting less finished and more cave-like, there were fewer torches... and then I ran slap bang into someone's chest.

He caught me in his arms. His hands were sauna-hot. It was the very last person in the world I wanted to meet. I had just crashed straight into Benedict Akil.

"Going somewhere in a hurry?" he asked in bored tones.

I shook my head.

"I need air. I can't breathe and I can't find my way."

He looked at me for a moment.

"Hmmm. Hold on."

He pressed me to him. I felt the earth dip away from me. There was a sensation of motion, fast and dizzying. I leant back from Benedict's chest and opened my eyes, but wherever we were it was pitch-black. I closed them again.

Minutes later he set me down. I looked around—we were somewhere in the gardens, under what looked like tunnels of pear branches. I was standing next to a wrought iron seat covered in climbing roses. I sank into it gratefully and breathed warm, blossom-scented night air.

"Can I assume that determinedly ignoring reality has finally stopped working for you?"

His voice was very deep and mocking. I didn't answer, mostly because I was still breathless, but also because he was right. Peter had warned me. I just hadn't wanted to know. Finally, I said:

"I know you don't like Oscar, but..."

He cut me off.

"Don't like! Good God, what's not to like? He's a terrific fighter. He looks good in a suit and he drives a shiny car. I can only assume he's a great lover—neither you nor Peter have complained—so as a boyfriend he's probably bloody marvellous. As a vampire he's a disaster. I don't dislike him. I despair of him."

"That's crazy. Why would you even say that?"

Benedict looked at me.

"Crazy? He runs headlong into every situation without thinking or considering the consequences. As a human that might be endearing, but in the undead it's likely to get you killed. That was bad enough when we lived in the shadows, but in this day and age it could spell disaster for each and every one of us."

I tossed my hair.

"I don't like you, and I don't trust you and I am not going to listen to you."

He snorted.

"Trust. That's a fine one. I have given you my protection. I am probably the only person in the bloody county you can trust right now."

I twisted a strand of roses around my fingers. In the moonlight, the petals looked white. They might have been pink or yellow in the sun. The leaves looked black.

"I can trust Oscar; he loves me."

Benedict snorted again. He had a good snort. He probably knew it.

"Love. He loves Peter too, but that hasn't stopped him taking one of the finest oncologists of your generation and treating him like a housekeeper. If he doesn't respect Peter's career and his integrity, what makes you think he will respect yours?"

I stood up.

"Are you suggesting that in the same position you would be any different? And are you really giving me relationship advice? What are you going to tell me to do next: listen to my heart?"

"In the first case, yes, I would be different. I might not respect your choices, but I would make damn sure you knew it up front, rather than breezing along and expecting everything to come out in the wash. And secondly, if you want advice here it is: keep your eyes open. And trust no one."

"Except you, of course," I spat.

"Except me," he said. "Though in a pinch, you could probably rely on Peter. And Camilla wouldn't hurt a fly."

"Well, excuse me for preferring Oscar's company to yours," I snapped. "He is sweet, and kind and loving. You are an autocratic moody tyrant. Doesn't the rest of this wretched Assemblage get sick of you throwing your weight around all the time like you are Jesus? This isn't the show dance finale in Strictly Come Wanking, you know."

He laughed and pushed me gently back down into the rose-entwined seat.

"At least I am this bad all the time, little tiger. As opposed to Oscar who is—what was it you said?—oh yes, who is sweet and kind and loving. When he is getting everything his own way. Let's see just how long that good mood lasts when you still won't let him drink your blood. Wait here and I will send him to you. You can ask him yourself. Oh, and Toni..." I glared at him. "Don't listen to your heart. It's a liar and a deceiver and brings nothing but grief."

He left me without a backward glance and walked off through the darkness of the trees. I watched him go until I lost sight of him in the soft moonlight. I decided to ignore him on the grounds that he was a complete arse. I put everything he had said from my mind, especially the bits that had come too close to the bone.

Chapter Seventeen

When I was little, I wanted to be an intergalactic princess. Maybe not with hair shaped like bagels, but definitely an intergalactic princess. As I got a little older and wiser and learned a little more science, I decided instead that I would be an Olympic show jumper. When it transpired that I didn't get on too well with horses, my career path had to take another subtle shift. I became torn between figure skater and gymnast. Everything changed when I was seven years old, when my hobbies became overshadowed by my Compulsion to raise the dead.

After that I didn't need to decide what I wanted to be—I knew. I was a necromancer, and that wasn't going to change. I only needed to decide how to pay the rent in between. Studying law pointed to a career path where I wouldn't have to work in the evenings. It would also come in useful if I was going to follow my forebear Ignatius Windsor's route to a happy and prosperous life. There's nothing like a good grounding in contract law if you want to cut bargains with the denizens of Hades. I hadn't tried it yet, but if I ever did, I had four modules in structured finance to teach me how to screw over the average British pensioner. I thought Azazel would be a pushover.

It dawned on me as a teenager that my views on what mattered in life differed from those of so many of my schoolmates... They wanted to marry millionaires, marry footballers, marry pop stars or TV presenters, and spent happy hours naming their imaginary future offspring. I never had a wish list for the man in my life. But now I had a man who seemed to tick every box I could have imagined. Gorgeous. Kind. Brave. Unafraid of commitment. Hot in bed. Plenty of money too, had that mattered to me, which it didn't... He was also totally unfazed by the undead.

So I sat on the bench trying to unscramble my brain. Claire was right. I was just being picky. Oscar hadn't lied to me—he had just assumed everything was obvious. And perhaps it would have been if I had spent the twenty-seven short years of my life living with a community of nightwalkers. But I hadn't, so everything was a shock to me. Was it insurmountable? Was it hell. I loved Oscar, and he loved me too. So, he came with baggage. If some of that baggage was Peter, so much the better. I knew I could make this work. I could prove Benedict wrong.

I had cleared my head by the time Oscar came wandering up through the trees. I stood up and walked over to him. I raised my face to his with a smile that I hoped contained all the love that I felt, and when he kissed me I kissed him back with enough passion—I hoped—to make up for having fled his bedroom in a panic earlier.

"Are you alright, dearest?" he asked. "You were there and then you were gone. Benedict told me I would find you in the arbour. My moonlight princess. You look perfect sat here under the stars."

"Promise not to name any constellations for me!"

He looked bemused.

"I do—but why?"

"I dated this Italian boy at college—we used to make love at night on Cabot Tower. He would name all these bunches of stars for me. Later I found out that not only was he doing the same for Claire on alternate nights, but he didn't have a clue what the stars were called. He just made up Italian crap because it sounded romantic."

Oscar laughed. He sat down next to me and caught my arm, pointing randomly at the sky.

"Look, Bellissima. There is the constellation of Linguine, the nymph of home-made pasta." He waved his arms in the air in the manner of a mad continental cook. "And there is the star Semi Freddo and behind it Gelato, the doomed brothers who fell in love with the goddess Pistachia and were punished by being crushed under a giant ice cream maker."

I stood up laughing and pulled him to me.

"You're daft," I said. "And I'm cold. Let's go back inside."

But when we reached the courtyard of The Stone House, we found Peter sitting on a stone lion. The light from the open doorway illuminated him. He had a determined air about him and a bulky holdall at his feet. I'd hoped for a shag. It looked more like I was getting a roommate and the wrong one at that.

"I really need to sort out your move tomorrow," I said. "I get the impression Peter doesn't plan to spend another night here. I hope he's prepared for what a mess Lichley Manor is in. Oscar, you say goodnight. I'll wait in the car."

Oscar kissed my cheek and I watched him walk over to Peter. They debated something for a few minutes. I looked around the car at the sea of crisp packets, old parking tickets, sandwich wrappers and petrol receipts that constituted my idea of interior décor. I thought about getting it valeted. Then I decided it would be easier just to lock Peter in for an hour. That should do it. At that moment, the man himself shouldered his holdall and climbed into the seat next to me.

"Let's go," he said. "Goodbye loathsome vampire residence."

I patted his hand as I reversed rather incompetently back onto the driveway.

"Are all your worldly possessions in that bag?"

"Pretty much; why?"

We trundled back onto the main road.

"Do they include a black suit?"

He shook his head.

"No, but I can buy a suit. I like shopping. Why?"

"I was hoping you'd come to a funeral with me tomorrow afternoon."

He looked surprised.

"Of course. I had no idea you had lost someone. Were they family?"

I explained about poor Jane Doe…

"…and so, it's really hard for my brother. But for me, it's like I failed this girl with the only power I have that's actually significant. I can't bear that they're going to close the investigation. I should have been able to help, but I couldn't. Someone killed her and hacked her up like a piece of salmon. And now they'll never be brought to justice. I'd just like a bit of support, and Wills will have to be in all stiff upper lip policeman mode."

Peter nodded.

"That's tough."

I pulled the car in vaguely parallel to the curb of my house. We took a handle each and lugged Peter's bag into my hallway.

"God, this weighs a ton, Peter. What's in it?"

He toed it into a corner by the stairs.

"Mostly textbooks. Do you want a glass of that cognac before we turn in?"

"Yes please. I'll use the bathroom while you get it."

I cleaned my teeth, scrubbed rather futilely at some grass stains and scrambled into pyjamas. On a whim, I took a look into my spare bedroom. Half of it was waist-deep in storage boxes. Some were mine. Others were Claire's. I rather thought one or two belonged to gaolbird ex-boyfriend. Behind them, the room was piled to the ceiling with tea chests of my parents' stuff. There might have been a bed in there… I couldn't remember. No one would be sleeping there unless I hired a skip. And maybe an interior decorator.

I returned to my bedroom to find that there was a man in my bed, drinking cognac and leafing through a hardback volume entitled *The Heidelberg Clinical Handbook of EKG Interpretation*. He put it to one side as I came in.

"This is the last of that bottle," he said. "Savour it."

I climbed in next to him.

"You're in my bed," I said, picking up the glass he had put next to my pillow and swigging. "Again."

He put a bookmark into his medical tome and leaned over to put in on the floor by the bed.

"I am," he said blandly.

I necked the rest of the cognac.

"Peter, I am not sure I should be sleeping with you."

"Why not. I don't hog the covers or snore."

"It's just weird."

"Toni, Oscar will never wake up with you in the morning sunlight. He'll never bring you breakfast in bed. He can't walk along a sunny shore with you. He won't take you shopping, or be your partner at weddings and funerals. He will never cook Sunday lunch with you, or buy you ice creams on a summer afternoon. He won't drink Pimm's with you at croquet matches and stop the drunken uncles groping your arse."

I bit my lip. He had a point.

"And you are saying you would? That you'd do these things for me?"

"Actually, I was hoping we could do them for each other. It's not like Oscar is going to do any of them for me either."

Oh. I processed that. I came to the conclusion that I needed to think more about other people. Maybe between the three of us, we could manage one functional relationship. Goodness knows I'd never managed it the conventional way. I relaxed into the pillows.

"You know, I think we could do that."

And we slept.

Chapter Eighteen

"IN SURE AND certain hope of the resurrection to eternal life through our Lord Jesus Christ, we commend to Almighty God our sister Jane Doe."

I held on to Peter's hand. The church had been stuffy and full of incense, and I had felt faint. Out in the sunshine by the grave, I was beginning to recover. Ancient, senile Father Denis was still waving round an ornate brass handled brush he kept dipping in holy water. Standing at the front as we were, Peter and I had been soaked by the time we had got to the Kyrie Eleison. Come the Liturgy of the Word, I had resorted to mopping up my face with the hem of my black dress. Peter, stripped of his usual uniform of heavy metal tee-shirt and black jeans, looked severe in a double-breasted morning suit and silk shirt. I noticed that he had kept his individuality up in a subtle way—his cufflinks were tiny gold skulls with ruby eyes. No matter—he was dripping wet too, and smelled decidedly of smoked frankincense and myrrh.

Not that there were many mourners to notice. Aside from Peter and I, Father Denis and Henry Lake were the only civilians present. The rest were all police.

"In the midst of life we are in death; earth to earth, ashes to ashes, dust to dust," Father Denis quavered. "The Lord bless her, and keep her..."

He dipped his sacred brush of soaking back into an embossed

pot. With a healthy flick of the wrist, impressive for someone who looked as old as Julius Caesar, he caught me full across the face with a little holy tsunami. I'd had the forethought to put on waterproof mascara that morning and bring tissues with me. I should have packed an umbrella.

"... and we commit her body to the ground."

I recognised most of the force present. Apart from my brother, there was Fiona Miller, the nice WPC who'd bandaged me up all those nights ago. She seemed to be trying to keep her body parts out of the reach of gropey George Allardyce. There were two others—a tall WPC with short blond hair and cool grey eyes, who I guessed was my brother's new partner in crime, and a short man with very unprepossessing features and sandy brown hair who I really couldn't place.

"The Lord bless her and keep her; the Lord make his face to shine upon her and be gracious unto her and give her peace. Amen."

Oh Lord, Father Denis was going for the brush again. I dived behind Peter who got the full force of the blast this time. When I peeped round, he was wiping his face with a large and beautifully ironed handkerchief.

"Is this an English custom?" he asked. "In Germany it's not traditional to try to drown the mourning party."

"It's a freaky Catholic Father Denis tradition," I said. "His beliefs sit at the bells and smells end of the ecclesiastical scale."

The coffin was lowered, and we all got a handful of loamy Staffordshire earth to chuck on top. I lobbed mine in with a heavy heart. Fiona sniffled. Wills looked white and pinched. Gropey George looked regal. Henry Lake just looked hot and sexy. I thought his mind was on other things, and I couldn't blame him. Like Peter, he was here in a supporting role and probably had a million better things to do with his day, like posing for a camera with a rapier in his hand, rather than lobbing some mud into a hole.

The funeral was minimal—those present had coughed up for the affair, me included. With the exception of George Allardyce, that meant dipping into somewhat limited resources. Only the wad of twenty pound notes languishing at the bottom of my handbag had ensured decent flowers. We had decided to skip a wake.

We were clustered around the end of a row at the Baswich Cemetery. The crematorium on the hill caters for those don't want to leave their loved ones for the worms, but Stafford folk are old fashioned. We like graves. There was a time when I would come here pretty much every night to assuage my cravings to raise the dead. For the past year or so, I'd been working my way through the little cemetery above my house, all four hundred and twenty-four of its occupants, but Bredon was the last corpse there I could put a name to. I could see a time when this would be my nightly haunt again...

My ponderings were interrupted by Father Denis leading us through a miserable and out-of-tune rendition of "The Lord's My Shepherd". The proceedings were at an end. We clustered together, exchanging rather desultory greetings and patting one another on the back. I tried to wedge myself firmly against Peter to avoid Gropey George patting anything at all.

"Sis, this is my new partner, Agnes," Will said. "Agnes, this is my sister Toni and her boyfriend, Peter."

I decided not to argue. We did lots of handshaking. Agnes had a firm handshake and a confident smile. She looked like she could run down dark avenues after lawbreakers without losing breath. I thought my brother had done well with the latest round of assignments. His previous partner had been a portly chap who had left the force to become a cheesemaker.

Wills finished the introductions:

"And Toni, of course you know Mark Darkover already, but I don't think he and Peter have been introduced."

I had no memory of ever meeting Mark or seeing him before, but I didn't like to look rude, so I just smiled as he shook hands with Peter. I didn't usually forget a face—or a name—but I couldn't place him. He grinned at me, as if he knew quite well that I hadn't a clue who he was. I decided to let it go and made conversation with Agnes as the gloomy little gathering drew to a close. At the earliest possible opportunity, we all bid one another a rather maudlin goodbye, and I walked back to the car with Peter.

"Who's Mark again?" he asked.

I was checking my texts. Yes! We could pick up the keys.

"I have no idea. I don't recall ever meeting him before. Peter, we have a housewarming to celebrate. If we break into Benedict's room before the sun sets, can we steal some more of that champagne?"

Peter unlocked my car and let us in. While I had been sorting out paperwork that morning, he had not only bought a classy black suit, but had indeed valeted the rust-mobile. Even the little knobs of baked on chewing gum had vanished from the dashboard. It smelt of lemon air freshener rather than old cheese crisps and I could see out of all the windows.

"Probably, if you fancy paying for it in blood. Personally extracted. Why don't we just go to a wine merchant instead?"

He had a point. We drove over to Whitebridge and bought a half case of something fizzy and French.

We didn't get to drink it. Our vague plan—such as it was—had been to pick Oscar up shortly after dusk, but when we arrived at The Stone House we found it in uproar. Even before we had parked, it was clear that were more cars than before. I could hear raised voices. There were people milling around. Most of them were complete strangers to me, but I spotted Camilla sitting on a stone lion looking tired.

"This doesn't look good," I said by way of greeting.

She hugged Peter and me in turn.

"It's not. A small coterie by Raunton Abbey was attacked last night. The vampire and her three mortals were all killed. Benedict's livid. He's demanded everyone assemble here for a grand conflagration on how to exterminate Marcello and his merry band."

She scooted up so that we could both join her on the stone lion.

"That sounds messy," Peter said.

I looked at him in surprise.

"Why? What makes you think that?"

He waved an arm around the courtyard. Two people were yelling at one another. There was some bad natured shoving going on by a Land Rover.

"Half these guys hate each other, and they all have massive egos. Pulling them together under one roof is a recipe for disaster."

That made sense. Camilla patted me on the arm.

"Oscar's gone, by the way," she said kindly. "Benedict sent him over towards Uttoxeter to sort out some vampire who gave a snippy response to his summons."

My heart sank. I hadn't realised just how much I was looking forward to seeing Oscar again that night, and now it looked as though I would miss him altogether.

"Did he leave a message?" I asked.

Camilla shook her head.

"No, sorry. To be honest, he seemed quite excited."

I thought about that.

"What does 'sort out' mean exactly in this context?"

She shrugged in an embarrassed way.

"Well, Toni. These are vampires. He's not going to fine them, is he? When Benedict says he wants something sorted out, that usually means he wants it to go away and never come back."

"No housewarming for us, then," I grumbled. "Can we hide somewhere?"

Camilla brightened and jumped to her feet.

"Let's try," she said. "I know a place. Follow me."

She headed towards the entrance, but we had been too slow. Before we made it to the doorway, it was blocked by a familiar and unwelcome silhouette. Benedict had arrived.

"When I said I wanted everyone here," he yelled, "I don't remember adding the codicil 'except for those who feel they have something better to do with their evening'. Or am I mistaken? It certainly doesn't sound like me."

Grace came out behind him. She was wearing another miniscule black dress. I figured it was a wardrobe stable for her. This one wasn't covered in blood.

"I don't know why you're so insistent that everyone should be here," she said.

The three of us tried to edge quietly away into the shadows. I thought we were doing well.

"No one standing in front of me is dead or being held hostage," growled Benedict. "It clarifies the odds nicely. I want a list. Who isn't here?"

Grace sighed.

"Give me five minutes," she said, wandering into the crowd of squabbling people. "I'll get you a list."

I thought that Peter, Camilla and I had almost managed a sneaky retreat when Benedict caught sight of us.

"Where are you going?"

"Just away," I said hopefully.

"No, stay there. I want you."

He stalked off into the darkness. We sat down with a sense of resignation on the stone lion.

"So close," said Peter. "So very close. Where are you girls going shopping tomorrow? Can I come?"

We sat at the edge of the flickering torchlight for a while vaguely discussing shopping plans. Camilla needed shoes. We told Peter what aftershave we thought he should try. I couldn't make out much of what was happening in the courtyard, but I could hear Benedict's raised voice much of the time, which told me it wasn't something I wanted to get involved with.

When Grace came back through the doorway, he returned.

"Well," he said.

She handed him a sheet of paper.

"Eight no shows," she said crisply. "Eight names, eight addresses. Happy?"

He gave her a look. It said we could assume not. He looked briefly at the list and then tore it in half.

"Peter Hilliard," he said, not looking up. "Take this. Visit each. None of them answered the phone. If anything looks odd, run away. Any questions?"

Peter stood up from the stone lion and pulled me with him. He took the list from Benedict's hand.

"Can I take Toni?" he said.

Benedict laughed.

"Take a picnic. But Peter..." We looked back at him. "If you feel the urge to do anything heroic, do please lie down until it goes away."

"I am no hero," said Peter with dignity. "Just a jobbing medic."

Benedict turned his gaze to me.

"And you," he said very kindly. "Do you think you could stay out of trouble for an evening perhaps? No headless corpses for a night? Just as a favour because I asked nicely."

I pretended to think about it. I would rather have gone home, but the alternative seemed to be staying here, which was worse.

"Just for you," I said, "I will leave the heads on."

I turned and stomped to the car. At least we got to leave. Just as I got my hand on the door handle, I heard his voice again.

"What the hell is that? An art installation."

I turned round to find Benedict staring at the heap-of-rust-mobile with revulsion.

"It's my car," I said, "and it's vintage."

"It might be the only thing I know that's older than me," he said with spirit. "Hilliard, take my car."

He reached into the pocket of his jeans and pulled out a bunch of keys. He tossed it over to Peter and disappeared once again into the confusion in the darkness.

Peter looked at the keys in his hand in simple disbelief.

"Es ist ein Wunder," he said. "A miracle. I am grateful to Benedict for something. I thought this day would never come. He's right about your car, though. The rust molecules are holding hands across the terrifying void."

"O. M. G," I said. "Let's for goodness sake get out of here before he changes his mind. I have fantasies about that car."

We waved apologetically at Camilla and legged it across the courtyard. The car was nestling under a tree glistening in the moonlight. The doors made lovely solid clunky noises as they opened and closed. The seat sort of hugged me when I sat in it.

"It's just delicious," I said as Peter started up the engine. He pressed a button and the roof kind of crept into the boot. "I don't have jewellery this pretty. Bloody hell, this seat is heated."

Peter slid gears into place. The engine made I-am-a-lion-hear-me-roar noises. We oozed out of the courtyard of The Stone House and nosed slinkily onto the main road.

"Tell me about these fantasies," Peter said as he tested out the acceleration and clearly found nothing wanting.

"Nope," I said firmly as we briefly left the road at the prow of a hill. "I can't risk distracting you. Watch the road."

Grace's list had four addresses on it, not one of which was close to a main road. We didn't care. Our first port of call was a smallholding at the top of Hopton Hill. By the time we reached it, I was breathless and laughing, and any melancholy left over from our earlier disappointment had been blown away by the wind in our faces.

"Tell me more about raising the dead," Peter said as we walked up a long, dark driveway. "Can you raise anyone who has died?"

I took my time replying because the surface was in poor repair and badly lit. The house we were visiting was set back from the main road, and while it was a clear moonlit night, straggly trees cut out most of the light as we walked down the slope of the drive to the small stone porch.

"Pretty much," I said. "It's harder the longer ago they died. Until a year ago, I hadn't managed to raise anyone who died much more than about a century ago. But I've been practising with older and older graves. I can go to nearly three hundred years now. I've raised all four hundred and twenty-four named occupants of Colton Hill cemetery."

There was a dusty knocker shaped like a fish. We rapped it a few times. The house had a neglected air. It didn't strike me as somewhere that had been invaded by rival vampires.

"You said you only raise them at night," Peter said. "Is that so no one finds out?"

"I can only raise at night full stop," I said. "It doesn't work in the daylight. My grandfather told me that the power of the undead is strongly linked to the night. I've tried raising in daylight, and it's like flicking a switch that's not connected to anything. I've even tried at sunset, or just after the sun is up, and there is nothing. No power. It's as though my necromancy just turns off and on with the sunrise and sunset. And I can always feel it when the sun sets, even if I'm indoors."

"Can you raise the same corpse a second time?"

"Lord, yes, though not on the same night. The second time is much, much easier, actually. There never seems to be any point, though. They rarely have enough to say to make it worthwhile. This house is depressing."

It had a mouldy, uncared-for and unloved look. Ugly statues lined the drive.

"Aubrey Cumberland lives here," said Peter. "He's probably the world's most depressing vampire. Oscar says he started reading philosophy in the 1850s and never recovered. I don't think he's ever learned to use a phone."

A light went on inside. We heard footsteps approaching the door and the door was opened by a pale, shrivelled vampire. The skin clung half-heartedly to his bones. He had a fragile, brittle appearance that I thought was probably misleading: the vampire presence I could feel was strong and vibrant.

"What is good?" he said, in a nasal voice that set my teeth on edge. "All that heightens the feeling of power."

"I believe so," said Peter politely. "Benedict Akil has summoned you and awaits your attendance."

"He that writes in blood and proverbs does not want to be read," said Aubrey helpfully. "Have you brought me blood so that that I may write with spirit?"

He stepped forward hopefully, his eyes on Peter's neck.

"Nope," I said firmly, seizing Peter's hand and dragging him back up the drive. "Not a chance."

I set a fast march and didn't let up until we were back in the car.

"He's quite harmless," protested Peter, restarting the engine. "He comes round to The Stone House occasionally spouting crap about isolation of the mind and begging for blood."

I nestled back into the heated seat of the car.

"That's all very well, Peter, but tonight he had been reading Nietzsche, so your jugular looked imperilled. I bloody hate Nietzsche. We had to study him at school."

Our next port of call was a longish drive away, somewhere tucked away by the Churnet River between Cheadle and Leek. The car took up the challenge of ninety-degree bends on single-track roads with much aplomb. On one blind bend, we took out a rabbit. I could guarantee it didn't suffer.

"I cannot believe you ran over that bunny," I said to Peter cheerfully, when I had a little breath back. "It didn't so much get run over as vaporised."

"They do that in all the posh restaurants," he said happily. "This is the most fun I've ever had with my clothes on."

The drive was indeed fun, but it was a waste of time. A fallen tree had taken out phone lines to the second residence on our list. The snotty blonde vampire who had eventually answered the door looked fearful when told she had missed Benedict's summons. I thought she was probably right to worry.

Our third port of call took us full across the county to Stonydelph. In an old rectory off the main road, I got the distinct impression that no one had answered the phone because they couldn't hear it over the deafening roar of the stereo. The sort of party I would have liked an invite to had clearly been in full swing since sunset. The willowy vampire who answered the door, sporting long white hair and not many clothes, apologised in an embarrassed way. I thought of asking if we could gate crash, but he was leching at my throat rather obviously, so we went on our way, serenaded by the dying strains of the Sisters of Mercy.

We stopped for coffee a little after four at an all-night garage. While we sipped at espressos, and the garage attendant gazed in lust at our car, I looked at the final address. It wasn't a million miles from my own house. It was…

"Peter!" I exclaimed. "This is Hugh Bonner's address. The farmer who introduced me to Oscar. I didn't realise until now because the name is different."

He took the paper off me and scrutinised it.

"Hannah Bonner, Bonner Farm, Colton. You are right," he said. "Do you know this place?"

I shook my head.

"He's pretty reclusive. His cowman is known for peppering trespassers with lead shot."

Peter restarted the engine.

"We'll take care to advertise our presence. Hang on."

The drive to our final destination took us nearly an hour and no speed limits were respected at any point en route. My seatbelt earned its keep. Bonner Farm was tucked away in a little copse at the top of Martlin Hill, but you had to drive up a long, exposed track to get there. The car purred its way up happily, and we pulled into a small farmyard. There were lights on in the house—hardly surprising in a vampire residence—but no one came out to greet us.

Peter turned off the engine and opened the driver side door. The usual revolting smell of farmyard drifted in. Always assuming I didn't get covered in blood tonight, I would still have to wash my hair just to get rid of the overwhelming odour of sheep. Talking of sheep, the yard was about four inches deep in sheep-related mud. I'd come across the word ordure in books. Here was a place it could come in useful in conversation. If I got out of the car at all, I would need new shoes.

"Can I stay in the car, Peter?" I whined. "Please."

He walked around to my side of the car and opened the door.

"Nein," he said firmly. "Auf keinen Fall. I bought this suit and shoes this morning, remember. We're going down together."

I got out of the car. Things squelched under my feet. And around them. We walked up to the kitchen door together. We were nearly there when a little warning light went off in my brain.

"Wait," I whispered. "Something's wrong."

Around us the farmyard was utterly silent. Not a mouse was stirring that we could hear.

"Are you sure?" Peter whispered. "What makes you think something is up?"

I shook my head.

"Hugh Bonner has four hundred sheep." I spoke as quietly as I could. "So, he must have dogs. In fact, I've seen him with a couple at the pub. But nothing has barked at us. Even though they must have heard the engine minutes ago and we're wandering around the house."

Peter nodded.

"God, you are right. And they must know we are here. Get back into the car."

We turned and headed back. I took out my phone and had even pulled up Camilla's number before realising there was not a trace of signal up on the hill. I stuffed the phone back into my bag. I could see Peter feeling in his pocket for the car keys but even as he took them out of his pocket, a dark figure barrelled into him and they both crashed into a pile of farm machinery and some rolls of fencing wire.

I was so shocked that I took a step backwards and fell over something lying in the mud behind me. I landed heavily in the farmyard sludge, whacking my leg on whatever it was I had fallen over. Fumbling around in the muck, I realised it was some kind of ditching shovel, with a long wooden shaft and heavy metal blade. Feeling that any weapon was better than none, I felt around for the handle, and hauled it out of the mud.

I scrambled to my feet. It was too dark to work out what was going on between Peter and his attacker, so I rifled through my handbag for my torch. I clambered to my feet, shovel in one hand and torch in the other. Shining the torch into the mess of flailing limbs and German curses emanating from the dark, I could see Peter was putting up a good fight for someone whose lower limbs were entwined with the pointy end of a rusty old haulm topper. But he was the one underneath, and—from the way he was moving—badly hurt. I hefted the shovel in my hands, misjudged the weight as it was nearly as tall as me, and fell over in the stinky mud again.

"Arse," I said distinctly, scrabbling around for the shovel and getting to my feet again. "Sodding bloody sodding sheep."

The torch was lying on its side, pointing vaguely towards the fighting men. Peter was losing the battle. His attacker was raining down punches and Peter wasn't blocking very many of them anymore. I took a better grip of the shovel this time, managed to get a bit of momentum up and brought it down about as hard as I could. I missed by about four inches and took a chunk out of the haulm topper.

The man attacking Peter let go and turned around to face me. He looked vaguely familiar. I thought I'd seen him somewhere recently, but couldn't place him.

"Stupid bitch," he said and stepped towards me.

But I had the measure of my trusty ditching shovel by now and I clubbed him with it in the side of the head with all my strength. The laws of physics were on my side and he dropped like a stone. The shovel and I, on the other hand, were also observing the laws of physics—conservation of momentum to be exact—so we carried on going. I let go a little too late and fell over again, fortunately this time landing on top of the unconscious man.

"Stupid shovel," I said, hauling myself back to my feet for about the hundredth time. "Peter, are you OK?"

I picked up the torch and squelched over to where he lay, still entangled in bits of machinery. I shone the torch in his face, which was covered in blood, accidentally blinding him at the same time. He winced and looked away.

"God, sorry," I said, averting the beam. "Are you alright?"

He coughed and spat out a mouthful of blood.

"No, actually. I think I have broken my ankle."

Some German swearing followed. I peered over at his feet. All I could see was mud. There might have been an ankle down there. In the darkness and the slime, there might have been evidence of life on Mars. I couldn't tell.

"Are you sure?" I asked. "Might it just be sprained?"

"I'm the doctor, remember," said Peter, a touch forlornly. "I think it's very much broken."

I looked around us. There was an unconscious man at Peter's feet. There was the first suggestion of light on the horizon.

"Look, Peter," I said. "We are minutes from dawn. I don't know what time the sun rises…"

"Three minutes past six," he interrupted.

I was thrown.

"What?"

He shrugged.

"Toni, I live with a vampire, remember. I know exactly when the sun rises and sets."

That made sense.

"Well, OK then. I was going to say we are minutes from sunrise and…. What time is it?"

He looked at his watch.

"It's quarter to six."

"OK, so it's quarter to six. We're not safe yet. Particularly being as—between us—we're armed with a ditching shovel and a torch and no bloody mobile phone signal. Peter, I'm going to see if there's a landline phone in the farmhouse, and try to call for help, because I can't see how to move you on my own. If there are any vampires near us, let's hope they're running for cover already."

Peter nodded. He looked grey in the pre-dawn light that was supplementing my little torch and the light of the farmhouse windows. I rather thought his nose was broken too, and his eyebrow, above the black eye that was healing, had split open.

"OK. Don't be long. And Toni…" I looked at him. He winked. "Nice work with the shovel."

"Thanks," I said. "Hang in there. I won't be long."

The farmhouse seemed deserted. Apart from the corpses that is. They lay in the hallway, blocking my path. They were a couple in their fifties, and I rather thought they had been Farmer Hugh's cowman and housekeeper. They were sprawled in a crumpled sort of way, their skin very white and shrunken. I could hear some flies buzzing. Lots of flies. My head span for a moment, and I hung on to the side of the wall for a bit while I threw up my coffee on the wooden floorboards. Under the vomit, I noticed a mound of the same greasy dust that had covered me when I banished Livia and Claudio. I got the impression that Hugh Bonner had ordered his last brandy at the Black Mitre. It seemed a shame.

I gazed at the scene in revulsion for a minute or so more before plucking up the courage to step over the bodies into the kitchen that opened off the hall. It was full of broken china and furniture as though an altercation of truly epic proportions had taken place inside, and—particularly repulsive—the bodies of four large dogs lay on the stone flagged floor. More things buzzed, and I gagged again, but there was no coffee left, so I leant on the table retching for a few moments.

When I had enough control, I averted my eyes from the dogs and walked through the door that led into a larger hall, with stairs leading to the upper storey. On a chunky wooden sideboard, there was indeed a phone. I realised that I should have asked Peter who to call... Before I could decide what to do, I heard his voice from outside yelling something at me. A warning? A cry for help? So help me, I didn't know. I ran back outside.

There was no one there.

There were no footprints other than ours and those of our earlier attacker. There were no tracks to signal the passage of a vehicle, and there was not the tiniest sign of Peter or the unconscious man, or who had taken them. They had gone as completely and as mysteriously as if they had been teleported into space by aliens. Where Peter had sprawled, bleeding, and asking me not to leave him for too long, there was just a smear or two of blood. The rusty shovel I had commandeered was sinking into the mud along with the keys to a sports car I wished I'd never set foot in.

I wanted to be capable and take control, but I couldn't. I wanted to know what to do, and to do it with wonderful efficiency. I wanted to be brave and competent and spring into action. Instead I just stood there in the mud in poor old Farmer Hugh Bonner's horrid farmyard, suffused with the stench of sheep, and burst into tears. As I stood there crying, the sun came up.

Chapter Nineteen

THE TRAIN CRASH had happened six years before, in the weeks between me sitting my finals and graduating. I was in that confusing world between being a student and having to finally earn myself a living. I wasn't sure about the concept of gainful employment, so instead of spending my evenings writing application letters to law firms, I spent them raising the dead and getting drunk, sometimes both at the same time.

You only get two guest tickets to your graduation ceremony, and I had no illusions that my parents would want either of them. Loving towards my brother, they had never shown the slightest interest in me. Had they been disappointed with my spotty academic record, floored by my choice of degree, and unimpressed by my failing to follow in their joint footsteps to Merton College, Oxford? Who could say...? They had also spent a total of about twelve months in the country since my tenth birthday, so I thought it unlikely that they would remember my graduation, let alone want to come.

I had asked my brother William and my grandfather instead. Neither of them had any better idea than me what I might do with a law degree from Bristol University, but they were happy to help me celebrate. I had moved into a bedsit for the final few weeks, unwilling to commit to a longer rental agreement. Claire would graduate with me, but she was spending the in-between weeks somewhere in Spain with a boyfriend.

Then it happened. The crash on the mainline that killed eighty-six people, including my mother, father and grandfather, and was never satisfactorily resolved. The railway ended up replacing two miles of track and all the signals, but no concrete faults were ever pinned down. I remembered my landlady coming in and sitting with me after the nice police constables had gone. She tried to comfort me. I just sat in her squishy armchair feeling helpless. That was the feeling: helplessness. Absolutely nothing I could do, not then or forever after, would change things. I could not alter the rather desultory way I had bid my grandfather goodnight the last time I called him. I had no time machine to go back and build a functional relationship with my parents. Those opportunities had gone for good.

But this was different. I had a chance to change things and I was bloody well going to. Peter had held my hand at Jane Doe's funeral. I was damned if the next one I went to would be his. I dried my eyes, blew my nose, and stopped feeling sorry for myself. What was my excuse after all? I wasn't the one with a broken ankle who had most likely been kidnapped by vampires.

I traipsed back into the house, picked my way over two dead people, the ashes of one ex-vampire, four dead dogs and a whole lot of bluebottles. They bothered me a lot less than the prospect of Peter joining them. If it had been night, I would have raised them and interrogated them. Instead, I picked up the phone and called Camilla.

She was remarkably competent and together. She assured me that every resource in the Assemblage would be looking to find Peter. She tried very hard to sound reassuring. She told me to get away from the farmhouse and get some sleep.

"Think about it, Toni," she said. "They are on the run. We burnt down their home a couple of nights ago. We killed their mortal supporters —there can't be many more left other than the man who attacked you tonight, maybe none. If they took Peter, it's not just to kill him. They probably plan to use him for ransom. And they are pretty much helpless until sunset. In that time, I am sure we can find him. Don't give up hope."

I wasn't planning to give up hope, but I certainly didn't plan on going to sleep. After searching the farmhouse and finding nothing useful, I drove home in the Spyker, taking the view that Benedict could have his car back when he woke up and noticed I still had it. I took the world's hottest shower, drank four cups of coffee, and shrugged into jeans, boots and a halterneck top. I was in work by seven thirty, a world record for me. I was going to play to my strengths: I found houses for people—maybe I could find the one that half a dozen desperate vampires were holed up in.

By eight I had acquired a list of the seven properties that Benson Hood had showed his mystery American millionaire around. We'd burnt one to the ground, and of the other six, I eliminated only two by phone. The other four were empty, and I decided to visit them in person. Bernie wasn't even in the office by then, so I wrote a note saying I was doing viewings all day, and headed out.

Naturally, the properties were distributed halfway around the county. After spending far too much time picking locks, I was also forced to admit that they were also all completely empty. My great idea had got me precisely nowhere.

It was well past lunchtime by then, so I drove back to the office, ate two Cornish pasties and drank more coffee, and worked through the file of properties I had prepared for Oscar the previous week. I didn't think a single one was secluded enough for what I was looking for. I was fast running out of ideas. I was also jittery and miserable because I hadn't raised a corpse for two days as well as having had no sleep. I was starting to feel helpless again.

"Those pasties are nothing like so nice as Amelia's," said Bernie, coming up behind my chair and stealing a piece of pastry with one hand while trying to stroke my thigh with the other.

I slapped him aside with a folder but couldn't be bothered with further retaliation. Something he had said had set off a tiny light bulb in my brain, but I couldn't quite work out why. What was my subconscious mind trying to tell me? I had no idea.

Unlike Peter, I didn't know when the sun would set. Just before eight, my computer assured me… more than half the day had gone, and I had made no progress. In despair, I rang Lewis Cadwallader at his home, and picked his brain for ideas. At least I could tell him why I was asking without restraint. He was suitably shocked, and suggested the derelict pumping station in the woods behind the Blithfield Reservoir.

"Do you know the one?" he said. "It's just where the reservoir meets the main road. It's certainly secluded and the sort of place they might go. You know the place I mean?"

I certainly did. I thanked him and hung up in a hurry. The pumping station seemed like a good bet. Not only was most of the building underground, but it was just minutes away from the cellar where Oscar and I had been imprisoned by Claudio Gambarini. In my panicked state, I had forgotten all about the cellar. Given that the two buildings were so close, it was highly likely that the vampires who had taken Peter had discovered the pumping station too.

I made the drive in record time. Closed in the 1980s, the station had quickly become a favoured haunt of the local youth. I had partied there myself as a teenager. These days, it was harder for me to see the appeal. A couple of burnt out VW Beetles were rotting by the entrance, along with some mouldy mattresses. The scrubby approach was littered with broken beer bottles, and less savoury items including the odd syringe and what looked like discarded condoms.

I took out my torch and picked my way to the doorway. The door had been hauled off its hinges and burned before I was born. Every now and then, someone in authority somewhere ordered the entrance boarded up, and layers of ripped off boards were piled up to one side. When the weather got colder again, they would go up in smoke nicely.

I was out of luck again—in the worst possible way. The vampires weren't there, but they had visited. At the very back of the station, down a flight of stairs and behind an elderly and foul-smelling sofa that I vaguely remembered from my own youth, a body lay sprawled. She had been hurled face down on the concrete, the single redeeming feature being that I only had to see the back of her head. I didn't have any doubt how she had died—her skin the same shrunken pale texture of the corpses I had seen the previous night. She wore a faded denim mini skirt, with a lace vest and hiking boots. She could have been me a decade ago. She probably came here to get laid. Or get high. Or just get away from her annoying family... she hadn't come here to die, but she was dead just the same. Damn it! Peter was not going to be next, not on my watch and not if I could stop it.

I called Camilla again. I felt bad that she would probably put steps in place to cover up what had happened to the dead girl I had just seen.

"Should we tell the police?" I asked when she had finished asking me questions. "They could help, surely."

"Oh Toni, we've talked about it," she said, "really we have. But these aren't vampires like Aubrey Cumberland. They are bad news, as bad as you get. We would be signing the death warrants of a lot of police." Like my brother. I decided she was right, but she carried on: "And Toni, it would also put the whole damn Heidelberg Accord into jeopardy if that happened. Imagine if the powers that be started looking sideways at the Mason-Schelling Act and maybe deciding that it had a bit of merit in it... Goodness knows where it would end."

"OK," I said. "I'll call you. But Camilla, last night, they drained this girl. I think they killed Hugh's coterie the night before—there were flies so the bodies weren't fresh. You realise this may mean they have just taken Peter so that they have something to feed on. I mean, we killed pretty much all the other living members of their crew the night Benedict burnt down Butterbank Lodge. How often do vampires need to feed?"

"If they are young, every night, ideally just after they awake," she said very slowly. "Oh my God, you're right..."

I thought I was. I would rather have been wrong.

"Yes," I said sadly. "Peter will die at sunset if we don't find him. So we have to find him."

I ended the call because I couldn't speak. I drove back up to the cowshed where Oscar and I had first been taken by the Gambarinis, and where I had banished Claudio. I didn't hold out much hope that they had returned since our escape, or that they might have somehow left me a sign of where they had gone next. But I was struggling to think of a single way that I could track Peter down before night fell. I had to find him before dusk. Somehow, I needed to do that. Camilla had promised that other people would search for him, but her voice hadn't held a lot of hope.

The cellar where we had been held was deserted. Benedict had complained about having to clean bodies up, and certainly there was no sign of the man Oscar had killed and drunk blood from. There wasn't a drop of blood or a trace of corpse to be seen. The manacles that had imprisoned us were still in place and hung as empty as when we had made our getaway. The mangled remains of my rape alarm lay in a corner. I had followed yet another dead end... I looked around the stone room. Had anything else changed? Only that the video camera had also gone.

I slapped my forehead with my hand. I had taken the data card from the camera, but never looked at it. Was it possible that there might be something there to inspire me? With no better ideas, I decided to drive home and see if I could access whatever was on it.

The card was still in the bottom of the handbag I'd used the night Oscar and I had been attacked. It didn't fit my own camera, and I couldn't find a slot in my laptop that would take it. I had a feeling there was a camera in one of the storage boxes belonging to gaolbird ex-boyfriend, so I hauled crates out of the spare bedroom and dumped them on the landing and in my bedroom until I found the two I was looking for: yellow plastic cases labelled 'Kit Maybury, you are a twat' in my own handwriting. I could feel time slipping through my fingers like sand, so I just opened both and poured the contents onto my bedroom floor.

"Peter, I have to find you," I said out loud. "If I don't, this house will never be tidy again."

There were some clothes, a games console, a pair of trainers, sunglasses and a snazzy watch I doubted had been paid for. There was an electric razor and three driving licenses in different names. I raked through a bunch of credit cards; not one bore the words Kit Maybury. At the bottom there was an expensive-looking camera. When it had fallen off the back of a lorry, it hadn't picked up a scratch.

I prised open slots until I found the one for a memory card—there was one in there already, which I chucked onto the floor along with everything else of Kit's. I tried the card I had taken from the cellar. Bingo. A perfect fit. The camera had no charge, so I scrabbled through the pile of stray belongings until I found a promising-looking cable. I plugged one end into the camera and the other into the wall. This time when I turned it on, it made a cheerful little beeping noise.

I fumbled through the controls until I worked out a way of playing what was on the card. There was a single block of video there, just thirty-two seconds long. I pressed play and it came up on the tiny two-inch screen on the back of the camera.

There is a man, covered in blood. It's still oozing out of a cut on his forehead. And one on his cheek. His lips are swollen. He doesn't speak for a moment, and then he says in a rasp:

"Diana, I want... I need... God, I am so sorry. Please, I don't want to ask this, but please do what they want. Please do what they say. I am scared. Diana, I don't want to die."

He drops his eyes and his voice trails off. For a moment you think you are watching his death.

Then he looks up with a completely different expression and asks brightly: "Will that do?"

From somewhere off screen a second voice says:

"Sure thing. We'll cut it there."

And the video ended.

I frowned. I pressed play again. And again. And again. Because I'd seen this man before. Now that I had time to look properly and think, I'd realised I'd actually seen him several times: once in the town square wearing a Barbour jacket, outside Amelia's house, and again last night when he attacked Peter in the farmyard. The man in the video was the man I had pegged as my plain-clothes policeman and the same man that I had clubbed unconscious with a shovel just hours ago.

Sitting on my bedroom floor, surrounded by piles of rubbish, my head was spinning. I felt the tiny clip of video held the key. I just couldn't see it. I tipped out my handbag so that everything in there joined the growing mounds of chaos and picked my phone out of the heap. I had to work this out.

I rang my brother, who thankfully picked up almost immediately.

"Hey sis," he said cheerfully. "Henry and I are just heading out to dinner."

"This won't take long," I assured him. "I need to ask you about the plain-clothes man who was looking after me last week."

"Mark Darkover? Yes, he was chuffed when he realised you didn't recognise him. I mean, he's good at his job, but he thought you'd spotted him several times."

Wills carried on talking but I had tuned out. The man in the Barbour jacket hadn't been tailing me. Mark Darkover had, but I'd never noticed him, partly because he was good at his job, but also because he looked so nondescript. He'd been pleased at the funeral when I clearly hadn't a clue who he was.

"Wills, sorry, I have to go," I interrupted. "Have fun tonight. Love to Henry."

I ended the call and sat in the crazy terrain that had been my bedroom minutes before. Time was passing, and I had to get my thoughts in order. I found a pen that had rolled under the bed, and pulled a scuffed volume out of the pile of Kit's belongings. Naturally, it wasn't a book—it was the instruction manual for a first-person shoot 'em up—but it had some blank pages at the back and I ripped one out. I wrote at the top:

Mark Darkover was the plain-clothes policeman.

Fine. That settled that. But if Barbour jacket man had never been following me, why had I kept seeing him? I hadn't worked that out yet, so I went back to something I did know. I wrote down:

The man in the video clip is Diana's Hansen's brother Louis.

Before Benedict had killed her, Grace's "little brunette" Diana had told us she had done everything to save her brother Louis. She'd been sent a video of him asking her for help. He'd been covered in blood and looking like death. It looked like he was being held hostage, and forced to make the film. But the end of the clip showed that he'd been faking. I guessed that they had cut off those last few seconds from the version they had sent to her. What had she said before Benedict ripped out her throat? Oh yes: "It was my brother Louis. There was so much blood." I was sure now that I had seen the same video she had described—I had just seen a few seconds more. I wrote down:

Louis Hansen is working for the Gambarinis.

But that still begged the question of why, if he wasn't following me, I had kept seeing Louis. Was it really a coincidence? I thought back. I had bumped into him in the square, and that probably was entirely by accident. If I'd never seen him again, I would have forgotten him completely. But I *had* seen him shortly afterwards. I'd seen him outside Amelia's house. Then it came to me in a rush. I'd seen him outside that house not once, but twice. The house with the cellar that was almost never used, the cellar that you could access from outside through the coal hole... The house of Amelia, who hadn't answered her door when I called round the other day... who had mentioned that her inside cellar door was jammed but hadn't been too bothered about it because she never went down there.

I remembered Peter's own words: "They target the homeless and lonely older people who live on their own."

I dropped the paper and pen and stuffed things back into my handbag. If I was right, my lovely Amelia Scott Martin had probably been dead for days, but if Peter was still alive, I finally knew where to find him.

Chapter Twenty

THE CAR ATE up the miles to Salt, but I was almost out of time. The sun was already low on the horizon and I had no idea if I was really on the right track. The certainty that had overwhelmed me when I saw Louis's video was fading. It was partly dented by heavy traffic, a raft of red lights and a combine harvester driving at about two miles an hour in the middle of the road. My patience had worn thin by the time the road was straight enough for me to overtake. I indicated my displeasure with the driver using the standard hand gesture and he responded by raising the grain platform in a cheery manner.

As a plus, though, by the time I pulled up to the kerb at Amelia's house, I was annoyed enough not to feel scared. I slammed the door of the sports car and stomped up the driveway in high dudgeon. There's nothing like righteous anger for filling you with courage.

I strode up to the front door and rang the bell. There was no reply. I rang it a couple more times to no effect. I reached into my bag for the lock picks. If there was anyone in the house who wasn't spending the day hiding from the sun's rays, I felt cross enough to take them on.

My bravery had flagged a little by the time I worked the lock open and stepped into the silent hallway. It was twenty to eight, and I knew time was very much not on my side.

"Peter!" I called. "Are you here?"

It wasn't really risky: anyone mortal in the house already knew I was here. Anyone dead couldn't hear me until the sun went down. I didn't hear anything back, so I walked on through into the kitchen, whacking my hip on a side table as I did so. I searched the tiny ground floor—hall, kitchen, drawing room—and what I found confirmed my worst fears. The kitchen was a mess. A tray of raw cupcakes sat on the counter, just ready to go into the oven. The batter had dried days ago to a tacky paste.

I went back into the hall and tried the door to the cellar. It was jammed fast. I kicked at it a few times to no effect. I knew from experience that Amelia didn't have so much as a screwdriver in the house, so I went back and searched the car. I found a longish metal thing tucked away with the spare tire. It probably had a special use if you wanted to change a tire or express road rage properly or something. I thought it could double as a crowbar. I wedged it into the crack of the cellar door and leaned into it. About the thousandth time I did so, the door splintered open.

I flicked on the lights and headed down. The fact that they were off reassured me. Vampires can see in the dark, but people can't, so anyone down there should still be sleeping the sleep of the undead.

Except for Peter.

The doorway opened on to a steep flight of stone steps, which led down to a large, low-ceilinged room. A pair of old fluorescent tube lights cast a sickly brown light on dusty flagstones. I didn't take in the rest of the room because Peter lay in a crumpled heap near the foot of the stairs, oddly draped over a heavy wooden ottoman. I saw why as I rushed down to his side. They had nailed him there.

I was almost gagging. Someone had used an industrial nail gun to drive three huge coaching nails through Peter's left forearm into the wooden chest. Blood had been oozing out sluggishly for hours, staining the top of the wood a slick, ugly brick colour. Red tracks had leaked over the edge and pooled on the floor. The thought that Peter had probably been pinned like this since dawn made my blood boil. Thankfully, he was currently unconscious, probably due to pain, exhaustion, or blood loss—or all three. Only the slick of sweat on his pale face and his uneven, stertorous breathing convinced me he was still alive.

I could tell from the blood on his right hand that he had been trying to free himself. I wondered when he had given up. I fitted my own fingertips over the wide head of one of the nails, but I could no more have pulled them out by hand that I could have pulled out my own teeth. I closed my eyes and told myself to concentrate. Then I opened them again and looked around me.

The cellar was about twenty feet square, and largely empty. Apart from the chest that Peter was slumped on, it contained a mound of coal, two large and very modern-looking roof-rack storage units and the dead body of Mrs Amelia Scott Martin. I had a feeling that the storage boxes were the modern equivalent of a fancy travelling coffin. The children of the night were meeting the modern age in their own way. I hoped two of them would meet their maker tonight.

First things first. I went far enough up the stairs to get some phone signal and rang Camilla.

"I've found Peter," I said without preamble when she answered. "I can't move him. You have to get people here."

She didn't waste time.

"Where are you? Give me an address?"

I rattled it off from memory.

"There's a cellar. He's down there. He's…" My voice falters. "He's unconscious, Camilla, and I can't free him. But listen, there are two luggage cases down there, big ones. Big enough for vampires to sleep in. I think he's meant to be their breakfast."

She interrupted me. She sounded despairing.

"Toni, dearest, listen to me: None of us is near you. Not one of us is closer than about twenty-five minutes away. If we had more time, I would suggest you try to stake them, but we don't. You have to get out of there before the sun goes down or you will die along with Peter."

"I can't leave him!"

"You need to get out of there. The sun sets in seven minutes."

I truly had run out of time.

"Camilla, how soon after sunset will they rise?"

She thought about it.

"I don't know, dearest. It depends—one minute, five minutes, maybe ten? All vampires are different. Most take a few minutes, though I know Benedict wakes immediately, Oscar too. And listen, the moment they do wake, we will send them to get Peter. They may well make it in time. Now get to safety. Here's what…"

She said something about safe distances. I wasn't listening. I disconnected the call and stuffed the phone in my pocket. I walked slowly back down the stairs and into the cellar. My brain was whirring but to no effect. I had no weapons and no plan. I shook out my handbag. Nothing helpful fell out. Lipstick and a packet of condoms were going to get me just as far here as they did the last time I'd visited a nightclub… absolutely bloody nowhere.

I took Peter's right hand in mine. It was hot and burning to the touch. He was full of fever and I wondered if the trio of rusty nails had been in place long enough for the likes of tetanus, septicaemia or meningitis to settle in.

"I won't leave you," I whispered. "I'm going to think of something."

"Just sweet," a voice behind me said. "You'd better get a move on then."

I dropped Peter's hand and whirled round. A man stood between me and the stairs. He had been better-looking without the livid bruises across the side of his face from where I had decked him with the spade, but this time I had no trouble recognising Diana's brother Louis Hansen. He was holding something in his right hand, but I couldn't quite make it out.

He grinned at me. I noticed with satisfaction that I appeared to have knocked out a couple of teeth.

"Not so brave without your shovel, are you," he said.

I looked at him with loathing. I had a strong feeling that he was responsible for the nails embedded in Peter's flesh and I intended to make him pay for what he had done. I didn't know how yet, so I decided to play for time.

"Your sister died for you," I said. "Did you know that?"

He paled and took a step towards me.

"Diana's dead? No, you're lying. I heard her speak to Marcello just days ago. You're just saying that."

He shoved me in my chest with his free hand, and I went flying onto my back, smacking my wrists on the stone floor. I was too winded to speak for a few moments, gasping for breath. Then I spat out at him:

"Benedict Akil ripped out her throat and she bled to death on the floor. For you. Because she cared about you."

I caught my breath again. I had wrenched my left wrist somehow and shards of pain were shooting up into my elbow and down into my hand. Louis was looking at me with a lot of hatred. I wanted to tell him the feeling was mutual, but I was struggling to speak.

A third voice interrupted our glaring competition.

"I liked Diana," Peter said.

He sounded very sick and weak. He sounded close to the end. I turned to look at him. His face was sickly pale, shiny with sweat. His breathing was irregular and shallow.

"I don't have any family," Peter said. He sounded contemplative, almost whimsical. "If I had a sister, I would have treated her better. She deserved better. Better than to have you for a brother."

Louis looked grim but determined.

"Enough of this," he said, moving towards me.

I tried to push to my feet but putting weight on my left wrist released shards of agony, and I ended up just scooting backwards on my arse. I bumped into something. I realised with a wave of nausea that it was Amelia's leg. Looking up at Louis, I saw for the first time what he was holding in his hand. It was the nail gun.

He reached out to take my arm with his other hand. I tried again to get to my feet and failed, clambering awkwardly to my knees instead and trying to scurry away from him. But he had caught my arm firmly and dragged me back along the floor towards the chest. I realised he intended to pin me there alongside Peter and began to flail in earnest. He lost his grip for a moment and I made a break for it, but he seized me by my hair and yanked me back down.

I twisted round to try to fend him off, but he was just a lot stronger than me. He dragged me by my hair over to the chest and then transferred his grip to my left wrist, which he wrenched across the chest. He took his eyes off me to flick a switch on the nail gun. It was just long enough for me to pull my knee in to my chest and then drive the heel of my boot into his crotch at as close as I could get to the speed of sound.

With a grunt he dropped like a stone, both hands clutched to his groin. The nail gun bounced across the floor, and the clip of nails fell out. I scrambled after it, hampered by having only one functional arm. I couldn't put any weight on my left wrist, and my left hand didn't seem to work well either. I grabbed the cartridge of nails with my right hand and looked round for the gun. It was partly underneath Louis, who had progressed to rolling around, whimpering, in something close to the foetal position. He was blocking my way to the stairs had I even wanted to go that way, so I tugged the gun out from under him and tried to load the nails back in.

If I'd ever used a nail gun before, things might have gone quicker. If both my hands had worked, that would have helped too. But I fumbled and dropped things for long enough that Louis managed to roll onto his knees. His face was white with pain.

"You are so going to pay for that, you dumb bitch," he said.

By wedging the nail gun in between my knees, I'd managed to get the clip of nails back in and close the little hatch to hold them in place. I picked the gun up and pointed the business end at Louis. There was a lever a bit like a trigger. I pulled it and nothing happened. Cursing I pressed another button and a light came on. As Louis lunged towards me, I pulled the trigger again, not sure what would happen or really where to point the thing.

There was a heavy clunk and Louis gave a shriek of agony. The end of a nail was sticking out of his thigh, and blood was spreading out into the fabric of his trousers. I was hurled onto my back by the recoil of the nail gun and accidentally let off another couple of nails, one of which struck the nearest fluorescent light tube, showering us in hot glass and leaving the cellar in a dim half-light.

Louis was still yelling. He tried to get to his feet, but the nail embedded in his femur was clearly causing him agony and he was staggering awkwardly. He took a step towards me and I let off another nail, which went straight through one of his ears with an explosion of blood and pinged off a wall.

"Jesus wept!" yelled Louis. "You shot off my ear."

The recoil smacked my head into the floor this time, and I dropped the nail gun. With a smug little click, the clip fell out again and rolled over to Louis's feet. He gave me a victorious look and bent to pick it up.

"Right," he said, stuffing it into a pocket. "Let's get this show on the road."

I struggled to my knees and tried to move away from him, but he was faster. He grabbed me by my hair again with one hand, and backhanded me across the face with the other. Stars went off in my head and the room spun around me. I was vaguely aware of Louis reassembling the nail gun and pontificating about all the things that were going to happen to me. They all sounded bad.

And then I felt the sun set.

I hadn't raised the dead for two days. I almost never let that happen because it made me so antsy. But between trying to engineer a shag with Oscar and getting sent around the county by Benedict, two nights had passed. As a result, when the sun fell behind the horizon, I felt the power rise within me. Even stuck down in the cellar, lying in a pile of glass shards with my head spinning, it filled me, hot and potent, and fizzy as champagne.

Louis was still speaking, but I wasn't listening. I looked across at Peter. He was still awake for now, looking at me with a tired gaze. I reached across the cellar floor towards him, and held out my hand.

"Hey there," I said.

He reached out to me with a look of weary confusion. I took his free hand. It was wet with blood and shook in my grasp. I held on to it for a moment and let the blood on his hand ooze into mine. That's the thing about necromancy: blood gives me power. It doesn't have to be my blood.

"Ich wußte, daß du für mich kommen würdest," he said softly.

I had no idea what he was saying.

"I know," I said gently. "It's going to be alright."

I let go of Peter's hand and pressed my own into the cold flagstones of the cellar. The power of the night soared up into me, and I breathed it in. I looked up at Louis, looming above me with a nail gun in his hand. He was still drivelling on about how I was going to die. I felt the rough stone, cold beneath my fingers.

"Amelia Scott Martin, I summon you," I said clearly and quietly. I could feel her spirit burgeoning at my words. "Come to me this night."

She rose neatly to her feet. Her hair was kind of flat on one side, and whatever blood the vampires had left her had pooled in her face to make one side livid and red. The other was as shrivelled and white and leathery as the other vampire victims I'd seen in the last two days.

Louis turned his head briefly to follow my gaze; the effect was gratifying. He gave an audible gasp and stepped away, his face white with shock.

"A fiend from hell," he uttered. "Denizen of Satan."

I looked at Amelia a little sadly. She would never bake cupcakes again, but at least she could get a fair whack at post-mortem vengeance.

"Kill him, Amelia," I commanded. "I order you to kill him."

'Yes, dear," she said rather uninterestedly. "Do you have anything to eat?"

She walked towards Louis. He raised the nail gun in front of his face and pointed it towards her. He clearly knew how to use it a lot better than me—he fired a barrage of nails at Amelia that would have fixed garden decking in place for a decade to come. They thunked into her flesh, a couple protruding from her face and two or three in her chest. She didn't seem to notice. She pushed his arm casually to one side and grabbed him by the throat.

An arc of nails flew across the cellar, thankfully missing Peter and I, but smacking into Amelia, the walls and ceiling—and the second fluorescent tube. We were showered in hot glass again, and plunged into near darkness.

There was a little light still, coming down the stairway from the hallway. It was enough for me to see Amelia's hand tighten on Louis's throat. He was scrabbling weakly at her hand and kicking out with his feet, but to no effect. Her knuckles contracted, and there was a wet crunching sound, as she crushed his throat. His head lolled backwards.

As he died, his hands clenched, and he released a final blast of nails. I winced, but they were none of them heading my way. A couple pinged off the ceiling and smacked into the two luggage cases at the far end of the cellar, reminding me that Louis had always been the least of the problems I had to face here. Louis was dead, but there were two vampires who weren't. My troubles were only beginning.

I looked down at Peter. There was enough light to tell me that he had lost consciousness again. I had to get him out of there before anything else in the cellar awoke. But I could feel myself slowing down. I hadn't slept for thirty-six hours and all I'd eaten that day was a pair of substandard Cornish pasties. I was starting to feel dizzy.

"Amelia," I called abruptly. "Come here and pull out these nails."

There was a nasty ripping slurpy noise. I looked round to find that Amelia, still grasping Louis by his throat, had taken a bite out of his shoulder.

"Amelia, stop that! It's disgusting," I snapped crossly. "Come here and do as I say."

She thrust Louis's body away and dropped it carelessly. It fell onto its face with a crunch. She stepped over to where I knelt next to Peter, looking a little resentful.

"I'm hungry," she said, her voice wistful. "So hungry."

"Just do this," I said firmly. "Do it now."

She reached down to the chest, and closed a thumb and finger around the first of the nails, pushing them into the bruised and swollen surface of Peter's arm to gain purchase. I was relieved he stayed unconscious as she squeezed them together, blood coating her fingertips. Then she slid out the first nail as easily as though it had been impaled in a sponge trifle, not three inches of human flesh and an antique chest. The other two followed. She dropped them carelessly on the stone floor.

Though Peter whimpered, he didn't wake, but blood began to ooze out of the punctures. I didn't think he could afford to lose much more. I tugged off my belt and tightened it around his forearm, just above the first of the wounds. It wasn't the world's best tourniquet, but it would have to do.

As I looked down at my handiwork, I heard a noise. As though things weren't bad enough already, in the luggage cases tucked away in the dark at the far end of the cellar, something was stirring.

"Oh God," I muttered. "Think, Toni, think."

There was the sound of a lid being thrown back, and in the darkness, I thought I could make out a figure sitting up. I looked up at the stairs, and the rectangle of light at the top of them. I didn't think I could get Peter up there on my own. Instinctively, I reached out my hand, still wet with Peter's blood, and pressed it into the stone floor. I let power flood me again. What was his name again? Louis something or other… I had forgotten his surname.

A woman's voice called from the dark.

"What's going on, Louis? I'm hungry."

Great. I was hungry. Amelia was hungry. Everyone was hungry. I was also weary and struggling to focus: what was his surname?

"Louis? Get a move on."

The figure moved in our direction. Then it came to me: Hansen. Louis' name was Hansen. I pressed my palm into the floor. Little chips of broken glass pricked into my skin, and I felt another rush of power as my own blood strengthened the pull.

"Louis Hansen, I summon you," I said. "Come to me, you murdering arsehole."

He moved clunkily to his feet. His head lolled to one side, and he had broken his nose when Amelia dropped him on the floor. A fist-sized lump had been gnawed out of one shoulder. I'd thought him good-looking once. He hadn't aged well.

"Louis, Amelia, I command you," I said. "Kill the vampires."

Chapter Twenty-One

I'D RAISED A right pair of shufflers that evening. They lumbered towards the figure in the darkness rather than springing into action. But I was counting on the element of surprise: zombies were a nightly feature in my life. In other people's? Not so much. Whoever the vampire was who had just arisen, it was unlikely that she knew what she was up against.

"What the hell?" I heard her say. "Didn't I kill you before? What the—"

Her words were cut off in a scream of pain. My eyes were getting accustomed to the dark, and I rather thought that a starvation-crazed Amelia was trying to kill two birds with one stone and eat the vampire's arm off. Louis hadn't struck me as a zombie with a lot of motivation, but given a clear lead he seemed happy to follow, and piled in with Amelia. The vampire went down in a pile of limbs and curses, some of which were entirely new to me.

I was under no illusions that she would stay down for long. Zombies are strong, yes, but vampires are stronger. And zombies tend to be slow and stupid. They are not given to improvisation. They would tear the vampire to pieces if she let them—I didn't think she would.

But I had bought myself a little time.

"Peter," I shook him. "Are you awake? We need to move."

He blinked at me and mumbled something. I took his uninjured hand in mine and squeezed it. It was burning hot to the touch and wet with sweat.

"Peter, we need to get upstairs."

He murmured something else. This time I could make out the word 'ankle'. Damn it. I had forgotten that, even before the vampires had taken him, Peter had broken his ankle. He didn't really look up to staggering to me. I doubted hopping was an option. I felt around on the floor to see if I could locate the nail gun, but I had no idea where it had ended up and the floor was covered in glass. Could I maybe help to tug Peter up the stairs, one at a time? Not with only one hand working myself.

Could I help tilt the odds if I could see what the dickens was going on? I scrabbled around until I found the torch that I had shaken out of my handbag, back before Louis and me between us had shot out the lights. Switching it on, I waved it in the direction of the scuffling.

My undead champions were struggling against a tall woman with long blond hair who was fast turning into a redhead in a most unbecoming and sticky fashion. Scratch that—Amelia had stopped struggling and lay in a twitching heap on the cellar floor. The blonde vampire had ripped her literally limb from limb, and moved on to Louis. She was going about it in a business-like manner, and I couldn't see him lasting much longer.

Even worse, behind her I could see the lid of the second luggage case moving. I looked around desperately. I was out of corpses, out of nails and out of ideas. Then I heard a horribly familiar sound. Louis's head rolled past me, bounced off the side of the chest and came to rest at the foot of the stairs. I looked up to see a furious bloodstained vampire storming towards me. She looked hungry. Behind her a second figure was coming to its feet.

I reached out again and took Peter's hand. There was no response, but it felt better to be holding on to someone. The time to run had gone with the sunlight. I hadn't been able to save Peter. In the end I hadn't been able to save myself.

"I'm sorry," I whispered to him.

Then I heard a soft noise on the stairs behind me and a figure moved to stand between me and the vampires. A figure in immaculate if inappropriate cream chinos and a white polo shirt. A figure with bright gold hair, cut not too short. My heart sang.

"I'm so sorry I'm late," said Oscar.

She flew at him in a fury, but he moved like smoke. He was already behind her, driving into her with enough force to slam her headfirst into the wall beside me. She rolled and whirled to her feet, but I could see just how outclassed she was; Oscar was already on to her again, using the momentum of her spin to help him hurl her straight into the opposite wall. He fought like a cage fighter, using the walls, the floor and even the ceiling as his weapons. My jaw dropped. You think you know someone and then you realise you just don't.

She hadn't been in the best state when Oscar had breezed into the room, and already she was floundering. Oscar hadn't even broken a sweat. I saw the flash of his teeth and realised he was smiling. The only time I'd seen him enjoying himself more was mid-shag, and to be honest, the difference was pretty marginal. All of which would have been more disturbing, except that he was busy saving my skin in the nick of time, and Peter's. You have to cut your boyfriend a bit of slack for that.

I moved to interpose myself between Peter and the fighters, taking him into my arms. As I turned back to watch, I saw the second vampire launch himself at Oscar's back.

"Oscar, look out!" I called, far too late.

But I need not have worried. Oscar must have heard him coming. The woman was rolling back to her feet, not as fast as before, and nowhere near fast enough to get close to Oscar. He landed a kick in her chest that drove her straight back into the wall, and somehow swung round at lightning speed to drive the same foot into the jaw of his second attacker, who was thrust back far enough and fast enough to trip over his own luggage case.

"Wait your turn, if you wouldn't mind," Oscar said amiably.

He swung back to the woman, who had pulled herself to her feet, but only just, and was leaning heavily against the cellar wall. She was far too slow in trying to put up any defence or protect herself, and Oscar moved right in and pinned her to the wall by her throat.

"Goodbye," he said, with great politeness.

Then he punched his right hand straight through the upper ribs of her chest, and tore out her heart.

It was as every bit as revolting as I could have imagined. There was an explosion of blood that left Oscar almost dripping. His right arm really was dripping, with blood pouring down and off his elbow. He tossed aside the heart like a balled-up tissue he'd finished with, and it bowled along the floor to rest next to Louis's head. I gazed at it in revulsion for a moment, but then I was distracted by the sight of the woman's body disintegrating.

After they die their immortal death, the chains that bind a vampire's soul to its body spring apart, and all the years that have passed since their death rush in. She decayed in just moments from a limp blonde corpse to a rotting heap and then to a wizened mummy that collapsed in on itself to form a familiar greasy dust. The butcher-shop trophy of her heart, unfortunately, continued to sit on the flagstones next to me and ooze. I cringed.

At the far end of the cellar, the fight was continuing. I could finally make out Oscar's new opponent, a bulky man with tightly curled light brown hair. He was both faster and fresher than the blonde vampire had been, but even I could tell he didn't stand a chance. The two moved fast, almost too fast for me to follow their blows and strikes, but Oscar was doing a lot more of the hitting and a lot less of the getting hit.

In the light I could see the other man's expression. It was grim and hopeless. He was fighting for his immortal life—and he was losing. Oscar, on the other hand, was fighting for the sheer joy of it. His teeth occasionally glittered in the half light of the cellar and his expression was one of excitement, not fear. Knowing that he was in no real danger, I didn't really want to watch. I leaned my cheek into Peter's shoulder and closed my eyes until some disgusting sound effects, including the noise of a major organ bouncing along the floor, told me this second fight had come to the same unpleasant end as the first.

"Were there just the two?" Oscar said hopefully, in the voice of someone who would like another couple for dessert.

I looked up. He stood next to Peter and me, his hair and clothes liberally splashed with gore. He was rather fastidiously licking blood off his fingers.

"Yup," I said. "Just the two, sweetie."

"Ah well."

He stooped to kiss my cheek, and I recoiled in disgust, but not quickly enough. He had blood on his lips, and I had no idea whose; the choices were wide open. He kissed his way down my neck and put a hand on my waist.

"I can smell your blood through your skin," he whispered. "Like caramel."

I realised with a sense of discomfort that the two fights to the death, with their literally heartrending finishes, had left him horny as a teenager. They'd left me feeling nauseous.

"Oscar don't. That's gross," I snapped. "And listen, Peter's really hurt, really hurt. He's so sick and he has a fever. Can you heal him?"

Oscar's face fell. He crouched down and stroked Peter's face gently. He shook his head

"I can't, no. Not something like this. But Benedict can, Toni, and he is on his way." A note of smugness crept into his voice. "I am faster than him, so I arrived first."

I sighed. Now my life was no longer in imminent danger, my exhaustion was threatening to overcome me, and I was able to give some attention to the agonising pain in my wrist.

"OK, we should wait. I don't dare to move Peter."

I leant my head back against Peter's shoulder. I would have liked to seek comfort in Oscar's arms, but they were covered in blood and bits of vampire innards, so I stayed where I was.

A deep and silky voice drifted nonchalantly down the stairs.

"Dear me, I missed more than the adverts and the trailers. A fine pair of corpses, neither sporting anything from the neck up;

I unerringly detect the touch of Ms Windsor. Dearest girl, you promised to leave the heads on this time. Did you forget?"

I didn't look up. There was nothing in the entire cellar I wanted to look at. I just turned my face slightly away from Peter so that Benedict would hear me.

"You need to heal Peter. I'm worried he's dying. You have to heal him now."

"Dying?"

Was I too tired to hear properly, because that sounded like genuine concern...? I looked up. Benedict was dressed as before in black jeans and a dark-coloured linen shirt, but he completely disregarded them as he knelt in the ichor and broken glass of the cellar floor. He took Peter out of my arms. I made a noise of protest.

"My dear, I do know what I'm doing," he said.

I watched as he gathered Peter into his own embrace. He frowned and closed his eyes. I felt his power rising so strongly I could almost taste it. I could almost stroke it with my fingers. It billowed. I closed my eyes—I could nearly see it... Then it ebbed and faded. I opened my eyes. Peter looked no better, and Benedict's frown had deepened.

"This isn't working," he said softly, in his deep voice.

The scream built in my chest. I let it out.

"Then make it work!" I shouted at him. "You sodding well make it work, you arrogant waste of space. This is your fault. All yours. Every bit of it. You sent Peter into danger without a second thought. You make it work, and you heal him, or I swear to God you won't make it to another sunset. I will come into your stupid bloody sauna and stake you through the heart with the sharpest, pointiest piece of tree in this whole county. I mean it. If Peter dies, I will kill you myself, and nothing and nobody will stop me."

There was one of those deafening silences that makes you wish a car alarm would go off. Oscar looked horrified. Benedict looked like Benedict. He ignored me and turned to Oscar.

"This isn't working," he said again. "He will need my blood to heal."

Oscar looked visibly shocked.

"You don't do that," he said. "You never do that."

"Well, this evening I am making an exception," Benedict said blandly. "If that's agreeable, of course."

The two vampires looked at each other in silence until I interrupted.

"What's wrong? What are you waiting for?"

Benedict ignored me again. He was still looking at Oscar, who was biting his lip with a look of indecision.

I raised my voice: "I said what are you waiting for?"

Benedict didn't look at me, but he did answer.

"Permission," he said.

He continued to look enquiringly at Oscar, who look conflicted but then shrugged.

"Of course," he said. "Of course you have my permission. I only hesitated because I was taken aback. I do realise the singular courtesy you are paying me. I am more grateful than I can say."

"If only that were true," Benedict interrupted. "Now that's out of the way, perhaps you could tell me why you are standing here pontificating instead of trying to track down the rest of this wretched band of incompetents?"

"I will do my best," said Oscar, and vanished up the stairs fast enough to spray me with blood as he passed. Benedict watched him go with a satisfied air.

"Do you really think Oscar can track them down?" I asked, largely to distract myself.

"God, no," he answered. "I shouldn't think so for a minute. I just find him extremely irritating."

He ignored my squawk of protest and tugged open one of his shirt cuffs. A cufflink pinged off and landed at my feet, and I retrieved it on autopilot. I recognised it from the other night: a tiny silver sickle moon, set with soft grey gems that I thought might be moonstones.

Putting one arm around Peter's shoulders, Benedict brought the other up to his mouth. I saw a flash of white tooth, and realised he had neatly punctured one of the veins on his own wrist. I winced, but it it hurt, he didn't show it.

He brought the dripping wrist up to Peter's mouth. I held my breath, but Peter just lolled there. He wasn't reacting; he certainly wasn't drinking. I thought again that he might be dying, and realised I might be about to compound a truly awful evening by crying in front of Benedict.

"Toni, talk to him," said Benedict, quite gently for him, but it was still a command. "See if you can get through."

I stroked Peter's uninjured hand, stifling a sniffle.

"Darling. Peter." What do you say? Pretty please, do drink the disgusting blood from the horrid vampire. What did I know? "Peter, try to drink. Please try. You need to try."

There was no response. Benedict's blood dripped uselessly down Peter's face and slid into his collar. I could barely hear his breathing.

"Can't you compel him to swallow?" I said helplessly.

Benedict sighed.

"He's unconscious and he's half a dozen heartbeats from turning into something you'd summon out of a grave in order to rip its head off," he said crossly. "I'm good, my dear, but as you so kindly pointed out to me the other day, I'm not Jesus. So no, I can't."

I sat in shocked silence digesting the implications of everything he had said. There were a lot of them, and none of them were good. Benedict was pretending he had forgotten my presence. He held his wrist in place a little longer, watching blood run down his wrist and into his shirt. Some of it dripped onto his jeans.

"Arse," he said succinctly. "You hold him."

And he transferred Peter rather hastily into my arms. Before I realised what was happening, he had pulled Peter's uninjured wrist to his mouth and ripped his teeth down it, opening the flesh up almost to the bone. I gave a cry of protest, but before I could do more, he had brought his own wrist up and repeated the gesture. This time I was sprayed with warm vampire blood, and had to blink it out of my eyes. Benedict had pressed the open wounds together, clamping his wrist to Peter's with his other hand.

"Is it working?" I asked.

Benedict rolled his eyes.

"I only just got rid of Oscar because he wouldn't shut up," he said in put-upon tones. "Should I have sent you with him?"

I shut up, partly because he had a point, but also because Peter did seem to be improving. His breathing was less shallow and bubbly, and he seemed a little less limp and comatose in my arms. We sat in silence, broken by the occasional sound of blood dripping onto the floor. There were people moving around upstairs, talking in low voices. I thought I heard Grace, but I wasn't sure. At one point a man's voice called down the stairs:

"Are you ready for us to start clearing up, sir?"

"No," said Benedict, clearly. "Wait."

After that, we weren't disturbed again. We sat in the dark together and I tried not to think about what we were sitting in. The remains of two dismembered corpses I had raised willy-nilly from the dead to save me, and the dust and blood of two vampires who had killed Amelia and damn near killed Peter and me too. When Peter began to mutter and struggle in my arms, Benedict took him back off me.

"I think he might swallow a little without choking now," he said conversationally. "Tell him to try."

Before I realised what he had in mind I saw the flash of his teeth again, and realised he had opened a broad slash in his own upper lip. He leaned forward and pressed his mouth to Peter's, forcing the blood inside. Peter flinched and tried to pull away.

"Drink, sweetheart," I said stroking Peter's cheek. "You're healing. Try just to swallow."

He seemed to relax and stop fighting and after another minute Benedict pulled away, letting Peter lean against the wall of the cellar. Astonishingly, the wounds he had opened up on his wrist, and on Peter's, had already healed. Peter's breathing was quiet and even. I looked closer, and saw that the nail punctures had vanished as completely as though they had never been there. Benedict looked across at me with blood on his lips.

"Am I forgiven?" he asked very sweetly. "Because this is the closest you will get to tears and excuses from me."

"No," I said, too exhausted and upset still to think about what he was saying.

"So hard-hearted," he said. "Come here and I will heal your wrist."

I lurched away from him in revulsion.

"Don't come near me! I am not drinking your blood," I yelped. "And it's fine."

He looked amused. He leaned very deliberately over to me, and took my wrist gently in his hands. I realised just how exhausted I was. I just couldn't be bothered to argue with him anymore. I thought I might curl up with my head on the blood-splattered chest and go to sleep if he would let me, or just lie there in the gore and the glass shards. I let him have my hand.

"It's broken," he said. "And you have a splendid black eye forming. But unlike Peter you are not suffering from imminent death. You won't need my blood."

I felt his power rise again, and this time it flooded into me. I looked up helplessly at him as it swept me away in a broad golden tide.

"I'm so tired," I heard my voice say as the deep waves of sleep enveloped me. It was the last thing I heard for a long time.

Chapter Twenty-Two

I WOKE IN my own bed. Alone. Nothing hurt, the room was a complete tip, and I had clearly overslept by hours. It felt like a perfectly normal weekday morning in my life. The past week might never have happened.

I opened the window and looked out. No corpses on my lawn. No EDL members lurking under the trees. The August sun shone down on the small village of Colton. My neighbours' net curtains were white and twitchy. A cat wandered across the road with something feathered and unlucky in its mouth. All felt right with the world.

I lay in the bath for an hour and deep conditioned my hair. Then I covered my body with the entire contents of an expensive-looking jar that Claire had given me the previous Christmas. I coaxed a comb through my hair—all the way—and I painted both my toe and fingernails with peach-coloured varnish. I lay on the bed staring at the ceiling while it dried.

I found clean jeans and a halterneck top. Neither was covered in blood. I dug out a pair of sandals that almost went with them and went to tell the coffee machine it had a tough task ahead of it. After two cups, I felt well enough to text Bernie and tell him I would be out for the rest of the week. After three, I frisked the kitchen for breakfast. Microwave noodles were invented for something; I'd finally worked out what.

There was an envelope on my kitchen table, bearing my name

in handwriting I didn't recognise. I was putting off opening it. It came from a part of my life that I was taking a morning off from. It could wait.

In the end I made it wait until I had drained the coffee pot. I opened it somewhat warily, but it contained my car keys and a single sheet filled with round schoolgirlish writing; the author still wrote her full stops as little circles, and her dots as little hearts.

Dearest Toni,

You were so brave last night! Oscar is really proud of you. I wanted to tell you that Peter is going to be fine, though he will probably sleep for a couple of days. I put you to bed (in case you wondered!) and your cottage is really sweet.

I also wanted to say: please, please, please get here before sunset to be safe.

Hugs,

Camilla.

I read it with mixed feelings. Firstly, Oscar hadn't really noticed me very much the previous evening, so I had a suspicion Camilla was just being nice about that. Secondly, I was pleased to know that Peter would be fine, but I'd not really doubted Benedict on that front. He didn't strike me as someone who made false claims. And thirdly, I really didn't want to spend the night at The Stone House. Camilla's pleas made sense—I just didn't like them.

I killed my bad mood by driving down to Lichfield and squandering some of Benedict's money in a boutique that was usually well out of my price range. I bumped into Will's gorgeous boyfriend, Henry Lake, while I was browsing for lingerie and we took time to share a glass of Pimm's in the wine bar next door. All of the women looked jealously at me—and so did half the men.

We chatted about his film—his big complaint was that the swords they were using were not from the same century as the storyline—and about my brother.

"Is he still hung up over Jane Doe?" I asked.

"He's alright, you know, petal," Henry said reassuringly. "He's just not used to failure. I've been an actor for ten years—it's mother's milk to me."

I was hung up on it too. I liked my corpses well interred and vintage. Jane was on my conscience: if I didn't bring her killer to justice she was going to stay there, forever nameless and unavenged. I had just the one thing going for me; to wit, raising the dead, and it was letting me down. It was letting Jane down. Neither Wills nor I would be happy until someone went to gaol for her murder.

We finished our drinks and parted ways. I drove home and put on one of my new purchases—a little black dress that was cut down almost to thong level at the back and which I hoped would give even Grace a run for her money. Then, with little enthusiasm, I drove to The Stone House and let myself in. It struck me that I had no idea where I was going, but I found Camilla in the hallway, arranging flowers.

"Is Peter awake yet?" I asked.

"No—but I think probably tomorrow."

She showed me into the cavern, which was no less lovely than before. Someone had lit all the braziers, and the soft scent of spice and wood smoke filled the air again. I found a pile of cushions behind a pillar, much as Peter and I had done before, and made myself comfortable. If I was lucky, no one would notice me.

I lay back and tried not to fret. I tried to think about the fact that Peter was better, that my dress was smoking hot, and that my nail varnish was perfect. But other thoughts kept creeping in. Like: if Peter was still unconscious, who was my boyfriend snacking on for breakfast? Or worse: if Peter was still out cold, was Oscar going to turn up in a minute looking all peckish and eying up my neck? The thought made me feel physically sick, so I pushed it to the back of my mind.

Benedict had accused me of desperately ignoring reality, but it seemed the best way to cope. Peter had told me that I would need to redefine what was normal in a relationship, but I didn't think I could. Vampires were not mortals, and they were different. Their way of living was different. And it wasn't going to be a case of pretending to like blue cheese when the truth is that it's horrid. Or faking that you were OK with lime in a gin and tonic instead of lemon when who the hell would be OK with that...? I didn't want to share my boyfriend. I certainly didn't want to share my blood. Bugger it, maybe I just wasn't a sharer. Maybe I was too bloody selfish to date a vampire. I went back to admiring my nails.

Figures began coming into the room. I closed my eyes, trying to see if I could tell mortal from vampire. It was a slight improvement on my previous attempt. I recognised Oscar from metres away, and eventually placed Grace too. After a while, some of the others began to feel more identifiable. They would be easier with names, I realised. Everything would be easier with a name.

I opened my eyes. Yes, there was Oscar, my delicious Oscar, looking, well, good enough to eat. And to my immense relief, he had a sated, well-fed look to him. I decided not to worry about how it had got there, and scrambled to my feet.

"Hey, you," I said, a little shyly, because last time we had met I had been sitting in a cellar full of glass-covered gore trying to avoid his kisses.

"Hello, my beautiful Toni," he said, in that rather formal way I liked so much. "I hope you are wearing that dress so that I can take it off you."

I blushed. I was, of course.

"Well, yes," I said. "But please don't tear it, because it was the only one in my size that they had, and you might like to take it off me more than once."

He leaned down to kiss me.

"When may I start?" he murmured. "Soon, I hope."

"Right now," I whispered back. "Please."

He slid his hands around my waist and pulled me in to him. Then he crept them to the hem of my dress and began to slide it up.

"Right here and right now?"

I squeaked and tugged it down.

"Stop that," I protested, realising he'd taken me somewhat too literally.

He laughed and slid his hands up and around to the neckline.

"Maybe here? Do I get in this way?"

I slapped his hands away.

"You don't, crazy man; don't you dare."

I tried to evade his grip, but I was laughing too hard to escape properly, and he moved his hands to the zip at the back.

"Ah. I have it now," he said with relish.

I managed to spin out of his grip but tripped inelegantly over the cushions I had been lying on and sprawled there on my back, laughing up at him. He flung himself down beside me.

"This is unexpectedly nice," I said. "I hadn't thought to enjoy this evening."

"No?" He sounded surprised. "I've always liked it here. I'd prefer to stay, but Peter hates the place."

I could see Peter's point. What usually made a home worth visiting was the hosts, but if you wanted to meet any agreeable people at the Assemblage you would have to bring them yourself.

"Were you here for long?" I asked, draping myself around him as much as I could.

He reciprocated, leaning back onto the cushions and hugging me to him. I let my head rest on his chest.

"Yes, most of my vampire years. I like working for Benedict— you know where you are with him."

I decided it was time to make another attempt at the question he had rebuffed before.

"Have you been a vampire for long?"

He began to slide his fingers up my thigh and under the fabric of my skirt. I moved his hand carefully to my waist.

"Not so very long compared to some," he said. "A little under three hundred years."

Three hundred years? I sat in stunned silence. Whatever I had expected it wasn't that. And he didn't think that was old for a vampire. Oscar didn't seem to have noticed my reaction. In his defence, his focus was on exactly the things I'd had in mind when I bought my dress. About the fifth time he began exploring under the hem I decided we should get a room.

"Maybe we should, um, be somewhere alone?" I suggested, trying to disentangle my legs from his hands and his exploring tongue from my ear.

"No one will mind," he said, his voice obscured by my hair. "They'd probably like the floorshow."

I poked him in a bicep, and he laughed good-naturedly, letting me go so that I could straighten some clothing. Quite a lot of it as it happened.

"As long as I am with you," he said. "Let me make sure we are not needed here."

There was no rancour in his voice, but I had to wonder if he'd really been joking... Still, he dragged me to my feet, and rather against my will tugged me over to where Benedict was sprawled in a chair. The man must have come in whilst I was canoodling with Oscar, but he already seemed to be squabbling half-heartedly with Grace over something. She was leaning over his chair, gesturing with her hands.

"Does it send the right message?" she was saying as we drew close. "I don't think it does."

"Christ, who cares," he replied shortly in his deep drawl. "I'm sick of the whole sorry mess. Let's be done with it at last. If I have to compel the bloody coroner's clerk once more, he's going to think I'm courting his daughter. And have you seen her?"

"Akil: please be serious for a minute. Would you consider whether this is the best path?"

He clasped his hands behind his head and looked up at her.

"I have actually thought about this, you know. I didn't live this long by making rash decisions." He caught sight of Oscar and me. "Ah, and talking of rash decisions, Oscar, this rather concerns you," he said, ignoring me as usual.

Oscar had become distracted by the view of my cleavage that standing up had afforded him.

"Of course," he said vaguely. "How can I help?"

"This evening I was contacted by the three remaining members of our visiting American cousins," Benedict said blandly. "They have petitioned me for clemency."

Oscar was silent for a moment.

"You've said no, of course," he said carefully.

Benedict didn't answer immediately. He looked up at Grace, who shrugged.

"You know what I think," she said. "I've said my piece."

"Indeed," said Benedict. "Several times." He put his fingertips together. "However, I am inclined to grant their request."

I couldn't hold myself back:

"What! These people killed Amelia. They killed Hugh. They damn near killed Oscar and Peter, not to mention me. They slaughtered that girl in the pumping station and Hugh's cowman and his housekeeper. How can you even think of letting them off?"

Benedict didn't look at me.

"Oscar, you can restrain your pet, or I will," he said gently.

Oscar pulled me to him.

"Hush, my darling," he said in soothing tones that had exactly the opposite effect.

He threw himself into the chair next to Benedict and tugged me down so that I was sitting at his feet. I sat, seething, as they talked over my head.

"Thank you," said Benedict nicely, as though someone had handed him a vol au vent. "As I was saying: I am inclined to give them the mercy they have asked for."

"Benedict, this isn't like you," Oscar said, shaking his head. "You've given them no quarter all this time. Why now? I can't believe you'd be happy with this as a solution."

Benedict pushed some ringlets out of the way with a careless hand.

"I didn't say I was happy about it," he said. "I'm not at all happy about it. I am just running short of alternatives."

Oscar got back his feet and began to pace.

"We should hunt them down," he said. "Hunt them down and kill them."

"With the greatest of respect, Wolsey—and yes that was sarcasm, just in case you've been in Germany too long—that's what you are here for. For some weeks now, I might point out. It's also what you've singularly failed to do."

Oscar stopped pacing and sat down again. He tangled his hands in my hair.

"I've not exactly been inactive, Benedict," he said stiffly.

"Granted, but—to use your own words—you've not exactly been productive either. I have put the full might of my resources at your disposal, and you have not exactly delivered."

Oscar worked his hands restlessly in my curls, wrapping and unwrapping them around his fingers.

"I need more time," he said. "Give me a little longer."

Benedict shook his head.

"I have run out of time."

I could see another proper row brewing. Camilla distracted me by wandering up with two saucers of champagne and plumping herself down next to me. She put the glasses on a small side table. They were full of a glittering apricot coloured liquid.

"Welcome to the harmonious peace of vampire central," I whispered. "God this stuff is nice."

"I wish they wouldn't fight all the time," she said. "Grace says they always have."

I thought about that.

"Oscar said he'd always liked this place; was he here before he took Peter to Germany?"

"Yes, I think so. Grace calls him The General. I think he always looked after anything to do with conflict for Benedict. Like a chief of police or military leader."

That fitted with the Oscar I knew. Or rather, the Oscar I was starting to get to know. I drank my champagne rather too quickly. I thought Camilla was wrong on one front: I was never going to get sick of the stuff.

Oscar had got to his feet again and was back to pacing.

"Why now?" he demanded. "Why throw in the towel tonight?"

Benedict continued to lounge in his chair.

"It may have escaped your notice, my dear man, but as of last night, I have another four bodies to dispose of," he said in very reasonable tones. "Another four snuffed-out lives I have to create some kind of back story to... More of us running round like headless chickens to ensure that no one asks the wrong questions or, as it happens, the right ones. I have had weeks of this, and the lies I am pasting over these events are wearing tissue thin. Modern forensics is not exactly on our side; I do not think we could stay out of the spotlight if one of the local constabulary started bandying words like "serial killer" around the station. Correct me if I am wrong, but please think about it first, because I very rarely am."

Oscar was still striding up and down, but I could tell he was buckling.

"I don't think you are making the right decision," he said. "I can't agree."

Benedict's hands were still clasped behind his head.

"Well in case no one noticed, I didn't send out a round robin announcing a show of hands," he said. "I've been civil enough to tell you of my decision in advance, but so that we are clear, it's my decision. This isn't a democracy—it's a dictatorship. There is no senate, no upper house, no lower house, and no anarcho-syndicalist bloody commune. There's just me. I think we are done here."

"How can you even think of letting them off?" I interrupted. "How can you let them go scot free?"

He deigned to notice me.

"My dear Miss Windsor, my resources are good, but they are not infinite. If I turn down this request, tomorrow night there will be another victim. Another Amelia, or if you prefer, another Peter. Which would you prefer, just out of interest?"

I turned my face away.

"Shut up."

"No, you started this."

I felt him come over as much as I heard it. He leaned down and hauled me to my feet by my upper arms. Oscar and Camilla seemed paralysed with indecision. Grace just looked mildly amused. I tried to turn my face away from Benedict again, but he did that super-irritating sexist thing of grabbing my ponytail and twisting me round to look at him.

"They will not get off 'scot free' as you termed it. Their punishments will be severe. Far more so than anything your English justice system would dish out for a similar offense, I assure you."

"I don't care," I shouted at him. "They nailed Peter to a chest and left him there in the dark. They killed Amelia. She was making cupcakes. She was probably making them for me!"

To my horror, tears started sliding down my cheeks, and he finally let me go so that I could hide my face in my hands.

"Believe you me, Miss Windsor," he said, very slightly more kindly, but not much, "I don't like the thought that someone can come into my domain and kill my friends any more than you would."

"You don't have any friends," I snapped.

"Christ almighty, Wolsey, you must have the patience of a saint," he retorted. "How you've managed a whole week without ripping her throat out is a complete mystery to me. I wanted to the first night I met her. She must be a bloody amazing lay."

I was so furious that without thinking, I snatched up my champagne glass from the little side table and hurled it at his face. He plucked it out of the air without seeming to try, catching the stem delicately between finger and thumb. He looked down at me in silence for far too long.

"Why is she even here, Wolsey?" he finally said in languid tones. Then he frowned. "Good God, why are *you* even here, man? If I'd found this waiting for me when I woke up, I'd never have made it out of the bedroom. I don't think I've ever seen breakfast so agreeably presented."

His voice had turned friendly, admiring, full of camaraderie...I looked at him in fury. I could see what game he was playing. He manipulated everyone... But Oscar didn't see it. He just preened visibly.

"My Toni is exquisite in all ways," he said. "We were hoping to head off, actually..."

Benedict smiled broadly. Was I the only person who remembered that he never smiled?

"You do that, dear man. You do that," he purred.

"You're just distracting him," I hissed.

"I know," he replied quietly. "And look how well it's working."

Oscar took my hand and pulled me into his arms.

"Come with me, my angel," he said, kissing my forehead gently. "You're upset. I'll take care of you."

He led me from the hall. I was too upset to protest. I cast a look of loathing back at Benedict, but he was making it very clear that he had forgotten my very existence. He had returned to his chair and was laughing at something Grace had said. He didn't watch us leave.

I dried my eyes and pulled myself together. I had no intention of letting Benedict ruin the rest of my evening. He had ruined quite enough of it already. Camilla had taken me to Oscar's rooms the first time. This time around, I made an effort to register the way.

They were as I remembered them, opulent but somehow cosy. The fire had been lit, and the lights were low.

"Where's Peter?" I asked as Oscar locked the door.

"In the bedroom," he said. "I think he may wake tomorrow."

I wandered through. Peter lay in the bed, pillows arranged around his head. His skin was still pale, but when I put my palm on his forehead, there was no trace of fever. His breathing was even. I moved the eiderdown to look at his wrist. It was free of scars. He had big hands, with long elegant fingers, good hands for playing the piano or the guitar. I held one to my cheek for a moment before pressing a kiss into the palm.

Seeing him lying so quietly filled me with resolution. And courage. And a thirst for vengeance. I didn't care what punishments Benedict had planned for the rest of the vampires who had hurt Peter so badly and killed my Amelia. I had my own plans. I would turn them into dust and ashes and nothing and no one would stop me. I lay down on the sofa and dreamed of sweet revenge.

Chapter Twenty-Three

I DIDN'T WAKE up until the alarm on my phone rang out shortly after six. I'd set it for approximately dawn and my necromancy told me that if I could only manage to find my way out this time, I would find the sun just peeping over the horizon.

I found myself curled up by the dying embers of the fire. Oscar had very nicely draped a blanket over me and peering around the room, I could see items of my clothing flung about. After a cursory hunt, I found my thong and sandals. Cursing myself for not having brought a change of clothes, I dressed once again in my tiny little black dress and stuffed my curls back into a plait.

I checked on Peter, but found him still out cold. His colour was good though, and I thought that Camilla and Oscar were probably right in expecting him to wake later.

Oscar, I now knew, spent his days in a locked chamber off the bedroom. Vampires, he'd told me as we rested in between making love, preferred to sleep in small, secure spaces, ideally far underground. I ran my fingers over the concealed panels of the entrance. It would have been impossible to distinguish them from the rest of the woodwork had Oscar not showed me where it was. Odd to think that as I wandered round his chambers, he lay just metres away, sleeping the sleep of the dead.

I collected my handbag and car keys. I had a lot of ducks to line up in some crazy rows and just fourteen hours to do it in. Because when the sun set that night, I planned to kill three vampires. I planned to kill them before they handed themselves meekly in so that stupid bloody Benedict could agree some stupid bloody pact with them.

I drove home as fast as the rust-mobile felt like travelling that morning. The sun was getting ready for a belter of an August day and my mind was clicking through the tasks ahead of me. I had a rough plan formed by the time I parked on the kerb and bounded up to my porch. It was on the lines of: first, find out how the hell you kill vampires; next, find the vampires; and then—finally—kill them. It needed fleshing out, but logically it was flawless. I was going to have to call in a lot of favours.

I needed to know how you killed vampires, because I couldn't banish a whole coterie all by myself. Anecdotal evidence suggested tearing out the heart worked. Benedict had mentioned stakes. The Internet had many, many other suggestions, but then the Internet also told me I could enlarge my penis with mail-order fennel pills and cure cancer by eating raw asparagus. The fact was, I had some vampires to slay and I didn't know enough about how to do it. But if I could track them down, I knew someone who really did.

First things first then: I called my brother Wills from the kitchen as I made my first coffee of the day. He sounded sleepy. Correction: he sounded asleep.

"Six thirty, sis. Better have a good excuse. Super good one."

"I need a favour."

"I guessed that."

He gave a great yawn. I took a deep breath.

"I need to see Kit Maybury."

There was a pregnant pause.

"Sis, fill in the form and come at eleven next Monday. You know the drill for visitors' hours."

"That's why it's a favour, Wills. I need to see him this morning. No later than nine."

"Are you crazy?"

"No. I'm desperate."

He didn't say anything for a while.

"Toni, I can't do it."

"Yes, you can."

"I don't like abusing my position. It's my job to uphold the law, not bend it."

"That's why it's a favour."

"I don't go round taking advantage of my uniform when it suits me."

"Yes, you do, bro. Letting your sister pad round the morgue playing Raise the Zombie with murdered corpses at two in the morning is not in your employment guidelines and you know it."

"That's in a very good cause."

"So is this."

There was another pause.

"Can you tell me what?"

"Nope."

"Toni, for crying out loud, this isn't like you! And he's bad news—you don't want him back in your life."

"I don't, Wills. You're right. But I still need you to do this."

There was another longer silence. There was a sigh, but it was one of resignation.

"Toni, you win. But never pull this again, alright?"

"I won't."

"Be at the main doors at nine. I'll have Agnes meet you there."

Kit and I had dated rather over a year before. My brother had teased me at Jane Doe's funeral about him selling drugs and jacking cars, but the truth was that Kit's main crime was boredom. He came from a good family, but ten years at boarding school had instilled him with nothing much more than a desire to cock a snook at authority wherever he could and damn the consequences. He stole cars but generally crashed them before finding a buyer and considered credit card fraud on a par with borrowing my bus pass. He was trouble, true, but he was also trouble in a charming package. He'd been fond of me, and dating him hadn't been as bad as my brother made out. I'd dumped him shortly before he was finally arrested.

He'd gone down for four years, which meant he would probably be up for parole in a few months. I'd visited him just once. He'd tried to persuade me to smuggle drugs through in my bra. I'd not gone back.

I showered and put on a tiny little denim mini skirt, long black boots and a low-cut black top. I blow-dried my hair into big shiny curls and put on mascara. I knew how to tilt the odds in my favour and Kit had never needed his women to be classy.

When Wills had said Agnes would meet me, my mind had done a blank. But I recognised the smartly uniformed officer who was waiting for me at the prison gates as my brother's new partner, the lady who had stood with him at Jane Doe's funeral. We shook hands rather awkwardly. Her cool grey eyes looked troubled, but if she had doubts, she didn't share them.

"I don't know what this is about," she said, "but Wills said it was important."

"It is," I assured her. "It really is."

You can't mistake the prison in Stafford for anything other than what it is. There's a seriously high wall curving round the whole building and remarkably few windows. There's heavyweight security that usually takes an hour to get through, though with Agnes at my elbow, we sidestepped most of the checks. The visiting room is like an aircraft hangar, a huge depressing room full of hugely depressed people. It smells of cheap food, smuggled cigarettes and broken dreams. This time around, we walked straight through it and into the main prison.

"We're not going to the visitor's area?" I asked.

Agnes shook her head.

"It's not open yet," she said. "I borrowed an interrogation room for us."

She led me through a maze of identical corridors to a small room. There was a desk with two nasty plastic bucket chairs. Kit was sitting in one. Now that I saw him after such a long time, I realised he reminded me a little of Oscar with his straight blond hair and blue eyes. But prison hadn't been kind to him—he'd lost weight.

And his perennial tan. And just a little of his sparkle.

He bounded to his feet and tried to hug me. Agnes interposed herself between us.

"Woah, Maybury, no touching," she said. "Sit down. No hands."

He sat down meekly.

"Toni, you have ten minutes. I'll be watching through the glass."

She shut the door behind her, and I sat down awkwardly opposite Kit. I'd rarely had the upper hand in our relationship. Today I needed to change that dynamic.

Kit gave me his melt-for-me grin. It was as good as ever.

"Toni girl," he said. "Makes my day to see you."

I sat down and leaned forward, tilting a little more than the odds in his direction.

"Kit, it's been such a long time."

"Looking good, Toni. I wish you'd come at opening hours. Do my reputation a lot of good to have the guys see you visiting me."

"Next time, Kit."

"Nice one."

There was a pause. I decided to break it.

"Kit, sweetie, here's the thing. I need a favour. I need it now, and if you can help me, I will owe you."

"Girl, unless you want some free-range cockroaches, I don't have a lot of favour to give here, and I don't think you want to smuggle those out in your bra."

"No, Kit, listen. I will tell you what I want."

And I told him. I told him twice to be sure. When I had finished, he shook his head.

"Maybe, and I mean maybe, but I don't know. What's your timescale? When are we talking?"

I took a deep breath.

"Noon today," I said firmly, "at the latest."

"No can do, crazy ginger lady. Can't be done."

I stood up and straightened my tiny skirt. I leaned forward over the desk so that Kit could lech down my cleavage about as far as my navel.

"I am so sorry to have bothered you sweetie," I said. "I hoped... well, never mind. Good luck with your parole."

"Wait!"

I waited. He ran a hand through his hair.

"Alright, I can do it. I'll do it. Where."

"At the café opposite St Mary's."

"OK, ginger. It's a deal. Now what's in it for me?"

I breathed out in relief.

"What do you want?"

"I want a character witness at my parole hearing."

"Done."

"And somewhere to stay when I get out."

"You are not staying in my house and pawning my stuff again."

He looked mulish.

"It's what I want."

I thought about it. I still had a wad of twenty-pound notes burning a hole in the bottom of one of my handbags. The Benedict Akil benevolent fund had so far paid for some of Amelia's funeral and a whole load of nice lingerie. I decided it could stretch to other, less deserving causes.

"You can't stay with me, but I will pay three month's rent for you," I said. "Fair?"

"More than, Toni, more than."

I stood up and looked down at my ex.

"Thanks, Kit. I appreciate this."

"Do you have to go?"

The words came out in a bit of a rush. I looked at Kit, thinner, paler and quieter than I had ever known him.

"I do, Kit. I'm sorry. They only gave me ten minutes."

"Stay until they come back then. I don't get a lot of visitors."

I sat back down again. Kit broke the rather strained silence.

"Do you still have my weights?"

"Gosh, I do actually. They are still in my bedroom."

"Next to your dead chandelier?"

"That's the one. Do you still have my CDs?"

"Sorry, ginger."

There was another silence. Agnes broke it by opening the door and coming back into the room.

"Time's up," she said.

"I know," I said. "Do I get to give Kit a hug?"

"I guess."

I hugged Kit carefully. He was bonier than I remembered.

"Good to see you, Toni girl," he said.

"You too, Kit. Good luck with your parole; I do mean it."

I left him sitting rather forlornly in the bucket chair and wended my way through the corridors with Agnes back to the entrance. I wanted to make more of an effort to get to know her, but my mind was on other things. We made the usual pointless comments about prison not achieving a lot and what might be a better way to help. We didn't come up with a way to change the world in the time it took us to get to my car.

"Well goodbye," I said, shaking her hand. "Sorry if I broke up your morning."

"It's fine," she said brusquely. "I had to be here anyway. There's a fence who's finally agreed to give us some names now he's tasted prison food. I'll see you."

I watched her walk back to the prison. She had a solid, confident, shoulders-back walk. The police service was lucky to have her. I thought Wills was lucky too and I hoped he knew it.

I drove to the café via the nearest supermarket where I took the time to work out the cheapest own-brand beer on the shelves. I bought six cases to be sure. In the gardening section, they had a watering can on special, so I bought that too.

I got to the café before noon, but even so my date was there before me, sitting at a table by the window and clutching a mug. I looked at him as I ordered tea and toast. His shaved head was starting to grow an uneven fuzz. He gave me a wary look as I sat down. He was wearing a hoody stencilled with the slogan: "God Hates Vamps". I thought he'd been wearing it the night he tried to kidnap me behind my house. I was meeting balaclava jerk for elevenses.

My brother had told me he'd put two EDL thugs away. If they were in prison, my charming ex would know them. Kit always knew everyone. And knowing Kit, they would probably owe him a favour for something. Kit collected favours like marbles. I'd seen him for ten minutes in two years and I owed him one already.

It had been a long shot, but I hadn't known who else to turn to. As I said, the Internet had suggested about eighty-seven different ways to kill a vampire. Crosses, ankhs, pentacles, garlic, pentacles dipped in garlic... you name it, someone thought it could kill Dracula. Various sites assured me the undead could be hastened back to their graves with red rowan berries, white hawthorn berries, black hawthorn boughs or the bones of golden eagles. Running water, holy water, water with silver nitrate solution in it—all bad if you believed everything you read. I hadn't a clue.

So, how did you go about killing the undead? Oscar could have told me, but I didn't dare ask. Peter might have told me, but he was out for the count. That didn't leave me with a lot of options. But the militant arm of UKAP? The people who wanted to wipe nightwalkers from the face of the earth and were cool with kidnapping and arson as part of the peace process? I somehow thought they would know. I hadn't been certain Kit could pull this off for me, but he had come through, and I was in his debt. The shaven-headed thug in front of me was my best hope.

"Hello," I said carefully as I pulled out a chair and sat opposite him. "I appreciate your coming to see me."

He looked nervous and I couldn't blame him. The last time I'd seen him, he'd been driving away at top speed after watching Bredon tear his mate's head off.

"S'OK," he said. "I guess. Some people I don't need to piss off told me to meet you."

I ate some of my toast.

"So," I said after I had failed to think of a gentle intro to the topic, "how do I kill a vampire?"

"Huh? I thought you were like friends with them."

"Things change. Tonight, I have to kill three vampires, and I need to know what's actually going to work."

"You and whose army?"

"Me and my army, actually."

"You better be good."

"We're alright."

He nodded and began to tick off his fingers.

"OK, they're not as tough as they like to think, and I know every way to take them down." His voice had come to life. "Here's the first thing: sheer physical damage will do it eventually, but you are talking getting squashed under a car crusher. Or, like, getting blasted into smithereens. Nothing much short of that works. I've heard of vamps having their legs and arms ripped off and three months later they're good as new."

"I saw one get crushed between a car and a wall. He was fine an hour later."

"That's it." He had become quite animated: he was clearly proud of showing off his encyclopaedic knowledge of vampire-slaying lore. We'd moved onto his specialist subject, and he knew it. He wouldn't be spending a lifeline or asking for a crystal ball. "The next thing is stakes. Stake through the heart, you know."

"Exactly how?"

"It's not easy. Got to be a fairly fresh, hardwood stake—elm, ash, oak, hornbeam. None of your pines or conifers and nothing too old. And you have to get right through the left side. So, like I said, it's not easy. Something you'd only get away with in the day."

"Fresh hardwood stake. Left ventricle. Got it."

"Then there's fire. Vamp blood is pretty flammable, so if you can get them going well, they'll burn all the way. Litre of petrol and a match. Woof. Bye bye undead guy."

"That's gross."

"They're just vampires, not people."

"What about crosses?"

"Don't work."

"Garlic."

"Nada."

"Holy water."

"Nope."

"Running water?"

"Urban myth—it's tidal water."

"Silver?"

"Silver weapons are good. They cut through vamp flesh well, and the wounds don't heal so quickly. And if you chain them with silver, they can't break free. Rhodium-plated silver is even better, if you can get it." He parted his hoody at the neck to reveal a grubby silver chain. "Art deco," he said proudly. "I wear it all the time."

"Sunlight."

"It's a sure thing. Takes a while—maybe twenty minutes—but they go up like Guy Fawkes. And they don't wake."

"Anything else?"

"Removing the heart entirely. I've never seen it done, but it's like one hundred per cent guaranteed."

"I've seen it done," I admitted. "It works a treat. Is that it?"

He ticked off a final digit.

"Beheading."

"What?"

"Beheading. Slice off the head. I've seen that done. Burst of blood and then dust time. Like, awesome."

I thought about that.

"Decapitation?" I asked carefully. "As in with a sword?"

"I saw it with an axe, but yeah, pretty much. You cut off a limb or so, and they shrug it off—but take off the head and it's hasta la vista time for toothy."

I drained my tea and stood up.

"Please don't take this the wrong way," I said politely, "because I'm grateful for your help. But I hope we won't meet again."

"Me neither," he said, sticking out a paw. "I'm never coming back to this county again. And good luck tonight."

We shook hands and I left him there. I would have liked some more toast, but my day didn't have a lot of wiggle room in it.

I drove next to the hills above Cannock. Henry Lake's Dad ran a small builders' merchant out of what had once been a stockyard. Mostly he sold sacks of hardcore tack, sand and gravel. I usually came up at the start of the winter for a couple of bags of rock salt to sprinkle on my front steps. Today, though, Henry himself was running the yard, lugging sacks around in the afternoon sun. I watched for a bit from the car—it was a hot day and he had taken his shirt off—before getting out and announcing my presence.

"Hey, petal," he said, coming over. "You want a big sweaty hug?"

"Yup."

Hugs duly exchanged, we sat on a low wall next to the car. Henry explained that filming had temporarily ground to a halt; the director had stormed off set after a row with the producer, setting the rest of the film crew adrift for a few days and giving Henry the chance for some family time.

"So, pet, what are you doing up here?" he asked. "Spot of DIY underway?"

"I'd like six bags of rock salt, actually," I said as casually as possible.

"Six sacks."

"Uh huh."

"In August."

"Um, yes please."

"Your call, but that's a lot of margaritas. I hope you've ordered enough ice."

I laughed.

"I like the idea. A swimming pool full of margarita."

Henry loaded up my boot with the bags of salt, and I counted out some notes into his palm. I was about to leave when another thought struck me.

"Henry, can I borrow a sword?"

He frowned.

"Yeah, sure. Any particular sword?"

"Um, I need the kind of sword that an English squire would have used in about 1700."

"That's very specific."

"That's what I need. Can you help?"

"I can, actually. It was made for a re-enactment fair, though, so it's more functional than pretty. And I doubt you would be able to lift it."

"Henry, I couldn't even lift the salt. Is it at your house?"

"It is—I will be back there at five. Do you want to pick it up then?"

I hugged him a second time.

"That's perfect."

"Um, pet, you going to tell me what you want it for? Just wondering."

I thought about it.

"No, but it's nothing bad, I promise."

"OK. Am I going to get it back?"

That was harder.

"Maybe..."

"Meh. Doesn't matter. Isn't worth a lot. You take care now."

I stole a third hug and drove back into town. It's hard to think of everything at once. This time, when I stopped at the supermarket, I bought a small shovel, a large knife sharpener, a Stanley knife and two whole roast chickens. Then I filled up the car with petrol and headed home. I packed my bag carefully—I would only get one chance—and just after five, drove to Henry and Will's house out at Hopton, not a stone's throw from the County Show Ground where Oscar and I had gone for our disastrous first date. They lived in a small barn conversion looking over Stafford towards Wales. On a clear evening, you can see the Wrekin Rock where it rises from the panhandle of the Shropshire hills.

I found Henry in residence, scrabbling through the garage.

"I've found it," he called when he saw me. "Give me a hand."

I made my way around the skeletons of two cars and a ride-on mower. Henry was up some stepladders, furtling around in a packing case that had been stacked across the rafters. I steadied the ladder and helped him down. He was carrying a long package, taped up in newspaper.

"Don't wander round town with this," he said good naturedly. "I don't know what it would get you on a first offence plea, but more than a flick knife."

I took it in both my hands. He was right—I could barely carry it.

"People fought with these? Seriously, Henry, this isn't a weapon; this is something you use for resistance training."

"Don't tell me you've ever joined a gym, petal."

He was right. The only time I'd ever picked up the weights Kit had left in my bedroom was to vacuum the carpet underneath. Still, the sword wasn't for me.

"It's for a friend," I said. "He knows how to use it."

"Didn't ask, petal."

"I know. And thank you."

I put the sword in my boot. There was just room next to the beer, the rock salt, the shovel, the Stanley knife, the roast chickens, the knife sharpener and the watering can. And the half case of champagne that Peter and I had never got to drink. I drove to the cemetery at Colton Hill. There were still a couple of hours until sunset; I rather thought I would need them both.

Someone once told me you could draw a circle with a rope and a stake. I didn't have a rope or a stake, and I couldn't remember what you were meant to do with them anyway. The little walled cemetery was vaguely round, and I decided that would do for me.

I should have brought a wheelbarrow. I lugged the bags around the graveyard perimeter, using my little shovel to draw a wiggly curve of rock salt just inside the wall. Five bags would have done it. It took rather over an hour.

I poured the beer into the watering can before diligently sprinkling it over my giant circle of protection, metre by metre. I unwrapped Henry Lake's sword. The very first time I had met him, little more than a week ago, Bredon had told me that with a sword in his hand, he would be the finest protector. I hoped he hadn't been boasting.

The sun still hadn't set by then, so I sat on Bredon's gravestone putting a good edge on the blade with the knife sharpener.

I waited until the sun's last rays were disappearing over the horizon. I opened my handbag and took out Diana's phone. Everyone had forgotten I'd got it. Not even Benedict had asked me for it back. I'd had a number of problems to solve today, but finding the vampires had never been one of them. I was going to call them. And they were going to come to me.

Chapter Twenty-Four

I'M A QUICK learner; my grandfather always said so. My teachers were less effusive, but then I did spend a lot of my school days sleep-deprived. And in between wrenching the dead from their graves and thrusting them back in again, my homework often fell through the cracks. But it's true: I pick things up pretty fast.

I hadn't been hanging round vampires for very long, but I had noticed a few universal truths. They seemed arrogant, quick to anger and given to grand gestures. I had a hunch that the best way to get what I wanted would be to piss them off mightily and impugn their courage. Or honour. Or anything else they felt strongly about. I wasn't going to be choosy.

I put through the call. Someone picked up on about the tenth ring.

"Well, well; you're supposed to be dead," said a harsh male voice, an odd mixture of Chicago burr and Italian musicality.

"Diana is dead." I drew in my breath. "But I am alive. Unlike the rest of your pathetic little Assemblage."

"Who is this?"

"My name is Lavington Windsor. We haven't met, but just so that you can place me, I am the person who killed Claudio."

There's a pause. Then:

"Go on."

"If you haven't got me in mind yet, I also killed Livia. Oh, and I

269

led Benedict to your little country pad out at Butterbank so that we could slaughter your sorry little mortal coterie and burn the place to the ground."

"Are you done?"

"Not nearly. Two nights ago, I led them to your little cubbyhole in Salt so we could mop up another couple of your family-sized pack of losers."

"What do you want?"

His voice was icy with rage. I heaped an extra coal on:

"If you don't mind me saying, you Gambaritos don't put up much of a fight."

"Gambarini. I am Marcello Gambarini."

His voice shook slightly

"Well Mr Gambarini, I am just saying. And now that things aren't going your way, you are snivelling up to Benedict. It's not exactly impressive. Round here, we'd say you got all the custard but not the mustard, if you get my drift, Mr Gambarini."

"I said what do you want?"

I ignored him. It always seemed to work for Benedict when he wanted to wind me up.

"I'm sitting here all alone, admiring my nail varnish, Mr Gambarini. Because I'm under Benedict's protection. So, once you have handed your sissypants arse over to him for general spanking, you won't be able to touch me. For the rest of my mortal life, you won't be able to lay a finger on me—or a tooth. How will that feel?"

"You tell me, Signorina. It seems to me that's what you want to do."

"Or I have another option. You three can come up here and try to take me out before you go crawling over to The Stone House. And we'll see who comes off best. How does that sound?"

"You are very full of confidence for one little mortal bag of blood."

"I think I can take you down. What do you think?"

"I am one of the Children of Diometes. I can drain your blood and wear your wishbone as a tie pin."

"Oh no! We disagree. How can this conflict ever be resolved?

"Where are you?"

"I'm in the churchyard on Colton Hill, you sun-phobic loser. Better hurry, because aren't you due to start grovelling soon? You wouldn't want to be late."

I ended the call. My heart was racing. What was I doing? Was I as mad as a box of frogs? It was too late to pull out now, but I wasn't just having second thoughts, but third, fourth and fifth ones. Calm, Toni, calm.

I thought they would come in a car: Claudio had driven to my house, and speed wasn't an attribute that Peter had mentioned when we'd talked about the Chicago Assemblage. Assuming they parked and walked into the cemetery, they would come in through the gap in the wall... Bredon's grave was almost at the farthest edge, so to get to me they would have to cross most of the cemetery. I was definitely in the best place. I had tried to ensure that my new best friends were most seriously pissed off: angry enough that they would come to attack me before taking up any offer of clemency; angry enough that they would want to gloat over killing me rather than simply rip out my throat. I thought I'd managed it.

I heard an engine and saw headlights heading up the hill. The road doesn't lead anywhere but the church, and in the two years I'd been raising the dead, I'd never met another soul up here that I hadn't summoned myself. I rather thought my challenge had been taken up.

The car drew to a sharp stop. The lights stayed on, but three figures emerged. They headed my way. My mouth was dry, and I was questioning my own sanity in setting up this insane encounter. Still, in for a penny... I knelt down on the ground next to Bredon's headstone.

"I'm here," I called.

I was aiming for confident and languid; I had to settle for not quavering too much. It's a bloody sight easier being brave and bolshy over the phone.

They walked slowly towards me, crossing the perimeter of my salt circle without seeming to notice it.

The man was tall; tall and wide. He had a swaggering gait. Something in that confident demeanour told me he expected to rip my head off and be back at The Stone House in time for the tea tray. The two women with him were so similar in stance and physique that I rather thought they were at least sisters, but more likely twins. They too moved in a way that told me they probably spent a lot more time doing weights than housework. I caught a glimpse of white-blond hair in the moonlight.

I waited until they were nearly in the centre of the graveyard. I took a deep breath and scored the Stanley knife across the palm of my left hand. I swapped sides and repeated the process on my right palm. I had no idea how deep was too deep, but I knew I needed a lot of blood. Maybe I had cut too deeply, because lots was what I got: it gushed out and dripped onto the ground.

I pressed my fingers into the soil. I felt the power coursing up through them. The blood pooled around my hands, glossy in the moonlight. I didn't need to say the names out loud, but I spoke them where it mattered... *Bredon Havers, John Doo, Maryrose Bletchington... Come to me*. I called them all and I felt them answer. Two zombies certainly hadn't been a match for a vampire; how about four hundred and twenty-four?

Have you ever taken the early train in from Stafford to London? You get to Euston station and the doors open. For a moment there is an empty platform, but moments later, it's heaving, as several hundred people tumble out of the carriages and begin the serious business of hating their fellow commuters. It didn't feel a million miles away from that—one instant I sat alone by Bredon's gravestone, and the next the hordes of the hungry dead surrounded me. More importantly, they surrounded my enemies.

I was almost too exhausted to breathe, but I pulled myself to my hands and knees. My muscles had turned to jelly, and my hands were shaking. I saw with some confusion that the blood dripping from them was being sucked into the ground. The soil drank it up, but stayed dry and dusty. No trace of moisture or colour remained.

Gasping lungfuls of air, I managed to inhale enough oxygen to speak.

"Kill the vampires," I said. I made it a command. "Kill them all. Don't let one escape."

My minions turned as one and began to close in. I couldn't see what was happening. I couldn't see a lot. My vision was blurry, and I felt sick. I slipped to one elbow.

"Mistress Toni," said a voice above my head. "Goodness gracious; are you hurt?"

It was Bredon. He sank to his knees next to me, oblivious of the tumult around us, his hands gentle as he helped me to sit up. I shook my head.

"Bredon, I am fine. I really am. Listen, you have to kill the vampires for me. I brought you a sword. You have to cut off their heads."

"A sword?"

His eyes sparkled. He seized the sharpened blade from where I had left it, leaning up against his headstone. He took it in both hands and whirled it experimentally above his head. He could whirl a blade alright. The man could probably have sliced moonbeams in half.

"Do you like it?"

"Like it!" He smiled broadly. "Dear heart, truly, this is a weapon for smiting your foe. I will be your champion."

"Remember: decapitate them."

He laughed out loud, the sound ringing across the crowded cemetery.

"Have no fear, Mistress. I know how to slay the undead."

And he turned and stepped into the fray. I had to laugh too, weak as I was. I'd spent half my day trying to find someone who knew how to slay vampires and he'd been here all along, waiting for me. I should have known—Bredon had told me the second time we met that they used to stake vampires in his day. I should have listened more closely.

It should have been a stupidly one-sided fight, but it wasn't. Vampires are just so bloody fast. Perhaps if I hadn't been so drained, I could have given better commands, but 'kill them all' had seemed to cover every base I cared about. And while there was enough moonlight to show me a lot of flying limbs—some of which were literally flying through the air, freed from their original tetherings—I was fuzzy on the details. I was feeling pretty fuzzy full stop.

The two women were almost surrounded from the moment I called my army from the earth. They disappeared under a mound of zombies like an apple core the wasps have found, and I saw Bredon, sword aloft, ploughing in after them.

But the man had been standing a little to one side and managed to spring free of the main horde before they could overcome him. I could see him on the edge of the mass, hurling zombie limbs to left and right. A head went whizzing past me and smacked into the tall cross on the grave next to Bredon's. I had a horrible glimpse of an eyeball pinging off at a tangent and turned hastily back to the main fray.

But in the darkness, and with the mass of flailing bodies, I could make out very little. It was dark. There was a fight... was that a severed leg or an arm?

In the end I closed my eyes and tried to home in on the vampires that way. Two were fading fast; I could feel their presences ebbing. One flickered out like a snuffed candle. The third wasn't going away in a hurry, though. In fact, it was heading my way.

I opened my eyes and looked up. He was tall, as tall as Henry, and huge shouldered. He was wearing a black silk evening jacket and dress trousers, but they'd been made in size extra muscly and he looked like his idea of chilling out was to arm wrestle a bus. He had zombies surging around him, and hanging off every limb. One arm hung limply at his side, and he was dragging a leg badly. Blood was flowing from a hundred bite marks, leaving splashes on his white lace-fronted shirt and the white tops of his jazz era shoes, but he was still managing to make unsteady progress towards me. My army of the dead was going to take him down, I had no doubt; the problem was, he might make it to me first. And quite soon.

I finally realised where my plan had a flaw.

Peter told me the Gambarinis could heal themselves. He hadn't been joking. I could see the holes closing themselves up gradually as I watched. My apathetic zombie horde was making new ones, but they just couldn't slow him down enough to save me. At this rate, my throat would get torn out long before his.

"Are you a Christian, necromancer?" His voice, with its soft Italian vowels, was thick with venom. "Better hope you know some short prayers. You don't have time for a full Hail Mary."

"Here's one," I spat back. "'Dear God, save me from smart-arse vampires with a terrible selection of one-liners.' Will that do?"

I hoped I sounded braver than I felt. I tried to scramble to my feet and ended up back on my knees. The world spun disobligingly around me. Up and down were usually easy to tell apart, but not anymore. I made another try at getting up, but the grass seemed slippery under my feet and gravity a lot stronger than usual. I began to crawl backwards away from the approaching vampire, but smacked into what must have been Bredon's headstone. Going around it seemed hugely complicated.

"Arse," I muttered. "This is so unfair. For crying out loud, there are four hundred of you, you useless shambling wrecks. Can you not take down one bloody vampire? Just the one! What kind of zombie apocalypse are you?"

My foe, Marcello I assumed, was drawing closer, close enough that in the moonlight I could make out his features. He must have been good looking before my minions got at him, with high cheekbones, broad elegant features and dark, springy hair that swept away from his face. But he was pock-marked with bites, even on his face and neck, and one ear had already provided some lucky revenant somewhere with an early evening snack. He was staggering his way towards me, step by step. One of his attackers was gnawing on an arm, another on a thigh, but he still carried on.

I felt the other vampire presence depart, winking out into the night. Two down, but they hadn't been the problem. The problem was starting to make faster progress, and I knew why. All this was taking far too long. My zombies were hungry and getting distracted. If this went on much longer, they would turn on me too.

The thought was like a bucket of water being poured over me. I got back to my knees and began to crawl round Bredon's headstone. If I made it out of the circle, I would be safe from the dead I had raised. But if Marcello made it out, so would he.

But as I looked up, I realised that wasn't going to happen. I was nowhere near the perimeter—and he had just broken free of the last of his shambling pursuers. He limped my way. When he came within a couple of metres he paused and reached out with his remaining functional arm to the grave next to Bredon's. He effortlessly snapped off the tall stone cross at the top.

He lurched to a halt above me and raised the cross above his head, four foot of solid granite. It seemed excessive. I'm not a big girl. A medium sized rock would have done. I looked up at him; was this it? Was this how it all ended?

Not quite. A figure barrelled out of the mass of slowly ambling undead. His weapon was shorter but not by much, and it was already dripping with vampire blood. He was just getting into his stride. He spun it around his head as easily as though it had been a bullwhip and sheared off Marcello's head at the neck and his arm at the shoulder.

I was showered with a wave of vampire blood. The cross flew into Bredon's gravestone and chipped off a corner. The separate bits of Marcello's body dropped to the grass; I watched in shock as the sands of time flowed across his piecemeal corpse and it rotted and then crumbled to powder.

Chapter Twenty-Five

BREDON DROPPED TO his knees next to me again, his face full of concern.

"Dear Mistress Toni, I was nearly too late. I despatched the first two before I realised that you were in danger. Are you injured?"

"I'm OK, it was just too much to raise you all," I said. "Listen, can you keep them off while I start to send them back? They look peckish and troublesome."

Bredon squared his shoulders. The role of champion was one he clearly felt he could embody with panache.

"They'll not get past me," he assured me, swinging Henry Lake's sword around in a move any musketeer would have been proud to master. "Just let them try."

Truth be told, my minion army wasn't particularly motivated, and none of them put up a fight as I sent them back. It took another slice out of my left palm to complete the task, but eventually there was just me, Bredon and the odd body part left in the cemetery.

I crawled to the edge of the graveyard. My circle of protection was down to a thread, a thin line of salt, each dismissal having taken its toll. I pushed my hand through it and broke it open.

"There's food in my car," I said, flopping onto my back. "I'm hungry, so you must be starving."

"It's true," he admitted. "I won't be long, Toni dear."

I lay on the grass and looked up at the moon. The clear sky around it was full of little stars. The world had three fewer vampires in it,

My plan hadn't been perfect, but it hadn't been a complete disaster either. I wasn't much as a military tactician, but what I lacked in strategy, I made up for in overkill.

I heard Bredon's footsteps returning. He was clutching a cooked chicken in one hand. I had a feeling the other one had already gone. He had also liberated one of the bottles of champagne. My heart warmed. Didn't I raise the best zombies?

I hadn't put much planning into our impromptu picnic. I had more been thinking that if I managed to pull things off, I could spend some time with Bredon. You can't go summoning a friend to smite your enemies and then banish them into their grave without so much as a thank you. And a snack… anyway, I had standards.

Not high ones, as it transpired. There was no rug, no glasses, no wicker basket and a general lack of strawberries and cream. I hadn't brought a radio or any china. There was just Bredon and me, sitting on the lawn covered in bloodstains. He cleaned his sword on the grass. I teased vampire dust out of my hair with my fingertips.

"I need to say thank you, Bredon," I said. "You were amazing back there. You saved my life."

He took both of my hands in his and held them.

"You give me life, young lady," he said. "I would do anything for you."

I blushed and sought for a way to change the subject.

"You're amazing with a sword, Bredon. Did you fight a lot of duels?"

"I did indeed, dear heart. We fought for sport, you know, rather than in anger. We would challenge each other on the slimmest of pretexts, and meet at dawn. Whoever won bought breakfast for all comers. Fine ale and a good roast of beef."

"Did you win?"

"Always, mistress. I was forever buying breakfast for my friends."

"Oscar is a wonderful fighter too," I said reflectively. "He gets enthusiastic about it just like you."

"Ah, your swain. How are things progressing? I have had no opportunity to enquire."

I thought about that.

"They're good, Bredon. I think. I have just wondered a couple of times... put it this way, he is very fierce."

Bredon lowered his chin into a palm. The moonlight shone on his curly brown hair.

"I think, Mistress Toni, if you will take advice from a man who is very much older than you but probably very little wiser, that when you seek through the world for love, you should first look for friendship and kindness. Without those, I think there is a great risk of the heart making bad choices for the head."

His words made a lot of sense. Was Oscar kind? He had been kind to me, coming to my office party, which must have been an absolute bore for him. And friendship? Well, we laughed together enough. Were we friends? It was too early to say.

"Is that what you did, Bredon?"

He was silent for such a long time that I realised I had made a dreadful English faux pas just asking the question. When he finally did reply, his voice was far away and sad.

"Yes, it was indeed. But others had different priorities. My dear young lady, this is a tale too mournful for your evening of victory. Instead, let us toast one another for the warriors we have been this night."

And we passed the bottle between us one more time. Despite the lack of accessories, it was a good picnic. The trick is to get the company right.

Two chicken wings and a few swigs of champagne did much to restore my equanimity. But once the adrenalin wore off the pain in my hands took over, and I had to cut our evening short. Looking at my palms, they were swollen, still oozing, and filled with soil. I thought they needed the attention of a doctor. Ideally, a Heidelberg-trained doctor with a really terrible bedside manner. I consoled myself with the thought that I couldn't possibly need another tetanus jab.

"Bredon, I have to go. I need to sort my hands out. Can you frisk the lawn for limbs? They will start to rot as soon as the sun comes up, but we should probably chuck them under a hedge or something."

"Of course, dear heart," he replied.

He sprang easily to his feet. The way I was feeling, in a week or two I might manage something similar myself, but not then and there. As it was, I just sat and watched him wander round the cemetery, pausing now and then to push a divot in with his heel, or gather something icky off the grass. I closed my eyes for a while.

"Mistress Toni, is this of use?"

I opened them again. Bredon was holding something out. I squinted in the moonlight. Thankfully not an organ of any kind. It was a man's signet ring, with a sea creature that might have been a crab or a crayfish carved into the top. I took it and wiped the blood off on the top of my denim skirt.

"It might be, actually, Bredon. I think one of the vampires must have dropped it. Thank you."

I pocketed the ring and attempted to stand up. With Bredon's help I managed it on the third attempt. I hugged him and then put both hands on his chest so that I could push up on to my tiptoes and kiss him on the cheek.

"Thank you. You're my hero."

He looked touched.

"You are more than welcome. I will always defend you."

He escorted me to the car before I dismissed him. I would have stayed until dawn, but I didn't fancy blood poisoning and I had a little more victory to celebrate before the sun came up.

I drove very slowly and carefully to The Stone House, gripping the steering wheel as gently as I could get away with. I parked with more than usual attention and levered myself out of the car.

I was still shaky, and leaned against the door of the Morris for a while, breathing the night air. The total exhaustion that had left me too dizzy to crawl had lifted. Probably to be replaced with shock and blood loss. I decided to ignore both. I had one last task in mind. I walked towards the entrance but as I got there, a figure emerged at speed from the darkness and hugged me. It was Camilla.

"Dearest, where were you? Peter and I were worried when you weren't here by sunset, especially now that Marcello seems to have gone to ground again." She paused for breath and finally caught sight of my appearance in the torchlight. "Oh my goodness. What happened to you?"

"I'm fine. It was nothing. Is Peter awake?"

She followed me into the hall, and I made my way to the spiral stairs that led to the lower floors.

"He is—he's just fine. Shall I find him for you?"

"Um, thank you. If you would. Listen, Camilla, I need to have a word with Benedict. Where is he?"

She winced.

"Rather you than me. He's in a bad mood. He's in his room—do you know the way?"

"Bizarrely and sadly, yes I do. Thank you."

"You're welcome. I'll find Peter."

She left me at the entrance of the long, windy dark corridor that led to Benedict's chambers. It was pitch black. I took a torch from the main corridor and, as he had, lit random torches along the twisting way. When I finally came to the black wooden double doors, I briefly doubted my own courage. But I had come this far. I banged firmly with the weighty iron knocker a couple of times.

"Yes," I heard his deep voice say. Just that. I opened the left side door and went in.

My bête noir was sitting at the heavy desk I had noticed before. He had tied his hair back from his face, and without the heavy frame of ringlets, he looked younger. If he looked crosser than usual, I couldn't tell. He had looked up as I entered, and if he was surprised, I couldn't tell that either. I came into the room and stood awkwardly by the bar, not sure what to say.

"Miss Windsor," he said politely. "I thought my evening could get no more sublime, but here you are to prove me wrong. Have you come to provide me with a little second breakfast, or is this purely a social visit?"

How did he do it? How did he get me that angry that fast? I was so furious that I seized one of the glasses off the top of the bar and hurled it at him.

"That's for your stupid bloody breakfast," I yelled. "And that's for your stupid sodding social visit."

He made no attempt to catch it this time, or the second one that followed. They shattered around him in a loud explosion of glass shards. Finally, I hurled the Gambarini's gold ring.

"And that's for your stupid clemency," I finished.

He moved then. He moved fast enough that I could barely follow, idly snatching the ring out of the air and leapfrogging elegantly over the desk to pin my hands behind my back and jerk me in up close against him.

I squeaked in pain as the move pressed my flayed palms against one another and to my surprise he immediately let me go.

"Show me your hands," he said.

I held them out, oozing blood and still covered in soil. Unexpectedly, he laughed.

"I see," he said, looking at the little gold ring with its carved crustacean. "I suppose I should have guessed. Did you get all three of them?"

"Yes," I said with some pride. "All three."

"Come through and wash your hands."

I followed him through to the bathroom where he filled the sink with hot water and gestured to me. Reluctantly, I immersed my hands. It hurt a lot more than cutting them open had.

"I was going to get Peter to dress them," I said defensively.

"I think I can do that much for you," he said. "I am somewhat in your debt you know."

"I didn't do it for you," I said hastily.

"Nonetheless," he said. "That will do now. Give me your hands."

I took them, dripping, from the sink and backed away from him, bumping up against the hot door of the sauna.

"I don't need you."

"You make that very clear," he said. "Almost every time I meet you. Give me your hands."

I let him take them, and closed my eyes as the rush of power flowed over me, like sherbet or cognac or the feeling of walking past a hot fire on a cold night.

"Hmmm. What a mess you've made," I heard him say. "Ignatius had a knife that would have done this quite neatly, you know."

I thought of the tiny golden knife in my great grandfather's chest with its sycamore flanges and sharp little blade.

"Oh that," I said. "Is that what it's for? I didn't know."

I looked down. My hands were still dirty, but whole again, and the pain had gone.

"Yes," he said. "So, my dear, what did you have planned for your victory celebration, apart from coming in here to rub my nose in it."

I had to laugh. He walked me to the door.

"Peter and I wanted to have a little housewarming with Oscar a couple of nights ago," I confessed. "I hoped we might try again this evening."

"In that case, I will give Oscar the night off," he said civilly. "Very few people surprise me anymore, Toni. You seem to be one of them."

I didn't say anything immediately. Benedict was being uncannily nice. But it's easy to be nice when everything is going your own way. Someone had warned me about that recently. I couldn't for the life of me remember who...

In the end, I replied only to the first thing he had said.

"Thank you," I said. "We would all appreciate that. I might try and clean myself up a bit first."

"Hmmm. I wouldn't bother."

"No?"

"My dear, you are covered in blood, and you look like you have been shagging in a graveyard. You are a vampire's wet dream."

In case I was in any doubt about what he meant, he idly slid his fingers round my waist and began to strafe his thumbs across the edge of my lowest ribs in a speculative manner. I removed his hands carefully.

"I'll bear that in mind," I said. "Goodbye."

And I let myself out.

I made my way to Oscar's rooms without getting lost. The door was ajar, and I could hear laughter. Camilla was sitting on the rug by the fire, and Peter was sprawled in a chair next to her. My lovely Oscar was perched on the club fender. He was wearing pale blue jeans and, as far as I could tell, nothing else. Eleven out of ten. I couldn't think of anything he would look better wearing. Apart from me. Or maybe a fireman's uniform.

"Knock knock," I said, closing the door behind me.

Peter caught sight of me and leapt to his feet. He ran across the room and I found myself being hugged to within an inch of my life.

"I was worried," he said. "What the hell have you been doing with yourself? You are covered in blood."

I hugged him back and thought about what to say. All day and all evening everything I had done had been about my obsession with vengeance, some notion of justice for Peter and Amelia that I hadn't been able to let go. If silly little Diana had to die for her desperate act of betrayal, then nothing less would do for the undead who had blackmailed her and put this whole hideous train of events into motion.

But now that it was done, I never wanted to dwell on it again. And I didn't want the scene around me to be tainted by it. I didn't want the laughter I had heard as I approached to give way to shudders of horror. There might be a time to talk about what had happened up on Colton Hill. That time hadn't come.

"It was nothing," I said hugging Peter back, and added with casual dishonesty: "None of the blood is mine."

He started to say something, to argue, but Oscar's voice interrupted him. Oscar had come to stand next to us and was looking down at me in a rather smouldering way that made my knees weak.

"Peter, don't you think you are rather hogging the girl to yourself?"

Peter laughed and let me go, and Oscar enveloped me in his arms.

"Good evening, my beautiful Toni," he said, and he leaned down to kiss me.

It was one of those kisses that started out as a gentle greeting but took a detour somewhere along the way. The gentle greeting became something very much more penetrating and very much less gentle, and before I knew it, I was pressed up against the door by a whole load of Oscar. One of the things that was pressing against me the hardest went a long way to convince me that I was indeed the very embodiment of a vampire's wet dream.

"You know, you could just give Camilla and me a tenner to go to the cinema," said Peter in an amused tone.

Oscar and I broke apart in some embarrassment and I straightened my clothes.

"Actually, I was thinking the opposite," I said. "I was thinking the four of us could do a little light housewarming. I have half a case of lukewarm champagne. We could pick up some fish and chips and a bag of ice."

"I have Twister," said Camilla, and the three of us stared at her. She shrugged. "I'm just saying."

As I said, the trick is in the company.

Chapter Twenty-Six

THE NEXT DAY was bright and clear. We slept through a lot of it

"Peter, this is the most depressing shopping trip I've ever been on."

"It was your idea."

"I know, I know."

Having sloughed away our hangovers with coffee and bacon sandwiches, I had decided to ruin the rest of our afternoon by going to choose a headstone for Jane Doe's grave. I couldn't quite decide why I felt so responsible for her. Neither Wills nor I had killed her. But I couldn't shake it—the feeling that I had failed to find justice for that poor dismembered girl, ripped up and discarded like so much litter.

Headstones are expensive, and this impulse would burn a substantial hole in the wad of cash lurking in my handbag. I had a feeling I would soon have to choose one for Amelia too. I'd felt uncomfortable taking money from Benedict. Still, if I had to make many more purchases of this kind, I would be tempted to swallow my pride and ask him for more.

The stonemason, or stonemasons, consisted of two brothers, Dorian and David Hattingley, who lived with their mother in a cottage over towards Etching Hill. They were sandy-haired, big-shouldered siblings with hearty voices and the musculature of men who tear up rocks for a living. I couldn't tell them apart. I didn't know anyone who could. Their office, such as it was, was the kitchen table in Mrs Hattingley's kitchen.

I'd been here just once before, six years ago. I had chosen the stone for the grave where my parents and grandfather had just been buried. Mrs Hattingley had been unexpectedly kind to me and given me chocolate biscuits.

She'd taught me history at school. Neither of us had enjoyed the experience. She hadn't passed on a lot of knowledge and I certainly hadn't passed any history exams. Whenever she looked at me, I was sure she was recalling my assertion that the Crimean war had been caused by criminals. Or the time when I had asked why the German forces hadn't invaded Britain via the Channel Tunnel.

'I would say that Lavington Windsor could do better," she had written in my final report, *"but I am increasingly of the opinion that she simply can't. The subject appears to be quite beyond her grasp, as does the timely attendance of classes or the handing in of any homework whatsoever."*

Still, she let me in very civilly and shook hands with Peter. We were led through to the kitchen, seated around the table, and fed strong dark tea. I'd had a quarter of a century to get used to builder's tea as a beverage. Peter just looked at it in horror and fed it to an aspidistra when Mrs Hattingley was looking the other way.

"So, dear," she said to me when all the usual pleasantries had been disposed of, "I understand you are after a headstone for that poor woman that the police found."

"Um, yes. I just thought she should have one," I said vaguely.

She looked enquiringly at me, but I pretended not to notice. I didn't understand my own motivations. I wasn't about to try to explain them.

"Of course, dear," she said. "Surely. Well here's the brochure."

The brochure was a bunch of photographs of headstones on a bulldog clip. I sifted through them until I found a plain black arch with old-fashioned lettering on it.

"This one," I said. "This will do."

She wrote something down on a piece of paper in the neat, round schoolteacher's script that I remembered.

"Of course. And what words do you want, dear?" she asked, pen poised.

I'd thought this through.

"In memory of Jane Doe," I said. "We will not forget you."

She wrote for a while, and then passed the paper over to me.

"Is this alright, dear?"

I looked at the paper.

'*Granite arch, gothic lettering*,' it said. "*To read: In memory of Jane Doo. We will not forget you.*'

I shook my head.

"No, that's not right. Jane Doe," I said. "You've written Jane Doo."

"That's how it's spelled, dear," she said, frowning.

"No, it's not."

"Oh, of course," she said with sudden understanding. "You're using the American spelling."

"What?"

She looked at me in exasperation.

"The American spelling," she said. "For someone you can't identify."

Little lights went off in my brain.

"Please explain this to me, Mrs Hattingley," I said as patiently as I could. "I obviously don't know what I'm talking about."

She sighed. I remembered that sigh. I had heard it emitted in my direction four or five times in every history lesson I had ever sat through, but right then and there I was too excited to care.

"You really never listened to a word I said, did you, Lavington," she said. "We even studied this in your third year." Her voice took on an authoritative, bossy air and she began:

"Going back to the fourteenth century, legal documents filed on behalf of 'the people' would use the names John Doo and Richard Roo to describe the populous. More recently the names John Noakes and Joe Bloggs were used." She could see I was struggling, and added snappishly: "It's a bit like saying Tom, Dick or Harry, or the man on the Clapham omnibus. Anyway, later the police used the names John Doo or Jane Doo for an unidentified corpse, but the practice fell into disuse. The American police used the same system, but the names morphed to John Doe and Jane Doe. Now do you understand?"

I shook my head, but I was starting to.

"So, John Doo," I said slowly. "His name wasn't John Doo."

"I don't know who you mean, dear, but no. It wasn't a real name."

"But he came," I whispered.

"What was that dear?"

I didn't answer immediately. I could have hugged her. I was beaming from ear to ear.

"I understand now, Mrs Hattingley," I said beatifically. "You're a wonderful teacher, and I never appreciated you."

She looked startled.

"Thank you, dear," she said. "How sweet. So did you want the American spelling?"

"Oh yes," I said. "Jane Doe. That's what we've been calling her. You know, Mrs Hattingley, I'm going to have to think about the wording a little longer. Let me give you the deposit for the stone and I'll call you in the week with the exact text."

I dragged Peter away with quite un-English haste.

"What on earth was going on in there?" he asked as he started up the car. "You look like you've just won the lottery."

"I feel like I have," I said. "Peter, his name wasn't John Doo."

"You said that before, and I didn't understand then either. And where are we going?"

"Oh, back to my cottage please, via the supermarket. OK, I'll try to explain. You know I can't raise someone unless I know their name, right?"

"That's what you said."

"Well, it's true. I can't. But there's a grave at Colton Hill for a man called John Doo. And Peter, I *have* raised him. I've raised him twice. I raised him last night in fact."

"And I still don't understand. Explain slower."

He drove on to Bower Lane and headed over towards the river.

"I didn't realise until this moment that John Doo couldn't have been his real name. It must have been the grave of an unidentified man. But I could raise him anyway. So even though it was only a name that he was given after he died, it was enough. And that means I should be able to raise Jane Doe."

"You can raise her as Jane Doe because it's her name now, even though you don't know what her name was when she was alive."

I nodded. I was certain it would work.

"Yes. Exactly. We've been calling her Jane Doe for months. It's pencilled in above her freezer; it's written on the tag on her toe and all over her notes. Father Denis buried her as Jane Doe, and it's carved into the temporary marker on her grave. So she's Jane Doe as much as John Doo is John Doo. And tonight, she can tell me who killed her."

Peter thought about it.

"What about the fact that she has no head or hands?" he asked.

"I've thought about that. I'll have to raise her with no circle of protection, otherwise she'll be raised without them and she won't be able to talk to me. It's risky, but I'm going to do it anyway."

"Do you want me to come with you? I had plans, but I could cancel. I'm meeting an old college friend for dinner—he is over from Frankfurt for a couple of weeks and I was going to ask if you wanted to join us. But I could tell him I'm busy…"

I shook my head.

"No, it's fine. I raise the dead all the time, Peter."

I had never wanted night to fall more quickly. I was counting the minutes until sunset and it was only afternoon. In the end we drove to Lichley Manor and I spent a couple of hours taking photographs and measurements to draw up better floor plans.

"What did you decide about doing this place up in the end?" asked Peter. "Oscar said something about asking you to hire an architect."

"I'm going to do it myself," I said contentedly. "I've always wanted to do up an old house. I sell these beautiful, ancient places all the time, and then you drive by six months later and the new owners have stuck in PVC windows and a hot tub. I know every craftsperson in the county, and I'm going to call in lots of favours and make this place adorable."

Peter laughed.

"You know, Oscar would probably like a hot tub."

"Well, they're tacky, and I'm English, so he can't have one. He can have a billiard room."

Evening came at last. I dropped Peter off at the bus stop and drove on to Baswich Cemetery. I parked the car and walked to Jane's grave. The black earth had been tamped down and a rectangle of turf pushed into place. The flowers I had bought were wilting and dried up, half the petals and leaves now scattered on the grass. The red dye on one of the ribbons had bled into the wooden marker at the head of the grave. Here lay a young woman, perhaps my own age, who had been slaughtered in the prime of her life. Tonight, I could begin the precarious process of seeking justice for her.

I had picked up the staples that any good necromancer needs—a loaf's worth of ham sandwiches and a few catering bags of crisps. I littered them around the fresh grave and sat down. This moment had been a long time in coming.

"Jane Doe," I said. I reached out for her. And there she was. She had always been there, waiting for me. I caught her in the butterfly net of my power. "Jane Doe, in peace I call you. I summon you this night. Come to me."

There was a little resistance, but she came, stepping out of the earth with a girlish little skip. She had long mouse-coloured hair and a round face. She was a little taller than me, a plump, soft creature with a childlike expression. She was wearing a white skirt with red poppies on it and a lacy white shirt. On a chain around her neck, a little pink crystal dolphin dangled. She was looking around herself in a rather bewildered way.

"Hello, hello," she said. "It's very dark."

Her voice was the voice of a child, of a little girl. She looked a little scared.

"Jane, I brought you some food," I said hurriedly, picking up a plate of sandwiches and holding it out to her. "You're probably hungry."

"Hungry," she said obediently and began to eat. "Yes, Jane is hungry."

I realised something in a rush that made me even angrier, if possible. Jane wasn't all there. She certainly hadn't had the mental capacity of an adult when she had been alive. My poor Jane had drawn every short straw going. Well, whatever support she had lacked in life, she would have mine in death.

"Tell me your name, sweetie," I said gently. "What are you called?"

"My name's Jane," she said. "Jellybean Jane."

I was confused. Had we wiped out her memory by renaming her? I realised the first plate of sandwiches had gone and hastily passed her another...

"Your full name, darling," I said. "What's your full name?"

"I'm Jane Allardyce," she said. "But Mummy calls me Jellybean Jane."

So her name had been Jane all along. But Allardyce? As in Gropey George Allardyce? My jaw dropped.

"Who is your mother, Jane?" I asked, my heart thumping at a thousand beats a minute. "Where is she?"

Jane began to cry.

"She died," she sniffed. "Mummy died and they said I couldn't stay. So I came here to Daddy. I knew the address and I caught the train. But he killed me. He said I could have a bunny rabbit as a pet, but he killed me."

My hands clenched into little fists.

"Did he have an affair with your mother, Jane?" I asked, unsure whether she would understand the question, but she seemed to.

"Mummy and Daddy got married," she said. "There are photos in a pretty book. She wore a big white dress."

I sat down on the grass, my head spinning. I passed Jane food while I tried to organise my thoughts. What did I know? Well,

George had recently married a rich widow. But now it looked like he had already been married. There was a word for that kind of behaviour and that word was bigamy. The truth would certainly cost him his seat in the House of Lords, as well as his rich wife. And probably a nice spell in prison along with all the people he had put there. Maybe wife number one had been bought off, but he couldn't buy off Jane—she probably didn't know how to lie, let alone what lies to tell. He'd had to find another way to silence his secret daughter.

So he'd killed her. Killed his own child and chopped her up to protect his reputation and his bank balance. Bigamy was a bad word. Murder and dismemberment were worse ones. Someone once told me that if you never tell any lies, you never have to remember anything. George Allardyce had told lie after lie after lie—and it seemed to be my job to make sure the truth didn't get buried and forgotten along with Jane.

If I told Wills, what would happen? Would DNA tests show Jane to be George's daughter? Might that be enough to start balls rolling? Probably not. Probably Wills would feel obliged to pursue things, he would lose his job and George would slip through the net like a slippery, gropey, murdering bastard. No. I needed another way.

I looked up at Jane. She was sitting on her own grave marker, eating crisps. I looked at the little dangling crystal dolphin. Maybe her mother had bought it for her. Certainly, George hadn't.

And then I knew what I had to do. Or rather, what Jane and I had to do together. I walked up to her, and patted her very gently on the arm.

"Come on, Jellybean Jane," I said. "Come with me in my little car. We're going for a drive."

Chapter Twenty-Seven

IT WAS EARLY evening, and I stood at my kitchen table packing the picnic hamper. I had found it the previous day at Penkridge market. It was lined in fabric printed with Union Jacks, and came with a vast rug in the same design. It was the kind of capacious basket that would fit comestibles for a hungry family of ten—or one small estate agent and her zombie. I'd included plenty of all the usual trimmings plus four pounds of strawberries and a pint of cream. Bredon—I had discovered—had a particular weakness for strawberries.

About a week had passed since our impromptu housewarming party. I had hired an extremely competent firm of builders to renovate Lichley Manor. They were unexpectedly free; their previous client, a reclusive millionaire, had vanished when his new home at Butterbank Lodge had burned to the ground. No one could get hold of the man. There are silver linings to all things.

I had made half a dozen rounds of shooter's sandwiches, and tucked the fat foil rounds into the basket carefully. I can't cook many things, but I am good at picnics. I added two litres of dandelion and burdock and a couple of bars of fruit and nut.

Lots of paper towels, some candles, salt, pepper... I was ticking off my mental list when the doorbell rang. Licking some butter off my fingers I went to answer it.

To my surprise, it was Camilla. She was carrying a large cardboard box that had been taped shut. Air holes had been punched in the top. It was emitting a low rumbling noise.

"Hello," she said. "I can't stop, but Peter asked me to drop this off. He said you would understand."

She followed me through and put the box on the kitchen table. I peeled off the tape carefully. A wide good-natured face stared up at me, tangerine-coloured whiskers bristling, a single white fang revealed by a yawn. Winchester, Amelia's vast and ancient orange cat, carefully climbed out of the box and sat on the edge of the table.

"Oh," I said in surprise. "Peter did say I needed a cat."

I looked at my new houseguest. He was licking a leg.

"I think you're meant to butter his paws," said Camilla helpfully.

I'd heard that. I found the butter dish and ineptly smeared some butter onto two fat, orange paws.

"Do I do the back ones as well?"

"I've no idea," confessed Camilla. "It's just something I heard. Listen, I have to go."

We watched as Winchester jumped down from the table. He parked his large furry rump next to the Aga, and began to lick his paws in earnest.

"Well, I think it's working," I said. "He doesn't seem distressed."

I walked her to the door.

"Are you seeing Peter tonight?" she asked, hugging me goodbye.

"No, he's meeting some friend from Frankfurt for dinner again," I said. "He asked me along but I'm busy too, as it happens. But I think he'll be here tomorrow."

And I waved her off. I headed back in and frisked the kitchen for cat-friendly food. I discovered a tin of tuna in the cupboard and a packet of ham left in the fridge. Winchester would live until my next supermarket visit. I wondered what Amelia had fed him on? Probably raised game pie. I hoped he could adjust to cat food.

My phone rang as I was tucking the last bits and pieces into my picnic basket. It was Wills. I had been expecting him to ring all week. I sat down.

"Hey, sis."

"Hey, bro."

"Um, so an odd thing happened this morning, Toni."

"Might it have concerned George Allardyce and Jane Doe?"

There was a pause.

"Well it might. I did wonder if you had anything to do with it."

"Well I might. Let's leave it at that."

"Probably best. We received a two-page confession from George. He admitted to the rather unexpected crime of being married to two women at the same time and the much more serious one of murdering his daughter, Jane, chopping up her body and then pulling us off the case."

"I'm happy to hear it."

"Well, you might be less happy to hear this: we went round to his house. Lulu—thank God—is on holiday with her sister. I say thank God because it looks like George hung himself two days ago after posting the letter. I've got a forensics team out there digging up the croquet lawn. In his letter, he said Jane's head and hands are buried under the red hoop."

He'd killed himself rather than face the music. My heart went cold. Then it hardened within me. George had made his choices. The important choice was the one he'd made when he lured poor, simple, harmless Jane to her doom by promising her a pet bunny rabbit. The rest? Well, Lulu was better off without him.

"I'm not sorry, Wills. It's not what I had planned, but I am not sorry."

"I can't say I am either. In his letter, he said the ghost of his daughter had begun to visit him nightly; she said she would rest once he confessed. Might you know anything about that?"

"What can I say, Wills? Guilt does strange things to a man. Or so I've heard."

"He claimed he panicked," Wills said. "Weeks back she turned up on his doorstep with a suitcase saying she'd come to live with Daddy now. Lulu was due back from the hairdresser in half an hour. He said he lost his head and strangled her and then realised he'd need to cover his tracks."

"We'll never know," I said. "But, Wills, when I panic, I drop things. Sometimes I stammer. I don't murder my family. Even when you are really annoying."

I stayed sitting at the table for a long time after that, looking rather blankly at the phone. Eventually, Winchester—paws licked clean of butter—began to butt up against my ankles. So I pulled myself together. I fed him on two slices of ham and a forkful of tuna after which he fell asleep in front of the stove. I picked up my leather jacket as I headed out to the rust-mobile. I didn't want to be cold after the sun set.

I had one more disagreeable task to get out of the way before my picnic. Peter was busy, and he'd told me that Oscar was engaged on some Assemblage-related business. That left the coast clear for me to do something I had been putting off for a while. I put the picnic basket in the car, along with the rug, and reluctantly drove to The Stone House. I couldn't procrastinate about this any longer—I needed to talk to Benedict Akil.

The drive was much more pleasant that the previous occasion—I wasn't bleeding heavily from open wounds for a start. Nor was I covered in gore and soil. But I was nervous. Benedict had said he was in my debt. I wondered how he would react to me trying to call that favour in.

I parked carefully in the courtyard. The usual flotilla of expensive cars was there. I tucked the rust-mobile in between an elderly red Bentley and Benedict's Spyker and let myself into the house. I rather hoped the man was in his room. I didn't fancy making an arse of myself in front of too many people.

There were some lights already lit in the twisting stone corridor, which was a good sign. I felt I'd walked along it far too many times already for one lifetime, and as I got to the dark wooden doors at the end my heart sank. Still, I'd got this far—the worst he could do was kill me. A maximum of twice.

I raised the knocker and banged it a couple of times. In the silence of the corridor, it sounded far, far too loud.

"Yes," I heard his voice, just as before.

I took a deep breath and went in. Once again, he was sitting at his desk. He was never going to be easy to read, but I thought he looked bored.

"Well, well," he said when he saw me, getting to his feet.

In a rush I said, "Do not say anything smarmy, do not say anything sarcastic and do not torment me."

"I see," he said. To my surprise he walked around the desk, took my jacket off me, and threw it onto a sofa. "What may I say, then, that won't win me a face full of glass? Can I offer you a drink?"

I perched nervously on one side of the club fender.

"Yes, please. I would like that."

He didn't say anything as he took a bottle out of the fridge and removed the foil from the top, rather more competently than I could. Maybe I needed more practise. I watched as he added a cube of sugar, a shot of cognac, and a dash of bitters to the glass before topping it up. My favourite cocktail, the Classic; heaven in a glass, and the only beverage better than neat champagne... he put it into my hand and sat on the other side of the fender. I sipped at my drink to mask my nerves.

"You and Peter have such reassuringly expensive taste," he said. "He absconded with a decanter of cognac the other day on quite the slimmest of pretexts."

"That might have been for me," I admitted, "and I'm afraid it's all gone."

"Why am I not surprised? So, is it safe for me to ask why you are here?"

I took another deep breath.

"I've come to ask you a favour," I said.

He looked down at his hands. He was still holding the champagne cork, turning it over casually in his fingers. He was wearing black jeans and a linen shirt in a very dark royal blue. The tight black spirals of his hair caught the firelight. I wondered how the hell he brushed it, because it looked worse trouble than mine.

"I feared as much. I hope it's only a little favour, Toni, because you cannot have my car."

I gave a gasp and burst out laughing. I couldn't help it. To my surprise he joined in.

"Well that's nice," he said unexpectedly. "I've never seen you smile before. It quite puts me in sympathy with Oscar. And makes it rather a shame that I don't think it will last."

"What do you mean by that?"

He looked back down at the champagne cork.

"I mean that I know what you've come to ask me, and you're going to be annoyed when I won't give it to you."

Oh. That was a bad start.

"I've come to ask you to release Oscar from his promise."

The cork twirled a little longer, and then he tossed it into the fire. He looked up at me. He had gone back to being completely inscrutable.

"Hmmm. I was afraid it was that."

"Well, will you?"

"No."

Damn it. I got to my feet and paced around the room. He watched me impassively.

"Benedict, this is crazy. You can't put Oscar's life on the line as hostage to my good behaviour."

"You say that, but I think you'll find it's exactly what I've done."

"Yes, but it's insane. I'm never going to do what you tell me to. Oscar won't last a week if you stick to this."

"Now you're just being pessimistic. It's been more than a week already. No, don't even think about throwing that glass."

I put it down on a nearby table with more force than was strictly necessary.

"You're just splitting hairs," I said. "A week, a month… this will never work out."

"Perhaps that's what I want."

I thought about what he had said… an excuse to take out Oscar? That sounded even stupider than expecting me to do as I was told.

"No, you're just being provocative. I saw Oscar fight in that cellar. He's amazing. You'd be crazy not to want that on your team."

"Perhaps," he said. "Here is the only offer I will make you, Toni. You can swear your allegiance to me directly, and I will release Oscar from his promise."

"That doesn't sound like a great deal."

"It is, however, the only one on the table."

I hummed and hawed. I was here because I couldn't have Oscar held accountable for what I did. Our relationship would never survive it, and right now our relationship was about as wonderful as anything that had ever happened to me. I'd had plenty of boyfriends and enough lovers to know that what we had was special. Because of my powers, I'd always been an outcast. While other kids were listening to assurances that the monsters under the bed weren't real, I was out raising them. Oscar didn't expect me to conform to a world defined by conventions. He would never make me feel like the freaky girl who hung out with the dead. Or the undead. I wanted this to work out.

I looked up at Benedict. Whatever game he was playing, no one had even told me the name, let alone the rules. I had a feeling he'd known all along that I would ask for this. Had he set me up?

"OK," I said ungraciously. "Fine."

"Thank you," he said. There was a pause. Then he added: "You know, Oscar very nicely went down on his knees when he did this."

"Nice try," I said with feeling. "I am never getting down on my knees for you."

"Ah well. Listen Toni, unlike Oscar, I insist that you know what you are doing with this. We nightwalkers are defined by our promises. We do not break them. If you had betrayed us like Diana, Oscar would have presented himself to me for punishment. He would have let me take his life without a second thought. Regardless of your low opinion, my dear, we have some sense of honour. So do not make me this promise unless you intend to keep it. Am I clear?"

"I suppose."

"Good. I will make demands on you only when they are essential, and when I do, I expect no arguments, no tantrums and no procrastination. Agreed?"

"Yes, I agree. But I won't give you my blood and I won't sleep with you."

His voice, when he replied, was amused.

"Hmmm. Those are two very weighty exceptions, Toni, my dear."

"And there is no wiggle room in either of them!"

"Very well, I won't demand your blood unless my life is at risk. And I won't make sleeping with me a condition of your loyalty. Though, Toni, I'm a vampire! And I have always had a weakness for redheads. I will probably ask you to sleep with me every time we meet. Now would be just fine, as it happens."

He got up from the fireside and walked over to me. He slid his hands around my ribs just under my arms and pulled me in until I was pressed against him from knee to chin. He dropped his sauna-hot lips to my neck and I felt his fangs graze my skin. He began to slide his hands downwards.

"I'm very good, you know," he whispered into my skin. "I'm better than Oscar."

With a sigh, I put my hands onto his torso and levered him away from me.

"Let me make you another promise," I said firmly. "I will never, ever sleep with you."

"Ah well," he said, walking idly back behind his desk and sitting down in the club-style chair behind it. "I hope you have a pleasant evening. Do drop in anytime if you change your mind."

I had to laugh. The man had no shame.

"I'll remember that," I said. "And good night."

I made it almost as far as the door before I remembered my final errand.

"Oh God, I forgot," I said, hurrying back to the desk and reaching into the pocket of my jeans. "I meant to give this back to you ages ago, but I kept forgetting. I hope you didn't throw the other one away."

And I dropped onto his desk the little moon-shaped cufflink he had lost the night he saved Peter in the cellar. It was platinum, of course, but I'd only realised that later. He picked it up and held it in his hand for a moment.

"Thank you," he said quietly. "That was unexpected. I am in your debt again."

"Well, I won't hold my breath," I said. "Much good it did me last time you said that."

I turned again to leave.

"Toni, wait!" he said urgently. "Wait please."

I turned back in some surprise and sat on the edge of his desk. He was looking at the cufflink. He didn't speak for a while. Then:

"Toni, what would it take for you just to walk away from this?"

The question came so out of the blue that I couldn't work out what he meant for a while.

"From what?"

"From all of this; from Oscar. What would it take to pretend you never met him that night?"

I looked at him as if he were mad.

"Are you crazy? That's not what I want."

"I'm well aware of that."

I thought for a moment. What was he actually asking?

"Do you mean never see any of you again, or just Oscar?"

"The former would be fine too, but yes, it's just Oscar."

"Would you release me from my promises?"

"Oh yes."

My head was reeling.

"Can I have your car?"

He laughed.

"If you want. But Toni, I am not talking about trinkets. Think about who I am. There is not much you can ask for that I can't give you."

I did think about it, and he had a point. Unlimited wealth? I had a feeling Benedict had been amassing the stuff since before it got monetised. Perfect health? Not a problem. Eternal life? Also available. Yes, if he meant what he said, there wasn't a lot he couldn't give me. And for what? I shook my head.

"I can't do it. Love is the only thing that really matters. Without that, what's the point of even being alive? It's why we get up in the morning. Or in your case the evening…"

He stood up. He picked up my jacket and walked me to the door.

"Ah well, I had to try. I didn't really think you would say yes."

I was still trying to work out what was in his mind. A thought occurred to me.

"Benedict, did you make the same offer to Peter?"

He nodded.

"I did."

"What did he say?"

"Ah, dear Peter. He told me to go fuck myself. In very eloquent German. He was really quite specific about it. Please don't do the same. My pride wouldn't take it second time."

"I don't speak German, but the answer is still no."

He opened the door for me and helped me on with my jacket.

"I did my best. Enjoy your evening, my dear."

The door closed behind me, leaving me alone in the corridor with my thoughts. They weren't very coherent. Why did Benedict care if I lived or died? Did it have something to do with my great grandfather? And why did the condescending pain in the arse want to separate Peter and me from Oscar? I had no idea, and speculation didn't seem useful. I resolved to put the matter from my mind and enjoy the rest of my night. It was easier than I had imagined.

I drove back to Colton and up the hill to the cemetery. I usually walked, but the picnic hamper was heavy, and rules are made for breaking. I spread the rug out on a nice flat bit of graveyard just next to Bredon's grave. I laid out cushions, candles and food. I arrayed china and chintz in all the right places. And then I summoned my friend and champion, Bredon Havers, to join me for dinner.

To my surprise, he was still wearing Henry's sword. I say wearing, because he had somehow acquired a belt from which it was hanging. The sight reinforced my thinking that revenants come back in the guise that they see themselves in. Bredon clearly thought of himself as my protector. I certainly didn't mind.

"Hello, stranger," I said. "I've come to ask you to dinner."

He joined me on the rug.

"And I am very happy to accept, young lady," he said, tracing the outline of the flags on the rug. "How fine; the Great Union flag. It's pleasing to see it hasn't changed in all these years."

We wined. And dined. We talked about this and also that. Bredon complimented me on the shooter's sandwiches. I complimented him on his sword belt. The rain held off.

I sensed something was on his mind though. I was reluctant to put a damper on our evening, but eventually I felt compelled to ask:

"Bredon, what's wrong? You aren't yourself tonight. I can tell."

He looked worried.

"Can you? It's just something you said when we were last together. You said that the bodies of my peers," he gestured around the graves, "would rot when the dawn came. Would I rot too?"

Oh, that.

"Yes, Bredon, you would. You can never go in the sunlight."

"I see." He was silent for a little. "You see, I'd been meaning to ask you to let me stay with you for the sunrise. I hadn't realised…" His voice trailed off. "I hadn't realised I would never see the sun again."

"Bredon, this is England, you know. We don't see it very often full stop. We get like three sunny days a year, and you know it."

Thankfully, I had made him laugh, and we spoke of other things. After all the food was gone, we lay on the rug and gazed at the stars.

"Sometimes I think the night sky is even prettier than the day," I said to him. "The moon, the planets, the little shooting stars."

"My father used to tell me the names of all the constellations," he said wistfully. "I never listened. Back then I didn't care. But if I am never to see the sun again, I would like to know them now."

Bernie wanted to shag me on the side while getting married to one of my girlfriends. Oscar wanted to drink my blood. Peter wanted me to mend the broken mess he'd made of his life. Christ alone knew what Benedict wanted, but I had a feeling that the list started with total control over my life and knowledge of all my innermost secrets.

And here was a man who only wanted to know the names of stars. It didn't seem like a big ask... I squeezed his hand in mine. OK," I said. "I'll get a book. We can learn together."

To be continued...

Acknowledgements

THIS BOOK STARTED out as a short story. I wanted to write about zombies from their perspective, not the point of view of their soon-to-be brain munched victims.

But that didn't happen.

Within two weeks, Toni had taken over and the short story was starting to look more like a novella. I gave up and told everyone I was writing an erotic vampire adventure. I decided my unexpected heroine could shag her uninvited two-dimensional toothy blonde love interest for a few pages and then I would get back to my paid work.

That didn't happen either.

Without me really planning it, Peter slid into the picture, and Benedict too. I took a fancy to the leggy Claire, the ethereal Camilla and the mysterious Grace. Toni's brother, meant to be a throwaway character to facilitate a scene with jokes about shagging sheep, felt too adorable to abandon so I wrote him a boyfriend. I was still writing, and my novella was nowhere near finished. Bredon filled my thoughts, but not only him; I'd become obsessed with Jane Doe. I hadn't even a vague idea of who had killed her, how or why, but I needed to find out. A hundred pages and counting...

Could it be a novel? Could it even be a whodunit?

It had also taken over my life without even trying. I was eating dinner with The Patient Spouse and Best Mate John a few weeks into the project. I'd cooked steak, I think, and as I stuck a fork into mine, my mouth opened and blurted out:

"If you decapitated someone, would the blood spurt out? And how long for? How far would it go? I mean, if you were inside, would it splash the ceiling?"

It's a testament to my two fellow diners that instead of dialling the emergency services, they simply put their minds to answering the question. Best Mate John even suggested reading H. Rider Haggard's *King Solomon's Mines* for inspiration.

I stopped writing four months later. The book was done. I planned to breathe a sigh of relief, set novel writing aside and get back to my paid work.

And that's never really happened. Indeed, as I start work on volume nine, I think it might not come to pass.

Thank you to The Patient Spouse for reading every chapter and giving me feedback. Thank you to my awesome sister Jessica and my unflagging co-conspirator Shelagh for constantly encouraging me. Thank you to my amazing agent Simon Kavanagh at the Mic Cheetham agency for loving my book and never doubting me. And finally to my editor Kate Coe at Rebellion, whose enthusiasm, if bottled, would eclipse tea, coffee and champagne as the beverages of happiness.

About the Author

ALICE JAMES WAS born in Staffordshire, where she grew up reading novels and spending a lot of time with sheep. She was lucky enough to have a mother who was addicted to science fiction and a father who was fond of long country walks, so she grew up with her head in the stars and her feet on the ground. After studying maths at university and training to be a Cobol programmer(!), she began writing novels to get the weird people in her head to go somewhere else. She now lives in Oxfordshire with a fine selection of cats, fulfilling her teenage gothic fantasies by moving into a converted chapel with an ancient spiral staircase—and gravestones in the garden. Her go-to comfort dish is a big plate of dumplings, her number one cocktail is a Manhattan and her favourite polygon is a triangle, though she has a soft spot for concave rhomboids.

FIND OUT MORE at http://www.alicejames.co.uk/.

FIND US ONLINE!

www.rebellionpublishing.com

/rebellionpub   /rebellionpublishing   /rebellionpub

SIGN UP TO OUR NEWSLETTER!

rebellionpublishing.com/sign-up

YOUR REVIEWS MATTER!

Enjoy this book? Got something to say?

Leave a review on Amazon, GoodReads or with your
favourite bookseller and let the world know!